I0680219

Fire Scion I: The Hidden City :

By Kathe Todd

The events in this novel begin nine years after the end of
Fireblood Chronicles III: The Fireblood Betrayed

Prologue: Waterdon

It was a sunny spring afternoon in Waterdon. Ragnar Gustafson and Ricard Boileau, two young adventurers on their way to call in on the eorl's steward in hopes of being offered paying work, had stopped partway up the steps leading to Wyrmshalla to admire the view to the east. They were new to the city, drawn here by the reputation it held across much of Agena as a place where things were happening.

Far off beyond the Brightwater, in among the mountain peaks, Ricard's sharp eyes picked up movement. He was the archer in their band of two, while burly Ragnar handled the heavy blade work. The two had struck up a partnership only a year before, but already they had enjoyed much success pillaging tombs and recovering stolen property from bandits.

"Hey," Ricard said, nudging his companion. "Isn't that a dragon?" He pointed, and as the pair stared into the distance Ricard realized there were *two* flying shapes. And they were coming this way. As they stood gawking a Waterdon city guard paused, amused at their unsophisticated behavior.

"That's not just *any* dragons," he told the pair. "Watch and you'll see somethin' you won't forget." The three stood there as the dragons drew closer, clearly visible now as the rays of the westering sun sparkled on their scales. One was red, and much larger than its companion. The smaller dragon was bronze in color, and probably no more than twenty feet from nose to tail.

Below the walls they were looking over was a farmstead with an enormous one-story farmhouse, and a tall cistern tower standing between the house and their vantage point. As the two young men gaped in disbelief, the larger dragon and the smaller came down in the farmyard – landing in an open space between tower and house. Then the two of them shrank in an instant, to be replaced by a naked woman and a tall, similarly naked youth. The two hurriedly stepped to the cistern tower and grabbed robes, which they put on before going into the house.

Ragnar and Ricard stood transfixed, hardly believing what they had just seen. That woman had looked awfully tasty, at least from this distance. Finally they turned to the guard, who was grinning at them in satisfaction. "Wha..?" was all Ricard managed to get out. The guard's smile got even broader.

"What you've just seen is The Fireblood. That's right, the one what saved all of Terris from the Soul-Devourer, Warden Bernadette Drakespring herself."

"Of course, that was all upwards of sixteen years ago now. I was just a tad when it happened, but there's books you can read that'll tell you all about it. She's got to be close to forty, but she sure don't look it! That boy's her son, they say he's fireblood too. Must be, if he can turn into a dragon like that. They say she had a mess of dragon kids, too. One of 'em lives right there at the farm with 'em, at least he used to before he got so big. Those kids must be why nobody hunts dragons anymore."

Chapter 1: Drakespring Farm

Bernadette and Andi, their robes wrapped tightly around them against the chill breeze, entered the front door of Drakespring House and found Erik in the kitchen, playing a card game at the dining table with Sigi, age nine, and Meri, now rising eleven. The leukalfar girl was as yet showing no signs of coming puberty, and Bernadette suspected her adopted daughter's people might be slower to mature than the races of men. The alfar lived for centuries, after all.

The three looked up as mother and son entered the room, their faces shining with welcome. Meri jumped up from her chair and came to give each of them a hug, while Sigi just grinned. He was a happy, usually placid boy – not nearly the terror his big brother had been at that age. Andi ruffled Meri's thin mop of silken, snow-white hair, saying "how you doing, Squirt?" She poked him in the ribs.

"Did you see Mondi?"

Bernadette smiled lovingly at the three of her twenty-three children who were in the room. As nineteen of those children were dragons who could *not* turn human, it was a good thing they were not present. Drachmondien, the only one of her dragon brood she'd brought home to raise with her human family, was more than fifteen feet long now and while still a child in some ways he no longer lived with them full time. He'd found a hunting territory in the mountains east of the Brightwater, and only visited at Drakespring Farm on occasion.

"We saw Mondi, and Zuunenwalt and Purpurflug were with him too" Bernadette said, speaking as much to her husband Erik as to the children. "They flew down from Sneyagflug's reach, and all three of them are planning to fly on south to visit with Sneyhimseel and Tapferverd for a while. Mondi wants to make the rounds and see how all his siblings are doing now that they've dispersed."

No one region can sustain too many large predators, and Iscandia had no predators larger than dragons. Those of the tribe who were hostile to humans had been driven out of many regions, killed off by adventurers at the behest of eorls for the most part. So as Andi's dragon siblings had grown larger, their education under the guidance of their father complete, the brood had split off into groups of two or three, occupying hunting territories that had been vacated.

In some of these regions the young dragons, able to speak the common tongue and given a much friendlier attitude toward humans by their mother (who, after all, was *usually* human), had been able to forge relationships with nearby human settlements. Some of them had even entered into commercial arrangements with them, offering services such as bandit and predator control, or sky rides for children, in exchange for items like beef. When they got bigger, in another decade or two, they'd be able to carry full-grown adults.

"I guess we won't be seeing Mondi for a while, then," Erik remarked in his deep voice. Now in his early forties, he'd maintained his powerful physique through many hours spent doing farm chores or working at the forge. He and Bernadette, and their marriage mate Andrion (Magister of the Academy at Eisenstag and currently there on business), also frequently quested together for fun and profit. Any silver strands in his hair went unnoticed among the pale gold.

"Where's Miss Riki?" Bernadette asked Erik. Andi's younger sister Erika, Erik's biological daughter, was thirteen now and had taken to regarding the rest of her family as something of an embarrassment – at least when she was with her friends. She had been best buddies since toddlerhood with Sintra, whose parents were employed at the Drakespring family's inn down the road. Sintra being a year older and also a full-blooded elf, the two of them were often running off to get into mischief.

Sigi spoke up, smiling. "Riki and Sintra went up to town to 'hang out' with Julia. I think they said something about going over to the construction project." Julia was the daughter of Alessia Adelini and Wolaf Blackknife, the proprietors of Valkyrie – the armory and smithing establishment near the Waterdon city gates. They were long-time friends and business partners with the

Drakespring clan, providing a retail outlet for the products of the Drakespring forge.

With peace in the land this past thirty years and more, since the end of the Elven Conflict, city walls had been ignored and Waterdon had expanded far to the west and north of its original boundaries. Bjorn Steadfast, once Bernadette's body servant, had been employed for most of the past sixteen years by Hegmar, Waterdon's foremost builder.

Hegmar's son Edmar had now come into the firm, but it was Bjorn he relied on for the design and coordination of any new houses that were built. Likely "the construction project" was whatever house Hegmar's crew were working on now, and that meant Andi's best friend Fjurbund (aka Fjuri) would be there as well.

Fjuri was the son of Bjorn and his wife Lifa, also a former body servant of his mom's and once (so Andi had heard, though he found it hard to credit) a formidable warrior in her own right. Fjuri was a few months older than Andi, and had an older sister, Anja, who was now off on her own. There was also a younger one, Edla, who was a little bit older than Meri. This year Fjuri's papa had decided it was time for him to work for his keep, and had put him on Hegmar's construction crew. He'd been getting some admirable muscles, but Andi thought it would have been more fun if he were free to do some adventuring instead.

Not that Andi himself had done all that much adventuring. He'd gone on a totally awesome quest with his papas Erik and Andrion when he was just a little kid, must be ten years ago. They'd gone to an ancient Norse tomb and killed a bunch of aptrgangr – the undead guardians that often haunted such places. There he had gotten the dragon spell that let his mom turn back into a human after the ancient dragon Sneyagflug had tricked her into turning into a dragon so she could be a mother to his dragon babies.

Since then, life had been pretty quiet. Awesome in its way – what other kid could turn into a dragon, and had nineteen brothers and sisters who were dragons too? – but there hadn't been any more exploring ancient tombs or fighting deadly enemies. His mom had never meant him to learn the dragon spells to turn into a dragon and back to human, he knew. And it had been entirely his own idea to make the potion that was required to prepare his body for the transformation. But she had gotten over being mad at him about it after a while.

Andi's dragon brother Mondi (his full name, Drachmondien, meant "Dragon- Man-Serve" in the dragon tongue) had conspired with him on that project. He couldn't have been more than six, and Mondi wasn't even a year old at that point. But dragons develop their minds really fast. Mondi could actually carry on a conversation by the time he was a month old, even before he could fly! The two of them had become fast friends from the time Mom brought him home, and they were still on a par mentally.

But Andi's human body was now beginning to go through the changes of adolescence, while Mondi was still just slowly growing toward eventually becoming a gigantic flying monster – who would still be living hundreds of years after Andi had died of old age. Andi felt a little proud that for now at least, his dragon form was bigger than Mondi. Evidently the extra five years of life made a difference.

Still, Mondi had no longer been able to stay in the house after he reached a certain size. Andi wished he could find a potion, a dragon spell, that would let Mondi turn into a human so he could continue to live with them. But he didn't have any access to dragon lore.

His papa Andrion (who, Andi was now old and knowledgeable enough to realize, was his biological father) had said that there had apparently been an effort thousands of years ago to destroy all the records that gave details about the relationship among dragons, the fireblood, and dragon priests. The dragon priests were all dead or undead now, but dragons lived on thanks to the late dragon god Tarragin; and his mother had appeared as the first fireblood to be seen in generations. He was the second.

Andi's mom spoke, pulling him from his reverie. "I'm worried about that girl. Sintra and Julia are older, and I think they may be leading her into things she's not ready to deal with." Erik looked up at her in surprise.

"It's all right, Berni," he said with a smile. "They're just enjoying their first taste of teenage freedom. What were *you* up to at that age?" Instead of mollifying Bernadette this reminder seemed to make her more concerned. She turned to look at her eldest son.

"Shall I run up to town and track them down, Mom?" Andi asked. His mother smiled at him. "Hey Squirt, Sig, want to go on a quest with me?" he queried his two younger siblings. The kids were excited at the prospect. Farm life was dull and boring, but the city (really, even after all the growth of recent years, only a middle-sized town) of Waterdon promised exotic delights.

"Back in two shakes of a dragon's tail," Andi said with a smile. He hurried down the hall and popped into the bathroom for a quick dunk in the hot bathing pool before drying off, donning his robe again, and putting on a pair of the clogs they kept there. He always wanted a bath after spending some time in dragon form. Next he went out the front door again and down the stairs to the lower level, where he and Riki now each had their own rooms. They'd been getting too big to share the nursery with the younger kids.

When he returned, jauntily dressed in dark leather trousers and boots and a deep green linen shirt, Bernadette (also now dressed) reached into a pouch at her side and produced a handful of gold. "Buy everybody some treats, love. See you all back here for supper?"

"Will do," Andi responded. Meri and Sigi trooped out the door behind him, looking forward to the "adventure" of a walk to Waterdon.

Chapter 2: Adventure Time

Meri and Sigi saw the walk to Waterdon as an adventure, but in fact the danger was almost nonexistent. Very rarely you might see a shri (sharp-toothed creatures like dog-sized rats) along the road, but expansion of the area's human population had driven out wolves, smilodons, and even most of the bandits. There was still almost always a band operating out of Brightwater Overlook a couple of miles from their house, but the once-bandit infested cave below the walls west of the city had been converted into aging caverns for a new cheese factory. The factory had been built right into the cliff face, another of Hegmar's projects.

The kids, in high spirits, skipped and ran – covering twice the distance needed. Andi, so much more mature at fifteen, strode along like a man. Indeed, he was beginning to look like a man. His mother complained that she had to buy him new clothes every three months, the way he was shooting up. He towered over her now, and looked likely to grow taller even than his father Andrion. Probably not as tall as Papa Erik, however. Nor as wide. He was slim and muscular, having spent many hours at sword practice and other active pursuits since he was four or five.

They stopped off at Waterdon Stables, greeting the old hostler. Sigi and Meri each took an apple from the barrel he kept, and went to give the treats to Sigrandil and Reshiva – the family's coach horses. The coach had had little enough use over the years since they'd built it, when Andi was just a baby; but as the kids had grown bigger the horses had gotten quite a bit more exercise. They were old and placid now, a perfect ride even for the two youngest members of the Drakespring clan.

Sigi smiled up at his big brother. "Andi, can we ride them up to town? Please?" Andi smiled back at him, but shook his head.

"They'll be too much trouble to deal with in the middle of town, and I was going to take everybody for roasted nut confections at the Horseman after we find the girls, remember?" Sigi's grin widened. He seemed to take more and more after their papa Erik with each passing year, though with his dark red hair he didn't much resemble him.

The three bade farewell to the horses and Skulvar, and continued on up the road toward the city walls. "Sigi, do you know where the new project is?" Andi asked his baby brother.

"Sure," he piped. Somehow, Sigi always seemed to know about everything that was going on. Maybe it was just that he was so lovable, everybody opened up to him. Under his leadership, the three of them took a left before beginning the climb to the city gates – on a new road leading west that might possibly be the best-paved road in Iscandia.

Chapter 3: On the Job

At the jobsite Riki, Sintra, and Julia stood off to one side admiring the construction workers as they labored at their tasks, staying out of the way of Bjorn and Edmar. Riki was a year younger than the other two girls, but the tallest of them – though it was possible Julia would someday match her in height. Her father Wolaf Blackknife was one of the few men Riki had ever seen who was close to her papa Erik, whom she strongly favored, in size.

Sintra, the eldest of the three, was beautiful in the willowy, graceful way of the alfar and less developed than her Norse friends were as yet. Her figure had changed little since the three of them were children together, but she assured them sagely that she would be catching up with them eventually. She thought it would be impolite to mention that she would probably still look like a young woman when they were crones. Certainly, she seemed to be on the same level of development with her friends when it came to their newfound interest in the opposite sex.

All three of them were quite tall for girls, taller than many boys their age, and this inclined them to be looking at older guys with interest. Now, some of the older guys were starting to look back. Riki had always been a pretty girl and at thirteen she was well on the way to becoming a beautiful woman – with her regular features, creamy skin, red-gold hair flowing to her waist, and sky-blue eyes.

They stood observing, making quiet comments to each other about this or that of Hegmar's crew and giggling together frequently – especially when one of the men would pause from his labors to give them an appraising glance. It was all so exciting! But secretly, Riki had eyes for only one of the laborers on Hegmar's crew: the foreman's own son, Fjurbund.

He was so gorgeous! Since he had begun working on the construction crew he had only grown more so. For one thing he was far taller than she was, though he was only a couple of years older. His skin was beginning to bronze a little from sun exposure with his new outdoor job. He was beginning to fill out, too, muscles rippling under that smooth skin.

Fire Scion I: The Hidden City

The fact that Riki had known Fjuri for as long as she could remember did not change the situation. She was totally, completely, in love with him! And he still treated her as if she were the pesky little sister that she had been throughout much of their lives, hanging around while he and her older brother Andi, his best friend, were going about their important pursuits. But now that she was a woman (she had had her first menses before the end of last year, an annoyance but Mama was firm she was *not* getting one of those amulets yet), other men were beginning to look at her in a way that told her her power was growing. Soon he would be unable to resist her charms! She hoped.

The girls' entertainment was interrupted by the arrival of the entire rest of the Drakespring Clan, junior division (not counting Mondi, who was very much a member of their family but now living mostly on his own). Julia was the first to spot them coming up the road, and she nudged Riki. "It's your brothers and sister!"

"Oh, no…" Riki groaned. Lately, it seemed, Andi had taken up the role of Guardian of her Virtue or some such rot. Mom thought that Riki was too young to be getting mixed up with boys, and he seemed to be on *her* side – when Riki thought, given how close they were in age, he should be supporting his sister instead.

Once at a family gathering Riki had heard Uncle Geri talking with Aunt Gytha, and he'd made some remark that suggested Mom hadn't exactly been sitting around on her hands when she was younger. Heck, she was married to two men at the same time and *that* wasn't usual. But though much of Iscandia might have thought their family situation was unconventional or titillating, Riki was here to tell them that all it meant for her was she had half again as many parents as most kids did, telling her what to do and when to do it.

Andi approached them, smiling. Larissa and Julia didn't seem to mind in the least. As far as Riki was concerned Andi was just another stinky boy, made stinkier by the fact that he could turn into a dragon whenever he wanted. Okay, maybe he wasn't all *that* bad. And she supposed that some people might find him good looking. He looked a lot like Papa Andrion, though his coloring was closer

13

to Mom's. But she didn't understand why her friends got all
nervous and excited when he was around.

"Hey, girls! I thought I might run into you here. Mom gave me
some money and I thought we could all go up to the Flying
Horseman for some roasted nut confections before Riki and the
kids and I have to go back to the farm. What do you say?" Girls
perplexed Andi, and filled him up with feelings he didn't know
how to deal with. But Riki was his sister, and he'd grown up with
Sintra and Julia so they might as well be his sisters too. With this
group, he could be suave.

Riki didn't miss the way in which he had slid "before Riki and
the kids and I have to go back to the farm" into his casual remark.
As if it were already understood that *of course* she had to go back
home with him. She sighed. Of course, she did. That was the
problem with living in a town like Waterdon. Really more of a city
these days, it might be rivaling Sylvanian if it kept growing as it
did. But it was still a small town, and her family was locally
famous. When she grew up, she thought, it would be nice to move
to Remus and live in Roma where nobody knew who she was or
where she was supposed to be.

Chapter 4: Spite

Riki and her friends, along with Andi, Meri, and Sigi, all walked over to say hello to Fjuri before heading back down the road that led up to the city gates. He watched them go, enviously. Andi's family was rich, and the kids didn't have to go to a job. Well, he admitted to himself, they lived on a farm and they had all had farm chores to do since long before he had become a construction worker. Plus, he sort of enjoyed working construction. It was a bit of a thrill to start out with his papa's drawings and end up with a real, three-dimensional house that people would be living in for generations. But still…

The Drakespring youngsters, along with Sintra and Julia, were greeted warmly by the city guards outside the gate and admitted to the city. Julia, alone of the six, had grown up within these walls. And only a few steps from the gates, at that. As the group came in, she maneuvered herself to the far side, away from Valkyrie and her mother's forge. Technically she was playing hooky, and should probably have been busy crafting armor and weapons as Alessia's apprentice – though she didn't really see *why* she had to become a smith. Their family was plenty comfortable, mostly because of the income from the arms and armor crafted by the Drakesprings. And she would probably just grow up and get married eventually. Why shouldn't she have some fun in the meantime?

The group managed to escape notice from Julia's parents and continued up the main street of Waterdon, heading for the Flying Horseman at the top. Though the Bathing Maiden, the Drakespring family business, was considered the premier inn in Iscandia, the Flying Horseman still got a lot of custom from locals and travelers who were in town on business. The Maiden's location on the road that led north, east of the city walls, put it off the beaten path – and most people who went there had heard of it first and sought it out.

The six of them trooped into the inn and milled around in front of the bar. The buxom barmaid, a Norsewoman in her late twenties who sent a thrill through Andi, identified him as the likely leader of the party and asked how she might help him. Britta, the older woman Andi remembered as the proprietress when he was a kid, had long since sold out and moved away from Waterdon.

"Go get a table, guys, and I'll be right there" Andi told his entourage. Sigi and Meri were first off the mark, and had soon claimed two of the inn's tables for them. Not many inns in Iscandia could handle a party as large as theirs at one table. Andi bought enough roasted nut confections for everybody, and got some jugs of water for them all. At home they were occasionally allowed to have ale or watered wine instead of water or milk, but Mom hadn't given him enough money. Throughout the exchange the barmaid dimpled at him – meeting his gaze with frankness as she leaned over the bar, and seeming to derive amusement from his discomfiture.

Gathering his dignity, Andi returned to the tables with his arms loaded down and they all fell to with glee. Sigi and Meri were particularly delighted to be having these treats in a relatively exotic location, but Riki and her friends enjoyed it too. After all, was this place not also full of interesting young men who could be entranced by their charms?

They were well into their snack when a youngish man, a sellsword from the look of him and nobody they recognized, came past their table. He looked to have had more than a couple of ales, and when he set eyes on Meri he reacted violently. "By the gods!" he bellowed. "What is it?" He drew a short sword, and seemed as if he were about to attack the leukalfar girl where she sat, eating her roasted nut confection and looking up at him in stunned silence with her not-eyes.

Andi jumped to his feet, eyes wide. "Waf-Ond-Nied-Lorn!" he cried, and the man's sword flew from his grasp. "She's my *sister*, you idiot!" Most people in Waterdon knew their family, knew that some of its members were out of the ordinary. And Meri, despite her alien appearance, was in most ways a typical eleven-year-old girl. Yeah, he knew there were a few who talked about her, said it wasn't right for a leukalfar to be raised with humans. But anybody who had come to know her realized she was as human as they were.

The stranger recovered himself after the shock of having his sword wrested from his grasp and hurtled across the room by someone who, if taller than he was, was obviously nothing more than a kid. "Your sister, punk? Who the hell has a stinking leukalfar for a sister? Does that mean you're a leukalfar too? I've gotta say, you have a lot more eyes than usual for your breed," he sneered.

Andi's fists were clenched, as he silently argued with himself. He had learned deadly battle magic when he was far younger than Sigi, all part of the preparation for his quest with his papas to retrieve the dragon spell to rescue Mama. But his parents, all three of them, had drummed it into him for years: don't use deadly force against anyone but enemies who mean to kill you. And clearly this jackass was just a posturing bigot, making himself look big and tough at the expense of a little girl. Punching a hole through him with a dual-wielded blast of fire and lightning was probably not a good idea.

"She may be a leukalfar, but she's a better human being than you are," he told the man quietly. Then he put his hands down at his sides, and turned to the stunned group at the tables. "I think it's time for us to leave," he said. "I don't like the smell of the air in here." The five youngsters stood up at once, tense and eager to get out of there. As they walked past the bar, huddled and silent, the barmaid looked at Andi in consternation and mouthed "I'm sorry."

Chapter 5: Decisions

Julia peeled off as the group passed Valkyrie, probably to endure a lecture from her mom about running off in the middle of the day with her friends. The rest of them continued out the gates of Waterdon and along the road, across two streams and back to Drakespring Farm. There was little conversation along the way, all of them burning with anger at the encounter. Leukalfar were not truly blind, and there were eyes encapsulated in the skin on their faces. Meri could not cry through them, but as in other human races her tear ducts were connected to her nasal passages and her nose, a little nubbin smaller than a baby's, was running as they walked along.

Sintra hugged Riki as they parted at the walk leading up the Drakespring House, before continuing on the Bathing Maiden. It had been her home since birth, though she had spent many hours at Drakespring Farm. She also bent to hug Meri, murmuring "it's all right, kid," and cast a plangent look at Andi before walking on.

Bernadette was in their outdoor forge working on some armor as her children arrived. She immediately saw that something was wrong, and her pique at Riki for absconding without permission was set aside. She put the piece of elvengild she'd been working aside. It would keep until she could pick it up again, and she followed the kids into the house.

As soon as all of them were inside, Meri turned and threw herself into her mother's arms. "Mama, he said I was a 'dirty leukalfar'!" she wailed, sobbing now. Bernadette hugged her adopted daughter tight, tears stinging her eyes. She had feared this since the day she'd brought Meri home. While she and Andrion were questing in a cave system far below a dypalfar ruin, attacked at intervals by leukalfar, she had killed Meri's true parents – only to discover that they had a baby with them. The six-month-old leukalfar girl, outwardly so different from other humans, had proven to be as sweet and loving as any human child could be. But humans' tendency toward fear and rejection of those who seemed different was one trait that ran deep.

Now, it seemed, it had caught up with them. Not that there hadn't been incidents before. Many people in Waterdon feared and hated leukalfar, seeing them as subhuman monsters who were to be killed on sight. Anyone who had ever quested in dypalfar ruins knew them as implacable enemies, alien and silent. The fact that Meri was a typical little girl, chattering childishly and snuggling up with her mama, could not override the revulsion brought on by her spindly build, eyeless face, and pale white skin. But never before had she been subjected to such overt hostility.

Erik had been working in the craft room and, hearing the commotion, came up the hall to the front room. He took one look at Meri, bawling in Bernadette's arms, and his heart sank. He loved the little girl as if she was his own, but he too had feared that she would face hostility and rejection as she went out into society.

Erik looked up from Meri, whose sobs were beginning to subside, to his white-faced and chastened-looking daughter and tall son. Andi's expression was grim, and it was clear he was struggling with a mixture of empathy for his little sister and anger at the man who had bullied her. To his papa's questioning look he replied through clenched jaws, "We were in the Horseman having some sweet treats and this Norse sellsword came up and pulled a blade on her. I used Repel Weapon on him, but I really wanted to incinerate him."

Erik stepped forward and enfolded his son in a tight embrace. He still topped Andi by a few inches, though the boy was now more than six feet tall. And not such a boy any longer. "I'm proud of you, son," he rumbled in his deep voice. "You did the right thing. People like that aren't worth the trouble of killing them."

Late that afternoon Papa Andrion returned, fast-traveling in from the Academy at Eisenstag. As Magister of that institution since months before Andi had been born, he had turned the place into a research facility that, in some ways, outstripped Remus' University of the Magical Arts in magical knowledge. He'd spent his first few years there in independent studies, and had developed a spell to materialize a tub of hot water anywhere. Not to mention the creation of the magic maps by which Agena's more fortunate citizens were able to travel anywhere they had previously been, in what seemed like moments. The actual time elapsed was longer, but at least the traveler was in no danger from bandits or hostile wildlife during the journey.

Now he had assembled teams of journey- and master-level mages, working on a wide range of projects to uncover the secret workings of magic. The knowledge obtained from this program was advancing mankind's understanding, and today's magic students had an education that went far beyond "read a spellbook and then practice." Andrion needed to check in frequently with his underlings at the Academy, and also travelled to Remus and other places around Agena on occasion, consulting with other mages.

Andrion had developed some much deadlier techniques for battle magic than had ever been seen before, and he'd taught some of these to Andi when he was quite young. Since then, the focus of Andi's magical education had mostly been on healing magic. His mom was an amazing healer, who had brought his grandpapa Francois back from a near-vegetative state after more than a decade of paralysis following a stroke. She'd taught Andi everything she knew, and if he chose to he might well make a career as a healer. Andi had still not made any career choices, however. The world was his oyster, with the range of talents and resources he had at his command, and he could do almost anything he wanted to. How could he possibly choose, until he'd had a few years to try things out and see what he liked?

Sigi and Meri were bedded down in the nursery, but Andi and Riki joined the family around the dining table later in the evening for a discussion of their adopted sister's situation. Mom seemed sad and regretful as she said "I've always feared this would become an issue when Meri got older. Do you remember, Andrion, when we found her – how I said she would grow up to be a liaison between the leukalfar and the rest of human society?"

Papa Andrion nodded thoughtfully. He vividly recalled that trip, more than ten years ago now, when he and Bernadette were questing in a leukalfar-infested cave system looking for the chemia book the dragon Sneyagflug had asked her to find. At that time, they had thought this was all they would need to do for him to aid his quest to stop dragons from returning to extinction.

Bernadette went on: "I think it's time we sought out Duraenis again. If anyone alive knows the leukalfar language and would be willing to teach it to Meri, it will be him."

Andrion replied "Do you think Duraenis is still alive? It's more than sixteen years since we left him at the Great Temple."

Bernadette nodded. "He'd lived for uncounted thousands of years before we met him, and had just gotten back control of the Great Temple after we killed his brother. I know he was hoping to bring the changelings back into the fold, to rekindle their worship of Apoldros. We haven't needed to return to recharge the Staff of Apoldros, since Lord Karazin was defeated and the staff was taken for safekeeping so soon after we left him. But I think it's likely we'll find him alive and well."

Andi spoke up, "Mom, if you're going to take Meri to the Great Temple, can I come along?" All three of his parents, and his sister as well, eyed him. "I really want a chance to meet a white elf!" he exclaimed by way of explanation. Mom and Papa Andrion's tales of their trip through the Eparchy and the killing of the vampire white elf Signis, had fascinated him since he was a kid.

His parents' gazes met around the table, and nobody had any objections. It was time for their son's education to include some real-world experiences – ones that wouldn't get him killed. "That'd be fine, Andi," Bernadette said. "How about you, Riki? Would you like to come along?" Riki had never had as much of a scholarly bent as Andi did, and at this stage of her life there were many other things she'd rather do than spend days in the frozen north talking with some old religious guy.

"Is Fjuri going along?" Riki asked, trying to sound totally casual. Andi pricked up his ears. This trip would be even better if he could have his best friend along!

"I'm sorry," Bernadette said, quashing his excitement before it could get underway, "Lifa tells me that he's going to be working on Hegmar's crew right through the spring and summer. You and he can take some trips together in the fall, Andi."

"Just curious," Riki murmured. "I think maybe I should stay here and help look after Sigi," she added virtuously. Bernadette gave a knowing smile, which wasn't lost on Andi. He knew his sister had a crush on Fjuri, but he didn't think Fjuri had even noticed.

"All right then," Bernadette went on, "Meri and Andi and I will fast-travel up to the Great Temple in the morning. If everything works out with Duraenis, we'll leave her there so she can start studying her people's language. Once she can talk with them, there shouldn't be any problems for her getting to know some of the tribal leukalfar and beginning to bridge the gap between them and the culture she's been raised in."

Chapter 6: The Great Temple

Going from a warm spring morning outside the front door of Drakespring House, Andi and his mom and little sister found themselves, seemingly in seconds, in an arctic environment at an hour that was impossible to determine. They arrived in a snowy courtyard outside a little stone house. Though Andi didn't know it, his mom immediately recognized it as the shrine from which she had plucked the Staff of Apoldros some sixteen years previously. At that time, the area had been strewn with rubble from a building that had been collapsed by the Archon Signis – a move that had failed to prevent Bernadette and her companions from killing him.

He had intentionally lured them here, having put out a false prophecy intended to lure a Netherblood vampire to seek out the Staff of Apoldros. With the blood of such, the legendary staff could be corrupted to permanently change the sun – making it possible for vampires to walk comfortably in daylight, and incidentally, perhaps, exterminating all life on Terris. His plans had not worked out all that well.

Signis' brother Duraenis, one of a handful of his race not to have been poisoned and corrupted by the dypalfar, had just taken over the place when Andi's mom last saw him. She was surprised and also pleased to look up and see the man himself standing with his back to them on the balcony above, looking completely unchanged.

At their arrival he heard them stirring and turned, astonishment painted on his pale features. "Fireblood?" he asked, not quite believing it was her though the woman had changed little enough in the years since last he saw her. But who were these others? The young man looked enough like her he guessed it might be her son, but why did she have a child of the changelings with her?

Despite his puzzlement Duraenis felt a surge of pleasure at the arrival of these visitors. It had been far too long since he had spoken with any beside the changelings. He had half hoped, all those years ago, that this woman and her companions might have spread the word, that others would come seeking to worship

Apoldros in the Eparchy. But none had yet arrived. He had been alone for centuries before they had appeared, save for remote communication with his four fellow Protectors manning shrines scattered around the Eparchy. At least now, he had companionship of a sort with the changeling descendants of his race.

Andi's mom led Andi and Meri, trailing behind her like baby chicks, up the nearest of a pair of semicircular ramps leading to the balcony on which Duraenis stood. "Duraenis," she said calmly, extending a hand. "It is good to see you still here. How goes your work with the changelings?" Duraenis, still half-stunned at the sudden appearance of this woman from the past, smiled.

"I am glad to see you as well, Fireblood," he replied formally. "Look around you and you will see what we have wrought since last you came here." He gestured off the balcony, a look of pride touching his features, and the three visitors looked down.

Below them were many of the leukalfar – but not as Bernadette had ever seen them before. Andi had never seen another leukalfar besides his sister, and Meri had never before seen another member of her race. She took them in with her not-vision, wondering at these people who were like her. Bernadette, who like most civilized people in Agena had known the leukalfar only as silent, scantily-dressed hostiles before she adopted her daughter, was amazed.

These were the leukalfar she had guessed at, the more so since discovering Meri in a baby carrier strapped to her dead mother's body. Unlike any she had seen previously, they were clad in long robes similar to Duraenis' but of less fine quality. They moved quietly and with dignity, going about the tasks of acolytes. Duraenis had gotten some of the changelings to return to the worship of Apoldros, just as he had hoped!

"I am so glad to see that you were able to bring some of them back into the fold," Andi's mom told the white elf priest. Andi was surprised that he looked no older than Papa Andrion, maybe younger even given that his white hair was the same shade as Meri's and had probably been that color his whole life. Papa Andrion was nearly fifty and had quite a few lines on his face, though he'd kept his body in shape over the years. But this guy's face was smooth, not young but sort of ageless.

"Come," Duraenis told them. "Let us take some refreshment and we will talk." At the word "refreshment" hunger hit Andi like a body blow. It seemed like it had been less than half an hour since his usual hearty breakfast, prepared by Papa Erik. But for some reason he felt like he could eat an entire good-sized mountain goat about now. As a dragon, he had actually done so. Flying really made you hungry.

Mom and his papas had told him about how the effects of fast-traveling on your body seemed to split the difference between the time it seemed to take and the time that had actually elapsed when you arrived, and Andi had certainly fast-traveled many times during his short life. But being here in the north, not to mention being fifteen, had him convinced it had been a *lot* longer than half an hour since his last meal.

Duraenis led them down off the balcony and into the building behind them. This had been completely rebuilt since Bernadette's time, she noticed. Andi had been told the story of their confrontation with Signis in detail many times, and he almost felt as if he was revisiting somewhere he had been before. Which, clearly, had changed a lot. There was no sign of the frozen leukalfar warriors and their mandimant pets. The halls were cold, but free of ice and there were no signs of ruination.

The throne of the Archon was still there, on an elevation at the back of the room. But the path to it was a series of stairs, so that postulants might approach. The room was large and airy, and off to one side there was a small, relatively cozy room with a fireplace in it that was many degrees warmer than the main building.

Duraenis beckoned them to take seats, and a leukalfar acolyte appeared and asked for his instructions. He spoke in the common tongue, which the robed acolyte seemed to understand. "Please bring hot tea, and some biscuits if you please."

The acolyte replied in the same language, slightly accented. "As you will, Archon." He (the figure appeared to be male) bowed slightly and exited the room.

Andi and Meri were taking this all in with something akin to awe. For Meri, it was her first contact with people like her. For Andi, it was standing on end everything he had ever learned about the leukalfar. His sister was clearly an exception. She'd been with them since she was a little baby, and had never known the life others of her race were leading in the mysterious caverns beneath dypalfar ruins.

Usually ebullient, Andi felt shy and constrained around Duraenis. This guy was the Archon of an entire religion, not to mention thousands of years old and one of only a handful of members of his race who had not been poisoned by the dypalfar. Andi's parents had raised him to respect all religious beliefs, without strongly adhering to any of them. He knew that the creator god Aderos had supposedly interceded to make their three-way marriage possible, and that the gods (not to mention the usually less-benevolent daimonic lords) were real. But these immortal beings did not seem to require worship from mortals, and his family had only occasionally made any gestures in that direction.

After tea and biscuits had arrived, the four of them relaxed a little. Andi could tell that Duraenis was burning to ask his mom about Meri, and it wasn't long before the question came. "Fireblood, how came you by this child of the changelings?" he asked. Bernadette took another sip of her tea, its warmth welcome even in this relatively warm little room.

"This is my daughter Merelle. Merelle, please meet Duraenis, Archon of Apoldros." Meri dipped her head, completely awed. Andi's mom went on, "When my husband Andrion and I were questing after a book far below a dypalfar ruin more than ten years ago, we chanced upon two dead leukalfar. I discovered that one was a woman, and carrying a baby with her. I could do nothing but take her in, and raise her as one of my own."

Meri had heard this story before, or a version of it. But the starkness of it as her mama related the events to Duraenis left her with a deep chill. She had been in the bosom of her family, loved, for as long as she could remember. But there was another life, a life that *should* have been hers – and *would* have been hers, had not her true mother died. Mama sensed the pain this had caused, and put an arm around her to reassure her. Whatever the facts of Meri's life might have been in the distant past, the fact was that *now* she had people who loved her.

Duraenis took a sip of his tea, as well. He seemed lost in thought. Finally he said, "This does you credit, Fireblood. I know that the changelings have been implacable enemies to all who intrude in their territory. But I have finally begun to reach them! The tribe living closest to the Great Temple have sent some to me as acolytes, and they have learned to speak the common tongue. Once again Apoldros has worshippers, and with every year more are coming from the tribal villages to join in His worship. I hope that someday we will be able to reach out to the other tribes scattered around Iscandia, and a détente will be reached between the changelings and the rest of humanity."

Andi's mom ate a biscuit, before taking another sip of her tea. Andi was trying hard, very hard, to restrain himself from eating every scrap of food on the table in front of them. When would it be dinnertime, he wondered? He hoped he wasn't going to faint from starvation before then... Mom said "This is my wish too, Duraenis! I have hoped from the first that in time Meri would be reunited with the people who gave her birth, as an ambassador from the rest of humankind. There is no reason for the changelings to lurk in the shadows, apart from all the other human races. But before she can do that, she needs to be able to communicate with them. And not just your acolytes who have learned the common tongue. She needs to learn to speak the leukalfar tongue, whatever that might be."

Duraenis was lost in thought for a while, pondering what she had said, and Andi noticed that somehow all of the food was gone. He did his best to ignore the complaints of his stomach, and to sit politely waiting for the old priest to respond. Finally, Duraenis spoke. "Our language is related to the tongues of the ancient eldalfar, though the dialect spoken by various tribes of the changelings differs somewhat from what we white elves spoke before the Betrayal. I would not be the best teacher, but I think I know someone who will do." He got to his feet saying, "Follow me, if you will...?"

The three of them got up and followed Duraenis through the corridors and passageways of the Great Temple complex, Bernadette hugging Meri close at her side. The buildings everywhere they went had been restored, debris hauled away, fallen masonry repaired, floors swept and maintained. Eventually they arrived in the central area: the large room where Bernadette, Andrion, and Nerissa had first entered on their trip here all those years ago. An impressive altar now stood at one side of the room, and there were wall hangings honoring Apoldros – chief of the gods, Father Aderos as He was known to men and dragons.

Several leukalfar acolytes were at work in the large room, either worshiping at the altar or performing more mundane chores. All work at the Great Temple was performed by these acolytes, who received room and board in exchange for their services. Duraenis led them to where a robed leukalfar woman was bent to her tasks, and said gently "Myrkra, I would like you to meet someone."

The woman stood and acknowledged the Archon with a bow of her head, hands together in a gesture of prayer. Then she tilted her head back up and moved it from side to side, scanning his companions with her not-vision. On seeing Meri she gave a barely-audible gasp, just a slight intake of breath. When she spoke, it was in heavily-accented Common: "Where this girl come... come from?" she asked.

"This woman," Duraenis said, gesturing to Bernadette, "is The Fireblood. She found the girl as a baby and has raised her as her own. The little one is called Merelle. Now it is time for Merelle to meet some of her own people, and to learn to speak with them. I am hoping that you and Mothris will undertake this task, and also guide her in the worship of Apoldros." The leukalfar woman was clearly looking at them all, but her attention seemed particularly drawn to Meri.

"Merelle," the woman said, "I am Myrkra, of the Ankhrazana tribe of the leukalfar. This boy my son Mothris." She gestured

toward the youth at her side, who if he were man and not alfar
would probably be a little younger than Andi. There was a certain
awkwardness about him, as if all of his body parts had not caught
up with each other – or he had not yet learned how to control the
body he had grown into.

"You want, you can live here in the Great Temple with us"
Myrkra went on. "You become acolyte of Apoldros and serve in
the temple. We teach you leukalfar speech, ways. This you want?"
Meri hugged tighter to her mother's side, but she spoke clearly in
response.

"Yes, I want to learn. I need to learn. But…" she took a
breath, and gathered her courage to continue speaking. "I'm afraid.
Afraid to be here by myself without any of my friends or my
family. It's cold here!"

Andi could see that Meri needed some support, and he spoke
up: "How about if I stay here too and we can learn together, Meri?
I could do that, couldn't I? Mom?" Bernadette bridled. She was
letting one of her children slip out of her arms, but did she have to
lose another as well? Yet Andi's offer was so kind, so loving. And
it would probably be a good experience for him. Maybe having a
man who could communicate with the leukalfar as well as a
leukalfar girl raised among men would help the cause (of bringing
these two disparate branches of humanity together peacefully) even
more.

"Are you sure, Andi?" his mom asked.

"Apoldros is Aderos, the dragon god, right?" he asked in
response. She nodded, not sure where he was going with this.
"Well," Andi continued, "I'm a dragon! At least sometimes I'm a
dragon. I think that being an acolyte of Apoldros for a time would
be… right, somehow."

Andi turned to Duraenis, and asked him "We'll be able to
leave after we'd learned what we came to learn, right? We don't
have to be acolytes for the rest of our lives?"

Duraenis shook his head, though his expression was one of
puzzlement. "Not unless you want to," he replied. "But what do
you mean, you're a dragon?"

Andi suddenly felt shy about revealing this detail about himself. But the cat was out of the bag now. "I'm fireblood, like my mom. When I was little, the dragon Sneyagflug had her create a potion, and drink it. It turned out that the potion and a dragon spell he had her learn let her turn into a dragon. And later, I made some of that potion and drank it too. I already had the dragon spell. I was just a kid – it seemed like a good idea at the time."

Duraenis gazed at him with sharp interest, silent for a time. Then he said softly, "I had heard of it when I was young, they said that the dragon priests could transform. But I thought it was just a story…"

Andi's mom broke in: "I assure you it's true. Both Andi and I can transform back and forth between human and dragon at will. I have nineteen dragon children scattered around Agena now, not counting this one."

Duraenis shook his head, then marshalled his thoughts. "Well, Fireblood, if you and your children are agreed on this they are welcome to stay. They will serve in the temple and learn about Apoldros, and in their spare time Myrkra and Mothris will teach them the language and culture of the changelings – or at least of their own tribe. Let's get you two some robes and some sleeping quarters, and then I'll turn you over to Myrkra so your education can begin."

Myrkra took the lead and led them down a passageway off of which several doors opened. It was warmer here, as if fires were burning somewhere nearby. One door led to a storage closet, where after going through piles of clean, folded acolyte robes she found one each for Andi and Meri. They put them on over the top of what they were wearing, and found that they were surprisingly warm. They came all the way down to the ankles, had long sleeves and hoods, and seemed to be made of an especially thick, soft wool.

Next, the leukalfar woman led them into a room that was outfitted as a bedroom. There were four beds in it, two on either side of a medium-size fireplace. Firewood was stacked beside the hearth, and a fire was laid on the grates but not yet lit. Andi couldn't resist showing off a little bit, and he stepped forward to set the wood ablaze with his fire spell. He'd had no real opportunities during most of his life to use battle magic on an enemy, but years of practice with targets had developed his skills – and his fund of magical energy had grown enormously over the years.

Duraenis and the two leukalfar acolytes seemed somewhat startled by this display, but they didn't say anything about it. Andi caught his mom rolling her eyes at him, however, and he winked at her – a sheepish grin curving his lips. She knew him too well. "That should be that, then," Duraenis said. "I look forward to having your children here with us, and I'm sure that they will be learning a lot. You can come back any time to visit and see how they are progressing."

Bernadette frowned for a moment as she thought of something. "Andi, I think you had better have my Agena map to keep with you. If anything comes up and you and Meri need to come home, I don't want you to have to fly there." Andi was big enough as a dragon that he could fly with a small, slender child like Meri on his back, and he had often taken her on rides. But this place was many, many leagues to the north and west of Waterdon and a trip like that would be exhausting. He might starve to death before they made it back.

"Good thinking!" he exclaimed, taking the folded map from her and tucking it into his acolyte's robe. Then he bent and enfolded his little mother in his arms, giving her a long squeeze and a kiss on the cheek. It seemed like only yesterday she had to bend to do the same to him! "Bye-bye Mama! Tell everyone I miss them – and tell Fjuri we'll be going on an adventure when I get back!" She reached up to cup his face in her hands and gaze into his warm brown eyes, so like his father's. Tears wanted to creep into her own eyes, but she held them firmly back. Her boy was growing up.

Next Bernadette turned to Meri and hugged her tightly, kissing her and telling her to be good and listen to her teachers. Meri grinned up at her. Now that Andi was going to be here with her, everything was going to be wonderful – and spending some time away from home was looking more and more like a fun adventure instead of an ordeal. "Bye, Mama! I'll be fine," she said brightly. "Tell Sigi to feed Sigrandil and Reshiva some apples for me, and tell Edla I'll see her before too long!"

Bernadette squeezed Duraenis' hand. "Thank you, Archon," she said seriously. "This means so much to our family, and I think it will be a good thing for the changelings as well as for my daughter." After thanking Myrkra and Mothris, who were standing by taking this all in, the priest accompanied The Fireblood back down the corridor to the main doors of the building. There, near the entrance to the Great Temple, he watched as she shimmered out of existence and returned to her home.

Back in Andi and Meri's new quarters, the roaring fire was already beginning to take the chill from the air. Both of them had lived their lives in the much warmer climate of the Waterdon area, and they could see that living here was going to take some getting used to. Myrkra turned to Andi and smiled at him, an expression that was a little alarming given the leukalfar woman's numerous sharply-pointed teeth. But her words were kind. "Welcome to the Great Temple, man-child," she said. "You have questions?"

Andi grinned at her. "Just one at the moment," he replied. "When do we eat?"

Chapter 7: Changes

Life in the Great Temple was not what Andi had expected. He had volunteered because of his love for his "other" sister, and a hope that this opportunity to connect with the race that had given her birth would be what Meri needed to make her way in life. Everyone in the Drakespring clan loved her, as did his grandparents on both sides. And she had a close friend in Edla Steadfast, Fjuri's baby sister. But it had been hard for her to fit in with the men and alfar of the Waterdon area, the "normal" human races who were all so much alike, because of her alien appearance. They didn't take the time to get to know her, they just looked and saw an unhuman monster – and rejected her.

Since Andi was an unhuman monster himself on occasion (fortunately, only when he wanted to be!), he had sympathy and understanding for her. Fjuri and a few of their other friends thought Andi's shape-changing ability was an awesome power, but many other people around town thought that he and his mother were abominations just for being able to do it. Mom had explained that he was always going to meet small-minded people, and he just needed to brush their stupidity and cruelty aside. That had made it easier to resist the temptation to waste that sellsword at the Horseman, when he had threatened Meri with a weapon and then, his weapon gone, cut her to the quick with his words.

The fact that Andi's parents were prominent and powerful citizens not only of Waterdon but of the entire province, and well-respected even in distant Remus, had shielded their children from some of the enmity that might otherwise have been leveled against them.

Riki was just a typical-seeming, pretty Norse girl and Sigi a loveable kid, perfectly ordinary in every way. But Andi's very early start in deadly battle magic; his fireblood status that let him learn dragon spells just by hearing them, and absorb the stones necessary to power them; and his ability to become a dragon just by speaking four short syllables, had all led to him being set apart. And then there was Mondi, one of Andi's nineteen dragon half-siblings. They had all hatched from eggs laid by his mother when in her dragon form, and the huge red dragon Sneyagflug was their father.

When she had been freed of her obligation to remain with Sneyagflug and their children, and had learned the dragon spell that let her return to human form, Andi's mom had brought Mondi back to Drakespring Farm to live with them. Andi, Mondi, and Fjuri had been inseparable back then – the two human boys learning to speak the dragon tongue and playing endless games with Andi's dragon brother. There had been a short period when Andi in his dragon form had been big enough to carry Fjuri on his back; but now Fjuri, who took after his father Bjorn (a man almost as big as Papa Erik), had gotten too heavy.

Now, Andi's life had changed in ways he couldn't have imagined. Every morning at dawn he and Meri rose from their beds and dressed. Before getting anything to eat, they went to the central altar of Apoldros and knelt to make their devotions. Much to his surprise, he found that silent communication with the Dragon God made him feel exalted in some strange way. Perhaps there really was some special connection between him, as a fireblood, and Aderos? Even the ancient dragons themselves revered Him as their creator.

Meri didn't seem to object to this, either, though he wasn't certain what she got from it. After that they made their way to the acolytes' dining hall, where they sat at long tables with other acolytes (all leukalfar, except for himself) and breakfasted on hot porridge with bits of dried fruit in it. This was accompanied by a coarse bread, different from the white rolls Andi was used to but somehow more filling, and gallons of hot tea. The tea had a flavor he had never tasted before, but he came to enjoy it.

The acolytes all had their tasks during the course of a day. There was time spent in worship or communion with Apoldros, and time spent performing the operations that were required to maintain the Great Temple: sweeping, cleaning, lighting of lamps and disposing of wastes, cooking, laundering of robes – the list was endless.

Andi's family was counted wealthy by the standards of Iscandia, but they had always preferred doing common everyday tasks for themselves rather than having them done by servants. From a young age Andi had learned to milk cows, care for the chickens, cook simple meals, clean up after them, wash and mend clothing, and more. So the chores he and Meri were assigned didn't seem particularly onerous.

The best part of the day, for both of them, was when Myrkra and Mothris would take time with them for language lessons, and discussions about the culture of the leukalfar. Andi was enough the child of both Bernadette and Andrion to be fascinated by this incredibly rare opportunity to see into a world that had been hidden from most of humankind (either man or alfar) for thousands of years.

Mothris, Andi realized, was close in stage of life (if not necessarily in age; alfar lived far longer than men) to himself. And the two of them had quite a bit in common. Though the leukalfar youth had chosen to come with his mother from their tribal village and take up the duties of an acolyte of Apoldros, he had many of the same concerns Andi did: what sort of adult was he becoming, what course would his future life take, and what exactly was the deal with those mysterious, utterly desirable girls?

Myrkra insisted that, as soon as Andi and Meri had picked up the basics of the leukalfar tongue, they would speak only in that. If either of them had completely failed to get what had been said to them, they could ask "asma courye?" which translated as "what meaning?" Myrkra would then run very quickly over the words they had missed in Common. But gods save them if they failed to commit these to memory and had to ask a second time.

Andi was reasonably young, Meri quite young by the standards of her race – and both of them were bright. In only a short time both of them were beginning to converse well in the leukalfar tongue (for though Duraenis, probably the last of the unchanged white elves, called them the changelings, they yet called themselves leukalfar – meaning "white elves"), and Myrkra pushed on to explain to them the beliefs and customs of her tribe.

Fire Scion I: The Hidden City

Before the white elves had sought refuge with the dypalfar ("deep elves") and become changelings, they had had writing just as all the alfar races did. But modern leukalfar, living in isolated tribes, no longer used the runes once employed by their ancestors. They'd adopted an oral tradition instead. They had very little commerce with anyone outside their villages, though some intercommunication was needed because young people needed to find mates they were not related to by blood.

Myrkra's tribe was hidden, locked away behind stone doors where no non-leukalfar had travelled for thousands of years. That Duraenis had been able to lure this many of her people down out of their mountain villages to rejoin with him in the worship of Apoldros was something of a miracle. Not just her people were here as acolytes – there was another tribe living within Nightvoid Cavern, and they too had been reached by Duraenis in his quest to bring the changelings back into the fold.

Andi found his fellow acolytes a prickly bunch, for the most part. The fact that he could speak their language, and that they knew he was an adherent of their religion, spared him from the overt hostility that might otherwise have erupted. But they were clearly uncomfortable with him, not wishing to prolong a conversation and reluctant to tell him anything about themselves.

Meri had more success. In contrast to the reaction she'd gotten from members of other human races, the leukalfar thought she was a cute little girl – and they were drawn to her. The leukalfar didn't have many children, and those they did have grew too quickly to adulthood and were dearly loved – not only by their parents, but by everyone in their villages. She soon had many friends among the people serving at the Great Temple. Andi at least had Mothris, and Myrkra seemed to be somewhat favorably disposed toward him – though she could be so irascible, it was sometimes hard to tell.

Spring had become summer, and days here in the north went on forever. Andi was able to get away from his duties and take Meri on dragon rides, flying high above the snow-covered wastes that surrounded the Great Temple. The valley immediately outside the cavern was clearly visible below, and he touched down to devour one of the smallish, striped and spotted deer that inhabited it. Meri had been familiar with her older brother's dragon form (and its eating habits) her whole life, and it didn't faze her in the least.

The two of them explored the Eparchy with Mothris accompanying them, traversing the shrines (still manned by their Protectors) and meditating within each of them. They met and spoke with some of the leukalfar in the caves, who were astounded that one of the "sou sepe" (Sky People, as they called all intruders who came down into their domain) was here, speaking their tongue.

And so the months passed, and as summer came near to an end Myrkra told them in leukalfar tongue, "I think it's time for you to come with us to the Canyons of Stone and visit with the rest of the Ankhrazana tribe. There is someone there I want you to meet, someone who can tell you things I do not know." She had come to love the girl Meri, so like a child of her tribe but so different, so open and ebullient compared with the reserve of the people among whom she herself had been raised. And the friendship that had grown up between her son and the boy Andreas amazed her. Perhaps his mother was right, and the rift between the leukalfar and the rest of humankind might be ended.

Chapter 8: The Home Front

Riki perched on the milking stool, wearing leather trousers and a canvas smock, and leaned into the cow's warm, hairy flank. "Oh Freydis," she sighed, "I have to admit that I really do miss Andi." There was deep love among all the Drakespring siblings, but Andi and Riki were so close in age that there had always been a certain amount of conflict between them as well. Yet now he'd been gone all summer, far longer than he had ever been away before, and Meri with him. She missed his teasing, his brown eyes alight with humor, even his show-off dragon transformations.

Not to mention, with both of them gone it had fallen on her to take on most of the farm chores. Mom was busy making enchanted Fireblood arms and armor, Papa Erik helping her. And Papa Andrion was usually busy with his magical studies, or away at Eisenstag leading his research teams. Sigi was some help. At nine he was more than competent to feed the chickens and collect their eggs, and help with the weeding. But milking the cows (the family still had two, Bloody Stupid Animal having been replaced with a springing heifer some years ago) and processing their milk was a task that called for some strength. She was the one who had it.

I can't help who I am, Riki thought forlornly. Erik was her biological father as well as her beloved papa, and he was nearly six and a half feet tall, still strong and muscular though he was now practically ancient (nearing 42). She was probably going to turn into some kind of freak of nature, an enormous red-blonde goddess who would have all the guys too afraid to speak to her. If only she could be petite like Mom!

Sighing again, Riki finished squeezing the last of Freydis' milk into the pail. The old cow, who'd been acquired by the family before she was born, wasn't putting out as much milk as she once had. As Riki untied the animal and shooed her back into her paddock, she mused that even if she hadn't been up to her ears in farm chores, this summer would probably not have been all that great.

Riki had a few other friends and acquaintances in her general age group around the Waterdon area. But her two best friends forever, since earliest childhood, had been Julia Adelini-Blackknife and Sintra Elendion. Both girls were a year older than she was, but Julia was the daughter of the Drakespring clan's smithing business partners and Sintra of Drelos and Larissa Elendion, long-time valued employees of the Drakespring clan's main business – The Bathing Maiden, just down the road. They'd been playing together since Riki had been old enough to walk.

It was almost like some kind of a conspiracy, Riki thought as she lugged the two wooden pails of milk into the house from the milking shed. Right after that day last spring when she and her friends had gone to the construction site, and there had been that trouble at the Flying Horseman after Andi came and got them, suddenly Drelos and Larissa insisted that it was time for Sintra to start developing some responsibility and she'd been inducted as a maid, table server, and kitchen helper at the Maiden. And about that same time, Alessia and Wolaf had also cracked down on Julia and begun demanding that she spend more hours at the forge, learning the trade her mother had plied for years before she was born.

Riki set up a filtered funnel in the kitchen sink, pouring off the morning's milk into a series of glass bottles which she then tightly stoppered and set into the cooling chest. When the milk had cooled some it would be sold, turned to cheese, or drunk by the family. This went on every single morning, rain or shine, too tired to arise at dawn or not. It's time for me to consider a career, she thought. One that does *not* involve cows!

Some hours later Riki had helped to prepare lunch and washed the dishes afterward, had done her personal laundry and hung it out to dry, had worked with Sigi to weed the tomatoes, onions, and potatoes, and had picked a large basket of tomatoes and set them cooking for sauce. They were going to have pasta tonight, Mom said – though she was planning on getting the noodles ready-made from the kitchen at the Maiden. This was a dish from Remus that had never completely caught on in Iscandia, though it was locally popular.

Now she had some spare time, but with none of her friends free to hang out with her Riki found herself setting up for some archery practice with Sigi. Every child in the Drakespring clan was introduced to weapons early, taught how to be safe with them. Iscandia had become a lot calmer during Riki's lifetime, the main conflict between the Remans and the Norse partisans gradually ebbing as home rule in Iscandia became more established. But it could still be a dangerous place, and Riki's parents had experienced it at its most lethal. They wanted all their kids to be able to defend themselves.

Sigi, Riki had to admit to herself, was just adorable. He had such a quality of openness, of innocence about him and was so sweet and loving that hardly anyone who met him failed to fall in love with him. She was happy to help her baby brother and pass along her superior knowledge and skills to him. After all, she was nearly four years older than he was, and had been drawing a bow since she was around five. Mom was one of the best archers Riki knew, and already she too was approaching the skill level where she seldom if ever missed – and could put a second arrow in the air almost before the first had found its target.

Admittedly, trees and buildings and straw-stuffed archery targets were not running toward you with murder on their minds. Riki wondered what it would be like to be shooting at real enemies, people (or creatures) that would kill you if you didn't kill them first. None of the Drakespring kids, not even Andi, had ever had to kill anyone – though Andi had once faced aptrgangr on a quest with their papas to find the dragon spell that turned Mom back into a human.

Riki, who had been three at the time, dimly remembered when Mom had been transformed into a dragon against her will. She had come back to them in her dragon form several times, and Riki had found it very confusing that this enormous creature spoke with Mama's voice. It had been a great relief for her a few weeks later to find Mama back in human form, carrying along her dragon brother Mondi (younger by years, yet mentally older), joining their family once again. And then after that Sigi had been born.

Sigi drew on the target, an uncharacteristic expression of grim concentration on his face as he took aim. Standing back a little, Riki assessed his stance. "Straighten up a little," she told him, putting her hand between his shoulder blades then sliding it down his backbone. "And hold your elbow up more. You want your forearm to be on a line between the target and your elbow."

Sigi made the corrections Riki had commanded, took a deep breath, then let it out. As he did so, he released the bowstring. The arrow (similar in construction to elven arrows, but with a blunted head intended for target shooting) flew to the target, piercing it near dead center. "Excellent!" Riki crowed, pleased that her instruction had produced such a fine result.

Just then a shout came up from the road below the farm: "Good shot, Sigi!" Riki swung her head. There'd been nobody anywhere in sight just moments ago, but now two figures stood there. As if they had fast-travelled… Riki took a couple of steps closer before she recognized the pair, who were even now coming up the walk toward the farmhouse.

"Anja!" she cried, rushing toward them. Sigi hung his bow over his back (part of the exercise was to do it in full armor) and hurried after her. The tall young woman walking toward them looked as if she might be an older sister to Andi, with her dark auburn hair and brown eyes. Her build was slim and muscular, and she was clad head to toe in elven armor. A daimonic bow was slung behind her, and various other small arms were hung about her person. Behind her, a still taller young man with a mop of unruly, dark brown hair and vivid blue eyes was similarly clad. He grinned at Riki and Sigi as they came to greet him and his companion.

After careful hugs (everyone in armor) had been exchanged all around, Anja looked about her. "Where is everybody?" she asked.

"Mom's in town running errands, and Papa Andrion is up at the Academy again," Riki said. "Papa Erik went into town but I think it was to visit with Uncle Geri and Aunt Gytha and their kids. That was later. Andi and Meri are up north somewhere, learning how to speak leukalfar!"

Anja looked a bit taken aback. "So it's just you two, then?" she asked.

"'Fraid so," Riki replied.

"Well, maybe we'll just hang out for a while then," Anja said. "I'm hoping it will be okay for Lars and me to stay here while we're in town, that's why we came here first."

"That should be fine," Riki assured them. "Papa Andrion is in Eisenstag for a few days, so you can probably use his room." Remembering her manners, acting as hostess to the young woman she thought of as an older sister (Fjuri's older sister, actually, though adopted) and her companion, Riki added "Are you hungry?"

Chapter 9: The Canyons of Stone

"Stay close, here" Myrkra commanded, as the small party made their way up the trail along a side canyon. They were no longer in the paths of the Eparchy that he, Meri, and Mothris had travelled during their tour of the shrines, Andi realized. Myrkra had somehow led them up a path that hardly deserved the name of trail, winding between large rocks, and now down into this narrow canyon.

Ahead, he saw a bridge of rope and mandimant chitin spanning the gap from one side of the canyon to the other. And on that bridge stood a lone leukalfar warrior, standing impassive at their approach. He supposed the lack of reaction was because Myrkra was in the lead, and he was the only one of their party who was not leukalfar.

Myrkra greeted the man (yes, Andi was beginning to think of the leukalfar as men and women, though technically in the parlance of his world humanity was divided into "man" – Norsemen, Remans, Afrans, and Galise like himself – and "alfar," the long-lived elven races). The ljosalfar, nachtalfar, sylvalfar, verdalfar, dypalfar, and leukalfar could theoretically interbreed with men, and his own race of "man" was supposedly a mix of the two – though Galise' lifespans were no different from those of other men.

The point was that they were all human, were all *people*. Myrkra and Mothris might have the ability to live far longer than Andi ever would (unless he opted to remain in dragon form forever and become, essentially, immortal), but they had the same general shape, the same concerns, the same aspirations as he did. Agena's other humanoid races, the catlike Gatti and the lizard-like Saurions, shared many of these traits as well – but they were not human.

Myrkra exchanged a few quiet words with the sentry. He "eyed" (leukalfar, without eyes, nonetheless left no doubt when they were "looking" at you) Andi with suspicion, but let the group pass unmolested. Some distance from the far side of the bridge, the trail dipped down along the canyon wall to its sandy, rock-strewn floor. There they met a leukalfar Watcher, much higher up in the tribal hierarchy than the lowly sentry had been.

Again, Myrkra and Mothris in the lead prevented the guardian from making any hostile moves before speaking with them. Andi towered above the leukalfar, and he was visible from a long way off to the curious not-sight of the leukalfar gatekeepers. It was a good thing, he thought, that he was accompanied by members of their own race. He suspected that his newfound facility in the leukalfar tongue would *not* have been enough to stop them attacking him, had he been on his own or in the company of, say, Fjuri.

At the bottom of the canyon, far down near the end where it dwindled to a narrow creek bed, two more guardians stood on either side of a seemingly blank rock face on their right. "Myrkra," one said, acknowledging her with a slight bow of his head, "you return to us?"

"Greetings, Arknis," the older woman replied with little warmth. "Mothris and I have come for a visit, and we have brought some strangers with us. The girl is Merelle, a child of the leukalfar raised by the Sky People, and the boy is Andreas. He is her adoptive brother, and is learning our language and ways."

Arknis fixed Andi with that leukalfar not-stare, then turned his "gaze" to Myrkra. "Pass then, Myrkra," he replied shortly. His fellow guard did something low down on the wall before them, and a grinding, scraping sound came to their ears as the central area of stone lowered itself into the ground to reveal a dark passage into the stone cliff. Andi couldn't resist practicing his language skills by inclining his head and saying, "Thank you, Arknis" in his best accents as he entered the tunnel. Arknis merely looked in his direction, making no response.

The tunnel put Andi in mind of Nightvoid Cavern, with its windings and luminescent plant life. The trip through it was far shorter, however, and in only a few minutes the party of three leukalfar and one Galise youth emerged once more into daylight. Ahead, a broad canyon opened before them. The path they were on climbed the side of it, and the space was crisscrossed with the familiar rope-and-chitin bridges. And lining its sides, and the sides of canyons leading off of it, were leukalfar dwellings. More than Andi had ever seen.

There were leukalfar everywhere! Going about their daily lives: gathering foodstuffs and chemial ingredients, cultivating small garden plots, dandling babies on their hips as they stopped to chat – all the activities of ordinary existence that Andi's mom had often spoken of when she discussed the leukalfar and her hopes for Meri and her future life. Oh, how Andi wished that she could be here now!

Myrkra turned to Andi and Meri and said "Welcome to the Canyons of Stone. This is the territory of the Ankhrazana tribe of the leukalfar." It was more than a village, Andi realized. Almost more like a city, or a city and its outlying areas. Some people liked living closer in, but others took advantage of the population center and its amenities (trade, support from their fellows) while staying a little further out where they had more privacy.

As the group proceeded up the main canyon people began greeting them. Well, greeting Myrkra and Mothris at any rate. Others were goggling at the strangers, and Andi suspected that the curious were eager to speak with their old friends – and harboring a hope that their curiosity might be satisfied. Mothris greeted several young leukalfar of a similar age to himself with the pleasure of meeting old friends. Clearly, not many his age had been drawn to the worship of Apoldros and service at the Great Temple, and he was glad to see those he'd left behind.

Those who came to speak with Myrkra and quiz her about the strangers were mostly met with formal courtesy. Then they came into an area where the canyon opened out into a broader, almost circular space lined, on several levels, with the dwellings of the leukalfar. A younger-seeming leukalfar woman, a small child at her side, cried out at their approach and ran to throw her arms around Myrkra.

"Madira!" the older woman cried, returning the embrace. "And Marsila!" she added, turning to the little girl. "How you've grown!"

"Greetings, Aunt Myrkra," the little one said in her lisping voice.

"Give me a hug!" her aunt demanded, stooping to the child's level and enfolding her in a tight embrace. Meanwhile Mothris was being embraced by the woman Andi took to be his aunt. She and Myrkra must be sisters, though it seemed there was a considerable age gap between then. Meri was taking this all in with an air of wonder, finally getting to see how much like her adoptive family the people who had given her birth could be.

Myrkra and Madira stood conversing for some time, and Mothris bent to give his little cousin a squeeze. Then he introduced her to Andi and Meri. Marsila looked up at Andi in awe. She had never seen one of the Sky People before, not even at a distance. Those leukalfar who were not on sentry duty or traveling on business tended to stay sequestered in their hidden villages, where outsiders never tread.

Wanting to put the little one at ease, Andi crouched down to her level. "Greetings, Marsila," he said, palms up in the leukalfar gesture that said "I come in peace." "My name is Andreas, and this is my sister Merelle," he went on. The small girl looked from him to Meri, then back again. She didn't understand.

"Your sister is one of The People?" she asked, confused.

"She was not born to us, but she has been a member of my family since she was a baby," Andi explained.

Marsila seemed to have gotten over her fear of the tall stranger. He spoke as one of her people, though his speech was somewhat stilted and his accent was strange. As he remained kneeling in front of her, she asked "Can I... can I touch you?"

Andi was a little surprised at this request, but he smiled at her and said "that's all right."

The little girl put her hands on his face, tracing its contours. His nose, so prominent compared with the tiny button of her own race. His eyes, big and with long lashes. His mouth, lips of a medium fullness in a compromise between those of his parents. Her mouth was open in surprise. Finally she put her hands down and said formally, "Welcome to the home of the Ankhrazana, Andreas and Merelle."

Chapter 10: Secrets of the Dypalfar

Some minutes later, the five of them continued on their way into the heart of the settlement and up a ramp to a large example of the typical leukalfar yurt. "This is my home, and Mothris'," Myrkra told the visitors. "My man Urgnis was on sentry duty some years ago and never came back." Andi winced slightly. It would be just his luck if it turned out that Urgnis was one of the hostile leukalfar Mom and Papa Andrion had killed while they were wandering around looking for the Great Temple with Nerissa back before he was born, before they and Papa Erik were even married.

"My sister Madira and her daughter live in the yurt next door with her man Dengan. They've been taking care of the place while Mothris and I have been gone." This was the most personal information Andi and Meri had yet heard from Myrkra, and it made them feel she had really begun to open up to them. Plus there was the fact that she had brought them here, to this hidden sanctuary of her people!

"Do all women of the Ankhrazana have names ending in 'a,' Myrkra?" Meri wanted to know. "No," Myrkra replied thoughtfully. "It's common and very popular, but not all of them do. Just like not all Ankhrazana men's names end in 'is.'" Everyone set down their packs and they took some refreshment, resting from their long trek. It had taken them most of the day to walk here from the Great Temple.

Andi checked his map, and saw that of all the places in this area he had been with it only the courtyard in the Great Temple where he and Meri had first arrived with Mom were showing, along with the four shrines. Seemingly, the magic map didn't acknowledge the places of the leukalfar.

But now that he knew approximately where this place was, Andi realized, he could go dragon and fly here whenever he wanted. Not that he would ever do something like that, coming here to this peaceful village as a fire-breathing monster, violating the trust Myrkra had extended to him by bringing them to her home.

Fire Scion I: The Hidden City

They were still resting from the trip, eating some flatbread smeared with a type of fruit preserve Andi had not tasted before (though he found it delicious; at his age, hunger added savor to almost anything edible), when people began dropping by to say hello. All those in the village who were close acquaintances of Myrkra and her family seemed eager to welcome her back home, even if it was only for a visit. She and her son had gone to join the service of Apoldros permanently, or at least she had. Mothris was young yet, and might still find that a life of religious devotion was not what he wanted.

And just by coincidence, the strange visitors were there in Myrkra's house and must be introduced to them, must speak with them. Some younger people, age-mates of Mothris probably, seemed particularly curious about the newcomers and asked Andi many questions. What was life for the Sky People really like? Was it true they were all bloodthirsty monsters, killing everyone they met on sight and stealing whatever they found from the underground places they hunted in?

Andi realized with horror that perhaps the answer to that last question was "yes." Not every Norseman, Galise, Afran and Reman (or elf) was engaged in plundering ancient ruins, of course, but it was adventurers like Fjuri's big sister Anja and her companion Lars, or like his own mom when she was younger, that the leukalfar sentries came in contact with. He found himself trying to change the subject. What did leukalfar young people do for fun in the evenings? Were there any interesting places nearby for them to explore?

As the late summer sun was beginning to slide toward the horizon, Myrkra shooed the last of their visitors away and announced, "There's some water in the basin over there. Wash your hands, then we're going next door. Madira is preparing us a feast." Andi looked up eagerly. It seemed like ages since their snack, and his stomach had been rumbling. Meri looked pleased, too. Now she was going to see what the people of her birth ate for dinner!

49

In the large yurt next door they were introduced to Madira's husband Dengan. He was a young leukalfar man of a similar age to Madira, and seemed remarkably cheerful for one of his reserved, clannish race. He was not at all put off having the strangers at his table (actually they sat on mats on the floor of the yurt, which was covered with mandimant chitin, in a circle around the fire) and engaged both Meri and Andi in conversation.

He was not one of the leukalfar sentries, they learned, but rather engaged in the limited agriculture the people practiced in their hidden canyons. Mandimants were kept for their chitin and other products, the eggs a powerful chemial ingredient. The Ankhrazana also had garden plots in which they raised grains, greens, potatoes, and various other crops. Having grown up on a farm, Andi found he had more in common with Dengan than he would have thought possible. But farming here was a communal activity, with those most apt to it doing the work and all members of the community benefiting from the produce.

Before dinner was served another guest arrived, the oldest leukalfar Andi had ever seen. If the alfar races lived for centuries, this man must be ancient indeed. Most of the leukalfar were very thin, emaciated-looking, but Gryndor had a little pot belly and a bit of flesh, hanging in wrinkled folds, around his chin. He was introduced as the tribe's Chanter, which Andi took to mean something like bard. He was bent, and walked with the aid of a stick.

Madira was very solicitous of the old man. Clearly, he was a highly respected elder. She provided him with cushions to sit on and a mug of hot tea before returning to her supper preparations. She must have been cooking since right after they'd parted this afternoon, to have gotten all this food together!

Gryndor's voice was mellow and powerful, and he too was very curious about Andi and Meri. "A leukalfar girl raised by the Sky People!" he exclaimed. "I have not heard of such a thing since ancient times. Not since the cursed dypalfar poisoned and enslaved us, made us as we now are, have any of the other alfar races, or any of the men, reached out to us in friendship."

50

"It's been a dream of my mom's for a long time," Andi explained. "Ever since she found Meri, she's hoped that it might be possible for leukalfar and the people who walk the earth above to meet in trade and friendship. The leukalfar people have many skills, and I know that men and the other alfar races would be happy to pay gold or trade steel and other metals for some of your potions and the things you make with chitin."

Gryndor seemed somewhat surprised at the boy's speech. That his people and the rest of humanity might reach a détente, might stop killing each other on sight, was not something he had ever considered possible. But were not the verdalfar and the Norsemen nearly as different from one another as leukalfar and ljosalfar? For that matter, he knew that saurions and gatti, not even human though certainly people, were able to move freely in Iscandia society without being harassed or murdered.

Now he wondered, might it even happen in my lifetime? Given the prickly and insular nature of his people, he didn't think it would be easy. But perhaps it was not impossible. "You're a Chanter?" Andi asked, breaking Gryndor's train of thought. "What is that, exactly? Do you sing and tell stories?" Gryndor pondered for a moment before answering. Both Andi and Meri were hanging on his words.

"Let me explain," he said, pleased that these young people hungered for his knowledge. It was, after all, what he was all about. "Many thousands of years ago, before the dypalfar forever changed our people – and for a while afterward, as well – the leukalfar had writing as did all of the descendants of the eldalfar. But after we had been enslaved for generations, and then when our masters vanished from this world and only a few scattered populations of the leukalfar were left behind, the knowledge of writing was lost."

"They vanished?" Meri blurted out. She could read and write and figure, and was starting to learn chemia, but had not yet studied much history. "What happened to them?" Gryndor didn't take offense at the girl's interruption. In their society, with children being born only rarely and grown in such a short time relative to their long lifespans, little ones were usually indulged and only rarely disciplined.

"Patience, child," the old man said. "After we have eaten I will tell you all. But as I was saying, without writing we needed a way to preserve the knowledge our people had, knowledge that must be passed down to each generation. So Chanters came to be. Those of us who had the aptitude, memories for detail that were nearly flawless, were taken as children and trained in the lore. Each Chanter must know all of our stories, and must tell these stories to the people. And each Chanter must pass down his or her knowledge to a successor. I have trained three such, and some of them have traveled to other tribes."

"Our stories are still growing," Gryndor went on. "It is not enough to remember the details of things that happened generations ago. We must find the new stories, things that are happening now, and tell them so that others can learn. The scattered tribes of the leukalfar are hostile to intruders, but Chanters can go anywhere. They pass on the new stories that they have learned, and learn the stories of other tribes. Then, in years or decades, they may return and add what they have learned elsewhere to the knowledge of our own tribe. Thus the history of the leukalfar remains."

Andi was awed. Poring over musty tomes in search of forgotten knowledge didn't have nearly the appeal for him that it did for his father and grandfather. But if the knowledge were living, told and preserved by speakers with the gift of a superb memory and good story-telling skills, everyone would want to learn what they had to tell. In fact, Papa Andrion had imparted many bits of lore to him – and these verbally-delivered tales had stuck with him far more than had things read in books. The same with Grandpapa Francois, though the old man was getting up there now and his mind sometimes wandered. The human element was an important part of learning.

Suddenly the area around the fire became a hub of activity as Madira and Myrkra, with help from Mothris and Dengan, began passing dishes around and laying bowls of food in the circle between the seated guests and the fire. They all had soon heaped their plates with food (Andi perhaps more than some others there) and fell to eating with enthusiasm. There was relatively little conversation around the fire for some minutes, as everyone was busy enjoying the delicious food.

Over the months he and Meri had been living and taking their meals at the Great Temple, Andi had gotten used to meals without the ubiquitous crusty bread rolls, white inside, which were the standard fare in Iscandia for every meal of the day. The food there, prepared by and for the leukalfar acolytes, was simple but plentiful and nutritious. Here, it seemed, Madira had gone beyond the usual to produce a meal that tickled the palate.

There was bread of a sort, again a sort of whole-grain flatbread. The rounds were large and soft, and were intended to be wrapped around a mixture of roasted goat meat, seasoned and chopped, and a medley of vegetables that were mostly unfamiliar to Andi but spiced in a way he found quite delicious. There was an assortment of sauces to be added, ranging from merely flavorful to mouth-burning hot (as a sometime dragon, he'd acquired a taste for such things). All of it was then rolled up and held in the hands to be eaten. A grain dish of some sort, slightly sweet-tasting and sticky enough to be best eaten with a spoon, accompanied the flatbread wraps.

It all tasted wonderful! Andi plowed into his serving and had seconds, with all the enthusiasm an adolescent boy can bring to the devouring of food. Meri however seemed somewhat put off by the unfamiliar foods. She'd been raised on the Iscandia Norse standards of meat and potatoes, bread rolls, and salads – and more exotic fare like the sandwiches and Dragon fries from the Bathing Maiden down the road from their home. With a little encouragement from her adored big brother, though, she ate what she'd been served. Actually, that grain dish wasn't too bad.

After everyone had finished eating, Madira and Dengan cleared away the plates and brought everyone mugs of an herbal tea sweetened with honey and whitened with what Andi took to be goat's milk. It wasn't his favorite way to drink tea, but it tasted good enough and he was lavish with his praise of the meal and thanks to Madira and her family for providing it.

Madira and Dengan joined them sitting around the fire after they had finished disposing of the dishes, cutlery, and bowls. Gryndor sat up a little straighter, sighing pleasurably. "Madira," he said, "That was a wonderful meal. Thank you so much for inviting me to join with you and your family. And your young visitors…" he gestured at Andi and Meri. "Now," he went on, "I think it is time that I tell the tale of how the leukalfar came to be as we are today."

Gryndor's audience was silent, looking at him in anticipation. For Andi and Meri this was a tale they had never heard before, information they were eager to learn. For the rest of them it was a familiar but much-beloved story, one they never tired of hearing from Gryndor. They had been listening to him tell it, from time to time, throughout their entire lives.

The old man began speaking, as the fire crackling before them gradually began fading into embers. "It was more than four thousand years ago," he began.

Madira broke in, asking "This is when you were a little boy, honored father?" Andi was shocked at the interruption, but he soon realized from Gryndor's reaction that there was a deep bond of affection between him and the young woman.

"Ahem," the old man said, then continued with the faintest hint of a grin, "No, young Madira, as strange as it may seem I was not even born yet. Indeed, my father and my father's father had not yet come into this world."

He went on, more seriously. "The white elves had been living in Iscandia for many ages, but the Norsemen had now come and were pushing us out of our ancestral lands. They were fierce, and had the working of metals, and though they quickly aged and died their children were without number. Our kin the dypalfar were hard-pressed too, but with their knowledge of machinery they had been able to carve themselves cities under the earth. Cities where the Norsemen could not come in force, for the ways were hidden and narrow and their metal servants, their automatons, guarded against all intruders."

The audience remained hushed, listening raptly as Gryndor's tale unfolded. "In those days," he said, "the white elves did not live in isolated tribes as we do now, but were a great nation. Though that nation was now severely damaged, and many had been killed while many others had fled for their lives, penniless refugees. There was one great leader of our people, and his name was Indinoris. He consulted with his counselors, and all agreed that he should seek out Mthragzam, the great leader of the dypalfar people, and ask that they give shelter to the white elves before we should be wiped out."

There was a slight murmuring in the dimness beyond the firelight, as those who knew what was coming commented on the story. Then silence fell again, and Gryndor continued: "Now at that time Mthragzam ruled in Undernight, a vast underground city where some of our kin still live to this day. And Indinoris went there with his court to meet with him. Long did they negotiate, and it seemed that the dypalfar held no great love for the white elves and did not want to shelter them from the attacking Norsemen. Finally Mthragzam said that they would allow Indinoris' people to come within and live with them in their hidden cities, but that they must agree to eat of a sacred mushroom before they would be let in. And furthermore, once they had come in, they would be required thereafter to serve the dypalfar."

Andi had heard some of this before, but it was news to Meri and she gasped audibly. How could the dypalfar, their fellow elves, have been so cruel and conniving? The story continued, as Gryndor said "Indinoris was very saddened, but he did not think there was any choice. There was nowhere else for his people to flee, and if he did not agree to Mthragzam's terms all would perish beneath the Norse assault that went on year after year, generation after generation. So he agreed, and he and those who were with him went down into Undernight and took of the mushroom."

"The mushroom had a powerful effect, and it changed our people in unexpected ways. Though we had looked much like other humans before, our noses shrank until they were little more than a nubbin, our limbs grew thin, and our eyes became tiny things – hidden beneath layers of skin. But yet we were not without sight. As the mushroom took some things away, it granted us the gift of the vision we now have, letting us see even in the blackness where other humans cannot. And it infected our seed as well, so that future generations who had never eaten of the mushroom's poison still showed the effects. The leukalfar had been transformed."

"This did not happen all at once," Gryndor went on. "Many of Indinoris' people had been wary of going through with the bargain, and when they saw what had happened to those who took the mushroom they fled. But they were killed by Norsemen or driven off. Duraenis and his brother Signis, together with the servants of Apoldros here in our northern fastness, were the only ones to survive unchanged."

Meri gasped, then getting a nod from Gryndor she asked, "But what became of the dypalfar, Gryndor? Why are we here and they are not?"

The old man nodded at her, smiling. "They had crippled the leukalfar, or so they thought, and enslaved us. And their underground cities had proven secure against the Norsemen, most of whom simply thought their enemies were gone. For many generations of men the dypalfar lived below while the Norsemen lived out their short lives above, unaware of what was happening beneath their feet."

"And then?" the girl prompted, agog to hear the answer.

"And then, the leukalfar arose and fought their masters. For more generations of men the conflict raged underground. And in Darkreach, the region where both dypalfar and leukalfar had originated, the dypalfar were also fighting the Auralfar, a race of elves who objected to the dypalfar's failure to honor their gods."

Gryndor went on. He might seem old and creaky, but his voice was smooth as silk, hypnotic. "The dypalfar technician Lord Dzurman had discovered the energy matrix beneath Og Vulanz on an island north of Darkreach, and he had built tools to harness its power. Now, as you may have heard, the dypalfar possessed a power held by no other race of humankind. It was referred to as the Joining. With this they could talk mind to mind over great distances, and thus did the scattered cities of dypalfar communicate with one another."

"And so, with the tools provided by Dzurman, it was decided that all of the dypalfar would travel to another plane – leaving Agena and its conflicts behind. There they would inhabit a world where there were only dypalfar – and what leukalfar slaves remained to them. For though the leukalfar had fought for generations to be free, many were still enslaved. Nor would their betrayers relent."

Andi couldn't resist interrupting at this point. "I was told that all of the dypalfar died, that their race was extinct," he said hesitantly. Gryndor nodded to him.

"And so," the old elf said, "it is thought throughout Agena. Everywhere there are the ruined cities of the dypalfar, where live the descendants of our people who were left behind. But nowhere is there a living dypalfar. Nor any of their mortal remains. For the truth is they did not die – they departed."

He went on, "Each group of the dypalfar had acquired for themselves the tools of Dzurman, and when the signal was given using the Joining, as the Dwelves in Darkreach were hard-pressed at the Battle of Og Vulanz, each opened a portal to the new world they had discovered, and all of their people went through it to the other side."

"Was it one of the planes of the Netherworld?" Andi asked. He'd been told of these. A few hundred years before he'd been born, a crisis had erupted in Remus in which dozens of such portals or "gates" had been opened and hostile daimons had poured through them to attack the human denizens of Agena. According to family legend, it had been one of his mom's remote ancestors who had been instrumental in aiding the last fireblood emperor to defeat the attackers and close the gates.

"The Netherworld has many planes, and they are not all alike," Gryndor responded. "Only one of the daimons might know one from another, and I doubt even any of those would know this one; else daimons would have been there. But Dzurman had discovered a realm, a pocket universe if you will, to which his tools would allow passage. Some of our people learned of it before the event, and they had been told it was a fair land, with trees and grass and lesser creatures but no men, no alfar, and no daimons."

"It sounds like a paradise," Andi murmured. The old man's hearing was still sharp (indeed, all leukalfar senses other than sight seemed magnified by comparison with his puny ones), for he heard the words.

"Yes, Andreas, a paradise. But a small one, I think. The dypalfar must once again delve into the earth to build their cities there, not because they feared attack but because there was not enough room on the surface for both their cities and the farms that would sustain their population. By now, though, the majority of the dypalfar people had been living underground for so many generations that most were more comfortable never glimpsing the sky. As is the case for many of our own people, though the Ankhrazana tribe have long lived above the ground. We might almost be counted among the Sky People, now."

Andi and Meri both pondered this. The differences between the race of alfar Meri had been born to and the race of men that produced her big brother were huge – yet there were so many similarities! Raised among men since infancy, Meri felt far more akin to her adopted family's people than she did to the Ankhrazana; but they called to her, in a strange way she didn't understand.

Gryndor continued his tale. "When all of the dypalfar people and their leukalfar slaves had passed through the portals, along with all of the goods that they needed to take with them, they left behind many of their enchanted automatons to guard the cities they had left behind. In order that none should ever follow them to where they had fled, it was necessary for one dypalfar volunteer at each portal to stay behind, to destroy the machine that had made the gate. And so the dypalfar passed from this world, and were heard of no more from that time to this. Though the leukalfar they left behind came to inhabit many of those cities, living in tribal societies, bereft of the technology of their masters or even of what technology we had possessed before we were enslaved. But we have remained!"

This apparently concluded the tale, and the old man took a large swig of hot herbal tea that Madira pressed into his hands. What a story! Andi thought. He wished Papa Andrion had been here to listen to it. The humans who currently ruled Iscandia had many theories about the disappearance of the dypalfar, and information about that vanished race and their technology was one of Papa Andrion's favorite fields of study.

He had worked with their family friend Diane Baudin (*nee* leBois) to build the Drakespring clan's wonderful hot bathing pool, based on borrowed dypalfar technology. That had been back before Mom, Papa Andrion, and Papa Erik had been married, the pool and Drakespring House itself surprises for Mom from her husbands-to-be. The pool and its surrounding tile had needed some maintenance over the years since, but the heating and sanitizing system had worked flawlessly. Andi had certainly taxed its capabilities to the fullest a few times in his life, being tossed into the hot water by Mama covered head to foot in grime.

"Thank you, Gryndor," Andi said respectfully. He felt like he and Meri had been given a great gift to be told this story, even if it *was* Gryndor's job. He also had the feeling the leukalfar had insights into the disappearance of the dypalfar that other races did not, being as it were on the inside of things, and that this story was probably the true one. "I have often wondered what really happened to the dypalfar," he continued. "So that was it, then? All of those portals are now closed forever, the machines that made them destroyed?"

Gryndor picked up his mug of tea between both hands, savoring the warmth. It was far warmer here in the Canyons of Stone than elsewhere in the Eparchy, but they were still far in the north of the province and nights got cold. "I have heard a tale," the old man said. He took another sip, drawing out the suspense. "But

I don't know if it is true." He "eyed" Andi and Meri, whose attention was fixed on him in suspense.

The old fellow took another sip of the hot brew, and smiled at them. He knew exactly what he was doing. "We Chanters," he explained, "strive only to pass on tales that we know to be true. They must have been witnessed by ourselves, by someone we trust, or have been passed on through generations of Chanters from one who was there or had it told to him or her by a trusted witness. Thus, we hope that we are keeping the true history of the leukalfar people, and not just spinning tales or legends. So what I am going to tell you now must be understood to be… rumor, perhaps. Or at least something that is not verified. Do you understand?"

The two youngsters nodded at him in unison. Others around the fire had dispersed to assist with the washing of dishes, and the preparation of dessert. "This story was told by one who was there to another, and from him to another, and then finally to the Chanter of a tribe I visited in my youth. It had been passed from her to her descendants, and finally to the one who told it to me while I was traveling, gathering more stories. In this way do the leukalfar maintain some unity as a people, for otherwise we would become nothing but a collection of little tribes, each cut off not only from the rest of humanity but from each other as well."

There was an interruption as more mugs of tea were passed around, along with some confections. These proved to be similar to the roasted nut confections so familiar to Andi and Meri, but seeming to have been pressed flat on a stone, baked over a fire, and then cut into squares. They were certainly delicious. Andi had been well-sated less than an hour ago, but he was already starting to develop an appetite. Meri too, in the way of most children, found she loved the sweet squares and also wanted seconds.

Some time later, Gryndor resumed his tale. "Where was I?" he asked, washing down the last crumbs of his dessert with a final mouthful of now-cooled tea. "Ah, yes. There was one portal, far to the west of here and still further north, where the one who was tasked with staying behind alone – presumably to die of starvation or be killed after he had destroyed the machine that had created the portal – did not fulfill his task. Moments after the last of his people had passed through the portal, as he raised his warhammer to destroy the machine, he was swarmed over by some of the leukalfar who had rebelled. They had been free of their masters for years, but had remained in hiding within the dypalfar city – seeking to free their brethren. They were well armed, and the last dypalfar guardian fell to their arrows before he could destroy the machine."

Meri and Andi gasped simultaneously. Then what happened? "This band of our people was well led, though the leader's name was not passed along with the tale. She decreed that they would not destroy the machine, keeping the portal open. In time, she hoped, they might be able to go through that portal and defeat the dypalfar overlords, freeing the leukalfar slaves they had taken with them. Their strength was not such that they could do this yet. But in the meantime, they would guard the portal and kill any dypalfar that should come through it, hoping to destroy the machine and close the last door through which they could be followed to their new world."

Gryndor ended his tale on a note of finality. What? This had been thousands of years ago. Surely, the leukalfar left guarding the machine must have been overrun and the portal closed. Or conversely, they must have built enough strength to have invaded the dypalfar paradise and killed their former masters, freeing the remaining slaves? The latter didn't seem likely, Andi thought. Both leukalfar and dypalfar suffered from the same problem all the alfar shared – their much greater lifespans were balanced by much lower fertility than that of men. Humans lived only a few decades, but they could breed like rabbits during that time – where a woman of the alfar was lucky if she could produce a single offspring during her long life.

This meant that it took the alfar a long time, many human generations, to increase their population. Any major battle or epidemic of fatal disease (though disease was less of a possibility, with magical interventions and panacea potions available to all) could devastate an alfar population and require centuries before they would recover. In the meantime, they'd have been overrun by men.

"Gryndor," Andi asked tentatively. "Do you think it's possible that the machine and the portal are still there?"

"I don't see how it could be," the old man replied. "Surely the dypalfar on the other side must have been aware that the portal was still open, and taken steps to eliminate it. But who knows? This tale was passed from person to person and then to a Chanter thousands of years before I was born." He saw them looking at him and added with a slight smile, "And no, I'm not telling you when I was born. Suffice it to say, it was a long time before *you* two were born."

Andi and Meri thanked the old Chanter, and shortly thereafter Dengan came to assist him back to his own yurt. Despite his advanced age, Gryndor still lived by himself. Darkness was no obstacle to the leukalfar, who could "see" as well in the utter absence of light as Andi could in daylight. Their sense was a psychic one, and did not offer the rich detail and range of colors his eyes could provide him when there was light – but it enabled them to move through the world quite well.

The two young people, one of them far stranger than any that had guested here before, gave their thanks and tokens of affection to their hosts and then were led by Myrkra and Mothris through the darkness to the yurt next door. The leukalfar didn't go in for torches much, having no need of them, and Andi stumbled slightly as he traversed the rough stone pathway between the dwellings. He was glad he didn't have to walk any further!

Chapter 11: Magic Map

Andi and Meri passed the night comfortably enough, buried under warm fur bedrolls in the home of Myrkra and Mothris. In the morning they rose and drank more hot tea. They were given a grain porridge quite similar to the breakfast fare they'd been enjoying at the Great Temple these past months, after which Myrkra told them, "It is time for us to return to our duties. Gather your packs, as we have a long walk ahead of us."

Andi smiled at her, reaching for the map Mom had given him. It had few markings on it at the moment, since it offered fast-travel access only to places the current bearer had visited while either in possession of the map, or as a companion of the person who was controlling it. Certainly some of Andi's most familiar haunts were there – Waterdon, the Bathing Maiden, Drakespring Farm – as well as some other spots he'd visited in company with his mother and this particular map: the Great Temple, Sylvanian, and Forestville, among others.

"I can take us back to the Great Temple without us having to walk it, Myrkra," Andi explained.

"Oh," she replied thoughtfully, "one of the magic maps. I have heard of them but I have not travelled with them. How does it work?"

"My papa Andrion made this one," Andi explained, showing her how it included not only Iscandia but the entire continent of Agena along with its major outlying islands. "That was when I was a baby, but they don't ever seem to wear out. It will take us anyplace I've been before with the map, or walking as long as the map was with me or with a companion when we went there."

"Well, go ahead and take us then," Myrkra said shortly. Andi had become very fond of the leukalfar woman, but she could certainly be curt on occasion. With her, Meri, and Mothris gathered around him he placed his finger on the marker for the spot where he, Mom, and Meri had first appeared last spring, and wished them all there.

They arrived in what seemed like a few seconds. Myrkra and Mothris both seemed a little taken aback, though the young leukalfar lad seemed exhilarated by the experience. "That was amazing!" he blurted, a break from his usual quiet and thoughtful demeanor.

Pleased by the reaction, Andi bragged "It'll take us anywhere that's marked, at least anywhere I've been before, in what seems like the same amount of time. Of course, more time will actually have gone past. But you don't have to walk, and you're not being attacked by bears or whatever along the way. So it's pretty cool."

Mothris peered over his shoulder, taking in the extent of the map. He had been born in the Canyons of Stone and had spent his entire life within a few dozen miles of there. He'd been dimly aware that there was a bigger world out there, but it had never really hit home to him until just now. Among his people, only Chanters and traders ever did much traveling. And as an acolyte of the temple of Apoldros here at the Great Temple, he would likely remain here for the rest of his very long life.

As Mothris was studying the map Andi scanned it too, trying to fix in his mind which markers represented places he had visited and which just marked major cities. The maps always showed the most important landmarks; but they would not take you there until you'd already visited them by more mundane means, while in possession of the map or as a companion of the one who held it. Hey, he wondered, what was that big symbol in the middle of a large island, far up to the north and west in the northern sea? Andi didn't remember seeing it when Mom had given him the map.

He racked his memory, trying to recall when it had first appeared. The symbol was of a tower, perhaps, pointed at the bottom and rounded at the top with what looked like a round-topped window in the middle of it. And the legend read "Mrzhgradfendz"! Clearly, a dypalfar ruin. But no dypalfar ruins were important enough to appear on the map before you had visited them, nor had he ever gone to one in that location.

Excitement gripped him as Andi realized what this must be: the symbol would have appeared on the map last night, at the moment when Gryndor had told him and Meri about the portal to the dypalfar's hidden realm. It was a quest marker! With The

Fireblood and two famous adventurers for parents, Andi had lived and breathed quests from earliest childhood – even if he'd only actually been on just one in his whole life.

He remembered from that time when he was five, how the quest marker for Gunderthal, the ancient Norse ruin where he and his papas had found the dragon spell needed to turn Mama back into a human, had appeared on both their maps when Mama, in dragon form, had told them about it. Papa Andrion had explained to Andi since then how, if you were given a true task to fulfill – a quest – the location of that quest would usually appear on the map.

Having somebody feed you a line, tell you "my sister is being held captive by bandits in Pine Hollow" when that was not true, would not produce a marker. However if there really was a place called Pine Hollow, and that person's sister was really there – even if she'd actually taken up with the bandit chief of her own free will – you might still get the marker. But if there were no such place, no marker would appear.

Andi took a deep breath, trying to still the racing of his heart. This was a real quest, the first one he had ever been given as an adult. Okay, maybe some people might not think he was an adult yet. But he felt like one. He was tall, and strong, and skilled with blade and bow and spell. Could anyone be more ready than he was to go off and perform legendary deeds? Hell, he was fireblood! What foe could stand before him?

Papa Andrion needed to know about this. And Mom, and Papa Erik, too. He knew they would be eager to join him in exploring this opportunity. What if they could follow the dypalfar into their new world? What secrets might be revealed? Unable to completely stifle his excitement, Andi turned to Myrkra as she was gathering herself to go back into the Great Temple.

"Myrkra, Mothris," he said, "thank you very much for taking us to your home. It means more to me than I can say, and the welcome your people extended to me, as one of the Sky People, was… amazing. But I think it's time now that Meri and I pay a visit to our *own* home. Would you like to come with us?"

Mothris looked interested, but clearly Myrkra was frightened at the suggestion. She stiffened, seeming to be searching for words, before saying. "Thank you, Andreas, for the offer. We would like perhaps, someday, to visit with your family in the lands of the Sky People. But for now, we have duties that we have been neglecting. We need to return to them. You and Merelle have made no vows, as yet, so you are free to go. I hope that you will be back with us before too long. There is still much we can teach you, about the leukalfar and about Apoldros."

"We'll see you when we get back, then," Andi said. He was sorry that he couldn't take Mothris along. He was sure his friend would have loved to have come, if he hadn't had his responsibilities. "Please tell Duraenis that we will return after we've spent some time with our family." He didn't mention that this time with family might involve a trip to the dypalfar world on the far side of a portal to another dimension! "Come on, Meri, let's go home."

Chapter 12: Homecomings

The long, late-summer day was drawing near to its end and three members of the Drakespring clan sat, contentedly enjoying the light on the mountains to the east, from a long wooden settee strewn with cushions. Riki had a sketchpad in her hands, and was using colored chalks to render her impression of the view that she'd known and loved her entire life. Her skills might not be equal to those of Fjuri's papa Bjorn, but she had some ability and had discovered that doing artwork gave her great pleasure. Papa Erik had been teaching her how to make jewelry, and her friends were eager to receive the pieces she made as gifts.

Bernadette was knitting a sweater. This had never been one of her great talents, but she was getting better at it and she wanted Andrion to have something warm to wear during those frigid Eisenstag evenings. He spent perhaps one week in four at the Academy now, as excited as ever by the projects his research teams were engaged in.

Between them sat Erik, an arm around each of his favorite girls. Well, Meri was one of his favorite girls and so was Anja. But these two would do nicely for the moment. He felt a great sense of peace, his tasks for the day done. All three of them had their feet up on a long, low footstool, custom-crafted like the settee by Bernadette's brother Gerard – now a member of the thriving woodworking and cloth-producing firm of Arngeld and Sons (though he was just a son-in-law).

Both Riki and Bernadette were bent to their work, so it was Erik who first spotted a familiar shimmer in the air on the road below the walk leading up to the house. He squinted a bit, making sure who it was. His once razor-sharp eyesight had declined a notch or two now he was in his forties, but he could still put an arrow into an aptrgangr's glowing eye-socket from fifty yards away, should the need arise.

"Andrion!" Erik called out, rising to his feet and stepping down off the veranda to go and welcome his brother home. Erik and Andrion, friends for years before Bernadette came into their lives, had become brothers on the day the two of them had married her, more than sixteen years ago now.

Bernadette and Riki were right behind him, and Bernadette sprinted ahead of him to throw herself into her husband's arms. Andrion's frequent absences had, in this case at least, served to make the heart grow fonder. He hadn't stayed home enough to let her get tired of him, perhaps. Though Erik had been right there by her side all along, and she certainly wasn't tired of *him* either.

Andrion's aging but still-handsome face was wreathed in a big grin as he saw his loved ones approaching. It was almost worth staying away, just for the joy of coming home again. After Bernadette had released him he was squeezed in an enormous bear-hug by Erik, and then Riki came smiling into his arms. At thirteen she might chafe at the restrictions her parents imposed on her, or feel frustrated at their seeming inability to understand her, but she dearly loved both her papas and she missed Andrion when he was gone.

Andrion had been away for more than a week this time, and he saw his daughter with fresh eyes. By the gods, he thought, she is turning into a beautiful woman! Life seemed to be passing by faster and faster with every year, and their babies were growing up. He missed his older son and younger daughter so much, and wondered what changes they were going through, way up in the frozen north.

After the three had thoroughly hugged and kissed him, Andrion looked around. "Where's Sigi?" he asked. Riki gave him an impish grin. "Wait for it…" she said, "aaand, there!" At that moment the youngest member of the Drakespring clan came tearing around from behind the house, in hot pursuit of Joqui Caron – the younger son of the Bathing Maiden's current head innkeeper, Remy, and his wife Hildi.

Lev Ciabalo, who had held the job when Bernadette first came to the Maiden seventeen years ago, had moved on to become General Manager. He spent a lot of his time elsewhere, promoting the Maiden across Agena and seeking out gourmet dishes, a passion of his, to offer in the Maiden's kitchen. He would stay at the Maiden for a few days several times a year, sometimes coming with his longtime friend and housemate Octavius Fibonacci. The two of them owned a house in the Alfarien district of Roma in Remus, and lived there together whenever one or the other of them was not travelling. They were both confirmed bachelors.

Sigi, close to catching his friend in whatever game they were playing, skidded to a halt when he saw the rest of the family gathered down near the road. "Papa Andrion!" he squealed, resuming his headlong pace as he rushed to fling himself into his papa's arms. Joqui, a fairly small and quite good-natured boy, just stood and smiled as he watched his friend's reunion. His own parents never left home, as they both worked and lived at the inn where he had been born.

Being surrounded by loving family members filled Andrion with joy, but at the same time there was a stab of pain as he thought again of his elder son and younger daughter. He knew that what they were doing was important, needed to be done so that Meri could fulfill the destiny fate had mapped out for her. But he wanted them back!

The group had just begun walking up toward the farmhouse when there was another shimmer in the road below. Though the magic maps worked differently for each user depending on their previous travels, they always chose the same arrival points. Andrion thought it had something to do with the dimensional matrices, and that these points were those most suited to materializing a traveler. Thank the gods, they never deposited you up to your waist in stone.

Only Joqui, still facing the road as he watched Sigi and his family come up the walk, spotted the two figures that materialized behind them. "It's Andi and Meri!" he cried out, excited. He thought Sigi's older brother and sister were really cool, being so different from everybody else he knew. Meri was one of a kind, a normal girl who looked totally freaky – and Andi could (and often did) turn into a dragon. He had kind of missed them during the months they'd been gone.

As one the Drakesprings whirled, beheld their missing family members, and rushed back down the walk to mob them. Soon Andi and Meri, grinning from ear to ear, were smothered in hugs and kisses, gasping for breath and laughing. Bernadette, who had so successfully held back her tears at their parting all those months ago, now had tears of joy streaming unregarded down her cheeks. Her babies were home!

Chapter 13: Stories

Joqui had gone back home to the Maiden, a mere quarter mile down the road, bidding Sigi a cheerful goodbye. He knew his friend would be eager to spend time with his brother and sister after their long absence, and he couldn't wait to tell his mama and papa the news.

Over the years of Joqui's life and that of his older brother Giscard, roughly the same age as Sintra Ventura, the Maiden had become a much more family-oriented place. There were still often naked people in the two large bathing pools (one in the original Maiden building and the other in the "new" northern wing, now sixteen years old), but there was also a child center on the far side of the northern wing where classes and activities were provided and parents could leave their children under the supervision of some of the Maiden's staff. This service had proven almost as much of a draw as the great food, entertainment, and attractive hospitality specialists that had made the inn one of the most popular in the province.

Back at Drakespring Farm, there was unceasing chatter as Andi and Meri were welcomed back into the fold – though Andi had been sure to mention, early on, that they were only here for a visit and had promised to return to the Eparchy before long. After Andi had dropped his pack in his room downstairs and Meri had taken hers to the nursery (which she still happily shared with her younger brother Sigi), they took a quick bath.

The entire Drakespring clan, or as many of them as could fit in the tub at one time, had been bathing together in this smallish bathing pool (less than half the size of the one at the Maiden) since they were old enough to be trusted in the water without a diaper. So nudity at home was something they scarcely noticed – though Andi had recently discovered an increasing sensitivity to the sight of *some* female flesh.

Papa Erik, whose attitude toward such things was a bit more relaxed than that of Papa Andrion, assured him that these feelings were a natural part of getting to be the age he was, and since it was girls who triggered them in him that meant he was growing up to be straight. He also explained that some men had those feelings for other men, hinting rather heavily that Uncle Lev and his housemate were among those. Andi guessed that explained why neither Uncle Lev nor his friend had ever married.

When Andi and Meri had emerged from the bathroom, refreshed and relaxed after all their travels (and Andi wondering whether he had enough magical energy yet to work Papa Andrion's hot bath spell – there'd been a definite shortage of hot water for bathing at the Great Temple these past few months), they sat with Andrion, Sigi, and Riki at the dining table while Bernadette and Erik worked together to prepare supper.

The arrival of her beloved, oft-absent other husband minutes before the arrival of her elder son and younger daughter had Bernadette sailing through food preparations with a song on her lips. Not that she was a nightingale, by any means. She had a pleasant, alto singing voice that stayed mostly on-key even if it had not much in the way of either range or volume. Erik smiled fondly at her, then as fondly at those gathered around the table.

Giving up his freewheeling, easy lifestyle at the Maiden for life on the farm with Bernadette, Andrion, and their growing brood of children had proven to be a happy life choice for Erik. The past sixteen years, except for that period when Bernadette had been stolen from them by Sneyagflug's trick and coerced into becoming mother to a new generation of dragons, had been almost unmitigated bliss as far as he was concerned. There were now so many people he loved!

The extra mouths for dinner had required some shuffling of the menu, and Erik dispatched Sigi on a run down to the Maiden for some provisions. Having a professional kitchen where fresh bread and other baked goods were produced six times daily only a short distance away was a huge convenience – even more so since, as the Maiden's owner, Bernadette never had to pay for whatever her family needed.

Sigi loved being sent to the Maiden on errands. It was a sign that he was one of the big kids now, trusted to go a quarter mile from home by himself and return with the goods. And he had friends there of all ages, from his best buddy Joqui to most of the Maiden's staff. Any child of the Drakesprings was regarded with favor by the Maiden employees, and Sigi was so lovable that he had almost everyone there (the women especially) wrapped around his little finger.

Sigi returned home a few minutes later, at a slower pace but still moving right along as Mama had said that they needed what he'd been sent to get before dinner could be served. It was getting pretty late, and he was starting to get hungry. Before long grilled lamb cutlets, mashed potatoes, fresh bread loaves, and a huge bowl full of seasonal greens were laid on the table. They all sat down to eat.

Home, I'm home! Andi thought, as he devoured the succulent meat, fresh greens, and bread still warm from the Maiden's ovens. His family was around him, and he loved them all so much – Mom, his two papas, even Riki though there'd been so much friction between them of late. It made him a feel a little sad to think that he had to leave again, but he hoped that some of his family at least would be coming with him and Meri on an exciting adventure before they had to go back to finish their time at the Great Temple. Despite the connection he'd felt with Apoldros during his time as an acolyte, Andi knew that a quiet life of religious devotion was not for him.

Conversation was bright around the table between mouthfuls, as the family consumed the delicious meal. Andi and Meri had already related much of what they'd been doing at the Great Temple for the past several months, but the story of their trip to the Canyons of Stone, and the secrets Gryndor had revealed, had not yet been told.

Andrion and Riki cleared the table, then shared the chores of washing-up. Riki had been born and raised here in Drakespring House, and had only the faintest idea of the ordeal others throughout much of Agena endured, as wash water had to be heated over an open fire. Here, you just pushed a button and then hot water came out of the tap until you were finished using it.

As the family was once again gathered around the table, ready to hear the full tale of Andi and Meri's months serving Apoldros and learning the ways and speech of the leukalfar, there was a rap at the door. It was now full dark, but the door was as yet unlatched. "Come in!" Bernadette called, and the door opened to reveal Anja and Lars – accompanied by Fjuri!

The Steadfasts' son, younger than Anja by some six years, now towered above his older sister and her companion. Riki's heart skipped a beat as she saw him coming into the house's main gathering room. He had been really more like a brother to her for as long as she could remember, but in the past year there was something different about him. He was becoming a man – a tall, muscular, fantastically handsome man.

True, Fjuri was not exactly Mister Charming when it came to social interaction with the ladies. But by the gods, he was so magnificent! His shoulder-length blue-black hair, deep blue eyes, chiseled features and the air of mystery that came with his reserved personality had turned him from "just that stinky boy who always hangs around with Andi" into Him. At Mom's suggestion Riki had kept a diary for years, and over the past few months that diary had become increasingly full of references to "Him." She was not dim-witted enough to actually name him in its pages.

Anja, Lars, and Fjuri were all astounded to find Andi and Meri among the family gathered at the table. With three Drakespring parents and four Drakespring children (dragon Mondi a member of the clan but unable to join them at table since he was little more than a year old), their table's eight-chair seating capacity was nearly exhausted.

Fjuri broke his usual reserve at the sight of his best friend from infancy. He'd accompanied his big sis and her companion here because he hadn't seen much of the Drakesprings since Andi and Meri went away – and it was a chance to get out of the house. "Andi!" he crowed, surging into the room as Andi jumped to his feet and the two bumped chests, slapping each other on the back in a masculine gesture of affection.

Shortly thereafter Fjuri bent to enfold Meri in a hug, too. He'd known the leukalfar girl since she was a baby, and though many people he knew in Waterdon thought she was an ugly freak or were afraid of her, he knew her as a sweet kid. Bernadette, Riki, Sigi, and Erik had of course been reunited with Anja and Lars yesterday, but Andrion had not seen them in some time nor Andi and Meri in months.

For her eighteenth birthday (Anja had been orphaned at around age five, and nobody knew her real birthday – but she and her adoptive family had chosen one) Andrion had presented Anja with one of his magic Agena maps and Bernadette had given her one of her magical amulets. In the time since then Anja and Lars, childhood friends whose relationship had deepened over the years, had been inseparable. They roved all over the continent adventuring and exploring, sometimes gone for months at a time.

There was much news to exchange on both sides. Anja's career as an adventuress, if lacking big important milestones like the destruction of Tarragin or the defeat of Lord Karazin, had proven to be longer and in some ways more productive than Andi's mom's had been. Bernadette still kept her hand in even now, but had largely retired from all that stuff after becoming a mother.

More chairs were pulled up, and if it was a bit of a squeeze they all managed to fit around the table. Bernadette carried in some tea, and a big platter of freshly baked pastries that Sigi had brought from the Maiden. Lucky she'd gotten extra, with all these additional young people around!

After everyone had heard about Anja and Lars' latest expedition, exploring ancient eldalfar ruins in Remus, it was finally Andi's turn to tell everyone about his and Meri's trip to the leukalfar village, and all they had learned there. "We're now able to converse pretty well in the leukalfar tongue," Andi said by way of starting the tale. "Of course, that's just the dialect spoken by Myrkra and Mothris's Ankhrazana tribe. But according to Myrkra, most of the differences between the way the tribes speak are in things like pronunciation or maybe special words that have been added to the language locally because of something they have in one area they don't have in another."

"Anyhow," Andi continued, as Meri looked on. She was pleased to let her beloved big brother be the spokesman for their group of two, but ready to chime in should he leave anything out. "Myrkra evidently decided that we had learned enough about the language and the ways of her people, that it was time for us to go and visit with them." He looked around him, sure that most of his audience didn't understand what a big deal this was.

"Mom, you were right! The leukalfar do have village life, and they live like most Norsemen and Galise do, too!" Bernadette smiled at her tall, beautiful son. Though he favored her more than she realized, he was more and more becoming the image of Andrion – the man she'd fallen deeply in love with no more than a couple of weeks after her arrival in Iscandia.

Andi went on. "We walked most of the day from the Great Temple, and were let into the Canyons of Stone – their hidden village. Everybody wanted to come and greet Myrkra and Mothris, and I think that some of that was they were really curious about us. Everybody thought Meri was adorable" – he gestured toward his little sister, who smiled brilliantly and pretended she was bowing to the audience – "and I think a lot of them were afraid of me. I'm taller than any leukalfar I've ever seen, and they haven't exactly had a happy experience with people who look like me. But people were really pretty nice to me, even so."

The audience was agog. For thousands of years the other human inhabitants of Iscandia – be they Norse, Galise, Afran, Reman, or any of the various alfar races – had regarded the leukalfar as twisted subhuman beings, a hazard to be avoided when exploring dypalfar ruins, and nothing more. Bernadette's adoption of Meri had begun a ripple of understanding, a realization among those who were close with her family that leukalfar were as human as any of the other races of men and alfar. But Meri and her adoptive family had a long way to go before the rest of Iscandia began to accept this idea.

After everyone had had a chance to digest the revelation that the leukalfar had more in common with them than anyone had realized, Andi continued his tale. "We met Myrkra's sister, much younger. I think it's pretty rare for there to be two children close together in age in a leukalfar family. Maybe for all the alfar races. She had a little girl who looked to be maybe six, really cute. Then we went to the yurt that was Myrkra and Mothris's home before they went to live at the Great Temple."

"It was right next door to her sister's house. We went over there for dinner after we'd had a chance to rest from our hike. And that's when we met Gryndor."

"Tell them about the food!" Meri broke in. Now that she'd had a chance to think about it for a while, it seemed to her that the exotic dinner they'd been served was really pretty good. At the time, she hadn't enjoyed it all that much.

Andi smiled at his sister. He'd been hogging the narrative, and was happy to let her have a little input though he was nearly bursting with the revelations Gryndor had provided. "The food Myrkra's sister Madira served us was kind of different, but it was good!" he said. "They seem to do a lot with flatbread, at least in that tribe. They don't seem to have any leavening, and no ovens either. But the meat and veggies they wrapped up in soft flatbread were amazingly delicious."

Riki chimed in with, "you think anything is delicious, Andi." He nodded, admitting the charge.

"It's food, isn't it?" he asked with a self-deprecating grin. Moving on, he resumed telling them about Gryndor. "Madira and her husband had invited an old man to join us. He was what they call a Chanter, and I think maybe he was actually an ancestor of her and Myrkra. She called him 'old father,' and they seemed to have a relationship that went beyond what you'd expect if they weren't related."

"A 'Chanter'?" Bernadette asked. Andi smiled at his mom.

"I asked him, and it's not quite the same as being a bard. More important. The leukalfar lost the use of writing when they were enslaved by the dypalfar. But they created the office of Chanter to be the official keeper of their lore, to remember all of the important information about their people and pass it on to future generations. From what Gryndor said, Chanters might be the only leukalfar who travel around from tribe to tribe, spreading knowledge and learning new stories from others. Most of the others seem to stay pretty close to the tribe they were born in."

Faces around the table nodded in understanding, and Andi went on. "After we'd all eaten, everybody gathered to hear Gryndor tell one of the Stories. I think it was a story that was familiar to everyone there, but he chose it because he knew Meri and I had never heard it. And it included information that men in Iscandia have wondered about for thousands of years."

Andi's audience was rapt now, eager to hear what he had to say next. Both Andrion and Bernadette were paying particularly close attention. "Gryndor told us of the time when the leukalfar had been hard-pressed by the Norsemen, close to being exterminated or pushed completely out of Iscandia, and of how they had come to be changed and enslaved by the dypalfar." Bernadette and Andrion exchanged glances. They had heard some of this from Duraenis when they had first visited the Eparchy in search of The Staff of Apoldros more than sixteen years ago. But Duraenis had been a sequestered acolyte of Apoldros, one of those few unchanged; and he had not known the full story.

Andi looked around him at the faces of his family. Though Anja, Fjuri, and Lars were not related to him, Anja and Fjuri's family had been so close to his while he was growing up that he felt they were cousins. "That was not all," he said. "Gryndor told us where the dypalfar went when they disappeared."

Chapter 14: A Setback

Meri was wilting. Fast-traveling always seemed to hit the young harder than it did adults, and the discussion after dinner had gone on forever, it seemed. Erik scooped her up, finally, and tucked her into her bed in the nursery with hugs and kisses. Sigi went to bed at the same time. The older members of the family, and their not-quite-family visitors, continued to discuss Andi's revelations as the hour grew later.

Andi couldn't believe it. Papa Andrion had wanted to know more about the dypalfar and their technology for as long as Andi could remember. Who *wouldn't* want the chance to talk with real live dypalfar and find out how their wonderful machines worked? But though he'd used every power of persuasion at his command, somehow he just wasn't getting through.

It was ridiculous to assume that the portal would still be there after five thousand years, Andi's parents had agreed, without the much-more-numerous dypalfar managing to come back through it and defeat the leukalfar guardians before shutting down the machine or destroying it so that the last remaining gateway to their new world would be closed forever.

Even if by some unimaginable chance the portal was still open, going through it could not possibly lead to a positive result. "But that's why we need to mount a serious force to go through it!" Andi insisted. His parents just sighed.

"Us, against the entire dypalfar nation?" Bernadette asked. After what seemed like hours of discussion, Andi realized there was no hope. He was not going to talk his parents into launching an expedition to search for the portal Gryndor had spoken of.

Admittedly, the old elf had not reported the remaining portal as fact – only as rumor or legend. But surely, there must be some truth to it! Andi knew when he was licked, though. His parents were strong-minded individuals, even easy-going Erik, and there were times when you just needed to back off and admit defeat.

"Okay, you're right," he said quietly, rising to his feet. "Tomorrow Meri and I will go back to the Great Temple and resume our studies with Myrkra and Mothris." His mom stepped up and enfolded him in a tight hug.

"Do you have to leave so soon?" she asked. "We've barely had time to spend together."

"Meri and I will be back for good in another few months," Andi promised. "I don't think either of us are planning to make a career as acolytes of Apoldros. But there's a lot more about leukalfar culture, and the details of their language, that we still need to learn."

Hugging him still harder, then looking up into his face and standing on tiptoe to plant a kiss on his cheek, Mom said "Get some sleep, then. I suppose Fjuri's going to camp in your room for the night?"

Since Andi had gotten his own bedroom in the basement, Fjuri had often spent the night there. Anja and Lars were bunking here while they were in town, sleeping in Papa Andrion's room as he and Erik slept in the house's main bedroom with their wife. "Yes, Mistress Drakespring," Fjuri chimed in. She had known that boy his whole life, had been present at his birth, and he still couldn't quite bring himself to call her 'Bernadette,' she thought. Sigh.

The party broke up, Andi and Fjuri heading out the front door and around the side of the farmhouse to go down the stairs to the basement. Riki went with them, as her room was also down there. She hadn't been able to get Fjuri's attention much tonight, with the excitement of Andi's return after months away and the additional thrill of what he'd had to report; but she was sure she had caught him glancing her way once or twice.

Chapter 15: Plans

Andi and Fjuri turned left through the door of Andi's room as Riki peeled off to the right. Her heart was beating fast as she closed the door of her room and then leaned back against it, eyes closed. Oh, Fjuri! Even as her heart was flooded with her obsession, her love for him, a part of her mind (the part from Mom, she suspected) was telling her, get a grip! This is just a teenage crush, and before you know it some other guy will come along to be the new Love of Your Life. She sighed. It sucks being thirteen, she thought, and made her way to bed.

In Andi's room, the two boys who had been best friends since long before they could remember undressed and climbed into their beds. Andi had gotten a second single bed installed when they'd carved his room out of the basement, some four years previously. In his mind, it was as much Fjuri's room as his. They were closer than most brothers.

After both of them had pulled the covers up, they lay there in silence for a few moments. Then Fjuri spoke first, which was unusual. "The secrets of the dypalfar!" he said. People who did not know Fjuri well assumed that he was slow, that his handsome exterior clothed a mind with little going on in it. But he was as bright as anybody. His parents, both former body servants for whom duty and life in general had always been a serious undertaking, had raised him to consider things slowly and carefully. And not to speak until that consideration had been carried out.

Andi looked straight up at the ceiling, his mind churning. He couldn't believe how completely his plans had been shot down! He had been so sure that his parents, Papa Andrion especially, would be thrilled at the story he had to tell and jump at the chance to mount a family expedition. This was his quest, his very first important quest as an adult, and while of course he'd be relying on the experience and battle skills of his parents he'd expected to take a lead role and a share of the glory when they broke through to the dypalfar world and returned with knowledge and treasures beyond imagining.

Instead, he'd been put in his place like some little kid, like what he was talking about was some imaginary crap instead of the first real lead anyone in Iscandia (besides the ones who had been there) had had to the disappearance of the dypalfar in the last few thousand years. He seethed with anger and frustration. Meanwhile, Fjuri was waiting for a response. "Andi?" he asked tentatively, wondering what was going on in his friend's mind. Andi seemed to have a lightning grasp of things that took him an age to arrive at.

"It's not right, Fjuri," Andi said, gritting his teeth. "They don't realize what an opportunity this is. It's right there on my *map!*" The fact that the map in question was his mother's, lent to him for the duration of his stay at the Eparchy, was beside the point. He had been in control of it and the quest marker had appeared after Gryndor had spoken with *him*. He was *sure*, absolutely convinced, that he was meant to go there and find the portal, travel to the dypalfar world, and… after that he wasn't so sure. Do *something*, something world-shaking. But his parents had refused to help him.

Fjuri remained quiet, watching his friend in the dim candlelight. In another minute Andi said, "We could do it ourselves, you know."

"Do it?" Fjuri responded, guessing what Andi had in mind but not quite willing to voice it. His whole life seemed to have been wrapped up in duty. Was he ready to take the leap, to break away from what he was expected to do?

"Go to the dypalfar portal," Andi continued, getting more excited as his mind leapt ahead to the possibilities. "I told Myrkra and Mothris that Meri and I would return after we'd visited with my family, but I didn't say when. We could go up and just look, see if the portal is there. If it's not, then we could just take you home again and go on back to the Eparchy."

"You want to take your little sister on a quest?" Fjuri asked disbelievingly. Meri was a cool kid, but what was she – eleven? You didn't take little girls into danger. Andi considered it for a moment.

"She's tough," he told his friend, "she's a fighter. Besides, she's leukalfar and even though I can speak their lingo I think we'd need her when we went to the portal. There'll be leukalfar there, and they might not hold their fire long enough to hear me out if we show up without one of their own kind."

Andi was lost in thought for another minute, reconsidering the idea. Was he just using Meri because it was convenient? "I'll ask her, before we decide whether to do it," he told his friend. "But if she says yes, are you in? It'll mean ditching your job with Hegmar's crew."

Fjuri considered. He didn't really mind working construction, even if he hadn't had a say in the decision for him to take the job. He was learning the skill set mastered long ago by his papa, earning spending money, and building some muscle mass to go with his height. The girls around Waterdon certainly seemed to be taking notice. And this was his duty, he'd been told. But for his whole life it seemed, Mama and Papa had been talking about Duty as if it were the most sacred thing in the world – when most times it wasn't even something you had chosen for yourself. Why couldn't he choose adventure, instead? "I'm in, Andi," Fjuri said.

"I knew I could count on you," his friend replied.

Chapter 16: Packing Up

In the morning Anja and Lars slept late. They were on vacation, taking a break to visit with family and friends and enjoy some of the fruits of their adventuring – no need to be up at the crack of dawn. Likewise Andrion, the oldest of the Drakespring clan and never an early riser even in his youth, caught another hour of sleep as his wife and fellow husband slipped from the huge bed they shared. But everyone else who had spent the night at Drakespring Farm was up with the chickens, looking forward to the day.

Erik switched off the milking chore with his daughter Riki, to give her a chance to spend some more time with her brother and sister before they left again – returning to the Great Temple for another few months of learning. Bernadette put a kettle on for tea and stuck a large skillet on one of the cooking fire's higher racks, where she began frying sausage patties and fresh eggs. Eggs were always in abundance on the farm.

Andi and Fjuri, after a hushed discussion of their plans as they were getting dressed in Andi's room, made their way eagerly to the table and began eating some slightly stale bread rolls. Halved and toasted over the fire, then slathered with farm-fresh butter, they helped to tide the two teenage eating machines over until the rest of breakfast was ready.

Bernadette was smiling cheerfully as she worked and humming a happy tune. It was so good to have the whole family here for a change! Even if they were soon to be losing Andi and Meri again for a while, her son's tale of the breakthroughs they'd made in breaching the gap between the leukalfar and the rest of humanity thrilled her and convinced her that it was worth the time they were taking. If they could eventually get some other leukalfar, perhaps a young Chanter or two, to come back to Waterdon with them and learn the common tongue, maybe the men and alfar of the region would begin to accept the leukalfar as just another branch of humanity. Including, most importantly, her beloved adopted daughter.

After all leukalfar were more human than either gatti or
saurions, both of which groups were tolerated as part of Iscandia
society. And as humans, they were little uglier if perhaps a bit
stranger-looking than uruks. Verdalfar could be found in all walks
of life in Iscandia, though they were in many ways as clannish and
isolated as the leukalfar in their hidden villages. She saw good
things ahead!

Both Andi and Meri were filled with mixed feelings as they
soaked up the wonderful comfort of sitting around the breakfast
table at home, eating delicious and familiar food prepared by
Mom. In one way they wished it could always be like this; and in
another, they were caught up by the excitement of the adventure
they were embarked on – Meri as the first leukalfar child raised by
men and Andi as the first man to be welcomed among the
leukalfar.

Riki had taken extra care with her dress and appearance this
morning, rising very early to take a bath and carefully combing out
her lustrous red-gold locks, donning her most fetching outfit. It
was becoming a little tight on her in some areas, pointing up the
amazing figure she was going to have in another year or two.
She'd hoped that decking herself out as a vision of female
loveliness might possibly get Fjuri to pay her some attention; but
now that they were all seated around the table it appeared she was
not nearly as entrancing as those buttered bread rolls. Both he and
her brother seemed to be a little tense and nervous, as if they were
simmering with suppressed excitement.

Shrugging, Riki helped herself to a bread roll and sat eating it,
talking with her little sister and brother instead. She was beginning
to think she might have to crawl into Fjuri's lap before she would
be able to get his attention. Erik returned inside with the milking
pails, and Bernadette sat down to eat some breakfast herself while
he poured the milk through a strainer into a series of sterilized
dypalfar metal cans. Without Andi here drinking his usual gallon a
day, they'd had a bit of a surplus lately and Bernadette had been
turning out a lot of cheeses.

Riki and Meri finished eating first, soon followed by Sigi, and the three of them headed down the hall to the nursery at the northern end of the house. They met Andrion coming out of the bathroom wearing a robe, and he stopped to give Meri a squeeze before continuing across to the master bedroom to get dressed. A little further along, they greeted Anja and Lars – also wearing robes but only just now heading *toward* the bathroom.

"Riki," Meri piped up as they came into the room, "could you help me get packed up for our trip?" Riki smiled warmly at her.

"Sure, kiddo. Do you want to take some more things from home?" The decision for Meri and Andi to stay after they'd arrived at the Great Temple had been very impromptu, and she hadn't been able to really consider what she might need before suddenly finding herself staying there for months.

Meri nodded. "I want some more warm clothes, for one thing. And, could I take my bow? I haven't been able to practice while we were gone, and I don't want to forget how to shoot." Excepting Andrion, whose skills in battle magic were so superb as to make other weapons unnecessary, all the Drakespring clan were skilled in archery. Not only could it be a devastating and silent long-distance weapon if you found yourself among enemies, but with a good bow and arrows you could feed yourself. The little kids started practicing with specially made child-size bows at around age five, and archery practice continued a few hours per week from then on. Meri, at close to eleven, was probably as good a shot as any leukalfar sentry.

"That's a good idea, Meri," her older sister replied. "It's still right over there on the wall where you left it. Anything else?" Meri stood looking around the room, a frown of concentration on her wrinkled, eyeless face.

"Um… You know, I'd really like to bring some presents back for the people at the Great Temple. Myrkra and Mothris especially, but also Duraenis and some of the other leukalfar acolytes who have been nice to me. What do you think? Can we ask Mom for something?"

"I don't see why not," Riki replied. She was thinking that what the people at the Great Temple were doing for Meri was probably a huge favor to Mom, so she might indeed feel like giving them some gifts by way of a thank-you. "Why don't you gather up your bow and quiver and all the warm stuff you want, and I'll go ask her?"

"Thanks, Riki!"

Riki returned to the kitchen. The bathroom door was locked and she could hear laughing coming through it. Anja always had loved their hot bathing pool. Actually, she couldn't recall anyone who'd ever used it who didn't. It was amazing how, for longer than Andi had been alive, it had been running perfectly – keeping the water hot and clean at all times. Her papas had worked with Aunt Diane on the project, according to family stories. It was one of the things that had gotten Papa Andrion really interested in the dypalfar.

Andrion and Erik had now joined Bernadette at the table, the boys having returned downstairs to gather up packs. Fjuri had brought one with him last night, planning to spend the night though he hadn't expected Andi to be here. Over his lifetime, he had frequently lived here for days at a time – his family and Andi's having been close since before he was born.

Riki came and sat down beside her mother as she was just mopping up the last of the egg yolk from her plate with a bite of bread roll. Her mom had always had a healthy appetite, as did she. Odd, she never seemed to put on any weight though. Mom might have gotten a little bit more rounded since Riki's earliest memories of her, not quite so muscular now she wasn't hiking miles, fighting aptrgangr, and plundering tombs on a regular basis. But now that Riki thought about it, she seemed hardly to have aged at all since Sigi was a baby. Her hair was still a rich light auburn color, nary a streak of gray. Maybe turning into a dragon frequently had something to do with it?

Riki put an arm around Mom's shoulders and gave her a squeeze. She was already the taller of the two. "Thanks for a yummy breakfast, Mom," she said. Bernadette smiled and kissed her on the cheek, but there was a bit of a question in her eyes. Since Riki had reached adolescence, she and her elder daughter had often found themselves in conflict. It reminded her vividly of what she had gone through with her own mother, back in the tiny Auverne farming village where she'd grown up. So while she was happy to accept affection from her beautiful daughter, she couldn't help wondering what Riki was up to.

"Want me to do the dishes?" Riki asked, her summer blue eyes (just a half-shade darker than Erik's) looking at her mother with complete innocence. Now Bernadette *knew* she was up to something.

"That would be lovely, dear," Bernadette replied. "And is there, perhaps, something I can do for you?" Riki grinned impishly. Her mom was most assuredly one of the sharper knives in the drawer.

"It's for Meri," Riki replied. "She wants to bring some gifts back for the people at the Great Temple who've been kind to them, especially Myrkra and Mothris and Duraenis. I was thinking maybe some amulets or enchanted necklaces, or rings. Or maybe a dagger or two, something nice that wouldn't be too heavy to carry and that would be items the leukalfar wouldn't usually be able to get since they don't trade with other human races and aren't bandits. What do you think?"

While Bernadette had never pursued conjuring, transformation, or illusion and had never gotten very good at battle magic either (why should she bother, when she was married to one of the foremost mages in Iscandia?), she was an acclaimed practitioner of healing magic whose fame had spread to more than one province – and she was one of the most skilled enchanters to be found anywhere on Agena. She had begun teaching each of her children healing magic from an early age, regarding it as akin to learning first aid.

Andi, pure Galise by heritage if born in Iscandia, had a greater fund of magical energy to begin with and had quickly taken to both healing and the battle spells taught him by his father. Riki was half-Norse though, and it had been harder for her to start learning to use magic. Yet she had found herself with something of an aptitude for enchanting, which hadn't much interested her brother. The pieces (mostly jewelry, some of it made by her father) she enchanted were not as powerful as those done by her mother – but they were still worth having.

"It's funny," Bernadette responded, "Your brother was just asking me the same thing a minute ago. Only he was hoping for weapons. I think he wants to impress the men in the village, and maybe his friend Mothris, with some of our craftwork. I told him to check in the forge. Erik's been doing some elven weapons I think the leukalfar might like to have."

Riki began running hot water into the sink, rinsing the breakfast dishes as she did so. There'd been little food left on any of the plates. "As for enchanted jewelry and so forth," her mother went on, "do you have anything on hand?" Riki had of course needed to enchant many pieces of jewelry and clothing, and destroy quite a few enchanted items, in the course of her education. But most of those she'd created had been given away to friends. The Drakespring clan was rich, by Waterdon standards, and she was a generous soul.

The girl smiled at her mother, then bent to her task. "Sorry, I'm tapped out. I've been so busy with farm chores since Andi's been gone, I haven't made anything all summer." Bernadette looked thoughtful. "Well, that's all right," she said after a moment, "I'm sure there are a few pieces in the craft room I can give Meri to pass out to her friends. Thanks for cleaning up, sweetie." With that she sailed from the room.

Riki smiled to herself, as she stood up to her elbows in the hot soapy water. Good old Mom. The two of them might have been at odds recently, but she was proud of her mother and knew that whatever happened, Bernadette would defend every one of her children with her last breath – even the scaly ones, who were now scattered around the continent.

Chapter 17: Departure

Everyone gathered outside the front door of Drakespring House to shower Andi and Meri with hugs, kisses and well-wishes as they and Fjuri shouldered their packs and prepared to set off down the road for Waterdon. The plan, as Andi had explained it, was for them to walk Fjuri back home and say hello to Fjuri's mom, Lifa, and his younger sister Edla – near to Meri in age and the leukalfar girl's best friend – before fast-traveling back to Myrkra and Mothris at the Great Temple.

Andi turned one last time as they struck the road, giving his family a brilliant smile and saying, "'Bye everyone! We'll see you in a few more weeks!" Bernadette stood between her husbands, each with an arm around her as they'd stood so many times before. She felt positive about what her children were doing, but wistful at the same time. As the kids walked out of sight headed south, they all dispersed back to the morning's chores.

Erik was soon at work in the forge, Andrion in the craft room, Sigi in the henhouse and Riki in the tomato patch. Anja and Lars invited Bernadette to come along with them on a hunting trip to the east, and she happily changed into some leather armor and grabbed her best bow. Fresh meat for the table was always welcome, though if they got a deer they'd probably donate it to the Maiden – where it could be hung in one of the inn annex's cold rooms until it was tender.

Down the road the three youngsters were silent, in a state of tension until they'd gotten out of earshot of the family behind them. Andi was about to broach the subject of the dypalfar portal quest, wanting to pitch it to Meri in a way that would not take too much advantage of the authority he bore. He'd never forgive himself if he pushed his little sister into something she didn't really want to do and then somebody got hurt.

She beat him to the punch, grinning from ear to ear with her sharp-pointed little teeth. "Well," she said. "Are we going?"

"Going…?" Andi responded, wondering what she meant. So far as anybody knew they were all going to Waterdon, to visit for a little while before continuing via magic map to the Eparchy.

"Going to see if the dypalfar portal is there!" Meri cried, her tone hinting that she couldn't believe he'd had to ask.

Andi smiled down at her. "Fjuri wants to come with me," he told her. "But you don't have to go if you don't want to. It might be dangerous." The little girl looked up at him with a pained expression.

"Don't be silly, Andi!" she said matter-of-factly. "I have to come along. If you and Fjuri go down into a dypalfar ruin without me, the sentries will shoot first and ask questions later. Then if you manage to keep them from killing you, that will mean you had to kill them, probably. And I don't think the people there guarding the portal will be too happy to talk with you if you come in shooting."

It was easy to forget, sometimes, that Meri was older than she looked. The leukalfar, post-change, were not a tall race. And they were so spindly (though Meri, who had never wanted for anything since infancy, was considerably more well-fed than most) that it was easy to mistake them for malnourished children. Her face aside, Andi's younger sister looked closer to seven than the nearly eleven she probably was.

"So I take it that means you want to come along, huh?"

Again, Meri fixed him with a look that said "boys can be *so* obtuse." "I brought my bow, didn't I? And I've got some useful necklaces and rings, too." Andi looked from his sister to his best friend, elation tinged with a hint of anxiety as he realized they were now committed.

"Well, Fjuri, it looks like we're really doing it! I think we should go up to Waterdon anyhow before leaving, and maybe you can sneak a few things into your pack before we use the map."

The three of them continued on the road, past the stables and a series of walkways, and through the main gates of Waterdon. They knew all the city guards by name now and the guard corps in turn were all very familiar with the Drakespring brood. Even Mondi, Andi's dragon brother, had been a frequent visitor to town before he got so large – though he usually just flew over the walls and came down in the street.

A few steps inside the gate they all greeted Alessia Adelini and her daughter Julia, working side by side at the Valkyrie forge. Then Fjuri pushed open the door of Brightsgate Cottage, the house where he'd been born and raised, and they trooped inside. Lifa and her younger daughter weren't in evidence, so Fjuri hurried up the stairs, calling "Mama?" There was no reply.

Edla now had the small upstairs bedroom that had belonged to Anja when she was small, and Fjuri had his own room in a small upstairs addition that overhung a workshop area built off the rear of the cottage. It was not huge, but it was big enough and gave him some much-needed privacy.

Calling down the stairs, Fjuri said "It's going to be really cold there, right?"

Andi nodded and said "Yeah, freezing. Bring some long underwear if you've got it. And stuff some gloves into your pack." In a few minutes Fjuri's pack (already heavier than it had been the night before, as it now contained several weapons) was stuffed with whatever cold weather clothing he could muster, and he returned downstairs.

"I'll bet Mama and Edla are either up in town shopping or out back doing laundry," he said. "We'd better hide my pack, or she's going to wonder what's going on."

Andi thought for a moment. He'd known Aunt Lifa, Fjuri's mom, all his life and she was a force to be reckoned with. Taller than his own mother by several inches as well as a few years older, the robustly-built woman had been orphaned in childhood and pledged her service to Eorl Ormund and the March of Waterdon while she was still in her teens. The eorl had given Mom Lifa's services when he made her warden not long after her arrival in Waterdon.

Mom had arranged for Lifa to be freed from her obligations and had given her and her new husband Bjorn (who had also been Mom's body servant, when she was made Warden of Westmarch) Brightsgate Cottage as a wedding present, way back before Andi was even born. The families had remained close in the years since. Cousin Anja, some six years older than Andi, had also been an

92

orphan. But Lifa and Bjorn had adopted her when they were married, and she'd grown up as part of the new Steadfast clan.

Having considered his choices, Andi said "Let's tuck all the packs under the table here, then you go check out back. If your mom's there, signal me and I'll move them out onto the step. If not, we'll take them over and I'll ask Julia to keep an eye on them for a few minutes. She's a good sport." Fjuri nodded assent. Julia Adelini-Blackknife was only a year younger than he and Andi were, and rapidly turning into an attractive young woman – in a sturdy sort of fashion. The three of them had been friends almost from infancy, though these days she was closer with Andi's sister Riki.

Riki! Fjuri's breath caught as he thought of that girl who, like Julia, had been a part of his life for as long as he could remember. Only two years his junior, she had been kind of a pest when they were younger. She was always either trying to follow them around and do what they did, whether invited or not, or refusing to have anything to do with them because they were, in her words, "stinky boys." But this past year had seen a change that left him with feelings he didn't know how to deal with.

Somehow, Erika Drakespring had transformed from a thorn in his side into an alluring creature of mystery who set his pulse racing every time she put in an appearance. It had never really occurred to Fjuri before, but Riki was beautiful. From her creamy complexion and glistening red-gold locks, the big blue eyes, sweetly curved lips, increasingly noticeable figure… Augh! Get a grip! Fjuri thought.

He couldn't imagine how there could ever be a romance between him and Riki. She was too much like a sister to him. But she had disturbed him mightily, and his usual response to her presence was to pretend very hard that he hadn't noticed she was there. And occasionally, to cross his legs or throw a napkin over his lap. It sucked being fifteen, he thought.

"Good idea, Andi," Fjuri said, stifling his train of thought. He walked to the rear of the cottage, opening the back door only halfway. He immediately spotted his mother and younger sister,

93

teaming at the chore of laundering the family's clothes at a wooden counter in which a pair of metal sinks had been set. "Mom, Edla, I'm home!" he called, cluing Andi that it was time to take the packs out the front door and set them off to one side where the three juvenile conspirators could retrieve them after taking their leave.

Both Lifa and Edla, who was now 11 and rapidly gaining height, turned from their work to greet the son of the family. Edla had taken more after their father, having hair of a medium brown instead of the nearly black color Fjuri shared with his mom. They both smiled warmly at him. "Did you enjoy your visit with the Drakesprings, Fjuri?" Mama asked. Fjuri walked forward and embraced his mother. She was tall for a woman, but now dwarfed by her still-taller son. Bjorn stood 6'4", and it seemed likely Fjuri would equal him when he'd finished growing.

Next, he hugged his little sister. He had to bend down still more to do it. Now, judging Andi had had enough time to dispose of the packs, Fjuri announced "I had a surprise when Ani and Lars and I got there – Andi and Meri were home!" Both Lifa and her daughter were thrilled at the statement. Lifa had always had a soft spot for Andi, first-born of her friend and benefactor Bernadette; and Meri was Edla's best friend.

"That's wonderful news," Lifa said. "Are they staying long? Will we get to see them?" Fjuri smiled.

"They're leaving again for the Eparchy really soon," he said regretfully. "But they're here now!" He was nearly knocked down as Lifa and Edla swarmed past him into the house. Andi had gotten the packs tucked out of sight in the meantime, and he and Meri stood ready as Lifa and Edla came in, eager to greet them.

Many hugs and greetings were exchanged, and of course Andi had to tell (with frequent contributions from his little sister) about all that they had been doing over the past few months. Edla took Meri upstairs to her room, to show her the latest picture books her papa had made. Bjorn was an amazing artist, and it gave him the greatest joy to express his talent by making wonderful illustrated books for his children. Not only Anja, Fjuri, and Edla had benefitted from these, but all of the Drakespring children as well.

The morning was wearing on and Andi was getting anxious about leaving. "It's been great seeing you, Aunt Lifa," he said sincerely. "And I'm sorry we missed Bjorn. Maybe we can say hi to him when we accompany Fjuri over to the construction site before leaving," he added with the slightest of nudges in his friend's ribs.

"The site?" Lifa asked, puzzled. "Fjuri, I thought you had gotten Papa to give you the day off?" Faster than was usual for him, Fjuri picked up his cue.

"Yeah, I thought it would be nice to have a day off. But Andi and Meri are leaving right away to go back to the Eparchy and Ani and Lars decided they were going off hunting today. I didn't feel like doing that, so I thought I'd go down to the site and get in half a day of work. I can use the money…"

This story passed muster with Lifa, who nodded and squeezed her son's hand. What a man he was becoming, and this indication of a responsible streak was welcome. She hugged Andi, then Meri, and finally Fjuri. "I hope you and Meri will be back with us soon, Andi," she said. "And I'll see *you* for supper," she added to her son. Meri and Edla made their goodbyes, then the three of them got out the door. After it was closed, they picked up their packs. The adventure was about to begin.

"So," Fjuri asked, as he shouldered his pack. "Where are we starting from?" Andi drew himself up to his full height of a little under 6'1", hunched his shoulders, and contrived to make his warm, friendly brown eyes look evil and mysterious.

"We, my friends," he said in a voice not his own, "are on our way to *Castle Hordenhaal*!"

Chapter 18: Heading North

Moments after Andi touched the map, the young adventurers found themselves standing on a chill and bleak-looking shore, snow falling through the darkness all around. Ahead of them loomed an ominous-looking edifice of stone, with a stairway leading to it flanked by hideous stone gargoyles. All three of them had of course heard the tale of Castle Hordenhaal, of how Andi's mom and his two papas had joined forces with the Daywatch Brigade and the beautiful, ancient vampire Nerissa to bring down her own father, the evil vampire Lord Karazin.

That was all long in the past though, before Andi's parents were even married. After Lord Karazin was killed and Bernadette had encouraged her to get cured of her vampirism, Nerissa had rejoined the Daywatch Brigade. But she'd taken time off from that to search for her mother Leandra, and eventually she had found her – hiding out in a plane of the Netherworld she'd entered through an ancient portal. That vampire woman, older even than Nerissa, had gone into hiding there to help foil her husband's plans to blot out the sun using The Staff of Apoldros.

Once Karazin was gone it was safe for Leandra to return home to Castle Hordenhaal. All of the family's vampire minions had been killed in the Daywatch Brigade assault, but some of their non-vampire servants remained. Leaving her mother in charge of the castle (and neglecting to mention this to anyone, lest her vampire-hunter friends go there and kill her mother as well), Nerissa returned to her work with the Brigade.

After years of working with them, acting as a liaison with vampires to try to convince them to take the cure, Nerissa had fallen in love with Count Radigar – a Norse vampire with a keep hidden deep in the woods of Lakemarch. He had agreed to be cured, and eventually Nerissa had retired from the Daywatch Brigade and married him. Leandra, thrilled that her daughter had found happiness as a mortal, took the cure as a wedding present to the couple. Castle Hordenhaal had been purged of its vampires, undead guards, and other unsavory creatures and was now much restored to the glory it had known centuries before.

Andi and Meri had accompanied their family here for the wedding, and had visited here once or twice since – which was why Andi had been able to use this as a fast-travel point. It was as close to his quest marker as the map could take him. A couple of guards manned the front doors, though the castle was not in any real sense a fortress. Its isolated, northern location had made armed invasion unlikely, except for that one time when the Daywatch Brigade had come calling.

The visitors were not recognized. On their most recent visit Andi had been ten and Meri five or six. Fjuri had never been here before at all, and as they came in through the doors he felt a chill run through him that had nothing to do with the temperature outside. At this hour, it seemed, most of the castle's residents were already abed; but downstairs in the main hall (which had now been divided into dining and cozy living areas) the three found Nerissa and her husband sitting in comfortable chairs before the fire, talking quietly. Radigar was a tall, handsome man, of a similar coloring with Fjuri and his mother. His blue-black locks were now beginning to show some silver at the temples.

"Aunt Nerissa!" Andi called, as he led his small party into the room. Nerissa looked up. She now appeared to be in her middle thirties, aging having resumed after her vampirism had been cured. She'd put on a little weight too, seeming somewhat plump and matronly after having given birth to the couple's two daughters. Valina and Serifa were now eight and five, and were fortunate to have the children of the castle's tenant farmers and servants to play with. Looking around at the massive architecture, Andi shuddered a bit inside as he considered what it would be like to grow up in such a place.

Nerissa rose to her feet, a look of bafflement on her lovely features. "Andi?" she asked tentatively. Last time she had seen him, he'd been about two feet shorter and a lot skinnier. The sight of Meri convinced Nerissa this had to be her friends' oldest boy, as what other child was likely to be wandering around accompanied by a leukalfar girl? The young man with them, she didn't recognize at all.

Andi gave her his most winning smile. Like his father Andrion, he had a smile that started at his warm brown eyes and worked its way down his face, and had been known to melt certain women on the spot. So far it didn't seem to be working all that well with the girls in Waterdon, but then the majority of the ones there had known him his whole life and were immune to his tricks.

"Surprise!" he announced. Followed by "Aunt Nerissa, this is my best friend Fjurbund Steadfast. And you know my sister Meri, of course." Radigar had come to his feet too, and Andi shook his hand. "Good to see you again, sir. I hope you'll excuse our dropping in like this." Radigar smiled pleasantly. He'd only met the Drakesprings on a few occasions, but knew that Bernadette in particular had been very helpful to his wife. She claimed that the love relationship of Bernadette and her two husbands was what had inspired her to take the cure, so in a way he had them to thank for the happy, loving family life he now enjoyed.

Nerissa looked around, as if expecting more people to appear. "Is it just you three, Andi?" she asked, puzzled. He grinned again and nodded.

"We're actually on our way to the Eparchy," he said. Nerissa knew the Eparchy well, having accompanied Bernadette and Andrion there on the quest for the Staff of Apoldros. "Meri and I just spent the past few months there, working with Duraenis' acolytes and learning the leukalfar language."

Nerissa was dumbstruck. So, Duraenis had succeeded in bringing some of the changelings back into the fold after all. She wished him well – after all, without his help they would never have obtained the staff. Though as it turned out, bringing her to the Great Temple had in fact all been part of a plot by Signis, Duraenis' vampire brother. "That's wonderful," she said in a moment. "Were you able to make friends with the leukalfar, then? I know that was always a dream of your mother's."

"Everybody loved Meri, of course," Andi replied. "Who wouldn't love a cute little girl?" Leukalfar complexion wasn't given to blushing, but Meri managed to look a little embarrassed anyhow. "It was a bit harder getting most of the acolytes to accept me, one of the 'Sky People' as they call us, but I did make friends with a leukalfar boy around my own age, Mothris. And his mother, who was our main teacher, took us to visit their village. We were both made welcome. I really think we're close to the breakthrough Mom's always wanted, and we may be establishing trade relations with the leukalfar before long."

Nerissa looked thoughtful. This was all so unexpected, and the boy had yet to explain why, if they were going to the Eparchy, they were now here on this island many leagues to the west. However, she decided to shelve that for the time being and offer her visitors some hospitality. "I'm afraid we've already eaten supper," Nerissa told the three of them. "But can I offer you some refreshment?" Breakfast had been several hours ago in subjective time, and seemed to have been much longer ago than that. As one, the boys spoke up: "Thanks, we're starving!"

Cocking an eyebrow, Nerissa hurried off to the kitchen. This place, once an unwholesome abattoir, was now a warm and tidy place where fresh bread was baked twice daily, and a wide range of savory dishes were turned out. There were some five dozen souls in all living on the island, most of them within the walls of the castle itself. Ermagard, the stout Norse cook, was relaxing beside the fire with her feet up while two apprentice bakers worked producing pans of sweet rolls. They would rest overnight and be popped into the oven before dawn, ready to provide breakfast for the castle's residents.

Ermagard hurriedly put her feet on the floor and stood up. "Madam?" Though the current masters of Hordenhaal were a lot less scary than those of thirty years before, Nerissa's aristocratic birth and centuries of life had given her an air of authority that few failed to note.

"We have some unexpected visitors, Ermagard. A couple of teenage boys and a girl of about eleven. What do you have that we can feed them?"

A grin spread over the plump woman's face. She'd raised a couple of boys herself and knew full well just how much food they could put away. You could almost just sit there and watch them grow, so she supposed it was no wonder they ate so much. There was a muslin sack of bread rolls left over from dinner on the counter, and a plate with a large mound of freshly-churned butter on it. "Here," she said to her mistress. "This will keep them from eating the furniture until I can throw together something more substantial."

Ermagard loaded the rolls and butter, a knife, a jug of milk, and three glasses onto a tray and handed it over to Nerissa. Thanking her with a smile, the countess carried the tray back to the main hall. She found her husband sitting at table with the three young visitors, whose attention (the boys' at least) was riveted on her and the tray she carried from the moment she appeared.

"Thank you, Aunt Nerissa!" Andi said enthusiastically, as he snagged a roll from the tray almost before it had settled to the surface of the table, then quickly slathered it with butter before sticking it into his mouth. "Ephcuse me," he said indistinctly. "Fash trabling always hash zhish effeck on me…" The other two young people also hastened to serve themselves.

The maps would take you places in what seemed like seconds and was really something like a large fraction of the time it would take to walk there (provided you weren't killed by bandits or eaten by smilodons along the way). But young people more than older ones seemed to feel the effects of that "lost" time strongly.

After most of the plate of bread rolls had been devoured and the gnawing hunger they (especially the boys) had been feeling was eased, conversation resumed. "So how is it," Nerissa asked casually, "that you three happen to be traveling here if you're supposed to be going to the Eparchy?" Andi smiled again, and launched into the cover story he'd prepared.

He'd known it would likely be too late for them to continue to the island where the quest marker beckoned by the time they'd gotten here. Fjuri's parents were going to miss him, and that was going to blow their cover. But he hoped, if they covered their tracks thoroughly enough, that they would have gone and found the dypalfar portal (or determined it was no longer there) before they were caught out. Then his parents (and Fjuri's, he hoped!)

would see that his quest had value, and they would be forgiven for lying. Andi hadn't worked out all the details, but he was sure everything would come out fine.

"We went back home for a visit," Andi lied smoothly, "and Fjuri was really anxious to go back with us. He hasn't had many chances to leave Waterdon the way I have. I've got Mom's Agena map with me, and I thought it would be cool if we visited some of the places that are on it before we get back to the Eparchy. Most of Mom's fast-travel points won't work for me, but I have been a few places with her and the map. So we came here. It's kind of like an adventure."

Nerissa gave him a knowing smile. She didn't know Andi all that well, but she didn't doubt that Bernadette's elder son was a bright kid with a good head on his shoulders, and firmly on the side of Right. How could he be else, sprung from that stock and raised by Bernadette, Erik, and Andrion? So the kids were just taking a detour, letting Andi's friend visit some exotic locations. That sounded fine.

As the last of the bread rolls were disappearing Ermagard emerged from the kitchen with another tray. She was stout but also tall and strong, years of kneading bread dough into submission having given her muscles a swordsman would be proud of. And she needed them. The tray was stacked high with cheeses, cold meats, fruits (many of them imported from the mainland; the Hordenhaal family was quite wealthy), and more.

The kids dug in with a bit more decorum now their initial ravenousness had been slaked. As Andi and Fjuri continued to eat, with some help from Meri (who was now beginning to feel very tired and sleepy, though she had risen from bed only a few subjective hours before), the conversation went on. Andi told Nerissa and Radigar about the past few months he and Meri had spent in the Great Temple, and about their visit to the leukalfar village. There was news to report about other members of the family, events in Waterdon, and so forth.

For their part, Nerissa and Radigar shared news about the Daywatch Brigade. After Radigar had taken the cure and before their marriage, he and Nerissa had worked together on the mission to either cure or kill all remaining vampires who posed a threat to Iscandia. In some ways, the two former vampires had become the carrot while the rest of the Daywatch Brigade became the stick. They confronted vampires with a choice: cease being a blood-sucking fiend, or die.

Some few were unwilling to give up their immortality (though for most who had possessed it for long, it had become a burden). Many of them died. But a third option for vampires had arisen, a movement that had gradually swept across Iscandia. These vampires pledged that, in exchange for being allowed to continue their undead existence, they would no longer treat humans as cattle. No sentient creatures would die to feed their blood hunger.

Any warm-blooded creature – goats, cattle, chickens – could provide a blood meal for a vampire. There was also a potion, though costly and not easy to obtain, that could suppress the hunger for a time. And so gradually, over the course of Andi's lifetime, the "vampire menace" in Iscandia that had necessitated the formation of the Daywatch Brigade had just... faded away.

Hmm, Andi mused. The "dragon menace" that had confronted Iscandia starting about the time his mom came here from Auverne had lasted for years after he was born. But with his nineteen dragon siblings and their father Sneyagflug actively working to establish friendly relations between humans and *drachen*, that too had receded. It filled him with a feeling of satisfaction that his family had been instrumental in relieving two of the most pressing threats to peaceful life in the province of his birth.

"So," Nerissa was saying, "Malden reluctantly concluded that the Daywatch Brigade's mission was done, and he released everybody. He and Frydda settled down and turned Daywatch into their family estate. Last I heard he was going to be a father – at *his* age!" Andi was surprised to hear this. Malden was already a middle-aged guy back when his mom was a sweet young thing. Okay, she'd been a lethal warrior with the abilities of The Fireblood. But anyway, the dude must be seriously *old* now. And he was popping out kids with one of his former Dawnguard fighters? Ew.

Nerissa went on, "Diane and Georges ended up moving to Alfenstein. You can imagine she couldn't stay away from dypalfar ruins. They came by for a visit a couple of years ago now, and mentioned they're involved with Miurlion doing his research on the archaeological site below Dypendwelve. Gods know how old *he* is, but he's a ljosalfar so I suppose he might be not that much younger than me. Their boy Edouard must be around Meri's age, and he seems to be taking after his mom. Very interested in all that old stuff."

The hour was getting late even for Nerissa and Radigar, and their three young visitors looked ready to fall asleep on the tabletop. Very little remained of the feast Ermagard had brought. "I think it's about time to find our young friends some sleeping quarters, don't you?" Nerissa remarked quietly to her husband.

"I have just the place," he replied with a smile. Soon the three were ushered up a stairway and down a long corridor, before being let into a room like a dormitory with six single beds in it. "The guards' quarters," Radigar said as he gestured around the room. "If we're attacked in the night, you'll be expected to leap from your beds and defend us. All right?"

Chapter 19: Flight of Fancy

In the morning the kids awoke early, light streaming in through the tall, glassed-in windows of their dormitory room. Autumn was coming here in the north, but as yet the days were long and there were still but a few hours of darkness. They'd all fallen into a deep sleep despite their unfamiliar accommodations, and now felt fully rested and ready to get on with their adventure.

They put on their warmest garb before venturing downstairs, leaving their packs in the room until after breakfast. There was a goodly crowd gathered in the dining area for the morning meal of warm, delectable sweet rolls, scrambled eggs for those who preferred them, fresh bread, fruit, and hot tea. A few of the castle people were taken aback at the sight of Meri, but others remembered her from her earlier visits and there was no overt hostility. She really was a pretty tough kid, and she was beginning to get inured to unfavorable reactions from men and alfar who had never seen a leukalfar close up before. Deep inside, though, it still hurt.

This is why I need to work to bring my birth people and my adopted people together, Meri thought as she bit into her second sweet roll. Mmm, good! When leukalfar travelled everywhere around Iscandia openly trading with the rest of the province's inhabitants, they would be no more out of the ordinary than uruks or saurions – different from the average man or alfar, but nothing to get excited about. Then it would be possible for leukalfar to be treated as people, judged on their own characters, and not seen as monsters to be shot on sight.

When breakfast had been eaten and Andi, Fjuri, and Meri had gathered up their belongings, they thanked Nerissa and Radigar for their hospitality and then left by the front doors. Andi walked them down to the spot where they'd arrived, then looked around furtively. "Okay," he said, clearly the mastermind of their dubious enterprise. "I'm going to have to get naked, then transform to dragon and fly to the island. It's a long trip, and I'm hoping there'll be some landmarks besides the dypalfar ruin leading to the portal. When I've got one, I'll be back in human form and then we can all go there. But you guys need to hang around here for a few hours until I get back."

"Why don't we walk down the beach a ways?" Fjuri suggested. They needed to get out from under the gaze of Castle Hordenhaal's gate guards, and hopefully find some shelter from the weather. Yesterday's blizzard had disappeared in the night and today had dawned clear, but it was still bitterly cold. The three of them made their way along the island's western shore.

Ahead and to the east was a "cove" where, Andi knew from the stories, his parents had moored the small boat they'd stolen when on a reconnaissance mission before leading the Daywatch attack. At that time the battlements had been manned by armed walking skeletons, but fortunately all those were long gone. Nor had they been replaced with human guards. What was there to guard against, here?

There was nobody to observe them as they made their way in toward the castle walls, finding a sheltered alcove where Meri and Fjuri could wait while Andi scouted ahead. On the walk there they'd gathered some driftwood, and they laid a fire – which Andi lighted with a fire spell. This elementary bit of battle magic he'd mastered long before he was Meri's age.

With the cheery blaze beginning to heat the space, Andi regretfully began stripping off his clothes. By the gods, it was cold! Soon he was nude, and had tucked all of the clothing he'd removed into his pack while still staying near the fire. He fervently wished that the dragon transformation would let you transform your clothing along with your body. Not even Papa Andrion truly understood the magic that created the transformation, though after much study he'd concluded that the extra mass came from (and was later returned to) a parallel dimension.

Naked, beginning to shiver despite the fire, Andi hung his pack over his head. His pack had been specially designed for this, its straps creating a loop wide enough to accommodate his neck when he was in dragon form. He smiled at his sister and his best friend, and said "Keep the fire going! I'll be back when I can but

I'll probably have to walk up here from the arrival point over at the front of the castle."

Andi stepped out into the open area beyond the alcove. Then he said firmly, "Mon-Drache-Ein-Korp!" and ballooned in a matter of moments from a tall, well-set-up young man into a bronze dragon more than twenty feet long from nose to tail. Behind him, Meri and Fjuri watched with a touch of awe.

Not for the first time, Fjuri wished wistfully that his name Fjurbund, a tribute to Andi's mom the Fjurblut, had somehow conferred on him some draconic characteristics as well. He could speak the dragon tongue like a native, and he and Andi sometimes used it as a sort of secret language between them; but there was no magic within him. None beyond the magic conveyed by the genes he'd received from his tall, athletic, and good-looking parents.

Andi turned his head on his long, serpentine neck and spoke in his dragon voice, an octave or so deeper than the one he had as a human. "Hang tight and stay warm," he said in the common tongue. "I'll be back as soon as I can." With that he flapped his long, leathery wings and took to the air. Before transforming he'd taken a bearing on the map, looking for a landmark to guide him to the north and east – heading for the island where, he was sure, the dypalfar portal lay.

Ah, Andi thought, as he pumped his powerful wings and rose to an altitude where an air current ran in the general direction he needed to go, it's good to be a dragon here! Despite the lack of insulating fat, fur, or feathers, his draconic fires burned so hot that he scarcely noticed the freezing temperatures. Riding the current he didn't need to flap his wings so often, but even the relatively slight effort of flying thus kept him warm as toast.

It appeared from the map that the island with the quest marker was at least 150 miles further north than the island on which Castle Hordenhaal sat, and around 50 miles to the east. Andi flew strong and fast, far faster than anyone could travel on the ground and faster even than any of Iscandia's birds. But it still took him hours to reach the island – and by the time he arrived a hunger had come on him that was so strong it nearly erased his conscious mind.

As soon as there was land beneath him Andi banked and came in for a landing. The icy shore was home to quite a few walruses, the massive pinnipeds that populated the shores of Iscandia's northern sea. They could be quite a threat to a man on foot, but to a dragon the size of Andi they were… lunch. Augh, that's so *good*! he thought, as the rich, fatty juices flowed into his mouth with each massive bite. He tore through one carcass, then chased down a second of the beasts and roasted it to a turn with Holocaust before digging in.

Sated and a little sleepy after the enormous, high-calorie meal, Andi considered his next move. He was getting concerned about Meri and Fjuri back at Castle Hordenhaal, and from his memory of the map the dypalfar ruin atop the portal was still another couple of hours' flight away. This island was huge.

Andi took to the air again, flapping higher until he had a good view of the shore. Dragon sight was hawk-like, a necessary ability for a species that hunted from the air. There, off to the east and north, he spotted what looked like a human settlement. Flying there swiftly he soon saw a ruined village below him. A stone jetty still jutted out into a small bay, and the foundations of a few houses yet stood; but there was no sign of any living inhabitants.

Touching down, Andi walked on all fours in among the remnants of the buildings, seeking a little shelter from the icy onshore breeze. Then, reluctantly, he cried "Drache-Mon-Zur-Heim!" and transformed, in a second or two, into a naked youth once again. One rapidly turning blue from the cold!

Andi clawed the pack off his neck and rummaged through it for his clothes, which he put on as quickly as possible. The clothes were nearly as cold as the outside air after having been carried around his neck at high altitude for hours on the flight here. They stole the heat of his body as they warmed, and it was minutes before he was able to stop shivering. Taking a page from the healing magic taught him by his mother, he used a little of the healing spell on himself and found the ill effects of cold receding.

Phew. Now, for the map. He unfolded it with fingers no longer numb from the cold, and found to his great relief that he was standing on a map marker. "Walrus Cove," it read. This must have been an outpost of hunters harvesting the fatty creatures for their meat and tusks, before the village had burned. Or perhaps it had burned after they'd hunted out the walruses in the area and abandoned it. Whatever the case, this spot had been significant enough to generate a map point and that was all that mattered.

Andi shouldered his pack once again, then pointed on the map to Castle Hordenhaal. In moments, he was back on the shore before the castle's walkway and beginning the trek around to the west and north, returning to the alcove where Fjuri and Meri awaited him. Fortunately, there was no one to see.

Chapter 20: Mobilization

Darkness had fallen over the land. Andi suspected that the magic map did not take the capability of flight into its calculations, and that the real time taken by his seconds-long journey from Walrus Cove to Castle Hordenhaal was based on how long it would have taken to sail there in a boat, perhaps. Whatever, though he'd left them in mid-morning and daylight still lasted long at this latitude in late summer, it was now pitch dark and freezing cold.

Mom had of course taught him a few spells she'd found useful in her life, and these included a light globe spell. It cast a small glowing orb a few feet above his head and followed him as he moved, lighting his path across the uneven terrain to the west of the looming castle.

Andi had only cast the spell two or three times, renewing the light that expired after a minute, before he came on the alcove where he'd left his companions. The fire was still glowing, though it was beginning to burn down to embers, and Meri and Fjuri were both wrapped in fur bedrolls and asleep, as close to the fire as it was safe to get.

Andi had a moment of realization as he saw them there, vulnerable. These were two of the people he loved, and they were going into who-knew-what peril just because *he* had encouraged them to join him in his quest. Was he acting nuts? In another moment the feeling had passed. Everything was going to be all right, great things awaited them! He was, after all, his mother's son.

Andi stepped into the alcove and poked up the fire. Meri and Fjuri had clearly been busy while he was gone, and there was now a large pile of driftwood stacked up ready to add to the blaze. He threw another couple of logs on the fire, then took off his pack and pulled his bedroll out of it before laying it on the stones at his feet.

Sitting on the bedroll, Andi continued warming himself by the fire and pulled some provisions out of his pack. He and Meri had made off with as many foodstuffs as they could from home, claiming a desire for familiar foods in the Great Temple and/or wanting to treat their new leukalfar friends with some exotic delicacies. Fjuri hadn't had the opportunity to similarly raid his family's larder, and that meant that they were shorter on rations than Andi would have liked.

Well, they could always kill a walrus and end up with enough meat to see all of them to the dypalfar paradise and beyond, Andi realized. He wouldn't even have to turn dragon to do it, as they had enough weapons among them to handle anything short of a mammoth. After Andi had quelled the rumbling of his stomach, he considered whether to wake his companions. He was excited and energized, eager for the quest. But it had, one way and another, been a long day. He decided instead to throw some more logs on the fire and then lie down wrapped in his bedroll, to catch a few hours' rest.

As darkness comes late, so sunrise comes early in northern climes in summer. In what seemed like minutes after he'd dropped off to sleep, Andi was wakened by the sound of seabirds, wheeling in the breezes off the west coast of the island. Daylight had arrived, and from the look of the fire it had been at least a few hours since he'd added those logs. He sat up yawning, loath to leave the warmth of his bedroll, and put a couple more logs on from the nearby pile. But his bladder was near to bursting, and he was soon forced to stand up, put on his boots, and pick his way across the rocks to another alcove where he could relieve himself.

Meanwhile Meri and Fjuri were stirring as well, and as Andi made his way back to their sleeping place he found both of them up. Andi waved to Fjuri, who was heading in the direction of their informal privy. Growing up with a flush toilet, an item that few in Iscandia had ever seen, had given Andi a somewhat different outlook on the usual bodily functions. But this wasn't his first time roughing it, and he knew what bushes were for. Or in this case, there being a notable lack of bushes on this island, secluded niches in the castle foundations.

Meri looked a little pained as she put on her boots and began adding layers. "You were gone an awful long time, Andi," she said with a hint of resentment.

"Sorry Squirt," he replied with a smile. "It took a few hours to fly to the island, and then fast-traveling seemed to take even longer. Too bad I can't just load both you guys on my back, huh?" She smiled at him. Andi was her beloved big brother, and he could do no wrong. He'd been her protector since before she could remember.

"Excuse me," Meri said, as Fjuri returned from his errand. Both of them had of course had to deal with finding a place to pee during the many hours Andi had been gone. When the three of them were together again, the fire blazing merrily and heating up the small space, they sat back down on their bedrolls and rifled through their packs.

"Sorry I couldn't snag any food from home," Fjuri said. "It would've been a dead giveaway. As it is, Mama will have known as soon as Papa got home that something's not right." Andi dug into his pack and handed Fjuri a couple of apples and a large packet of trail bread. This concoction of dried meat, dried fruit, flour and suet provided a major burst of calories and nutrition in a small, long-lasting package – if it wasn't exactly what you'd call delicious.

"I figure we're going to have at least a couple of days' lead time on them, maybe longer. That should get us to the portal, and once we've proven it's there they will have forgotten how mad they are." I hope, Andi added silently. Again, that nagging doubt cropped up and he stifled it.

In his whole life, Andi had never really been in trouble. There was deep love and acceptance in his family, with three parents watching over and raising the kids, and no mischief he'd gotten into as a child had ever resulted in more than a scolding. Nor had he ever really gone beyond the bounds his parents had set. There hadn't been many. Be responsible, be kind – that was about it. But now, he felt that they had failed to realize that his time had come – that he was a man now. Was it too much to ask, that they would give him a little assistance on this first important quest that had come to him?

111

"It's time for us to armor up," Andi told his troops. He was being responsible, and he didn't think he was being unkind. So it must be all right... right? Each of them had managed to stuff clothing that was both warm and protective into their packs, along with far more foodstuffs than Andi's parents realized had been taken, and quite an assortment of weapons.

Both Andi and Fjuri had brought their current sets of elven armor, crafted for them by Andi's mom. Neither of them really understood what it meant for them to have this, how many pieces of gold it would cost for the average adventurer to own set after set of this armor, custom fitted to his body and replaced as that body changed. Fireblood arms and armor fetched a premium in Iscandia, and some people journeyed to Waterdon just to buy it. But Bernadette had lovingly kept both the boys in elven armor, light and protective, since they were four and first beginning their weapons training.

Fjuri's armor was already beginning to get a little snug. When crafting a new set for either of the boys, Bernadette always made it a little roomy. But this set had been made last spring, and already he had grown nearly an inch. In addition there was the muscle he'd added working construction the past few months, and the layers of warm underwear. He could still move, though.

After a summer spent mostly performing religious rituals and janitorial chores, Andi had no such bulking-up to boast. He was a little envious of Fjuri's impressive physique. Not that he didn't have muscles – the farm chores he'd performed since he'd been old enough to be trusted with them, along with regular sword practice, hunting, and other such activities had left him, at fifteen, looking muscular but lean. Andi wondered what effect, if any, regular dragon transformations had on his human body. Both his biological parents had muscular builds (though Mom's had softened somewhat with age), so perhaps this was just the way he was supposed to be.

The boys helped each other into their armor, and Meri got herself into her own armor. Mom had crafted this, too – all the Drakespring children had armor of some sort. Their lives on the farm might be settled and peaceful for the most part, but her younger life seemed to have inspired The Fireblood with a desire to err on the side of caution. No child of hers was going to be caught unprotected, if push came to shove.

Meri's leather armor, modeled for the most part after that worn by the Guardians, had an additional feature not found on any other leather armor ever seen in Iscandia: plates of daimonic metal, sablium infused with daimon blood, had been affixed to it front and back to provide extra protection from collarbone to hips. The leukalfar were, by and large, a fierce people. And the Drakesprings could be, too.

When all of them were fed and fully kitted up, Andi led his companions out onto the rocky shore and pulled out the map. "Ready?" he asked, and received gleeful nods of assent. In moments, so it seemed, they were standing on the desolate shore halfway between the abandoned jetty and the ruined buildings of Walrus Cove.

Chapter 21: Walrus Cove

"What happened here?" Fjuri asked, looking around at the ruined buildings in the rays of the westering sun. Once again, the magic map had decided that quite a few hours ought properly to have elapsed since they departed the island on which Castle Hordenhaal sat. Andi had heard both Mom and Papa Andrion bemoan this aspect of travel by map. Even though Papa Andrion had been able to create this map, he still didn't know everything about how they worked and why they worked that way. So much of the knowledge of the Ancients had been lost in the mists of time.

"I think this was a Norse outpost for hunting walruses," Andi said. "It looks like they've been gone for a long time, but this is the best fast-travel point I could find in a hurry. You wouldn't believe how long it took to fly here. Or how hungry I was when I arrived!"

"Hungrier than you usually are, brother? Unbelievable!" Meri shot back. Andi just grinned at her.

"I'm feeling a bit peckish now, as you mention it" he replied. "How about you?" They all acknowledged that a bite to eat would not be unwelcome. Rather than dip into their stores, Andi strode down toward the shore. In the years (decades?) since the settlement had been abandoned, populations of walruses had returned and there were half a dozen lying on the beach. They went underwater at night to feed on seaweed and shellfish, Andi had learned. But in the daytime they mostly just rested ashore, soaking up what little heat the northern sun provided.

The beasts were quick to rouse if anyone approached them, and could be dangerous – though they couldn't really outrun a human if the person was agile enough. Nor could they climb rocks. Andi, Meri, and Fjuri stood on the half-ruined stone jetty, scanning the shore of the small bay to either side. They didn't want to trigger a mass attack. Walruses were not as social as humans or even mammoths, but if you attacked one in too close proximity to others, you might find yourself mobbed by angry critters that weighed more than a ton apiece.

Meri's not-sight quickly picked out a target. "That one, I think," she said quietly to her brother. Andi turned to look. The walrus in question was resting on the shore nearest to the jetty they stood on, and no others were near enough that they would likely come to its aid. For whatever reason, a wounded walrus never sought the sea as an escape from attacking humans. Perhaps worse things than two-legged predators awaited an animal leaking blood, should it decide to swim for it.

Both Meri and Andi strung their bows, nocked arrows (they'd "borrowed" some of Mom's finest, no blunt-tipped target arrows here) and pointed them at the walrus. Fjuri was not much of an archer, but the power of those muscles behind a blade was not to be discounted. He'd be in at the killing stroke, if one were needed.

"Now," Andi murmured softly, and the two shot as one. Meri's arrow struck the walrus in its nose, penetrating through the sinus cavities but not reaching the brain. Andi's, with a lot more force behind it, hit it in the neck in the area above the shoulder – near as one could tell on an animal packed deep with blubber. It sank almost to the fletchings, and the creature responded with a roar of pain from the two shots.

With a wave for his companions to follow, Andi surged off of the jetty and onto the shore on the side where the wounded walrus was moving. It spotted them with its beady little eyes and began humping its way toward them in a fury. As they'd hoped, it was far enough from its fellows that none of the other walruses along the strand had joined its charge.

"That's right," Andi said, "come a little closer please…" The enraged behemoth continued up the beach, finding the rocks beyond the sand uncomfortable to cross. But it was in so much pain from the two arrow shots that it no longer had any thought beyond attacking, and killing, the enemies that had wounded it. Its fellows relaxed on the sand, oblivious to its plight.

Andi and Meri put two more arrows into the creature, but still failed to find a vital spot. It became even more enraged. Fjuri had drawn his sword, which had been difficult indeed for them to pack without it being noticed, and stood ready to meet its charge. As the wounded animal, now running blood, approached them, he dodged to the side and brought the sword down, hard, on its head. The sharp weapon sliced through hide and blubber and bone, to penetrate the skull and the brain beneath. With a groan, the enraged beast collapsed on the rocky shore, dead almost before it had stopped moving.

"Go Fjuri!" Andi crowed, impressed at the force and effectiveness of his friend's blow. Fjuri was four months the elder and had been taller than Andi throughout their lives, so his strength was not unexpected. But still... The three of them, panting slightly with the excitement of the hunt, stood for a few moments looking around them. Nope, the rest of walruses on the beach were acting as though nothing untoward had happened. Good!

Now, they had a ton of freshly-killed animal to butcher, and Andi and Meri were better-equipped to deal with this than Fjuri was. They'd been raised on a farm, where killing animals and processing the carcasses was a normal part of life. After they'd all caught their breath, Andi began directing their efforts. "Okay," he said. "Let's all get on this side and see if we can heave him over."

Some hours later the three adventurers were gathered in one of the more complete of the village's ruined houses, licking the grease off their fingers as more walrus steaks smoked over a driftwood fire. They'd suspended the meat on wet sticks over a fire made smokier by added seaweed, and they hoped that by morning it would have shed enough moisture to keep for a few days in this chill climate as they began their trek to Mrzhgradfendz and the dypalfar portal.

Andi and Fjuri split watches during the night, keeping the smoky fire going and looking out for any signs of hostile activity. They decided to spare Meri and let her sleep, as it wasn't likely she'd be able fight off anything that attacked them without help. Fortunately she was unaware of this, or they would have had an argument on their hands.

Dawn came, and the wayfarers woke and gathered themselves for the trek north. Mrzhgradfendz was north of the centerline of this large island, and looked like it might take days to get there depending on the weather – and on what might be out there looking to stop them. Walrus steaks were rich and filling but fishy-tasting, and the three Waterdon kids had already had as much of them as they wanted for the time being.

This was likely to change after they'd been out in the weather for a while and had run out of more appealing food; but for now they breakfasted on trail bread, taking the steaks they'd smoked as provisions for another meal. Andi had found a cast-iron teakettle in the ruined house they were occupying, and a well several dozen yards north of the village's center provided fresh water – so they got to wash their trail bread down with tea.

Andi slapped his forehead as he realized how little provision his plans had made for water. They had all brought filled skins, but none of them had considered that they were going to an island. Who knew whether there would be streams, or more wells, where they could replenish their supply on their journey north? Maybe we can melt snow in a pinch, he thought.

For now, they filled what skins they had with water from the well and tucked all the smoked walrus steaks, likely to remain edible enough in these temperatures for the foreseeable future, into their packs. Faced with the reality of the conditions he and his team were facing, Andi experienced a tremor of doubt. But he stifled it with a will. They would triumph!

Soon they had finished with breakfast and were ready to move. They were armed and armored, and had enough food to last them for days. On the northern edge of what had once been a town Andi picked up a faint trail. He hoped it would take them where they wanted to go.

Chapter 22: Discovery

As late afternoon came on, things were quiet at Drakespring Farm. Riki had finished her farm chores and was now taking an enchanting lesson from Bernadette. Since the girl showed some interest and this was a useful skill, she wanted to advance her knowledge in case she wanted to make a career of it.

In the culture of Iscandia women who married and then sat around looking pretty and socializing with their friends while the men provided a living were the exception. There were women in every walk of life, from farmers and smiths to mages and soldiers. And though the Drakespring clan was wealthy and could probably afford just to lie around and collect the profits from the Maiden without lifting a finger, Bernadette and her two husbands believed in everybody pulling their weight. Idleness led to dissatisfaction, boredom, and trouble.

Andrion was also in the craft room. As Anja and Lars would be staying in his private quarters while they were in the area, he'd taken the collection of books he'd recently brought from the Academy at Eisenstag and piled them on a table in one corner of the room. He was trying to piece together the answer to a magical mystery from a dozen scattered sources, and the project involved a lot of reading.

Erik had finished the smithing he'd been doing, taken a bath and was now in the kitchen trying to decide what to cook for supper. Both he and Bernadette enjoyed cooking, so they often switched off at the chore and sometimes even cooked together. He smiled as he recalled the time, so many years ago, when she had first learned he had this ability. She had been so outraged to learn he'd been cooking for the Steadfasts, but had not done so for her!

Sigi was down at the Maiden playing with Joqui and would be having a sleepover there, and their guests were also planning to dine at the Maiden; so it was just the four of them to cook for. Perhaps he could come up with something a little special. He missed Andi and Meri, and the vibrant energy around the dining table when the whole family was here.

As Erik was squatting, peering into the opened door of the cold chest to see what was on hand and seek some inspiration, there came a knock at the door. Before he could get back onto his feet and go to open it, it opened and Lifa came inside, closely followed by Bjorn. Her face was tense, mouth grim, as she said "*Please* tell me our son is here, Erik."

Uh oh. Erik, flabbergasted, stepped forward to take her hands. He looked at her, then into the face of Bjorn – a man as wide and muscular as he was, and nearly as tall. "Andi and Meri left here with Fjuri right after breakfast. They were going to drop him off at home and say goodbye before leaving for the Eparchy again. Didn't they make it?" His calm, friendly face radiated concern.

Lifa's, however, changed from anxiety to anger as she began connecting the dots. "They *did* come to the cottage to say goodbye, around midmorning. And then they left, and Fjuri said he'd decided to go over to the construction site and get in half a day's work."

"But he never showed up at the site," Bjorn put in. He, too, looked like he was beginning to get angry. Both Lifa and Bjorn were former body servants, and though they were usually fairly reserved they were not people you wanted to meet on the wrong end of a sword.

Erik's mind was churning as he led the Steadfast couple down the hall to the crafting room to discuss the situation with his marriage mates. He had a sinking feeling he knew exactly what had happened, but he could scarcely believe it. Andi had always been such a well-behaved kid, and not given to sneaky behavior. "Berni, Andrion – trouble," he said in his deep voice as the three of them came into the room, just loud enough to be heard. Bernadette, Andrion, and Riki all looked up, worried.

Some fifteen minutes later, projects and supper preparations forgotten, they were all gathered around the dining table discussing the situation. "I suppose it's possible," Bernadette mused, "that Andi and Meri decided to take Fjuri to the Eparchy with them. He really missed spending time with Fjuri these past few months, even if he did make at least one young friend among the leukalfar."

"Fjuri wasn't entirely happy being put on the construction crew while Andi was off having what he thought of as 'adventures,'" Lifa admitted. "He knows all about the lives we led back in the day – gods know, Bjorn has made him an entire library of your adventures, and ours as well. And he's become such a young man, this past year (yes, oh yes he has, Riki sighed to herself). I suppose we were fooling ourselves if we thought he'd be satisfied moving right into a steady job and a settled life in the city. Look at what happened with Anja!"

Anja, Lifa's elder daughter, was the orphan who had set her on the path of a loving family life from one of selfless (and likely someday fatal) service to the march. Although it gave her heart pain to know that her beloved little one – not so little, now – was putting her life at risk killing bandits and exploring haunted tombs, there was some part of her that was proud of the girl for being as brave and effective a warrior as she had been at that age. Though it seemed Anja had rather more fun doing it than *she* ever had.

Bjorn rumbled in acknowledgement of the truth of his wife's words. He was angry at his son for ditching his responsibilities, angry at Andi for leading him into it. Yet he was wise enough in the ways of the world to understand what was probably going through the boy's mind. He himself had been recently orphaned at that age, and he knew full well – it sucked being fifteen.

"I don't think there's any choice about it," Bernadette sighed with an air of finality. "My original map is the only one we still have with the Great Temple on it, so either Andrion or I is going to have to go up there and see if that's where the kids went. And if they didn't, I'm afraid I know what the next step will have to be. Lifa, do you want to come along?"

Lifa smiled at her friend, the first such expression to cross her face since she and her husband had arrived here.

"More than anything, Bernadette. But I can't leave Edla."

"Bring her down here!" Erik boomed. He loved kids, and they loved him. All of the Steadfast children were honorary Drakesprings, in any case. Lifa turned to Bjorn.

"Will that be all right, dear?" she asked. His expression was a little forlorn. He had a job and responsibilities he could not abandon, but he didn't much like the idea of being left all alone while his son was missing and he couldn't join the hunt. On the other hand, they could hardly leave a girl Edla's age to hang around the house by herself all day while he was at work.

Bjorn smiled at Erik, an expression with a hint of pain around the edges. The two of them had been good friends for fifteen years or more, and despite his misgivings he appreciated the offer. "I think that'll be for the best. Edla's over at Valkyrie right now, but I'll go get her and bring her back here." Edla was three years younger than Julia, Alessia and Wolaf's daughter – but the two families had been next-door neighbors for many years, and it had been no problem to leave her there while they walked to Drakespring Farm hoping to track down their wayward son.

"I'll go pick her up and bring her back here, then," Bjorn said. It was clear that just having a plan was making him feel better about things. "Lifi, are you and Bernadette going to leave right away?" Bernadette spoke up, having had more experience with fast-traveling than either Lifa or Bjorn.

"I think we might be fainting with hunger if we don't eat first. Bjorn, why don't you and Edla come back and expect to eat supper here? Anja and Lars are eating at the Maiden, but they should be back later this evening. Then after we've had something to eat, Lifa and I will pack up and go. It'll probably be morning in the Eparchy by the time we arrive."

As she said this, Bernadette made eye contact with Andrion. They had been together for most of her adult life, and it wasn't often they needed words to communicate. He nodded slightly, indicating he thought this was a good plan. He *hoped* they would get to the Eparchy and find Fjuri now enrolled as an acolyte of Apoldros – or maybe just seeing the sights. But he trusted his wife to cut to the heart of the situation, and if it turned out they had a quest to go on, he was ready. He might be pushing fifty, but mages lived longer than most men. He was still in possession of all his faculties, and so for that matter was old Faramund up at the

Academy – a man who'd looked like he was in his seventies fifteen years ago, and still looked much the same today.

As Bjorn set off for Waterdon to collect his daughter, Erik got busy putting a meal together. His original plan, a special supper for himself, his wife, his co-husband, and their not-quite-adult daughter, had gone out the window. Now he was looking for something simple and quick that would feed an additional two adults and one pre-teen girl.

Lifa, feeling anxious still despite the plan in place, continued sitting at the dining table and engaged Riki in conversation. By the gods, the girl was lovely. Not that her own Edla, or Anja for that matter, was not also lovely. But Riki was so clearly the feminine version of her father Erik's godlike splendor. The girl was going to get awfully tall though, Lifa feared, taller than she herself was – and she was considered tall for a woman.

It was going to take a very special man to pair with her, Lifa thought. She felt a pang of sympathy as she realized how unlikely Riki was to find that special man among the boys her age in Waterdon. Well, she was only thirteen. There was no hurry, and there were many travelers coming through here all the time. Perhaps someday, in another five years or so, her eyes would meet the eyes of the One who would claim her heart – as had happened to Lifa when Bjorn came into her life.

Meanwhile Bernadette, as prone to anxiety as Lifa, had decided to let Erik handle the supper preparations while she went to the master bedroom and craft room and began putting together a pack for their trip. She hoped she wouldn't need that much, but it was better to be prepared. An hour or so later they had all fed well on a one-pot meal of chicken and vegetables, served with the ever-present bread rolls. Bernadette and Lifa rose from the table as soon as they'd finished eating, anxious to be on their way.

Bjorn had been thoughtful enough to bring along some gear for Lifa. This included her old steel armor (which she could still fit into after sixteen years and two kids, thank the gods) a short sword and dagger, and a pack with some changes of underwear. Her eyes shone as he handed these over to her. When they had met both of them had been recent warriors, and it was this as well as their mutual orphanhood and status as body servants that had bonded them together – on top of a profound attraction.

Anja and Lars had not yet returned from the Maiden by the time Bernadette and Lifa were geared up and ready to leave. The young people were no doubt carousing with friends and acquaintances in the convivial atmosphere that prevailed there in the evenings. Neither of the two mothers, their thoughts grimly set on their missing children, gave it a thought.

Lifa received deep hugs and kisses from her husband and younger daughter, and slighter hugs from Erik, Andrion, and Riki. Then Erik, Andrion, and Riki gave Bernadette hugs and kisses, wishing her success. All three of them were really, really hoping that the situation would turn out to be as simple as Andi and Meri having "abducted" Fjuri for an excursion to the Eparchy. Erik and Andrion, at least, did not really believe it.

Chapter 23: Seeking

Outside the door of Drakespring House Bernadette touched the Great Temple on her map, and in moments she and Lifa found themselves standing in the courtyard where she, Meri, and Andi had arrived last spring. Bernadette turned and smiled at her companion. "It's just like old times, huh?" she asked cheerily. She was hoping to break the tension, but it was clear from the effort Lifa put into her response that it hadn't really worked.

"Except no Andrion," Lifa replied with a smile that seemed a little forced. The three of them had gone on the quest for the Staff of Zauber together, early in Bernadette's career as The Fireblood.

It hadn't been dark yet when they'd left the Waterdon area. At this season sunset was still late and dawn early, and the sun had already risen on the Great Temple; but there was little sign of activity. Bernadette now knew her way around this place somewhat from her visit a few months before, and she led the way into the nearest building.

To her pleasure, Bernadette immediately spotted Myrkra. Years as the mother of a leukalfar girl had sensitized her to the differences among individual members of the race, and she had no trouble distinguishing one from another. In the years before she had found Meri, they had just been adversaries to be disposed of, studied as little as possible. Now that she realized they were fully people, with lives that meant as much to them as her own did to her, she shuddered at the callous way she had slaughtered them in times past.

"Myrkra!" Bernadette called, approaching with Lifa at her side. Lifa had not been with them on their original trip here, having been ensconced in Brightsgate Cottage and taking care of Anja with assistance from Bjorn at the time. So she was a bit distracted, taking in the exotic surroundings and the several leukalfar acolytes who moved quietly about the space. To her, as to Bernadette, these people had only been enemies to kill.

The leukalfar woman turned in surprise at the call. "Fireblood? Is all well with Andreas and Merelle?" She had expected them to return by now, and seeing the children's mother instead filled her with apprehension. Bernadette's spirits fell as she knew the kids had not come here. That left only one more likely destination, and none of them had it on a map.

Sighing, Bernadette told Myrkra "I sincerely hope all is well with my children, and with the son of my friend Lifa here," gesturing toward the tall and well-armored woman at her side. "The problem is, we don't know where they are." The little woman's eyeless gaze focused on her for a few moments, as if not understanding what had been said.

"They left home," she said finally, working it out, "and you thought they had come here with the map you gave them. But they did not."

As they spoke, Myrkra's son Mothris came up to join the conversation. His mother turned to him and quizzed him in the leukalfar tongue: "Andreas and Merelle left home but did not come here. Did he say anything to you before they left that would indicate he planned some other excursion?"

Courteously, Mothris addressed his reply to Bernadette and Lifa in the common tongue, which he spoke fluently but with an accent. "Andreas said only that they were going home to visit with family for a while," he told them. "He did ask Mother and me if we would like to come along. I would have liked to… but I have responsibilities here." He stood lost in thought for a moment, thinking the situation over. "There is one thing," he added. "We used that map to come back here from the Canyons of Stone after our visit. Andreas was very excited about something our Chanter Gryndor told him the night before, and then when we got here he was looking at the map and it seemed as if something had been added to it."

"A quest marker," Bernadette said, nodding grimly. "He showed it to us when they got home, but we didn't study it. His fathers and I didn't think that it made any sense to investigate this supposed dypalfar portal. It must surely have been closed for thousands of years, and even if it were not I can't see how any small party of people could invade the dypalfar paradise without being killed out of hand. We told him to forget about it, and he seemed to accept that. But I'm now sure that he and Meri, with Lifa's son Fjuri, have gone to see the portal for themselves."

Myrkra considered, then suggested "Now that you know they did not come here, can you not just travel there and rescue the children using the map by which you came?" Bernadette shook her head.

"I don't have that marker on my map," she said ruefully. It was inconvenient, if you were carrying on the activities of ordinary daily life, to be carrying around a map on your person at all times. Erik and Andrion each had his own Agena map, and unless they were traveling they usually left them sitting atop the chest of drawers in the bedroom – too far away to trigger a quest marker if they were told of a quest location in a room at the end of the hall. Generally, you needed to be in close physical proximity to the map for this to happen.

Andi had told them that it had taken an all-day hike to reach the Canyons of Stone, the village of the leukalfar tribe to which Myrkra and Mothris belonged. Bernadette hated to have to ask, but she didn't see any way around it. "Myrkra, I need to go and speak with your Chanter, so that I can get the dypalfar portal location marked on this map. I know it's somewhere on this big island, but I need to know the exact location." She showed her the map.

"Fool boy," Myrkra muttered. "I can hardly believe he would take his little sister into danger like that."

"Fool boy, indeed," Bernadette responded. "But he would have had a hard time convincing her to stay behind. When she's with her big brother, she's fearless. And she does have some skills. She's an excellent archer. I'm not so much worried about them getting killed by wildlife or hostiles as of starving or freezing to death up there. I don't think there's all that much living so far north."

"Well," Myrkra concluded, "we must do what we must. I think we had better take Mothris along as well – he can carry the provisions. Madira, Marsila and Dengan will be pleased to see us again so soon, at least." Seeing Bernadette's look of question, she added "My sister and her family. It was at their house where our

Chanter told Andreas and Merelle of the dypalfar portal. It's not even official lore, just a story. Boys!"

"Please wait here," Myrkra said to the two women, and to Mothris added "Put up a pack for us with some water and food for the trip, and get our traveling cloaks. I'll go talk to Duraenis and explain why we must leave our duties again for a while."

"Thank you Myrkra!" Bernadette called after her as the leukalfar woman bustled off. Her son hastily departed in another direction to fulfill the orders he'd been given, leaving them standing there in the midst of the Great Temple.

As it seemed they would have some time in which to wait, the two anxious mothers paced around the room, taking in the statuary and religious symbols. "You wouldn't believe what a change this place has undergone since Andrion, Nerissa and I were here and killed Signis," Bernadette remarked conversationally. "It was all fallen stone and icicles hanging from the ceiling, and undead frozen leukalfar and mandimants everywhere. I guess since Signis was a vampire, the living conditions didn't bother him. And he was furious at his god for having failed to protect him. He'd decided the way to get vengeance was to destroy Apoldros' church and kill off all its worshippers. He would have succeeded too, if it hadn't been for his brother Duraenis."

Lifa thought back to that time. She had been idled for months, just hanging around the Bathing Maiden with nothing to do while Bernadette went questing with one or the other of her lovers for companions. She'd made some friends there during that period, but life had been lacking in purpose. Then one day Bernadette and Andrion had returned with the adorable five-year-old orphan girl, and everything had changed. A head injury or possibly the emotional trauma of the dragon attack that had left Anja (a name Bernadette had chosen for her) orphaned and homeless had also stripped her of her memories. In very little time, she had begun to think of Lifa as her mother. It was only a few months later that Lifa and Bjorn were wed and the three of them became a family forever.

Meanwhile Bernadette and Andrion, later accompanied by Erik, had been off on a grand quest to find The Staff of Apoldros and defeat the evil vampire Lord Karazin – and she and Bjorn, caring for Anja at Brightsgate Cottage, had felt a tinge of regret that they hadn't gotten to participate in that. Were it not for Anja, they might well have all joined the Daywatch Brigade. Well, Lifa certainly didn't regret the way things had turned out. Now if she could just get her hands on her great hulking dolt of a son!

Mothris returned, burdened by an armload of cloaks and a large backpack. He grinned at them shyly, a somewhat disconcerting expression with those pointed leukalfar teeth. The "changeling" leukalfar had been greatly altered by the poison fed them by their dypalfar masters, but it had not changed their underlying humanity. They still smiled and laughed among themselves, at least.

Myrkra was next to arrive, and she took her cloak from her son and then held the pack for him while he got into it. She'd brought some walking sticks, and passed them around. "The trail is narrow and steep in some places," she said matter-of-factly. "Best not to slip and fall to the bottom of the canyon." With that she led them down a series of corridors, and as soon as they had stepped out into the courtyard fronting the Great Temple the cold bit through them like a knife. Bernadette and Lifa halted the procession for a moment as they retrieved cloaks of their own from the packs they were wearing.

Several hours and numerous sentry checkpoints later, the small party arrived through the secret passageway into the Canyons of Stone. All around them people stopped and stared at the two strange non-leukalfar women accompanying Myrkra. She'd brought a non-leukalfar boy, the first such to visit this hidden village in lore or memory, just a few days before. Now here were two more. Would the Sky People soon be invading en masse?

Andi, clearly not yet full grown and wearing a cloak over an acolyte's robe, accompanied by his leukalfar sister, had provoked curiosity among the villagers. These two somewhat grim-looking Sky People women, armed and armored, created a wave of uneasiness and they did not find their passage delayed by people crowding in to bid Myrkra and her son welcome.

They made their way to the hut of Madira and her family, next door to Myrkra and Mothris' own. It was late afternoon and the young leukalfar woman, "helped" by her little daughter, was preparing supper for the family. Dengan had not yet returned from work in the village gardens. With autumn coming soon to this northern clime, there was much harvest work to be done.

Madira dropped what she was doing, astonished. She had not expected to see her sister for another month at least, perhaps longer if there were early snows. In the worst of winter, the mountainous trails between the Great Temple and the village became impassable. "Myrkra!" she exclaimed, even as little Marsila hurried over to give her aunt and cousin hugs. "You've brought us more visitors?"

Myrkra's expression was a mix of pleasure at greeting her beloved sister (alfar families with more than one child were rare, and though she had already been an adult when Madira was born she had treasured her from that day to this), and annoyance at the errand that had required this journey. They spoke in the leukalfar tongue, as Madira had only a few words of Common. Most who remained in the village and didn't venture outside except perhaps for sentry duty had no need of it; though Myrkra and Mothris, on their infrequent visits, had begun teaching it to Madira and her daughter. A command of the common tongue was a requirement for acolytes of Apoldros at the Great Temple, and a course of it occupied most novices for the first few months before they took up their religious duties.

"It's boy trouble I'm afraid," Myrkra told her sister acerbically. Madira glanced at Mothris. "Not that boy," Myrkra said, "though it's probably just a lack of opportunity for him. It's a wonder any of them survive to be men," she added with a shrug. "Young Andreas, the Sky People boy who was here a few days ago."

"Oh, I liked him!" Madira said with a smile. What a surprise and delight it had been to come face to face with one of the dreaded Sky People and find him polite, amiable, and somewhat shy.

"He's a nice boy, I think," her sister replied. "But while he and young Merelle were here Gryndor told them that old story about the surviving portal to the dypalfar paradise. I think he was just flattered at how interested the strangers were in his stories, and I thought I heard him telling them that it wasn't necessarily Lore, just a tale. But the boy seems to have decided he'd been set a quest to go find it. Now he's run off and we need to talk to Gryndor so his mother" – a nod indicated Bernadette – "and the mother of the friend he took with him" – another gesture, this time toward Lifa – "can go track him down before he gets eaten by a snow troll."

Without eyes, a wide-eyed expression was one the leukalfar could not convey easily. Madira managed it, somehow. "Oh dear," she replied. Turning to Mothris, she said "Mothris, will you please go to Gryndor's yurt and ask if he can join us for supper? Tell him there are more Sky People for him to meet, I know he'll be eager to come then." Bernadette and Lifa had been standing there the while, listening to this exchange in a language they did not understand. But you didn't need to know what the words meant to get some sense of what was passing between the sisters, especially considering their purpose here.

As Mothris hurried out of the yurt, Myrkra turned to her companions. "We're fetching the Chanter now, and he'll join us for supper as it's getting to be that time." To her sister she added with a hint of amusement, "There'll be no trouble serving an extra five people for supper, I suppose?" Madira looked a little concerned. Mothris by himself could eat more than she and her daughter put together. And that Sky People boy, Andreas, had more than matched him. Did all Sky People eat like that, or was it just adolescent boys?

Bernadette, an old hand at meal planning and having frequently been called upon to feed a horde of unexpected visitors, intuited the situation in an instant. Hauling her pack down off her back and rummaging through it, she began pulling out some of the provisions she'd packed. "I have some food with me, if it'll help," she told Myrkra. Lifa too had packed along food, also from the Drakesprings' kitchen as she hadn't had the chance to go home between learning Fjuri had run off with Andi and embarking on their hasty trip to the Eparchy.

Between them they handed over a dozen hard-boiled eggs, a couple of half-wheels of cheese, a quantity of dried beef, some somewhat stale bread rolls, half a dozen apples, and some trail bread. Madira smiled at them, appreciating the gesture, but a little unsure what to do with some of the items she'd been given.

The apples and eggs were familiar, the trail bread similar in appearance if not in composition to something the leukalfar made for travelers; but they did not keep cattle, and neither cheese nor beef was an item on their list of usual foods. Being provided with a dypalfar metal plate, raided from some dypalfar ruin and traded with another leukalfar tribe generations ago, Bernadette sat a half-wheel of cheese on it and then pulled a dagger with which to cut off a slice. Madira did not flinch. In her young life, sheltered in their secluded village, she'd had no contact with any who meant her harm. True, people on sentry duty out in the canyons sometimes disappeared or were found dead; but no enemies had come to the Canyons of Stone in time out of mind.

Bernadette nibbled the slice of cheese she'd cut, smiling at Madira. Then she cut another sliver and proffered it to her hostess. She'd made this herself from the milk of their two cows, and in keeping with her own preferences it was mild and slightly sweet-tasting. Madira hesitantly put the small piece of cheese to her mouth and bit off a little, then chewed it. Then she had another bite, and smiled. "This is good!" she said to her sister. "Try some!"

Soon everyone in the room was munching on cheese. Bernadette sliced up some of the bread rolls and toasted them over the fire, showed the leukalfar women how a slice of cheese could be melted onto bread. By the time Mothris came back, accompanied by the aged Gryndor, they had all eaten a few slices of toast with melted cheese and some chunks of dried beef (which Madira had discovered was pretty similar to dried goat, if less flavorful) were simmering in a pot with some herbs. In a while, fresh vegetables would be added.

Bernadette was burning with eagerness to talk with Gryndor and learn where her son and daughter had taken Fjuri. Fifteen years ago, she would probably have buttonholed him and demanded the information, then dragged Lifa out of there to fly home (with the map; not literally, though with her dragon transformation ability that was also an option) and gather reinforcements before rushing to the rescue. Now, older and wiser, she was attuned to the social situation she was in. She had wished for détente with the leukalfar people for many years, and here she was being made welcome in a leukalfar household. A few hours' delay could surely not spell the difference between life and death for her children.

So, Bernadette set aside her anxiety and just enjoyed the gathering. Dengan arrived, bringing with him more fresh vegetables, and Bernadette helped Madira cook. The language barrier was something of a problem. But they were both mothers, both familiar with the challenges of keeping a family fed. Lifa contributed as well, and in no more than half an hour after Dengan had returned (during which time more slices of toasted bread with melted cheese had been enjoyed) the group sat around the fire to eat a stew of beef and vegetables, the flatbread leukalfar ate at almost every meal, and an additional dish of mashed root vegetables seasoned with sweet spices and topped with something that looked like butter.

Bernadette guessed that the leukalfar must be domesticating and milking the goats that roamed everywhere in Iscandia. Which meant they could probably produce their own cheese, if they wanted. Goats didn't make nearly as much milk as cows did, but you didn't need to feed them as much either. If she had longer to spend here, she thought, she might be able to teach the villagers how to make goat cheese.

Finally the meal was concluded and it was time at last to broach the subject that was the reason for their visit. Bernadette felt torn. She would happily have lingered for hours, learning all she could from these people and especially from the old Chanter.

That the leukalfar's oral history was so tightly regulated had been a surprise to her, and both she and Andrion had been thrilled at the possibilities this held.

Never mind musty tomes, these people had kept their history alive through a succession of human recorders, each of them tasked with preserving only the facts. What long-forgotten lore might they reveal? The rest of humanity, having remained literate, had left the remembering to the books and then forgotten the books were there, for the most part.

After the supper dishes had been taken away, Bernadette spoke. They had arranged for her to be sitting beside Myrkra. On her other side was Lifa, and on Myrkra's other side sat the old Chanter, Gryndor. As Bernadette spoke, Myrkra translated. And Gryndor's words came back to her through the same channel. "My son, Andreas," she began (it appeared the leukalfar were a formal enough people that they did not tend to shorten people's names into nicknames), "was very excited by your story of the last remaining portal to the dypalfar paradise," she said.

Bernadette waited as Myrkra translated, then translated Gryndor's response. The old elf had a somewhat rueful expression, as if he now regretted telling the impressionable youngsters about the rumored portal. "He told them it was just a story," Myrkra said. "I don't think they understood about the difference between a story and Lore," she added editorially.

Bernadette considered the cultural gulf between her children and Myrkra's people. Meri might be of the same race, but she was as much a Drakespring as any of them and she would not have picked up on the context of Gryndor's story any more than her brother would. "I'm afraid that Andreas was convinced he had a quest to visit the place you told them of, and learn whether the portal still exists. He tried to get his family to come with him, but we told him it was not sensible. He's fifteen years old and sure that he's a man now, so he brought his best friend and his sister in on it and went anyway. I need to get the location of that dypalfar ruin, so we can go find them and rescue them before harm comes to them."

After Myrkra had finished translating this Gryndor's shoulders slumped, and his face took on an expression of woe. After a few moments he spoke again, and Myrkra translated the words: "I am sorry, Fireblood, that I have been the cause of this problem for you." Gryndor had learned, somehow, who she was. The legends of The Fireblood reached even among the Ankhrazana!

The translation went on: "A story that came down but was not through the accepted channels claimed that the last of the portals which the dypalfar opened on the night when the entire race disappeared was not closed. A party of our people, who had been in hiding, killed the dypalfar soldier tasked with destroying the machine that had created the portal, and they kept it open. This was in a city far to the north, on a large island north and west of where we now sit. Whether that portal still exists, whether any leukalfar yet guard it, no one knows. Does this answer your need?"

Hearing this Bernadette pulled out her map from where she kept it folded beneath her armor. Breath bated, she unfolded it. Though she had carried this map for more than sixteen years and it had been folded and unfolded times beyond number, it never wore out. That was part of the map's magic. Heart pounding, her eyes went to the upper left corner of the map. This one covered only Iscandia and some of its outlying islands, but the island in question was there. And seeming to glow upon it, north of the midpoint of the island's centerline, was a black symbol with the legend "Mrzhgradfendz" beside it. Yes!

Bernadette smiled brilliantly, her eyes alight with triumph. "It worked!" she crowed. Beside her, Lifa's dark blue eyes were also glowing. Soon, they would have their kids back – safe at home. And then, those kids would be grounded until their twenty-first birthdays, if not longer. "Thank you, Gryndor, I have the information I need," Bernadette said so that Myrkra could relay her response. She was sitting cross-legged, enjoying the warmth of the crackling fire, and she suddenly realized that she felt exhausted.

Bernadette turned to Lifa. "How do you feel?" she asked. It had been early evening when they had left Drakespring Farm, after which they'd arrived in early morning and spent several hours hiking through the canyons to get here. Now it was early evening getting on toward mid-evening, and neither of them had slept since the day before. Or was it the day before that?

Lifa, a few years older than her friend, took time for an internal examination and discovered that she was trembling on the edge of collapse. "I think we might need to take a nap before we try to go home," she admitted – though her desire to get moving, to be on the way to rescuing their children before something awful happened to them, was burning within her.

Bernadette sighed. "I think you're right. If we fast-travel again without resting we may arrive in a state of collapse, and that's not going to help anything. The kids have a couple of days' lead on us by now, but we can catch them. They'll probably get bogged down once they get to the island, if it's anything like what I imagine. Maybe we should just stay the night here."

Chapter 24: Heading Homeward

At Bernadette and Lifa's request, Myrkra conveyed their thanks to Gryndor for the information and to Madira and her family for the hospitality, then led them to the yurt next door. Bernadette was happy to use her fire spell, not much use in battle but great for starting fires, and there was soon a cheery blaze in the hearth. She recalled a time sixteen years ago when she and Andrion, in company with Nerissa, had sheltered for the night in a similar yurt. This place felt much homier.

Lifa was bemused as they removed their armor and wrapped up in double layers of fur bedroll to sleep. Though she had long since gotten used to the leukalfar child her friend had adopted, and happily accepted her as a friend and companion to her own daughter, she had always seen adult leukalfar as strange, alien, enemies. Yet after an evening spent in the company next door, she found herself thinking how lovely Madira was. She had a sort of internal beauty that shone through her exterior like warm lamplight.

The two women fell into a deep sleep, more exhausted even than they had realized. Fast-traveling could be very upsetting to one's body's sense of time, with consequences that might take days to overcome. Yet early the next morning, after a perfunctory breakfast (the now-familiar leukalfar flatbread, heated over the fire until soft and wrapped around a filling that seemed to be made of soft fruit and nuts and was quite delicious), they were back into their armor and picking up the map again.

Myrkra and Mothris didn't mind being taken by magic map back to the Great Temple, rather than having to spend most of the day walking there along steep and rocky paths. It appeared to be midday when they arrived, for the straight-line distance was not that great. "Thank you so much Myrkra, Mothris," Bernadette said as she and Lifa prepared to leave for home. "Without your help we would not be able to go to the kids' aid."

Myrkra pondered. "You are going to this Mrzhgradfendz, then, on the northern island?" she asked. "That's right," Bernadette told her, "after we go home and gather some more people and supplies. It's likely to be an arduous journey, and we have some preparations to make before we can leave."

"Suppose," Myrkra continued, "that you are not able to catch Andreas and Merelle and their friend before they have arrived at the dypalfar ruin. What will you do then?"

Bernadette made to reply, then looked stricken as she thought it through. "Oh crap," she muttered. "If we go there we will run into the leukalfar who are living in the ruin, whether there's any portal there or not. Andi and Meri both speak leukalfar and with Meri there they will probably get through all right. But we'll just be invading Sky People and we'll have to fight them."

Myrkra nodded sagely. At this point Mothris, who had followed his mother's train of thought and was thrilled to the core as her meaning became clear, spoke up: "I'll have to come with you!" he said eagerly. "With me along, you won't have to fight the guardians at Mrzhgradfendz. You can rescue the kids, and then we can all go home. And I'll get to see Andreas' home in Waterdon!" he added, excited at the thought. Bernadette looked to Myrkra. The woman seemed to keep a pretty tight rein on her adolescent son, and she was a little surprised she would encourage him to run off and abandon his responsibilities in the temple of Apoldros.

Myrkra nodded once again. "Mothris," she said a little resignedly, "I am not sure whether the life of an acolyte is really what you are meant for." She spoke in the common tongue for the benefit of Bernadette and Lifa. "I sincerely hope you will not seek to become a sentry as your father was," she went on, "but it may be that Apoldros has some other plans in store for you. I believe it may be time for you to go to the lands of the Sky People and see what there is to see. Help these people rescue their children from their foolishness. And perhaps, like young Merelle, you may also become an ambassador from our people to those who live always above the earth."

This was a long speech from the leukalfar woman, and her audience took it in with solemn attention. She seemed to have made the decision to let her son go free and seek his destiny. In a race that had so few children, this must surely be one of the most difficult things a mother could do. For Mothris, the words were the answer to his innermost hopes and prayers. He honored Apoldros and was pleased to have been able to come here instead of spending the rest of his life stuck in their village – but now the entire world was opening up before him!

"Thank you, Mother!" Mothris said fervently. He embraced her formally, a few inches taller than she was. Along with their eyeless faces and spindly limbs the Change had made the leukalfar the shortest of the alfar races, both mother and son well below Lifa's height.

"I think you may want to gather a few things before you leave," Myrkra remarked coolly. "And then I'm going to have to explain to Archon Duraenis why he has lost another acolyte."

Bernadette and Lifa stood talking quietly with Myrkra about the joys of raising teenage boys until Mothris returned, still in a state of excitement, with his pack bulging at the seams. Goodbyes and thanks were said, then the Waterdon women stepped out into the courtyard with their young leukalfar companion – Myrkra going as promised to explain the situation to Duraenis. Bernadette smiled at Mothris, a great deal of sympathy for him shining in her sea-gray eyes, as she flourished the map and wished them all back to Drakespring Farm.

Chapter 25: The Rescue Party

Mothris had now experienced fast-travel twice, both times moving from the village in which he'd grown up to the familiar courtyard in the Great Temple. Now, after a moment or two of swirling darkness, he found himself looking at... more darkness. They were standing on a road that ran down a broad valley.

To their left a long farmhouse loomed, a bright dypalfar lamp illuminating its front door. Beyond that stood the walls of an immense city. The biggest working of humankind Mothris had ever seen was the Great Temple, and few of his peers growing up in the Canyons of Stone had even seen that. The walls of Waterdon, well-lit with lamps and with the windows of houses glowing atop them, were almost beyond comprehension.

But he was not afraid. His whole life, since that time when Father had not come back, Mothris had felt that the world was a much bigger place than people in his little village knew – and he was eager to get out there and seize it. This was it! The start of everything he'd dreamed about! He could hardly wait to meet the rest of Andreas's family. The two Sky People women led him up the walk to the farmhouse, and they went inside.

The evening was getting on, and the supper dishes had been cleared, but everyone was still awake and the room was crowded. After finishing his day's work, Bjorn had walked down to join the Drakesprings for supper. He was delighted to share this meal with his grown-up daughter and her companion, a rare treat. Anja was only in the Waterdon area a few weeks a year, these days – though he hoped she and Lars might someday get married and settle down not too far away.

Everyone looked up with excitement as Bernadette, Lifa, and Mothris came in. Cries of "Mama!" from Anja, Edla, and Sigi intermingled with "Berni!," "Lifi!," and "Mom!" from Andrion, Erik, Bjorn, and Riki. For a moment, Mothris felt very much the outsider. Just like Andreas' mother and her friend must have felt in his village, he realized. After all the various family members had given and received hugs, Bernadette was quick to bring their guest into the fold.

"Everybody," she said smiling, "I'd like to introduce you to Andi and Meri's friend Mothris. Andi has already told everyone about you, Mothris." She went around the room, marking off Andrion, Erik, Bjorn, Riki, Sigi, Edla, Anja and Lars. She doubted that Mothris had a prayer of remembering all the people he'd just met, especially considering they were so different from the people he'd been raised with; but the leukalfar, it proved (or at least Mothris), had a surprisingly good memory for faces and names.

Everyone except Sigi and Edla were eyeing Bernadette and Lifa with questions in their eyes. Clearly, they had *not* returned with Andi, Meri, and Fjuri in tow. And that meant the kids had gone someplace else. Someplace they were not eager to contemplate. Bernadette looked around the room, and sighed. She tried to put a jolly face on it, though her heart sank at what they were going to have to go through. If only Andi had used a little more sense!

Eh, she thought, he probably has more sense at fifteen than *I* did. I thought I was ready to conquer the world, but fortunately there weren't too many opportunities for it in Pied de Puce. That tiny farming village in Auverne had been Bernadette's birthplace, and it wasn't until she was in her early twenties that she'd traveled to Iscandia and discovered her destiny as The Fireblood.

"The good news," she announced at last, "is that Mothris is here to help us in our quest to rescue Andi, Meri, and Fjuri. His presence in our party will assure that we don't have to fight his people, and he can act as a translator for us." Her audience was agog, waiting for the other shoe to drop. "The bad news is it appears our wayward children have decided to follow Andi's quest marker to the supposed site of the dypalfar portal on Skarhalfn, an island far north and west of here. We are going to have a trek on our hands."

The news delivered, Bernadette's nostrils flared as she sniffed the air. "Is there anything left to eat?" she asked. Erik, who'd been standing taking in her words, hurried over into the kitchen area and began rummaging in the cold chest. In a minute or two he'd produced a platter with some cold sliced meat, bread rolls, cheese, and fresh fruit. Bernadette stepped up to him and gave him a deep kiss. "Thank you, love!" she said before digging in.

Lifa joined her. Both of them felt ravenous after traveling from breakfast to past suppertime on no more than a token amount of food. While they ate like starving shria, a buzz of conversation arose around the room as the adults considered the quest at hand. Not all of them would be able to come along, but who would stay behind?

Erik took Bjorn aside. "It looks like you and I might need to be the ones holding down the fort," he said. "I don't think this is going to be a situation for brute force, and somebody's got to watch the little ones." He lumped Riki into the category of "little ones," though clearly she was rapidly becoming a woman – and posed her own set of problems.

Bjorn pondered, and had to admit Erik was right. He had responsibilities he could not just cast off to go running after his wayward son. With Edla staying here during the day while he was at work, Lifi would be able to join the search party. "Would it be all right if I bunk here for a while?" Bjorn asked his friend.

Erik smiled at him. "Sure, you can sleep in my room if you want. You'll like the bed."

Erik's bed, custom-made to accommodate his 6'5" height, would be a treat to a man like Bjorn – only an inch or so shorter. Erik expected Andrion would accompany Berni, so he'd have their gigantic master bed all to himself. It was past bedtime for the youngest members of the group, and Bernadette roused herself from stuffing her face (now beginning to feel sated) to haul Sigi and Edla off. Edla was getting too old to bathe with boys, or so she thought – so Bernadette just got them to clean their teeth, kiss and hug everyone goodnight, and get tucked into bed in the nursery.

"Mama," Sigi asked sleepily as she pulled the covers up and planted a kiss on his forehead, "will you be gone when I get up?"

"Probably not," she replied. "We have to figure out who's going on the trip to find Andi and Meri, and we probably won't leave until after breakfast." He smiled at her. Of all her children,

Bernadette thought fondly, he was the sweetest and most easy to love. He was a child of Erik's spirit, if not of his body.

"See you in the morning, then," he smiled.

Lifa joined her to kiss and hug her own baby, pre-teen Edla. As the two of them left the nursery, she spoke quietly with her friend. "I think we're going to want to launch our expedition second thing tomorrow morning," she said. "I guess Bjorn and I can share Erik's bed tonight?" The house was very nearly full.

"That'll be fine," Bernadette replied. She herself was looking forward to spending the night sleeping with both of her husbands.

When they got back to the front room, Anja and Lars were saying "Of course we're going to come! Do you think we'd let Fjuri go wandering loose in the frozen north and not try to find him?" Riki didn't want to be left out. She was not the warrior maiden Anja had been at her age, but she wasn't completely useless in a fight either (she assumed; she'd spent many hours shooting arrows at targets and game, though she'd never actually been up against an enemy that wanted to kill her), and this was her brother and sister they were talking about. Not to mention Fjuri, the boy who seemed to have the power to derail her usually hard-headed thought processes by glancing at her with his deep blue eyes or flexing some of those muscles he'd recently acquired. Sigh.

Riki's hopes of joining the expedition were soon dashed. Mom put her foot down, and there was to be no argument. The party would include herself, Lifa, Andrion, Anja, Lars, and Mothris. The six of them all had skills that would be invaluable in the search for their missing family members. Riki was crushed, and flounced off to bed close to tears. How could they just... *discount* her that way? In her heart of hearts she knew Mom and her papas didn't want to put her in danger, and that was a more important reason than a lack of questing skills on her part. As she lay down in bed and closed her eyes, the thought came surging up again: "It sucks being thirteen."

Chapter 26: The Hunt Begins

In the morning all arose early, excitement making it impossible to stay asleep any longer. With the house full of people like this there was heavy pressure on the house's lone bathroom (still miles ahead of most homes in Iscandia, where a wooden washtub filled with water heated over the fire did for bathing and most people used chamberpots if they didn't have an outhouse). Bernadette, Andrion, and Erik had bathed the night before, so they didn't have to use the tub this morning.

Bernadette and Andrion had quested together in the north many times in the past, and they had some very good long underwear to put on. Erik smiled and gave his wife a warm hug as she began digging out her woolies, then said "I'll go get breakfast started." She gave him a bright smile and returned his hug with a kiss on top. Marrying two men at the same time had been looked on as eccentric at best, if not outright scandalous, all those years ago. But the relationship had worked out very well, and now the three of them could not imagine doing without each other.

Mothris had been tucked up for the night in Andi's room in the basement, across the hall from Riki. He suspected that his friend's sister was considered an attractive young woman among the Sky People, and that likely his friend was accounted handsome. But having spent his entire young life, before this past summer, with only his fellow leukalfar and the elderly white elf Duraenis for reference, he still found the Sky People too alien-looking to feel any attraction.

Before lying down to sleep he'd spent minutes just studying the room. He craved new experiences, and he wished Andreas was here so he could ask him about the different objects in the room, and what they meant to him. It certainly appeared that Andreas's family was rich beyond any understanding of the term among the people he'd been raised with.

Mothris awoke feeling a burgeoning wave of anticipation coupled with anxiety. For the first time in his life he was completely on his own, away from his mother and the extended family of his village, away from the protective environment of the

143

Great Temple. He was seventeen years old, not accounted a man yet among his people. Yet Mother had *urged* him to take up this quest, helping to rescue his friend and his little sister from the situation they had gotten themselves into. And without his help, he realized, it was unlikely that the quest would succeed. It bolstered his confidence as he understood what an important person he had become.

He gathered his gear and exited the room. He was lightly dressed. Another benefit of the Change, along with the leukalfar sight that needed no light, was their ability to withstand cold. It went against any sense, as they were relatively small among humans. They were nearly hairless, having only a thin fall of pale white strands on their heads, and there were certainly no fat layers to provide insulation. Yet any leukalfar, lightly clad, could remain comfortable living at the bottom of a dank pit or among snowdrifts – as was often the case in the Canyons of Stone in the wintertime.

Riki, already lying awake in her bed, heard Mothris leave Andi's room and decided to get up. She might be getting left behind, but this morning she was seeing that as more of an opportunity to help Papa Erik take care of Sigi and Edla. As much as she wanted to be a part of the quest to rescue Andi, Meri, and Fjuri, another part of her was willing to admit that those who were undertaking the task seemed to have it covered pretty well without her – and staying here at home, warm and safe, was probably going to be a lot more enjoyable than freezing her toes off in some northern wilderness.

Everyone eventually converged on the kitchen, where Erik had decided to scramble a couple of dozen eggs and serve them up with sausage, bread rolls, and a bowl of plums. It wasn't often they had this many people in the house. Though Andi and Meri were gone the addition of Mothris, Bjorn and Lifa, Anja and Lars more than made up for it.

He piled the food onto large platters and let people help themselves. There weren't enough places at the table and some people sat on extra chairs around the room, their plates on their laps. Before long everyone had eaten, and those who were leaving began to gather up supplies and equipment.

Though Bernadette doubted there would be many enemies roaming the icy wastes of Skarhalfn, and they didn't intend to do any fighting in the dypalfar ruin Mrzhgradfendz, it was better to be prepared – and she ran around like a mother hen with her chicks, making sure that everyone had all the gear and supplies they needed. Lifa, older than her and a mother herself, took it with bad grace but with understanding.

Sigi, really pleased that Edla was staying with them, led her back to the nursery so they could play together. She was more Meri's friend than his, being close to two years older; but the two could still enjoy each other's company. Riki, aligning herself with the grownups, set to work gathering up plates and began washing the breakfast dishes. Papa Erik came over and bent to give her a squeeze across the shoulders and a kiss on the cheek by way of thanks for her helpfulness.

Within an hour armor had been donned, weapons gathered, provisions and potions packed. Children and stay-behind spouses had been kissed and hugged, and it was time for the party to leave. The six companions had two Agena maps plus Bernadette's original Iscandia map on them, which they hoped would be enough to help them get around in a hurry. Bjorn had already departed for the job site where he was acting as construction foreman.

As Erik, Riki, and the two younger children stood watching outside Drakespring House's front door, Bernadette gathered her companions around her. Andrion was as concerned as she was about the missing kids, but in this he deferred to her and Lifa as the leaders of the party. Bernadette had a very good idea where Andi would have started his quest. It was the closest fast-travel point her map had to Skarhalfn, and she stabbed with a finger while gathering her will to encompass those around her. They were off to Castle Hordenhaal.

Chapter 27: The Wilds of Skarhalfn

As Andi, Fjuri, and Meri made their way up the faint trail
leading north from Walrus Cove, they felt a mixture of excitement
and trepidation. Had this really been such a good idea? The boys
were as big and strong as many grown men and had been training
with weapons since they were little kids; and Meri, if small, could
hold her own with a bow against most antagonists. But were they
prepared to survive the trek across the freezing wastes of this bleak
northern island?

The three didn't talk much as they walked along. The boys
had Meri walk between them – where Fjuri, in the rear, could keep
an eye on her and she'd be somewhat protected if anything
attacked them. It's all going to be okay, Andi told himself. It
wasn't as if they were stuck out here. If they found themselves
engulfed by a blizzard or running out of food or water he could just
transport them all away to safety with the map – back to Castle
Hordenhaal, to the Eparchy, even back home to Waterdon.

But the humiliation of aborting the quest to go running home
with his tail between his legs was not something Andi was willing
to face if he could avoid it. Besides, he knew, he and Fjuri were up
to their necks in trouble with their parents – it would just be wrong
to get into all that trouble and not have anything to show for it.

The weather wasn't all that bad as they walked along. Indeed,
it wasn't as cold here as Andi had expected. He supposed the fact
the island (Skarhalfn, he'd realized, after studying the map some
more) was surrounded by water meant that it stayed a little warmer
than areas of the continent to its south. There was no snow falling,
though clearly a lot of it had fallen in the past. Some areas of the
terrain through which they walked were free of snow, though, and
there was a surprising amount of life. Most of the vegetation was
short and scrubby, but there were some tall evergreens growing in
clumps here and there.

He was relieved to find there was water to drink, too. Small
lakes dotted the landscape between the hills, and though most of
these had ice on them it was thin and could easily be broken
through to fill a water skin. They saw rabbits and foxes, both

seeming to be slightly different from the familiar species in the Waterdon area. They were blotched white and brown, like the landscape, and would probably be turning full white as winter came on. After all, it *was* still summer. Their ears were smaller than those of the rabbits and foxes Andi knew, too. Probably a useful protection against frostbite.

With little wind and a mix of blue sky and clouds, it was almost pleasant. The terrain wasn't particularly rugged, the trail running up and down and curving around the sides of the steeper hills. They seemed to be climbing slightly as they headed north toward the quest marker that had lured them all here.

After a couple of hours of walking, Meri asked for a halt. "Hey, big brother," she said to Andi in her piping voice, "your legs are a lot longer than mine. Do think we could take a little rest and maybe have a snack?" Though the boys could probably have kept going for hours more without a rest, food was already on their minds. In near-freezing conditions, everyone needed to eat more.

They were approaching the crest of a low hill, on which a stand of tall fir trees was growing. There were some medium-sized boulders scattered around, and the moss on them looked like it might be softer than sitting on the ground. "Sure, Squirt," Andi said cheerfully. As they moved closer to their goal, he was beginning to feel more optimistic about things than he had when they'd first set out.

They took off their packs and set their weapons carefully aside, before taking seats and rummaging through their belongings for food and water. They still had some trail bread, and those smoked walrus steaks had not yet begun to seem appealing. Their water skins they'd carried near their bodies, keeping them warm enough not to freeze solid; but the water was still chilly and all three of them wished there were some hot tea instead.

"Andi," Meri asked, as she sank her sharp little teeth into a hunk of trail bread, "why do you suppose this trail is here? Do you think the leukalfar in Mrzhgradfendz come down to the coast?" Andi considered as he chewed. He was his father's son in many ways, and his active mind had been spinning explanations as they walked along.

Mouth cleared with a swallow of chill water, he at last replied: "There's no stone, so this is a path not a road. And it looks like it once got a lot of use. But you probably noticed there's bushes and little trees starting to sprout in it. I think it was probably the people at Walrus Cove who had some reason to come in this direction, and the trail's been abandoned since they left." He took another bite. "I suppose we'll know when we get to where it's going. If it goes all the way to Mrzhgradfendz that'll suggest they might have been raiding the ruins for treasure over a fairly long period of time."

Meri nodded. Then after she'd washed her snack down with a gulp of water, shivering a bit as it went down her throat, she returned her water skin to its hanging place and stood up, dusting off her long-fingered hands. "'Scuse me," she told her two male companions, "I've gotta go…" With that she moved over into the stand of trees looking for a likely bush to squat behind. Lucky boys, they could pee standing up and do it almost anywhere unobtrusively. Down slope a little ways, Meri worked her way into a small thicket with an open space in the middle of it and began the laborious task of unfastening the lower part of her armor and dropping her underwear so she could relieve her aching bladder.

Oh! The air was so *cold* on her bare legs and behind. She squeezed hard, trying to finish her business quickly. Leukalfar she might be, and cold didn't bother her nearly as much as it did her Sky People parents and siblings; but she'd been raised in a much warmer climate and she wasn't used to such temperatures.

Happily fastened back up again, Meri was just making her way toward a gap between the bushes so she could return to the group at the summit of the hill when she heard a noise that made her blood run cold. "Areugh, hunh, hunh… areugh!" The unmistakable warning growl of a bear! While bears never came into the area around their home, Meri had encountered them while hunting with her parents on more than one occasion.

148

Unlike smilodons or wolves, which would simply attack you on sight, bears would usually try to warn you away from where they were denned or foraging. Meri must have stumbled into this one's territory without realizing it. There was a lot of icefruit growing in the area. She'd left her bow back with her pack, not that she'd be likely to stop a full-grown bear with arrows before it had had a chance to chop her into mincemeat.

"Andi!" Meri wailed, hoping that the bushes would not muffle her cry too much for her to be heard. "There's a bear!" she shouted. Some thirty feet away through the bushes, both boys heard her cry. They heard the bear as well, and grabbed their weapons before moving toward where it was snarling out its defiance. "Stay there, Meri!" Andi shouted back. She was his responsibility, and if anything happened to her on this trip he would never forgive himself.

It sounded like good advice. Meri huddled down in her little thicket, hoping that the bear would not notice her. She wasn't really happy about having her brother and Fjuri taking the animal on without help, either, but there wasn't much she could do. The two tall boys stalked toward the bear, which was now standing on its hind legs and looking really menacing. It was a brown bear, one of the largest types.

Andi motioned to Fjuri to separate from him, and they approached the belligerent animal from opposite sides – making it hesitate to charge either of them. Fjuri had his sword out, not the ideal weapon for fighting an animal that stood a foot taller than you and had claw-tipped forelegs that could just about knock your head off with a single blow. If you had to kill bears, you were better off peppering them with broadhead arrows from a hundred yards off, with some hope they wouldn't be able to reach you before they died.

Or I could go dragon and just toast him, Andi thought – but quickly rejected the idea. If he burst through his clothes and armor, ruining them, he'd have to *stay* dragon because he wouldn't have anything to put on afterward. Which would mean he couldn't go down into the dypalfar ruin. He had his bow strung and an arrow nocked, but at this range he'd never be able to stop the bear in time. Even with Fjuri attacking from the other side, there was a pretty good chance somebody would get hurt. And if it were him, they'd have nobody to use healing spells.

All this passed through Andi's mind in an instant, and he knew what he must do. Bow held down at his side, facing the enraged beast standing only a few yards away, he took a deep breath and cried "Ruh-Trau-Stil-Rir!" Calm washed over the bear, freeing its mind of fear and aggression. It dropped to all fours and wandered off a short distance, looking as though it had forgotten what it was doing. Andi knew that situation wouldn't last long.

"Come *on* Fjuri!" he shouted at his friend, and they sprinted back up the hill to collect their belongings. Andi picked up Meri's pack and bow as well, and they made their way hastily down to the thicket they'd heard her calling from a few moments before. "Meri!" he called in a much softer voice, as he approached where he thought she was hiding.

"Here, Brother!" she responded as quietly. "Is it gone?"

"No, but I quieted it down for a while," he replied as they zoomed in on her location. The thicket was too tightly interwoven for them to come through without getting scratched up. "Hurry up and come out! We've got your stuff, but we need to get out of here before the bear comes to his senses."

Meri wasted no further time in wriggling out between the branches and grabbing her pack. Then the three of them moved off down the hill in the direction they'd come from, striking the trail well below the crest where they'd stopped earlier and moving over onto the hillside on the far side of it. They crept along warily, keeping eyes and ears open for the bear they'd just met or any others that might happen to be hunting for berries (or fat, juicy humans) in these woods.

After a quarter of a mile or so they felt it was safe to circle back and resume walking on the trail, which continued to offer an easier way through the increasingly thick undergrowth. After an hour had passed and there'd been no further attacks, they all began to relax a little. Fjuri, too, had been thinking about things. "Hey

Andi," he called past Meri, who was once again walking in front of him, "How do you suppose bears and foxes and rabbits got here to this island? I can imagine walruses going anywhere there's water, but wouldn't a rabbit freeze or drown?"

"I think maybe this island wasn't always an island," Andi replied after a moment. "There are some little islets off to the south of here between Skarhalfn and the Iscandia mainland – I saw them when I was flying over from Castle Hordenhaal. From what Grandpapa Francois told me once, thousands of years ago it was much colder than it is now, and sea level was lower. That chain of islands might have been a bridge connecting the two land masses, and the animals could have come across that way."

"Huh," Fjuri responded. "Maybe it wasn't an island when the dypalfar went through their portal. That might be why they were being so hard-pressed by their enemies." Conversation subsided for a while after that. The land grew more rugged, rocky scarps rising and forcing the trail steeply up and down or back and forth in switchbacks. Soon the three were puffing, and Fjuri could see that Meri was beginning to flag. Little kids, even tough little leukalfar kids, just didn't have as much stamina as people his size did.

"Hey people, what do you say we break for lunch?" he suggested. Andi turned and immediately understood that Meri, at least, was in need of a break. They were at a higher elevation here than they'd been a few hours ago, and it was quite a few degrees colder. There were still a lot of trees, though, if also more snow on the ground.

Andi spotted what was probably a deer trail (they'd now also seen both deer and elk, though only from a distance) departing the trail and leading down through a light coating of snow over a thick cushion of pine needles around a large boulder. On its lee side they found a little sheltered hollow where a fallen evergreen tree had come down beside a slight overhang. It wasn't a cave by any means, but the area between the rock and the log was free of snow. Andy broke handfuls of small dry branches off of the log, making a spot where they could sit as well as giving him an armload of kindling.

He began laying a fire up against the rock, saying over his shoulder "Meri, Fjuri, could you see if you can find us a little more firewood? Oh, and watch out for nasties!" The two smiled and set off, hands on weapons and alert for danger, to see what they could come up with. Meri was able to break many smaller branches off of the lower reaches of the evergreens, fairly dry and free of snow. Meanwhile Fjuri got the wood axe he'd brought along out of his pack and chopped them a few larger logs from downed trees in the vicinity.

Andi had started his kindling with a fire spell, and soon after Meri and Fjuri returned with their contributions that little fire had become a roaring blaze. It quickly heated the rock face above it, and that heat was reflected out into the sheltered space where the three of them sat along the fallen log. Fjuri got some of the smoked walrus steaks out of his pack, where they'd been wrapped in some of the waxed paper their trail bread had come in, and a little work with a dagger soon produced sharpened sticks to skewer them on.

Each of them held one of the big, fatty steaks over the fire on a stick, as children in another universe would toast marshmallows. Though the meat had smoked above a slow fire overnight, it still had some moisture in it and soon sizzling juices were beginning to run out and drip into the fire. They had to be careful lest they incinerate their food as the rich, fishy walrus fat produced sudden flare-ups.

Somehow, after hiking in the cold for all these hours and having nothing hot to eat or drink since this morning's tea, the walrus steaks seemed more appealing now. When they were hot enough each of them plucked one from the fire and gingerly picked it up with two gloved hands, sinking their teeth into the rich flesh.

They'd left the teakettle behind in the ruins of Walrus Cove, but Andy managed to produce individual cups of tea. He'd brought along an invention of his mother's for tea while traveling, little muslin drawstring bags full of finely crumbled tea herbs. They steeped much more quickly that way. Each of them had packed their own mug, and they filled them with water from their skins and set them on the ground before the fire with a "tea bag" sunk in each of them. Then he applied his fire spell, slowly and carefully, until the mugs were hot and the water in them boiling.

By the time they had cooled enough to be handled, the tea in the bags had steeped enough to produce one mug of nice, hot tea each. They fished the bags out of the mugs with a spoon and laid them on a patch of clean snow to cool and drain. Andi took charge of them after they'd finished their break, removing the spent herbs from the bags and tucking the bags into the top of his pack. They'd need to be rinsed out before being used again.

The rich, hot meat and warm tea (sweetened with a little honey) had restored them all. Fjuri dumped some snow on the embers of their fire lest it somehow set the woods ablaze, and the three of them went on their way in relatively high spirits. As they continued along the abandoned trail, climbing uphill and down, the clear skies of morning began to give way to a gray overcast that made it hard to tell what time of day it was.

Fjuri happened to be looking up the trail as it climbed steeply before them – going between two large rocks like the one where they'd stopped for lunch. His blood froze, and he hissed "Andi!" His friend's ears were sharp and there were few sounds here in the wilderness to distract him from the sound of Fjuri's exclamation. He looked back sharply, to see Fjuri pointing up the trail, beyond him.

Meri, too, had turned at the sound and was now following with her leukalfar sight the direction Fjuri was pointing. By the gods! Crouched atop the smaller of the two rocks that flanked the trail ahead, no doubt waiting for its dinner to deliver itself, was one of the largest snow cats the kids had ever seen – dead or alive. Andi and Meri's mom had a magnificent cloak made from a single snow cat pelt, and that one must have been pretty good-sized. But these were another of Iscandia's creatures the three hadn't come up against very often in their young lives.

Before Andi could think what to do next, Fjuri had drawn his sword and Meri, lifting her bow and taking quick aim, had put a deadly arrow into the cat's chest. With a shriek of rage, it launched itself at them from the boulder – hitting the ground perhaps fifteen feet away from them and coming fast though blood was running from the wound. "Kraf-Luft-Struung-Wund!" Andi cried, blowing it back some twenty feet downslope from the trail just as it had nearly closed the distance.

Mom had schooled Andi well in the use of dragon spells. As one who was fireblood, he could learn these spells easily – and absorb the stones needed to power them into his body. One of things she had taught him was the limitations of dragon spells. Calm would not work on sentient creatures like dragons or humans, or even on very large animals like mammoths. And the degree to which the Gale spell could hurl your enemies away from you was partly dependent on the mass of the enemy. This cat had not gone very far, nor was it taking very long to get back on its feet again.

In pain from the arrow lodged in a lung, it wanted only to kill these strange creatures who had hurt it. As it gathered itself for another charge Meri put another arrow into it, this one a little off to one side where the foreleg met the shoulder. She didn't have a good angle for hitting its heart, as it was rushing toward them. Peeling off to the side she shot again, sinking an arrow into the cat's neck this time. It was beginning to slow.

Andi considered using his bow but decided it would take too long to bring their attacker down. Instead he slung it behind him and dual-wielded lightning, sending a powerful bolt of electricity sizzling toward the injured animal. It was knocked off its feet, shrieking in pain and rage, and as it made to get up again Fjuri reached it and ran his sword into its side, between the ribs just behind the left shoulder. Its heart pierced, the cat gave a guttural sigh as its last breath departed from it – and lay still.

Its three mighty slayers stood around in excited relief, chests heaving. That was too close! After everyone had taken a few breaths, it was Andi who spoke first. "Nice work, Meri," he told his little sister. Just because she wasn't apparently an adolescent yet didn't mean she was to be discounted in a fight. She came from fierce people, both those who gave her birth and those who had raised her as their own.

"You too, Fjuri," Andi added – not wanting to slight his friend's quick action. Spellcasting and then launching that dual blast of lightning had taken a lot out of him, and he might have had some trouble finishing that snow cat off without the help of his sister and friend. Meri, broken from her temporary paralysis, had a dagger out and was on the carcass in another breath.

"Should we take the hide, Andi?" she asked. One of the lessons instilled by Mama and Papa Erik throughout their lives had been not to kill anything needlessly. And if you must kill, you make as much use as possible out of what you had killed. That "what" might be "whom," as in bandits or Insurgents or renegade vampires, was not something they'd emphasized.

Andi considered the sad corpse of the cat as it lay there in a snowbank, its life's blood already congealing around it in the freezing conditions. "I think the hide's too chewed up with all your arrows, Squirt," he told her. "I'll just get the fangs and eyeballs then," the sweet young thing replied, and bent to her work.

The three of them, with the resilience of youth, soon recovered from the aftermath of the adrenaline that had surged through them minutes before and continued on their way. The trail, which had stood them in good stead this entire day, suddenly dived down from the ridge they'd been climbing – veering from its straight course toward Mrzhgradfendz – and widened out into a sort of plaza, clearly of manmade origins.

For a moment or two the trio stood side by side, taking in what lay before them. There was a ruinous-looking wooden hut off to the left, pushed up against the hillside. It no longer had a roof, but some of the walls still stood. To the right of that were a couple of wooden carts lying topsy-turvy, one missing a wheel and the other with a broken axle. And beyond those was surely the entrance to a mine of some kind.

All of them had visited mines in the past. It could be fun to heft a pick and then take your ore to be smelted, though only Andi among them had actually done any smithing. His mom was a master smith with a reputation that spanned Iscandia and beyond, his Papa Erik nearly as good in his own way. If he hadn't had so many other possibilities clamoring for his attention, Andi could well have considered a career as a smith. He got a lot of satisfaction from working with his hands.

"I think we know now what the trail led to," Andi told his companions. They nodded silently. "I wonder if maybe the village on the coast wasn't just a sideline, a way to supply the miners with food and oil and make a little money on the side. Then when the mine was tapped out, they all packed up and left."

Like most mine entrances, this one had a wooden door. But it was hanging open, one hinge rusted away. From the look of the place, it had been more than a generation since men had last been here wresting riches from the earth. This could possibly be a good place for them to shelter for the night; but they approached with caution. Lots of other… things… might also think the abandoned mine workings a likely den.

As nearly as they could tell through the cloud cover the sun had sunk most of the way down the western horizon and was soon to depart, leaving them in darkness. Andi and Fjuri, Meri a couple of paces behind with her dagger drawn, approached the yawning mine opening with considerable trepidation – sniffing the air. There was a musky animal scent as if a smilodon or perhaps a bear had denned here in recent years. But it was old, muted. Meri's sense of smell was more acute than the boys', and she shortly announced "I don't think anything's living here right at the moment."

Fjuri had his sword drawn, while Andi had raised a globe of magical light to give them some illumination as they stepped inside. To one side of the entrance was a pile of rusty mining implements – picks, shovels – and a pair of dusty barrels that looked still intact. Andi breached one of them and discovered a couple of torches inside – and some wizened, hardened objects that he suspected might have been apples or maybe potatoes at some time before he was born.

Surprisingly, the torches were still soaked with oil and flared to life in an instant as he touched them with his fire spell. All three of them soon realized that they must have been treated with rendered walrus fat. The stuff was useful beyond a doubt, and lasted for a long time if there was nothing to eat it up; but gods what a reek! Making a great show of trying to hold his nose while holding a torch in one hand and his sword in the other, Fjuri grinned at his friend and they proceeded deeper into the mine.

As they went down the broad rock-hewn passage, heavy timbers overhead, the three saw further evidence of the mining activities that must have gone on here for quite some time. If Andi's theory was correct, the mine had produced enough ore that its operators had decided to build a village at Walrus Cove. But the workings were not as extensive as they'd expected. Maybe, after all, the mine had been a chance offshoot of the walrus-hunting operation and not the other way around.

Andi and Fjuri might be well-grown and on their way to becoming men; but within both of them lurked the children they had been – with imaginations that expected there would be precious gems, overlooked ore veins, or other treasures to be found here in the abandoned mine. They were therefore somewhat disappointed to find nothing left behind here but things that were broken or of no further use. The miners had followed a vein of ore, and when the vein had been exhausted they'd packed up anything of value and left the rest behind.

Meri was just glad to have reached something like shelter before it got dark. The abandoned mine was as good as a cave, maybe better as it had smooth, level floors and ceilings well supported by still-strong timbers. The temperature down here was much warmer than up on the trail, sheltered from the wind. And as they'd now explored every foot of the workings and found no sign of current occupation by animals or people, they should be safe here for the night.

Andi and Fjuri concluded the same, and they returned to the entryway and spent some time propping up the mine's wooden door. There was a pile of spare pit props stacked nearby, and they were able to close the door and then place several of the props at an angle between it and the well-packed earthen floor. Only a force strong enough to obliterate the door would be able to come through it now, until they removed the props.

The three of them, feeling tiredness washing over them now that they knew they could finally relax, returned down the main shaft and through a couple of turnings to an area that had apparently been an encampment for the miners. There was a stone fire ring below a vent hole that would carry away smoke, and even a small underground stream flowing past. Some of the "waste" left behind by the miners included an assortment of cast iron pots, judged too heavy and not valuable enough to be taken away with them when they left.

Fjuri happily pulled out his wood axe and went to work on another pile of unused pit props. Some of them became kindling, others "logs" for the fire Andi soon lit with his fire spell. Having fire at his command was such a useful thing, he wondered why everyone did not learn the spell along with their ABC's.

The fireplace still had an iron spit standing across it, and a hook on which to hang one of the pots. A pity we didn't kill anything more edible than that smilodon today, Andi thought. A nice leg of goat or haunch of venison would be perfect right now. Despite Mom's warning that they were not good to eat, Andi had tried smilodon in his dragon form. However, no amount of Holocaust roasting was enough to kill the pungent, gamey carnivore flavor. Herbivores and creatures that ate both plants and animals were tasty enough, but he'd just as soon save smilodon steaks for the point where he was close to starvation. Yuck.

Well, they still had a good quantity of semi-smoked walrus steaks. There is one hell of a lot of meat on a walrus. And they also had a pot, fresh water to hand, and bags of dried herbs and vegetables. Time to try a "trail stew." Both Mom and Papa Erik had touted this dish, one they'd eaten on many a wilderness quest. Andi dunked up a quantity of water in a medium-sized stew pot, and hung it over the fire. Then he tossed in some of the dried stuff he'd taken from home, and while the water heated he cut up some of the walrus steaks on an earthenware plate, small chunks he hoped would have time to tenderize while the stew simmered.

At home all of them would probably have cut out the massive ribbons of fat from the meat. In Waterdon it never really got that cold. Here, they welcomed its richness. When the stew had simmered for an hour or so Andi ladled it into bowls using his tea mug, and they all blew on it impatiently waiting for it to get cool enough to eat. After the long day of trekking through the frozen wilderness and fighting off hostile wildlife, it smelled amazing!

When the last of the stew had been scraped from the pot with slices of toasted stale bread and happily devoured, the three of them sat around the fire on their bedrolls feeling replete, happy, and pleased with themselves. What a day it had been, and they had come through it without a scratch! Tomorrow, they hoped, they would reach Mrzhgradfendz.

Chapter 28: The Journey Continues

Down inside the mine (High Crest Mine, the map declared, though there was no indication of what had been mined here) there was no difference between day and night. As the three exhausted youngsters slept, wrapped snug in their bedrolls, their torches went out and their fire burned down until it was only a few embers.

It was Meri who woke first – she who was best able to cope with the darkness. Sure, Andi could throw up a globe of magical light. But she needed no light at all. Better than a cat or a dragon, a leukalfar could see in utter blackness because their sight was not as that of other creatures. No wonder so many of them stayed far below the earth, in the dark places where their enemies would not go.

Meri checked some nearby barrels and found more torches. Their fire had been large, and the embers still had some heat to them. Using some slivers of wood left over from Fjuri's chopping the night before, she blew them into a slight blaze and used it to light the stinking, walrus fat-soaked torches so that they glowed brightly. Just as darkness was no barrier to a leukalfar's sight, so a sudden increase in visible light did not blind them. The "blind" leukalfar could see far better than anyone else could, if without nuance of color.

The sudden light woke her two companions, and both boys were soon sitting up and yawning. They felt well-rested after their long day yesterday, and both of them were fairly well starving as well. Eating enough calories to keep a fifteen-year-old boy going in a chilly northern clime was no small task.

Fortunately, they still had a good quantity of trail bread. They hadn't brought enough supplies for a long trip though, Andi realized as he devoured a cold hunk of the stuff. They built up the fire again and heated water for tea, which was nice. But if they hadn't killed that walrus they'd have been nearly out of food by now. Somehow, when he and Fjuri had hatched this plan, it had all seemed a lot simpler. Well, they'd just have to kill some game as they continued their journey. Unlike the barren, frozen wasteland

Andi had expected, Skarhalfn had proven to be as full of life (if not human life) as anyplace in Iscandia.

Soon, they were ready to leave again. Though a wildfire hardly seemed likely here in this cavern of stone, Fjuri dutifully filled the stew pot from last night at the little stream and used the water to douse their campfire. He had been thoroughly trained by his own parents and Andi's as well. They left the pots and other items behind, so that this place might provide shelter and comfort to some other travelers after they'd gone.

Andi took one of the torches Meri had lit, Fjuri the other and once again, Meri walked between them. She liked doing that, actually. It made her feel part of the team, not a tag-along kid; and safe as well, between her adored big brother and his big, strong friend. Fjuri had never been mean to her, as had some other people she'd met.

When they came to the door they'd barricaded the night before, Andi handed off his torch to Meri while he removed the pit props so the door could fall open again. He wished he had the wherewithal to repair the missing hinge, as he thought this place a good shelter and worth keeping up; but they really had no way to do that. Likewise, they didn't know what to do with their blazing torches once they'd gotten outside. After some discussion they just laid them down in a snowdrift that ran along one side of the open area leading to the mine, where they hissed and went out.

They explored the ruined shack, but found nothing of value there. "Well troops," Andi said enthusiastically, "onward to Mrzhgradfendz!" Fjuri and Meri grinned at him, and they fell into line behind him. But the trail they had been traveling all day yesterday had ended at this spot, and it was time for Andi to find a new way for them to continue to the north.

He surveyed the terrain for a moment, scanning around them for a likely route. Studying the map, which showed his location as an arrow that rotated as he did, he launched them back up the trail to the ridge it had departed from yesterday evening, then made a sharp right and continued along the ridge. There was no trail here, and the going was considerably harder than it had been throughout their trek yesterday. But the snow on the ridge was not as deep as on either side, there was little growing on it, and it was heading in the right direction.

Andi paused for a moment and turned to his followers. "We're running low on food," he admitted, "so it'd be good if we could kill something while we're walking. Meri, if you spot any rabbits see if you can get them with your bow. Fjuri, you want to borrow my bow?" Fjuri had been training in weapons since he and Andi were not yet five, though back then it had all been fun and games. With his size and reach edged weapons gave him a big advantage, and he was not the bowman most of the Drakespring children were. On the other hand he was no stranger to the bow, and he usually hit what he was aiming at – with a force that Meri, a better shot, could not equal.

He grinned at his friend. Their personalities were such that, while Fjuri had always been and would remain the larger and more muscular, it was usually Andi that took the lead when they were together. "Good idea, Andi," he said. "You want to take my sword?" Even weaponless Andi was far from helpless, with his dragon spells and battle magic. But it seemed a good idea to have something to flourish should they need to menace anyone they ran into.

The weapons swap completed, Andi turned and led them along the ridge. As is generally the case in hilly country it eventually petered out, and they found themselves climbing the next one through snow that seemed to be getting thicker. By the gods, it was cold! They were managing to keep reasonably warm through the effort of hiking, but they were burning calories like crazy and it seemed like they had been traveling for no more than a couple of hours before Andi felt his stomach rumbling again. What he wouldn't give for one of Papa Erik's mammoth breakfasts: piles of fluffy scrambled eggs from their chicken flock, with crispy bacon on the side and unlimited fresh bread rolls slathered with fresh butter…

Andi realized that his mind was beginning to wander. Spending a long time in freezing conditions seemed to affect your brain, somehow. He was jolted out of his food-based reverie by a quick *thrum* behind him and Meri's triumphant cry, "Got ya!" She skipped downslope a few yards to the corpse of a rabbit, pierced through by an arrow from her bow, and hoisted it aloft with a grin. As little as she was, Andi observed, the cold didn't seem to be getting to her as much as it was to him.

Meri retrieved her arrow and labored back up the snow-strewn slope, the snow squeaking underfoot, until she was back on the ridge they'd been traversing. She pulled a handful of leather thongs out of her pack and tied one of them around the rabbit's hind leg, then hung it from a ring sewn to her pack. In these temperatures, cleaning and skinning it could wait until they settled down to camp.

Meri looked up at her brother, than back at Fjuri – the two boys towering above her. "One down, two dozen to go," she said with a smile. Andi grinned back at her. Too true. At the rate he was burning fuel he was going to need half a dozen rabbits to himself (mmm, sizzling with juices as they roasted over an open fire…) just to make up what he'd used since they left the mine.

In fact Meri's sharp sight and deadly accuracy did get them a further three rabbits as they picked their way along. Andi was beginning to revise his expectation that they might reach Mrzhgradfendz before they had to camp again. Without the trail, moving through this wilderness was much slower going than it had been on their first day of travel.

Leaving one ridge they found that their path no longer ran along the ridges. So they picked their way down a snowy hillside to the bed of a smallish stream that was running in the right direction. At the bottom of the slope they ran across a deer trail, which was a relief. Andi had certainly spent a lot of time hunting in the wilderness of Iscandia, but this was the first time he had needed to rely on the skills he'd learned for survival.

He halted their march again, and Fjuri and Meri gathered around him. "I think this might be a better opportunity for us to find some larger game," he told them. "Lots of creatures must come here to drink. But that includes predators, not just the ones we're hoping to kill for food. So stay alert!"

They both nodded at him solemnly, then Fjuri (also suffering from visions of hot food) asked "Are we going to take a break soon? I'm starving."

Andi thought it over. "As soon as we get to a wide spot where we can make a fire, I think we'll sit down and toast those bunnies Meri's carrying. We need to keep our strength up!" Both his "troops" grinned in eager assent. They pushed on, finding it easier going alongside the stream though the trail they followed was narrow.

There *was* more wildlife here, though fortunately they didn't encounter any bears, wolves, or smilodons. The water in the small stream, which was barely half a dozen feet across and probably nowhere more than two feet deep, was still mostly free-flowing at this season – though ice was beginning to form around the rocks that littered its bed.

Meri got another rabbit, spotting it on the far side of the stream as it unwarily approached the water to drink. Then the three of them stood there looking at the dead rabbit for a moment, considering. Meri wouldn't be able to retrieve it without getting her feet wet. Fjuri realized this and said, "No problem – I'll be right back!" He backed up a bit, then took a running leap and jumped across the water without any difficulty. Gods be thanked, the ground was too hard and frozen for him to slip in mud on the far side and land up to his elbows in icy water. That would have been *really* embarrassing.

In another moment their supply of rabbit carcasses had increased to five, and the small party continued on their way. The thought of those rabbits hot and sizzling was beginning to weigh on Andi's mind, and as they came to a spot where a second, even tinier stream joined the one they were traveling along he was just about to call a halt. The banks on the far side of the little tributary were relatively level, offering them a spot where they might be able to make a fire and rest for a while.

Just then Fjuri spotted it – a young cow elk moving downhill along the little rivulet, picking her way delicately as she headed toward the larger stream and a place where she might be able to drink more fully. "Shh!" he hissed, halting Andi as he was about to announce their stop. There was no sound but the babbling of the brook beside them as he drew the bow, a magnificent recurve daimonic one (Andi's mom believed in giving her kids the best, as their skills increased), and took careful aim. The elk was not yet aware of them, seemingly trying to drink from the smaller stream as she walked along its course, finding the water too shallow and mostly frozen over.

Andi and Meri were both riveted as Fjuri lined up his shot, the bow creaking slightly as he drew it to its fullest. Then he let the arrow fly, leaping toward the young elk faster than a thought. It missed. No, not entirely. It struck her, but Fjuri's intended killing shot landed between the shoulder blade and the rib cage, lodging in the elk's left shoulder joint and making it impossible for her to run away at speed. It was not a shot that would bring her down in a hurry.

As she turned and bolted back up along the course of the little rivulet above them, Fjuri cursed "By all the hells!" He set off at a run uphill, the others following him, as he drew another arrow from his quiver. The elk, crippled by the arrow lodged in her shoulder, was unable to use that leg and she was slowed down a lot. She was losing blood, too, and as the surge of adrenaline that had swept over her when she was hit began to fade, her pace faltered still more.

"We can catch her!" Andi urged, as the three kids pushed up the hill. This was far more exertion than simply hiking along beside the gently rising streambed, and the three of them were soon breaking out in sweat beneath their armor – a situation that could prove fatal in these freezing conditions. But the boys were ravenous, and Meri's instincts had her as caught up in the chase as they were. They pushed on.

The elk, beginning to stagger now, crested a rise where the small stream she'd been running beside fell down from a meandering path across a small, snow-covered meadow. Her three pursuers, panting, were only a few feet behind her. With the terrain now level and her hunters at her heels, she put on a burst of speed and opened a gap as she bounded through snow a couple of feet deep – heading for another sharp rise on the far side of the flat area.

As the kids came up onto the surface of the meadow, they paused gasping for breath as they watched the wounded elk quickly running away from them. Even hobbling on three legs, she had a turn of speed they couldn't hope to match – especially not in snow this deep. "I don't think she can last much longer," Andi panted. That he, Fjuri and Meri could also not last much longer at this pace went unspoken. "She's going to collapse from exhaustion in another minute. Why don't we just take a little rest?"

Both Fjuri and Meri had gotten some additional arrows into the rear of the elk during the chase. They were protruding from her hindquarters, and blood was now running down her hind legs and staining the snow. At the least, there wouldn't be any trouble tracking her in this white wilderness.

The elk had reached the far side of the meadow and was now struggling to climb the hillside beyond it, but her hunters could see that she was reaching the end of her strength. Fjuri scooped Meri up onto his shoulders as he observed how difficult it was for her to get through the deep snow, even following in Andi's footsteps. In a minute or two they'd reached the lighter snow of the hillside and were closing in on their prey again.

Suddenly, another patch of white seemed to detach itself from some trees on their right, and with swift strides it closed to the foundering elk and grasped her by the head. In another moment it had snapped her neck, and her struggles were done. The three kids, shocked and disbelieving, stared in horror at this apparition that had seemingly come out of nowhere. "It's a snow troll!" Andi cried.

Chapter 29: Ghrztum

"Ruh-Trau-Stil-Rir!" Andi cried, though he wasn't sure it would do any good. Snow trolls were near the upper size limit of creatures that could be pacified by Calm, and furthermore they were sort-of on the borderline between animals and sentient creatures like humans or dragons. If Calm didn't work, he wasn't sure what they would do next. It was going to take more than a few arrows to put this one down, that was for sure.

It seemed to be working. At least, the troll had set down the elk he had been about to carry off and was not attacking them. But it didn't have that dazed, sort of "I forgot what I was doing" look that hostile creatures got after they'd been zapped with Calm. It was gazing at them questioningly, and its attention seemed to be focused on Meri. Fjuri had set her down when they reached the hillside, and the three companions were now standing in a semicircle around the fallen elk and the creature that had suddenly appeared to claim it.

Meri had her bow drawn. She never met a snow troll before but had heard enough about them to know there wasn't the slightest chance that an arrow from her was going to stop this one if it decided to attack. She could only pray that Andi's dragon spell had erased the hostility you would naturally expect from one of these beasts, and would give them a chance to flee. Or that Andi would run it through with Fjuri's sword, or something!

She was trembling slightly as she held her shot, waiting for a sign that the troll was going to attack them. But it wasn't cold, or fear, that set her shaking and put the accuracy of her shot in danger. It was anger. How dare this big heap of white fur just stroll out from between the trees and make off with *their elk*?! They had worked *hard* for this elk, and she had been really looking forward to gorging herself on the hot, juice-dripping meat.

Meri continued holding her shot, quivering, as she realized that the troll was gazing right at her with an expression of... surprise? Its surprise was as nothing to the surprise of Meri and her companions when, a moment later, it rumbled deep in its throat and then spoke, in passable leukalfar tongue, the phrase "Little one?"

Meri released the draw on her bow, keeping the arrow nocked on the string but pointing it down toward the ground, as she tried to take in the fact that a troll… a *troll*! had just spoken to her in the language of her people. Andi, too, was dumfounded. Sure, trolls were almost like humans in many ways and far smarter than most animals. But a troll had made a noise that sounded like speech instead of just attacking them – astounding!

Evidently it was Meri's presence and not Andi's dragon spell that had stopped the enormous creature from attacking them. As the three travelers, still panting from their chase of the elk, studied the troll more closely they realized it was wearing a leather harness of some sort, with a club hung from one side and a leather pouch, tanned white like its fur, on the other.

It spoke again, once again addressing Meri: "Why are you with these Sky People?" it asked, gesturing at the two tall boys flanking her. "I'm her brother!" Andi spoke up in leukalfar tongue, angry at being talked about as if he weren't standing right there. Now it was the troll's turn to stare in disbelief. One of the Sky People, speaking the language of the leukalfar? Sensing that apparently the troll (if that was what it really was) wasn't going to just charge them with that club flying, Andi continued "Who are you?"

Shaking his head, still having a hard time making sense of what he was hearing, the troll said after another couple of moments, "My name is Ghrztum, son of Indinala and Skarnoris of the Mirskhrazana tribe of Mrzhgradfendz," he said formally.

"You're a leukalfar?" Andi asked in disbelief.

Ghrztum glanced from Andi to Meri, and said pointedly "And you are her brother? Obviously, I'm adopted."

This fellow was a lot smarter and more articulate than they'd initially thought, Andi realized, and he apologized hastily. "Your pardon, Ghrztum, for my rudeness. I am Andreas Drakespring of the Sky People and this is my sister Merelle Drakespring. She was born to the leukalfar, but has lived as a member of my family since she was a baby. My large friend here is Fjurbund Steadfast, and I'm afraid he does not understand any of the leukalfar tongue."

Ghrztum nodded, then his face split in an enormous and truly frightening grin. He gestured to the dead elk, rapidly cooling as it lay crumpled in the snow at their feet. "May Apoldros smile on you, Andreas and Merelle Drakespring," he said. "I suppose you were planning on having this creature for your midday meal?" Fjuri had slung Andi's bow over his back, and was standing there trying to take in the conversation from the participants' body language and gestures. If only there'd been more time for him to study leukalfar! He and Andi had both learned the dragon language when they were little kids – though once Andi had begun transforming into a dragon, it had become his "native tongue" in a way.

Andi smiled back at Ghrztum. "Yes. I was thinking we would gut it and then carve off some steaks to roast. We were hoping to make it to Mrzhgradfendz today, so we didn't want to spend too long cooking and eating. Is it far from here?"

Ghrztum considered them. "Not so far for me, or for you two maybe. But the little one can't move that fast through this snow. By the time you can make a fire and do some cooking, I think it will be too late. But there is a cave near here. Shall we go there and eat?"

Andi didn't see why not. That elk must weigh three hundred pounds at least, representing far more meat than they could hope to carry. The bulk of it would have been left for the wolves, so why not share it with their new leukalfar/troll (Trollfar?) friend? "Ghrztum wants us to go with him to his cave so we can all eat the elk. All right with you guys?" he asked Meri and Fjuri. Meri of course already knew what the troll had asked, but Fjuri needed to be brought into the loop.

They both nodded enthusiastically, and Andi told Ghrztum "That sounds fine!" Before he could utter another word the troll, who was at least seven feet tall and heavily muscled beneath his thick white fur, scooped the elk off the ground and heaved it over his shoulder. "Follow me," he said, and began striding off in the direction he'd come from earlier.

Chapter 30: Camping Out

Once again, Fjuri lifted Meri up and she scrambled up onto his shoulders as he held Andi's bow in his left hand. Meri thought the view from here was great, not dissimilar from that she'd enjoyed from atop Papa Erik when she was younger – though Fjuri was neither so tall nor so massively muscled as her papa.

The boys, fairly starving now, made haste to keep up with Ghrztum as he strode across the snowy hillside and around a ridge into a stand of medium-size trees. It looked as if a wildfire had swept through here, killing many of the tall evergreens and offering a temporary opportunity for a grove of shorter, deciduous hardwoods to spring up. They came to one that stood some thirty feet high and spread more than as wide, with one particularly sturdy forked branch at a height of about eight feet from the ground.

From old blood stains and other evidence Meri and Andi guessed Ghrztum had used this tree for these purposes before. He lifted the elk up by the hindquarters until its rear legs were caught in the fork of the long, sturdy tree branch and it dangled down, limp. Then he produced a long, wicked leukalfar knife from his harness and in one quick motion, nearly severed the corpse's head so that what blood was still flowing within the carcass would drain out onto the snow below. Though the tree was nearly leafless, the snow cover was light beneath its branches and there were areas of bare dirt showing among the drifts.

Andi and Meri watched with equanimity, Fjuri with a bit of a shudder as the troll next inserted the tip of his blade just above the animal's breastbone and ripped up, through the thick-pelted hide, muscle, and underlying tissues to open its abdominal cavity. He took particular care as he neared the top of the cut, not wishing to pierce the glands there that could burst and spoil the meat with their foul contents.

If I were in dragon form it'd already be digesting, Andi thought with a pang. He was so *hungry*! Of course, had he gone to dragon form he'd have been three times as hungry. A dragon was like a huge furnace that had to be fed constantly – one of the reasons he had decided they should keep hiking, instead of him flying ahead while the others waited in the snow, and turning Mrzhgradfendz into a fast-travel point as he had done earlier with Walrus Cove after his flight from Castle Hordenhaal.

As the kids stood watching Ghrztum quickly and efficiently removed all of the elk's internal organs and dumped them onto the ground a few paces away. He grinned at them knowingly. "The wolf brethren will be happy we were here," he said. The liver, still warm, he held back and cut off a fairly large chunk of it, offering it to Meri. Mesmerized if a little repulsed, she took it from him solemnly and put it into her mouth. She was not the ravenous eating machine her brother and his friend were, but she was getting hungry enough to consider eating almost anything. Hmm, it was good! Warm, a little bit rubbery, but it tasted like… sustenance!

Seeing her reaction, Ghrztum offered another slice to her with a grin. After they'd known him for a while, Andi thought, they might come to see this expression for the indication of friendliness that was apparently meant. He was already coming to like the enormous, white-furred fellow. But as yet, the sight of all those teeth gleaming down at you from nearly seven feet off the ground was unsettling.

Ghrztum handed around slices to each of the boys as well, and while raw liver had never been on the list of favorite snacks for either of them it was *food*; and they happily ate it. When the glistening, deep red-brown organ had been pared down to about half its original size the troll nodded and dropped the rest of it into his gigantic mouth, lips smacking and emitting little grunts of pleasure. After swallowing he said, "That was good, eh?" then resumed working over the elk carcass.

In another few minutes he'd removed the rest of the internal organs and stripped off the hide. He held it one huge paw, and asked Andi "You want to keep this? Make leather?" The leukalfar used mandimant chitin in many of the things they made, but leather, clay, reeds, and other natural materials were also in use. "I don't think we want to carry the extra weight," Andi told him. "I'll take it then," Ghrztum said, and rolled it up into a more compact package. He cut a thin strip of sinew from one of the elk's hind legs and used it to tie up the hide. Then he slung the stripped carcass over a shoulder and carried the rolled-up hide in his other hand.

They set off walking again, and soon picked up a sort of trail across the snow-covered hillsides. Andi suspected this was a way Ghrztum came often, when he was hunting away from the cave he'd mentioned. He sure hoped they would reach it soon. A few bites of raw liver had only served to remind his stomach of its grievances, and it was now screaming at him in earnest.

In perhaps fifteen more minutes they rounded another ridge and a large cave opening appeared before them, with a ledge around five feet deep fronting it. "Home!" Ghrztum said cheerfully, adding "for the moment, at least. I'm on a foraging expedition but I'll probably be going back to the city soon."

Fjuri lowered Meri to the ground again and the three kids walked inside. The cave entrance was fairly broad, more than fifteen feet across, and perhaps ten feet high. It narrowed as it went back from the hillside, giving onto a passage no more than six feet wide at the back but still tall enough for the troll (let alone them) to stand upright. Beyond the passage it opened out again into a roughly circular chamber nearly thirty feet across.

Only a little dim daylight reached this far from the cave opening; but after setting the deer carcass and rolled hide down on a raised stone platform near the rear of the chamber, Ghrztum made his way quickly to a fire ring wherein a banked fire still harbored glowing embers. In moments he had added some fuel to the fire and blown it into a merry little blaze. Then he took a couple of torches lying beside the fireplace and lit them, before inserting them into sconces carved in the rock of the cave walls.

"That's better," he said. He grinned at Meri and added, "My adoptive people think I'm handicapped because I can't see in pitch darkness like you can. But they keep me around because I'm twice their size and don't mind going outside to hunt." As the flickering torchlight illuminated the chamber, Andi realized that it was stacked with provisions: jars, bales of hides, sacks he presumed held some kind of foodstuffs.

Without access to the agricultural opportunities the Ankhrazana had in their Canyons of Stone, the Mirskhrazana must have been living on mushrooms, mandimant byproducts, and whatever else could grow deep within the dypalfar ruin they inhabited. Having Ghrztum as a member of the tribe must have led to a big improvement in their diet.

"I see you have some rabbits, Little One," the troll said gently to Meri. The rabbits! She'd nearly forgotten them, with all that had gone on in the last hour. "I was thinking we might have them as... an appetizer while we wait for the elk to cook. Is that all right?" Meri wriggled out of her pack and quickly picked the stiffened corpses from the rings they'd been dangling on.

"Here!" she said, "Sure! But they're frozen solid..."

"I think I can help with that," Andi said. He took the rabbits from Meri's hands and laid them on the stone floor of the cavern, then stepped back a little and applied a gentle, diffuse fire spell to them. At this intensity he could continue the spell, regenerating his magical energy, almost indefinitely; and in two or three minutes, fur only slightly singed, the rabbits were once again soft enough to be gutted and skinned. Ghrztum watched with fascination.

"Nice trick, Andreas," he remarked in his bass rumble. "You a mage?" Without breaking the spell Andi nodded.

"Battle and healing mostly," he said. "If you need a cut healed, I'm your man."

Actually his modesty covered a huge pride in the delicacy of his work. The focusing and fine-tuning of spells like fire, frost, and lightning had been one of Papa Andrion's foremost contributions to the magical arts during his tenure as Magister of the Academy at Eisenstag (an office he had held since before Andi was born). Papa Andrion could direct battle spells to punch a hole the size of an arrow shaft through an enemy, or make a host of adversaries in a swath fifty feet wide feel *very* uncomfortable. Not to mention use dual-wielded spells to cut dypalfar metal like it was soft cheese. Andi's education in these techniques had begun a decade ago, and if he didn't yet have quite his father's fine touch he was better at it than almost any other mage in Iscandia.

Meri insisted on processing the rabbits herself, and after they were ready to cook the troll gave her a couple of spits for them. In the meantime, the little fire had become a roaring blaze and then died down again to something more appropriate for cooking meat. There was no shortage of firewood in the forest outside the cave.

Roasted over a hot fire, the rabbits didn't take too long. Andi and Fjuri dug hunks of trail bread out of their packs and demolished them, the savory smells of the cooking meat driving them insane with hunger. The fact that they'd made contact with the leukalfar tribe living over the hoped-for dypalfar portal let Andi believe that they would be welcomed and fed soon, and that they didn't need to keep a reserve of food. Besides, he hoped there might be some leftovers from the elk.

Meanwhile, Ghrztum set to work butchering the elk carcass into smaller pieces. You could spit a whole, stripped carcass (legs cut off at the first joints, body cavity stuffed with herbs or cut apples and pinned shut) and turn it on a spit to cook the whole thing at once. But that took many hours, and they were all far too hungry to wait.

The rabbits were sizzling and done enough, and Ghrztum used padded gloves to pull the spits from the fire. Then, after adding a few logs to the blaze, he laid an enormous rack across it supported on four legs. Andi wondered where the leukalfar had gotten the iron. They didn't seem to work metals, though the dypalfar who had Changed and enslaved them were masters at the craft. Perhaps these items had been salvaged from the ruins of Norse settlements on the island.

Ghrztum covered the rack with pieces of elk meat, including some steaks around two inches thick as well as bigger pieces. By now the cooked rabbits had cooled enough to be handled, and the four of them dug in with enthusiasm, just holding them in their hands and gnawing the meat off the bones. There was one rabbit apiece for Andi, Fjuri, and Meri – and two for their host. Since it was his fire, they felt it was a fair trade.

Meri was already beginning to feel as though her gnawing hunger had been satisfied by the time she'd finished eating her rabbit and licking the juices and grease (not that there was much of that, on game animals in this northern wilderness) from her fingers. The boys were just getting started.

The smaller steaks had been turned, and were now done enough to be taken off the rack. Other pieces of meat took their place. The entire little cavern now smelled of cooking elk meat, and the crackling of the fire played counterpoint to the sizzle and pop of steaks on the rack. Both Andi and Fjuri (and, one might guess, Ghrztum) were slavering in anticipation of the feast. The three Waterdon kids had gotten their plates, along with forks and sharp knives, out of their packs so that they could tackle the sizzling elk steaks with a little more decorum.

An hour or so later, as afternoon was giving way to evening, everyone in the little cavern was feeling truly replete. The fire had been built up twice more and the rack was still completely covered with pieces of elk. Smoking the meat was impractical here with the size of the cavern and a desire on the part of its inhabitants to breathe; but they could cook it thoroughly and carry it off, and in this climate it would stay edible for weeks.

Now that hunger was finally sated, and they were all feeling warm and comfortable, it was time for quiet conversation. Andi felt a little fuzzy after the morning spent hiking in the snow and his recent gorging on elk meat; but he was burning with curiosity. How had Ghrztum come to be adopted into the local leukalfar tribe? What was the situation in the dypalfar ruin where they made their home? And most importantly, was the dypalfar portal still in existence?

The fact that there *was* still a leukalfar tribe living within the dypalfar ruin that sat above the supposed dypalfar portal seemed like powerful evidence that the dypalfar had not sent a force through to round up the remaining leukalfar before destroying the portal. But Andi supposed it didn't really guarantee the portal remained. An invading force from the dypalfar paradise might just as well have killed anybody guarding the device, then quickly destroyed it and the portal it was creating – thousands of years ago – before being overrun themselves.

Ghrztum, too, was very curious about his guests. "Andreas," he said as they relaxed around the fire, taking a break from eating, "I have never actually met any Sky People before. You and your friend Fjurbund are not as I had expected." So, the Norsemen had been gone from this island a good long time.

"If I might ask, Ghrztum, how many years have you?" Andi replied. The troll pondered for a moment, seemingly counting. Trolls had math?

"I am told that I was a baby not yet walking on two legs when my mother and father took me in," he replied thoughtfully. "Since then I have seen twenty summers. And you?" He was not much older than them! That was a surprise, but maybe not. How long did trolls live, anyhow? Andi suspected that Ghrztum would not have much information about the people (he could no longer think of them as animals) who had given him birth, any more than Meri had known anything about the leukalfar before their journey to the Great Temple this past summer.

Andi replied, "My friend and I have fifteen summers, though he will be sixteen years in another month and I not sixteen until early next year. We are not considered full-grown by our people, though I think we're getting there." He smiled winningly, and Ghrztum chuckled. From his viewpoint, no doubt, they were just kids.

"How came you to learn the leukalfar tongue, you and your adopted sister?" This question really bothered him. So far as he knew, the Sky People were the inimical enemies of the leukalfar, intruders in their underground lairs who must be killed on sight. Yet these two had been taught to speak with them?

"Our mother had occasion to meet one of the last of the white elves who had not undergone the Change, about a year before I was born," Andi said. It was a long story, and his agile mind went into overdrive as he strove to shorten it. "Last spring, she took us to visit with him. Merelle and I were invited to stay at the Great Temple and become acolytes of Apoldros along with leukalfar from the Ankhrazana tribe. Two we met there taught us the language, and later took us to visit at their village. They live above ground like the Sky People."

Ghrztum felt as if he had been struck by lightning. The Great Temple! The Ankhrazana! The white elf who had lived for all the thousands of years since the Change, unchanged! These were like legends to him, stories he had heard from the Chanter of his tribe. And these chance-met visitors were somehow linked to it all. Had Apoldros himself come to earth and commanded Ghrztum to take up a sword and follow him, he could not have been more stunned.

From Ghrztum's poleaxed expression, Andi had struck a nerve. At about this point, Fjuri spoke up. He was so shy, it was rare to hear him volunteer something in company. But sitting there listening to a conversation he could not understand was finally beginning to get to him. "Andi? How about if you start translating what you're saying? I'm beginning to feel kind of left out here."

"Oh, sorry!" Andi exclaimed, chagrined that he'd been so rude as to completely ignore the fact that Fjuri wasn't able to be part of the conversation. He filled his friend in on what they'd been discussing for the past few minutes, and then took a little time to give Fjuri some of the key words and phrases in the leukalfar tongue. He'd picked up the dragon tongue quickly enough, so he ought to be able to at least have some idea what was being said in leukalfar before long if they just kept translating for him.

Ghrztum recovered himself while the exchange was going on between the two Sky People youngsters. It appeared that Andreas was trying to teach his friend, Fjurbund was it (what strange names these people had!), the language of the leukalfar. He should certainly learn it, if he was to come among them. It was what people spoke. He was proud to be a person, rescued from the life of a wild beast by the chance circumstances that had led to his being adopted by the Mirskhrazana.

"These things you speak of are amazing, Andreas," he said at last – then waited a moment so that Andreas could translate what he'd said. "It is a big world, and a strange one. But what brings you to our island? You said you are going to Mrzhgradfendz?"

Andi felt a strange fluttering sensation in his chest as he considered what he would say next. This might be it: the end to their harebrained quest, if Ghrztum's next words were to be something along the lines of "Oh, that's a story we tell. The portal was overrun and the machine destroyed thousands of years ago, or so it is said." But they were so close to their goal!

He answered seriously, almost quivering with anxiety to hear the response. "Gryndor, the old Chanter of the Ankhrazana, told us of this place. He said that there was one last portal from this world to the dypalfar paradise, that had not been destroyed when the dypalfar fled all those thousands of years ago. I have a magic map," he added, pulling it out and displaying it for Ghrztum's benefit, "and a quest marker appeared on it. The way the maps work, you will usually only get a marker if the place you were told about has an important quest connected with it. So we just had to see for ourselves."

This was all duly translated as Ghrztum sat pondering Andi's words. Then as Andi fell silent again, he said, "A portal to the dypalfar world! That might explain it!" The three kids were staring at him, eager for him to speak further. He smiled at them. "Within the Mirskhrazana there are certain societies. I am among the Gleaners. We gather food, tend mandimants, and some of us – me, mostly, go outside the city to hunt and gather wild foods under the sky. Not many of my tribe are comfortable being in the open spaces, but I think it's in my blood."

Ghrztum thought he detected a trace of impatience on Andreas's features. He couldn't be certain, as Andreas and Fjurbund were the first Sky People he had ever met and he wasn't used to telling from their facial expressions what they were feeling. They were certainly odd-looking people, nearly hairless like the leukalfar but with eyes like trolls and those enormous, prominent noses that neither the people of his birth nor those who had raised him possessed.

He continued: "Besides the Gleaners there are the Sentries, who are trained in the arts of combat; the Crafters, who make clothing and weapons and all sorts of useful things; and the Priests, who worship Apoldros and lead others in His worship as well. They are also our mages and chemiasts. And there is another society, one with relatively few members and of a very secret nature. They are called the Keepers, and their province is the innermost heart of Mirskhrazana, many levels below the entrance to the city. The Keepers' Sanctum is hidden behind a series of locked doors where none may enter save them, and even then I have heard that each door is heavily guarded against intruders."

"The Keepers," Ghrztum went on, "fill their ranks with only the wisest of our numbers, those who have proven themselves. Many who begin as Sentries or Priests will later become Keepers. And they are sworn to secrecy, never discussing what goes on in the Keepers' Sanctum with anyone, not even their wives or children. They will only say that they are fulfilling a sacred trust given to them by our remote ancestors, from the time when the dypalfar departed and left the city of Mrzhgradfendz to us."

Andi and Meri were staring at the troll, who had already begun to seem like a friend to them though he'd been terrifying on their first encounter. His eyes were shining, and each of them was thinking "It's true! The portal is there!" How they might be going to reach it for themselves they could not yet imagine, but at least they now felt that this quest had not been in vain.

Once again, Andi brought Fjuri up to speed on what Ghrztum had said. Fjuri was as excited as they were. The troll went on, "I think that you three definitely need to come to Mrzhgradfendz and meet my people. They will be astounded! If there is indeed a portal to the dypalfar world in the Keepers' Sanctum I don't know whether you will be allowed to see it, but at least you can visit our city. And maybe you can help me with my load. I was planning to leave for home soon anyhow. As you can see, I've got almost as much as I can carry."

Their conversation continued on into the evening, as more logs went onto the fire, elk meat was finished cooking and taken off the rack to be replaced with more from the pile of raw pieces on the stone slab. By the time the travelers were yawning they had all eaten quite a bit more of the elk meat – and all three of them

were thinking wistfully of some vegetables, fruit and bread as a
break from the enormous quantities of meat they'd been eating
today.

Still, their bellies were full. Ghrztum had told them many
details of his life growing up in Mrzhgradfendz with his adopted
people, and what he knew of the trolls (not a lot, since other than
the fact he *was* a troll everything he knew of them was passed to
him by his adoptive parents). Clearly, Andi thought, there was a lot
more to trolls than anyone in Waterdon had realized. He knew
Mom and Papa Andrion both would be fascinated to know they
were so much more human than anyone had thought, and would
probably want to study them.

For their part, the Sky People youngsters told their furry new
friend about life in Waterdon, the political and economic structure
of the empire, details about their own families, and some about the
Great Temple and the resurgence of the worship of Apoldros that
had begun there under the guidance of Archon Duraenis, among
the last of the unchanged white elves.

Toward the end of the evening Fjuri, who had a good ear for
languages and was quick to learn them, was picking up a lot of the
conversation without Andi's translation and was even able to speak
a few words himself. He'd better pick it up fast since they were
about to go meet Ghrztum's people, he thought, and not a one of
them spoke either the common tongue or dragon language.

There was one detail about themselves that none of them
mentioned to Ghrztum. Perhaps in the fullness of time it could be
revealed to their new friend, but for now Andi thought it better not
to bring it up. Telling people you'd just met that you were
fireblood and could transform into a dragon usually led to flat-out
disbelief or demands for a demonstration, in his experience. So he
asked Meri and Fjuri, in their own language, to keep quiet on the
subject.

The kids laid their fur bedrolls out around the fire pit, and
soon drifted off into exhausted sleep. Ghrztum had made himself a
bed of leaves and branches in a depression over near one wall of
the cave, liking the softness but needing no blankets. He was

covered head to toe in luxuriant, double-layered white fur. After butchering the elk earlier he'd stepped outside the cave and wiped himself down with clean snow, leaving his coat pristine. "Good night," he rumbled to them as they all began drifting down into tired sleep. "Tomorrow, we go to Mrzhgradfendz."

Chapter 31: The Shining City

Meri was the first to arise again, beginning to feel a little chilled. The fire still had some glowing coals in it, and she stirred them up with the hard stick Ghrztum had been using for the purpose last night. It would soon to be time to shovel out the fire pit, she thought. This had often been one of her chores at home. It's funny, she mused. Here she was on a real adventure with Andi and Fjuri, traveling to strange places and meeting people she had never dreamed existed; and yet some things were just the same.

After adding wood to the fire and fanning it into a blaze, she put on her boots and a cloak and walked out through the passageway to the outer cave, then away from the cave entrance a way to squat and relieve herself. She hadn't seen any sign of a chamberpot, and supposed Ghrztum wouldn't bother with one since he was likely here by himself whenever he was out foraging. Most "deep-down" leukalfar were likely too agoraphobic to be comfortable roaming around outside.

As she returned to the cave she found Ghrztum sitting up. Lucky him, he didn't have to get dressed. "Good morning, Little One," he said in his deep voice. Meri supposed that they were all "little ones" compared to him. Even Papa Erik would be dwarfed!

"Good morning, Ghrztum," she replied, managing to pronounce his name (which sounded a bit like throat-clearing when he said it) passably. She knelt on her bedroll and began rummaging through her pack, pleased to find she still had a package of trail bread. She thought she had eaten enough elk yesterday to last her for quite some time to come.

The boys began stirring too, though likely under other circumstances they'd have been happy to sleep until noon. Meri had noticed that about teenagers. Meri offered some of her trail bread to Ghrztum, thinking it only polite. "Thank you," he said with a slight smile, accepting the morsel between thumb and two fingertips. It was scarcely a bite for him. He popped it right into his mouth to show that he trusted her not to give him anything nasty, and after chewing for a moment remarked "That is *good*! What is it?"

She smiled back at him. "We call it trail bread," she told him. "Our mom makes it from grains and dried meat and dried fruit, and I think nuts and some honey and maybe some beef fat. It keeps for weeks if you store it wrapped up, and it's really filling. Of course, you can get tired of almost anything after a while."

"Hmm," the troll mused, savoring the last of his small mouthful before swallowing. "I have most of those ingredients right here. Well, no grain and no honey, and it would probably have to be bear fat. But maybe we can try to make some after we get home to the city. It might make a nice treat. Meanwhile, I have some dried icefruit you might like. And there's still plenty of elk." Meri made a slight face at the mention of the elk.

"Icefruit sounds nice," she told him.

Within an hour everyone had had something to eat and was fully dressed and packed up, ready to leave – except Ghrztum. He of course didn't need to get dressed and he wasn't carrying a pack. But he had exited the inner cave and returned shortly with a good-sized sledge. It was crafted out of mandimant chitin and bone, held together with sinew, and was beautiful to look at.

The three travelers helped him gather and load the stored foodstuffs in the inner cave onto the sledge, piling them high. Then he secured the load with a length of rope woven out of some kind of plant fibers, and they helped him push it back out of the cave. Ghrztum had brought in quantities of sand and used it to cover the floor of the passage, which meant that the sledge could glide fairly well. They had a bit of a chore to get it out of the outer cave and down onto the snow to the east.

The troll studied the load on the sledge for a moment, then addressed Meri. "Merelle, do you think you would like to ride on top of the sledge? We have a few hours to travel, and the snow is deep in places." Andi was pleased at Ghrztum's concern for Meri. It seemed she had acquired a new big brother, older and furrier than the other two (Fjuri was, for all intents and purposes, another of her big brothers).

"Sure!" she chirped. Andi gave her a lift up, and she found a nearly comfortable seat wedged in between a stack of what she thought were hides and soft bales of what was probably some plant product. The load was a little top-heavy, so as Ghrztum strapped himself into the harness attached to the sledge for pulling it, Andi and Fjuri each took one of the handles at the rear. They didn't need to push, only steady it.

And so, the last leg of their trip to Mrzhgradfendz began. The weather was marvelous for this far north, sky clear with only a few puffy clouds and no snow falling. With excellent visibility on all sides, they found that the wildlife of the region was staying out of their way. Andi would be willing to bet there were not many creatures on this island or perhaps the whole of Agena – other than a dragon – that would voluntarily tangle with a full-grown snow troll.

Andi and Fjuri had to hustle to keep up with Ghrztum's pace. They were travelling on a trail Andi assumed the troll had created for himself, beating the snow down into a layer of ice over which fresh snow fell, during his trips out foraging on behalf of his tribe. As with the Ankhrazana, the leukalfar in Mrzhgradfendz lived communally – each person in the tribe doing what he or she was best at, and everyone sharing the fruits of each other's labors. It wasn't a bad way to live, though he doubted it would work in a society as large or as far-flung as the empire.

After an hour or so they took a brief break, so that everyone could relieve themselves and the boys could munch some food out of their packs. Though the trail was good footing and they didn't have to actually push the sledge, their fast pace in this cold environment was burning fuel at an accelerated rate.

In another hour they came up over a rise, and the three travelers from Waterdon got their first glimpse of Mrzhgradfendz. It was beautiful! The classic dypalfar architecture was familiar to all of them from expeditions with Andi's parents. They'd even visited Undernight, Papa Andrion collecting a few dypalfar artifacts while Erik and Bernadette stood guard and the kids (Sigi, only five at the time, had not been included on this field trip) oohed and aahed at the strangeness of the place.

"That's it, huh?" Andi asked, though the answer was pretty obvious. Ghrztum halted from the labor of pulling the sledge to turn back and grin at his new friends.

"Pretty impressive, huh? Wait'll you see what it's like inside. The last foreign Chanter that came through said Mrzhgradfendz was the best-preserved dypalfar city he had ever seen."

They continued on their way, winding through switchbacks down into a long and broad wooded valley with a fair-sized stream running through it. Meri, able to relax and enjoy the view, was taken with the beauty of the place. Nothing like home, of course, but there was something about it that called to her. She'd been told that her birth parents had been living deep, deep below a dypalfar ruin like the one on the hill. But raised as she had been, she couldn't imagine living that way. She wanted a warm, cozy house at night and the sun overhead (preferably, shining from a clear sky) in the daytime.

The little caravan had a good straight run through the valley, beside the stream. At this season ice was only just beginning to form around its edges. Andi had a thought, and asked Ghrztum, "Do you have salmon in the river here?" In leukalfar the word was a little more generic. Salmon could sometimes be found in pools where the deep leukalfar lived, but it was the only fish they knew. They had no words for "Betanid" or any of the other myriad little fishes to be found in the quiet inland waters of Iscandia.

Again the troll paused briefly to turn and grin at them. "More in the springtime than now. They go someplace else, I think. Then in spring they come and swim up all the little streams to lay eggs, before returning down them to the sea. We eat a lot of salmon in the spring." After another moment, he added "the eggs hatch and there are little ones, but we think it's better to leave them alone. Not worth the trouble of catching them – and better to wait until they are bigger!"

Andi could well imagine his new friend polishing off half a dozen whole adult salmon by himself – possibly, raw. From what little he knew of snow trolls (to which knowledge Ghrztum had added but little during their talk last night) they ate pretty much anything that they could get their hands on – with a preference for fresh meat. But he suspected Ghrztum's dietary habits had been warped by his leukalfar upbringing, much as Meri's had presumably been changed by growing up with his family in Waterdon.

There were so many new things to think about! Andi had expected adventure to be all about the excitement of life-or-death situations, about using his combat and battle magic skills to get them through danger, with some kind of glittering reward at the end of it all. Certainly, there had been some of that. And he was coming to appreciate what his papas had long known – there's nothing quite like the feeling when you realize you are alive and whole, and your enemies are dead.

But he had discovered an unexpected benefit on this quest: his mind was being opened to new ideas, things he had never imagined. The hunger to learn more about the world was rising within him – and the excitement, as he realized that hunger would soon be answered, filled him with elation! He was his father's, *and* his mother's, son.

After traversing the valley they passed through a broad, snow-covered meadow as they neared the hilltop on which Mrzhgradfendz sat. Now, Andi and Fjuri added their efforts to Ghrztum's, as they climbed the final grade before reaching their goal. It was approaching midday, and both of the boys were beginning to feel as though (despite the recent surfeit of elk in their diet) that an entire roast elk would go good around now. Though Meri hadn't had to put out any effort at all on their journey, she too was beginning to get hungry. And her butt was beginning to get sore from riding on the less-than-cushy collection of foodstuffs beneath her.

At last, they had a straight shot up a snow-covered slope to the gleaming walls of Mrzhgradfendz, now close at hand. The three travelers were surprised to see the place looking deserted. There was no sign of guards, as the sledge approached a large pair of dypalfar doors that led into the heart of the city. "The

187

Mirskhrazana don't post guards outside their city?" he asked
Ghrztum.

The troll turned his head, while continuing to pull the heavily-
laden sledge up the slope. "Against whom?" he asked. "You three
are the first intruders to have arrived here in *my* lifetime. Anyhow,
my people don't much like to be out in the open. You'll find
guards after we get inside." Leaving the sledge at the bottom of a
broad flight of steps, they climbed to the top. Then reaching the
doors, Ghrztum pushed them open. They had arrived at
Mrzhgradfendz.

Chapter 32: In Pursuit

It was still daylight outside Castle Hordenhaal when the rescue party arrived. They had gotten their start much earlier in the day than Andi and his companions. Bernadette, side-by-side with Andrion, led the group toward the front doors of the castle. Castle this might be, but it was not really a stronghold. The place and its occupants had fallen to an invasion by only around thirty warriors from the Daywatch Brigade some sixteen years before.

Now, the guards on duty recognized some of the members of the group. Bernadette and Andrion had been here several times in the past, and had been among the wedding guests when the Lady Nerissa and her lord had married some nine years before. "Fireblood," one said with respect as he opened the doors to them. "I think it possible my lady is expecting you."

Bernadette nodded and smiled at him tensely. As fear and anger roiled inside her, she was finding it hard to be polite. Inside, both Bernadette and Andrion were struck by a feeling of déjà vu as they traversed the short hall to look down from the balcony on the room below. They had been here on several occasions now, but on their first visit the place had been filled with vampires – the tables in the hall below littered with gruesome corpses.

Nerissa and Radigar, at table with their little daughters, Nerissa's mother Leandra, and most of the castle folk as well, looked up as Bernadette, Andrion and their party came down one of the staircases from the balcony. Nerissa rose to her feet. "Bernadette!" she exclaimed, "so good to see you! I'm afraid I have some idea why you may be here."

Though the party had left Drakespring Farm after a hearty breakfast what seemed like minutes ago, all of them (Mothris in particular) found that the sight of food on the tables filled them with a certain… peckishness. This was a familiar phenomenon to all of them but Mothris, whose experience with fast-travelling was as yet slight. They hung back, hoping to be invited to join the family for supper.

Radigar also rose, smiling with genuine warmth. "Bernadette, Andrion, so good to see you. Erik's not with you?" Bernadette returned his smile.

"He's home watching the rest of the kids," she replied. Nerissa spoke to a serving girl who was just clearing away some emptied serving dishes.

"Helga, would you please ask Ermagard to send out some more food? And set six more places for dinner, if you will." To her guests, she said "As I assume you've just come here by map, you all could probably use a bite to eat. And I'm sure we'd all like to meet your companions." She was burning with curiosity about the leukalfar boy. He was only the second leukalfar she'd ever met socially.

In a minute or two the six newcomers had been squeezed in around the hall's main table, and it was time for introductions. Bernadette did the honors. "Nerissa, Radigar, this is our friend Lifa Steadfast. She was my body servant at one time, and she and her family have been friends with ours since before the first time we came here. The young woman is her daughter Anja Steadfast, and the young man there is her companion Lars. We also have Mothris of the Ankhrazana tribe of the leukalfar, an acolyte of Apoldros at the Great Temple. I suppose you know why we've come?"

Nerissa smiled, though her deep blue eyes had a look of sympathetic motherly pain in them. "I am guessing you might be seeking the whereabouts of a couple of tall lads, one who looks remarkably like you two and another who resembles Lifa? And a small leukalfar girl who goes by the name of Merelle?"

"On the money!" Andrion exclaimed. "You've seen them, then?"

"They were here a couple of days ago," Radigar replied. "We gave them a late supper and a bed, and in the morning they were supposedly off by map going back to the Eparchy."

"I was afraid of that," Bernadette said. "Lifa and I went looking for them at the Eparchy first thing. Now I have to wonder if they just stopped off here for a visit on the way. Andi might have wanted to show Fjuri some of the more interesting places he's been."

At this juncture some more plates of food arrived and the six visitors (Mothris in particular, though the food was unfamiliar) dug in for a few minutes before the discussion resumed. Nerissa ate a few more bites of the vegetable casserole on her plate, looking thoughtful. Then she spoke. "Bernadette, it's possible your wayward children really did go to the Eparchy, but they hadn't gotten there yet when you were there looking for them – since they came here and stayed overnight before going there. Why don't we host everyone here for a day or two while you or Andrion goes to see if they got there? No point in everyone getting completely map-lagged."

"That's not a bad idea, Nerissa," Bernadette said. "Andi and Meri are *supposed* to be going back to the Eparchy. They're not finished with their education there. But Fjuri is playing hooky from his job and his responsibilities, and they should *not* have brought him along. Did Andi mention anything to you about a supposed portal down in the bowels of a dypalfar city on an island northwest of here?"

"Not a word," Nerissa replied. "He claimed he and Fjuri were just taking a little detour before they all went to the Eparchy, as if it had been all been arranged that he was going to accompany them."

"Wait'll I get my hands on that boy," Lifa muttered – though it wasn't clear which one she meant. Andi was usually the ringleader when the two of them got into trouble, but Fjuri had begun kicking over the traces of his own accord, recently.

"While Andi and Meri were visiting with Mothris' people in the area of the Eparchy Andi picked up a quest marker on the map I lent him," Bernadette explained after eating a couple more bites of food. "We were afraid that they might have gone looking for the island and its dypalfar city. But maybe they really did just return to the Great Temple after leaving here. I'll have to go check."

They concluded the meal, and most of the castle folk left the table after eating to get back to their chores or return to their quarters for some quiet time with their families before sleeping. The little girls said goodnight to the guests, then were led off by their grandmother to get ready for bed. The count and his wife, however, lingered to converse with their guests. There was sweet wine and brandy, little cakes, and tea to be enjoyed sitting around the living area near the large central fireplace.

Bernadette enjoyed the opportunity to relax, but she was too anxious to put their quest out of her mind. What if Andi, Meri and Fjuri had *not* gone back to the Eparchy? What if they were wandering around on that island, fighting off bears and snow trolls, or stirring up a hornet's nest of hostile leukalfar? While Meri's presence might stave off hostility, it was no sure guarantee of a welcome. The leukalfar had inter-tribal warfare just as did the rest of humanity. She knew she was going to be completely beat by the time she got back here, but she didn't think she could rest until she found out for sure.

Standing, Bernadette said "Nerissa, Radigar, thank you for your hospitality. I know I'm not going to be able to get to sleep until I know whether the children are safe. So I'm going to hop over to the Great Temple now. The rest of you might as well just relax here and enjoy our friends' hospitality for a while. It'll probably be around twenty-four hours before I can return. If Fjuri's there, Lifa, I'll bring him back with me. Mothris, do you want to accompany me? If it turns out Andi and Meri are there, we won't need you to go with us and you can just get right back to your acolyte duties…"

Mothris looked as though he'd been put on the spot. He was quite enjoying this expedition with the Sky People, seeing parts of the world he'd scarcely imagined before, eating exotic food, and improving his command of the common tongue. But on the other hand, he had his duties. "Um, Mistress Drakespring" – "Bernadette, please" – "Bernadette, if you wouldn't mind terribly much I'd like to stay here. I'm already feeling pretty sleepy from the fast-traveling, and this might be my only chance to explore a real castle…"

Bernadette smiled at him. He was older than her own boy, she thought, but the alfar seemed to mature somewhat more slowly than men. And he'd led a pretty sheltered existence. What boy wouldn't want the chance to see more of the world, to have some adventures? "That's all right, Mothris. I'll see you all when I get back, then." With that she came and squeezed Nerissa's and Radigar's hands, hugged and kissed her husband (who gave her a somewhat troubled glance and wished her good luck), and went back out the front doors of the castle. She shortly vanished from the island.

After another hour or so Radigar and Nerissa found accommodations for their visitors. The castle had once held many more people than it now supported, many of them blood-sucking fiends under the control of Nerissa's late and unlamented father, the evil vampire Lord Karazin. While they enjoyed their aperitifs, maids were at work preparing beds for everyone.

Andrion missed the warm body of his wife beside him in the bed he'd been given. Over the years of their marriage they had often been apart, his magical researches and role as Magister of the Academy keeping him from home at frequent intervals. He supposed Erik, who almost always stayed at home, must feel her absence now even more than he did. He certainly hoped Berni would return from her expedition to the Great Temple with good news, and they could all just go back home.

Huh, he mused, whatever news she brought, she was going to be beat when she arrived. Her body would feel the time that had actually elapsed locally rather than the few seconds that appeared to pass when fast-traveling. And she was leaving on a twenty-four-hour trip just at bedtime. She never seemed to age, his beloved – she looked the same now as she had nine years ago. But even so she was nearly forty, and would surely be exhausted on her return. He rolled over, pulled the thick comforter up around his chin, and drifted off to sleep.

Everyone got up in the morning, glad of the night's rest, and breakfasted with their hosts and the castle staff. It was certainly cold out, but conditions weren't unbearable and the five visitors wandered around at will, exploring the public areas of the castle, visiting with Leandra and the girls, Valina and Serifa. Leandra's private garden, once overgrown and abandoned after she had fled to another dimension, had now been restored to its former beauty – and the girls loved playing there whenever the weather permitted.

The older woman, who had been an immortal vampire for centuries and had taken the cure less than ten years ago, was aging well. She looked far too young to be a grandmother. Nerissa and Radigar's young daughters were beautiful, and Andrion mused that their parents had better find a way for them to meet some eligible young men before too many more years had elapsed. That his own daughter, Riki, was approaching that age now had not yet completely sunk in for him. Somehow, she was still his little red-blonde angel – a perfect blend of his beloved Berni and his equally beloved brother Erik.

Mothris was able to spend some time talking with the girls, too. They had met Meri on several occasions, most recently during the kids' visit a few days ago, and they were curious to talk with another person like her. Having never encountered leukalfar in any other context, they just assumed that he was another of a kind of particularly different-looking people, who seemed pretty normal despite their appearance. Older people were less accepting, but he could see that it might very well be possible for him to become an ambassador of the leukalfar to the Sky People.

As a member of the Ankhrazana, Mothris was in a unique position. They were the only tribe they knew about who had chosen to make their homes above ground, and after many generations of living thus they had become the least agoraphobic of the leukalfar tribes. He was perfectly comfortable walking around outside, nothing but sky above, and after knowing Andi for the past few months – and now meeting his family and these other Sky People – his command of the common tongue was becoming near-perfect. And he was losing his shyness around them.

So the day passed away pleasantly in visiting and relaxation, though among all of them there was a slight undercurrent of tension. Would the kids be all right? Or would they be chasing them to this distant island on Bernadette's map? As suppertime approached both Lifa and Andrion became increasingly anxious. If her estimate of the time required for the round trip was correct, Bernadette should soon be returning to them – with or without Fjuri.

They all gathered in the castle's great hall for dinner: Nerissa and Radigar, Leandra, Valina and Serifa, the castle's other residents, and the five visitors. In honor of their presence Nerissa had arranged for Ermagard to lay on a special feast. In this northern clime they were always looking for an opportunity to celebrate and raise their spirits, and more feast days were celebrated at Castle Hordenhaal than in most of Iscandia's cities.

The drink flowed, and everyone in the hall partook of a wealth of dishes prepared by Ermagard and her hard-worked crew. The centerpiece of this was a whole yearling bullock, roasted for hours in the castle kitchen's massive fireplace. The festive atmosphere came close to distracting Andrion, Lifa and their companions from the anxiety that was pressing more and more on them as the time for Bernadette's return came nearer.

They had all come close to eating their fill and dinner plates were being whisked away to be replaced with small ones on which dessert would be laid, when there was a small stir and one of the castle's men-at-arms (of which there were few, these days) escorted a small, slumping figure to the balcony. Bernadette Drakespring came down the stairs into the hall.

Both Andrion and Lifa, though somewhat numbed by food and drink, were on their feet in an instant. Fjuri's not with her, Lifa thought. We still have to go find them. Andrion was aware of what it meant that Berni was alone, but his immediate concern was for her, herself. She walked like a woman finding it hard to remain upright, and as she got closer he saw that her eyes were reddened, dark circles beneath them, her auburn hair hanging lank. It had been days of actual time since she'd been able to bathe, he realized. He didn't mind going a few days between baths but Berni took one every morning, if she could.

He rushed to her and enfolded her in a firm embrace, kissing the top of her head. She hugged him tightly – anger and fear and frustration, along with love for this man who had swept her off her feet so many years ago, fighting a losing battle against complete exhaustion. It seemed as if she and her companions had spent maybe three hours eating and socializing with Nerissa and Radigar, some fifteen minutes ago. Before that, there had been a few minutes after they'd eaten breakfast in Drakespring House. In the real world, some thirty-six hours had elapsed. And at the moment it felt as if her body had lived every one of those thirty-six hours without a rest.

"Oh, love," Bernadette managed after a moment. "I am so tired! And so hungry! What is there to eat?" Andrion took his wife's arm and led her over to the table, where another chair was brought in for her to sit on. She collapsed into it like a dropped sack of potatoes, her pack hitting the floor a moment before. There was a big glass of water sitting on the table in front of her and she seized it like a person dying of thirst, her throat working until she had drained it. It was not just food and rest that you needed after a day and a half of elapsed real time.

Nerissa, anticipating this, had motioned for faithful Helga to go to the kitchen and fetch the plate that had been prepared against Bernadette's return. Ermagard had been keeping it warm near the stove. In moments the food had arrived, and Bernadette smiled wanly at the familiar, beloved faces looking at her anxiously. "Short story," she croaked, "they weren't there. Wait a couple of minutes and we'll talk more." With that she attacked the plate before her with a will. Those who knew Bernadette knew her to be a woman of appetites, and this had not changed much as she got older.

After Bernadette had devoured all of the food on the plate, then moved on to the dessert which had been belatedly served (and downed another two glasses of water along the way) she heaved an immense sigh. "Oh!" she said, sinking down in her chair as if she meant to continue to the floor, "That's better! Thank you, Nerissa, for thinking of me."

Realizing that everyone in the vicinity was looking at her with bated breath, eager for her report, she continued "I'm sorry, there really isn't a lot more to tell. I arrived at the Great Temple in early morning and found Myrkra there. She was surprised to see me, and after I explained why I'd come she told me Andi, Meri, and Fjuri had *not* come there. I think it's safe to assume that our harebrained adventurers have found some way to get to that island. As will we... but not until tomorrow. Andrion, take me to bed!"

Chapter 33: The Dragon Edge

For almost the first time in the history of their relationship, Andrion was awake and out of bed before Bernadette was. He'd had trouble getting up early his whole life, and it had often been a point of conflict between them when she, a natural early riser, would be frustrated and less than understanding if he failed to get out of bed when she was eager to get moving.

He woke at what seemed an appropriate time, anxiety about the kids eating at him, and made his morning ablutions while she slept on. He gazed at her sleeping face. The dark circles were gone, and in the utter relaxation of sleep she looked closer to the twenty-two she'd been when they first met than the thirty-nine she was now. His heart skipped a beat and he realized he'd forgotten to breathe. From the first moment he had seen her, his heart had been in her hands.

She seemed as if she might have recouped her energies, and Andrion knew she would not want to waste time. Who knew what peril their kids, and Lifa's son, were getting into while they slept? So he stepped close to the bed and planted a warm kiss on Bernadette's forehead. Her eyelids fluttered and she woke, gazing up at him with love. "What time is it?" she asked sleepily.

"Can't say," he replied, "but the sun's up over the horizon by a bit."

"Oh!" she cried, and jumped out of bed. She was wearing her linen underclothes, a nod to the frigid nights in this northern climate. Somebody had slipped into the room early and built up the fire in the fireplace, so it wasn't horribly cold in here right now. Bernadette stepped close to Andrion and gave him a deep kiss and a full-body hug, before looking around for the rest of her clothes. She'd kill for a hot bath right now, but didn't think she wanted to take the time.

They met with their fellow guests at the breakfast table, and discussed the situation over eggs and sausage, mountains of bread rolls fresh from the castle's ovens, applesauce, and (something you didn't often see in Waterdon) kippered small ocean fish. They were salty and smoky and a little oily, and seemed somehow just the thing to fortify themselves against the cold.

Bernadette addressed Leandra, who had lived here on this island for more centuries than any of them could imagine – though she would not have been born, of course, until millennia after the dypalfar had departed for their "paradise." "Are you at all familiar with this island, Leandra?" she asked, proffering her spread-out map where only the single quest marker for Mrzhgradfendz showed within its featureless outlines. A few river courses were marked, but nothing else.

Leandra looked at the map, where the legend "SKARHALFN" appeared across the center of the island. "I believe the Norsemen were the ones who named it Skarhalfn," she replied thoughtfully. "There were some hunters and miners there at one time, but not recently. I don't believe the dypalfar ruin there was associated with any particular great treasure, to make it worth the trouble of getting there and fighting one's way through the usual hordes of hostile leukalfar." Mindful of the company, she looked up at Mothris and said "Sorry. Our peoples have a lot of history to get past."

"Well," Bernadette said, after polishing off the last bite of her second sweet roll and taking a big swig of hot tea to wash the sugar from her mouth, "unless the kids just randomly ran off to one of the other points on my map where Andi had been with us, they have to have gone to the island. So how did they get there? Are there any boats missing?"

In addition to a small rowboat, usually kept moored at a small mainland bay to the west, the island now sported half a dozen fishing boats. They were tied up at the "inlet" where Bernadette, Andrion, and Nerissa had come seeking a back way into the castle during their search for Leandra and her laboratory some 16 years previously. Chickens, goats, sheep, and cattle were all raised on the island – but the human residents' diet included a lot of fish.

"All boats are present and accounted for," Radigar informed her. "The kids have to have left by magic map. Would there have been another fast-travel point closer to Skarhalfn?" Bernadette studied the map for a minute or two, traveling back in her mind to the places they'd visited with Andi over the years of his life. Even places like her birthplace of Pied de Puce in Auverne would have been available to him, but clearly they would have come here only because it was their closest launch point for Skarhalfn.

Andrion watched as the wheels turned in his wife's head. He was bright, certainly – one of Iscandia's foremost scholars. But Berni had a mind that could, when she applied it to a problem, dart to a solution like a striking snake. Love surged in his heart as he saw her eyes light, the answer in her grasp. "He went dragon!" she declared.

Of course. This island, Skarhalfn, was probably only a few hours' flight to the north and east. Carrying the map and his clothing, Andi must have found a fast-travel point on the island and used the map to transport himself back to Castle Hordenhaal. After that it would have been the work of subjective seconds to transport himself, Meri, and Fjuri back to Skarhalfn.

Bernadette's eyes were troubled as she continued working out what Andi must have done. "He's so small in his dragon form, he must have been nearly starving by the time he arrived," she said. "But he definitely did make it, or Meri and Fjuri would still be hanging around here. And that means there's a fast-travel point and something to eat there. Good, I'm going to need it."

As Bernadette and her son had found, the dragon that appeared when they transformed was of a size directly related to how many years they had been alive – much as it would have been if they had been born as dragons. When Bernadette had first made the transformation, tricked into it by the enormous and ancient dragon Sneyagflug, she had been quite small relative to him. Nine years later, her dragon form (known as Schunmurte, Beautiful Mother, to her dragon consort Sneyagflug) was considerably larger. Andi as a human now towered above his mother, but his dragon form was still far smaller than hers.

Andrion quickly worked out what Bernadette was getting at. "So, you'll fly to the island with your map and then come back and get us?"

"Right," she said, standing and giving them all a brilliant smile. "Let's gather up some supplies, and get my flying harness." Years before, after dragon transformations with her son had become a regular part of Bernadette's life, she had crafted a sort of "necklace" for herself that would hold a full pack's worth of things she might need.

The weather this morning remained relatively good, no snow blowing at least. Bernadette gathered her flying harness, with a full set of warm clothing and some other essential supplies, while the rest of the party raided Castle Hordenhaal's stores for some additional traveling rations. Before long Bernadette thanked their hosts for their hospitality and Andrion accompanied her as she walked down the shore for a way. Most of their companions had seen her in the nude before, but she still preferred to do this privately.

The five of them would once again be forced to remain, enjoying comfortable accommodations and good food, while Bernadette flew to Skarhalfn and then fast-traveled back. None of them knew how long this would take, though Bernadette thought that the flight itself should take only a few hours. As a dragon she was now more than thirty feet from nose to tail, and a powerful flyer. But how much time would elapse while the map did its magic? Only time would tell.

Bernadette stripped down and hastily stuffed her clothing into the flying pack, then draped it over her head. She was already covered in goose bumps, and beginning to shiver. Andrion held her close, then kissed her soundly before backing off. When his wife became a dragon, she needed a lot of room. She smiled at him brilliantly, the love in her eyes so intense it still nearly knocked him off his feet after all this time. Then she got down to business, before she should turn an interesting shade of blue.

"Mon-Drache-Ein-Korp!" she cried, and became in an eye-blink a good-sized red dragon, scales glistening in the morning sunlight. Andrion took her in with a bit of awe. He liked her a lot better as a human – she was much more cuddly, for one thing – but her dragon form was pretty impressive. "Have a good flight!" he called to her, as she spread her wings and began beating her way up into the sky.

"Thanks, love," she called in her much-deeper dragon voice. "See you in a few hours, I hope."

Chapter 34: Landfall

Oh, that's better! Bernadette thought, as she winged her way to the northwest. In her dragon form, and as long as she kept moving, cold environments didn't bother her at all. Visibility was good, only a few puffy clouds in the sky, and after rising to a few hundred feet above the surface of the sea she thought she could just see Skarhalfn on the horizon. It was somewhat mountainous, gleaming white in the morning sun.

As always when flying she found the view fascinating. You could get a much better grasp of the land (or sea) from up here, see how it all fitted together. Powerful, leathery wings pumping, she glanced to her right and noticed a chain of small rocky islets running in a line from the Iscandia mainland toward the island that was her destination.

Bernadette's dragon form had much more endurance than did Andi's, but after having to flap for half an hour or so she decided to climb higher until she found an air current moving in the right direction. That enabled her to glide, flapping less frequently, and the northwest coast of Agena was spread out before her like a map.

Within three hours of flying thus the island came below her, and she circled down – scanning the near side coast for evidence her children had been here. Pink stains streaked the snow along the shore, and she came in for a landing to examine them more closely. Aha, there was evidence here that at least one large animal, likely one of the walruses that had scattered at her approach, had been thoroughly devoured. There were little bloody scraps of hide and tusk, but not much else, and there was some evidence of charring. Gotcha, Andi, she thought.

She was feeling a little peckish herself after the long flight, but it could wait for a bit. So, he grabbed something to eat as soon as he got here. Then what? A careful look at the coarse sand that ran from the waterline up to snow-covered rocks some distance away revealed no signs of human footprints. So he must have flown off again. Bernadette launched herself into the air again with an effort, and rose in spirals until she was a thousand feet or more above the ground. Then she began flying in lazy circles, looking for landmarks.

What ho, was that some human habitation she spotted over there to the east a few miles? She flew lower and soon realized she was looking at a ruined village, complete with a stone jetty still thrusting out into the waters of a small bay. She touched down in an open spot among the remnants of the buildings, a fairly tight squeeze. This place looked like it might have been home to as many as fifty people at one time, though that time was likely decades ago.

Well, only one way to tell for sure if this was Andi's fast-travel point. Steeling herself for the shock of cold, Bernadette cried "Drache-Mon-Zur-Heim!" and shrank in an instant to a smallish, pale-skinned and shivering woman of middle years. Hastily she rummaged through the pack she'd brought with her and began donning garments until she was well-insulated enough to withstand the icy wind blowing in off the shore.

After she was fully dressed Bernadette was still shivering violently, and she used a touch of her healing spell to still the reaction to cold. She'd discovered this side-effect of healing magic quite a few years ago. Now that she was feeling better, she began walking around. It didn't take her long to discover the evidence that someone had camped overnight in one of the less-ruinous of the village's houses. And her map, when she got it out, announced she was now at Walrus Cove. Eureka!

Convinced she had picked up the trail, Bernadette briefly toyed with the idea of going dragon again and flying up to the dypalfar city. It would certainly save time. But if a full-grown dragon showed up it might spook the local inhabitants, nor did she want to be going there without Mothris. Better to just fast-travel back to Castle Hordenhaal and get some rest and food before bringing the entire party here to Skarhalfn using the map. If she were back in dragon form she could probably have caught one of those walruses; and it would certainly have seemed a delicious meal to her in that form. But standing here being human, she felt that some bread and meat that had been properly cooked seemed more like the thing.

Moments after reaching this decision, Bernadette found herself standing once again in the fast-travel arrival spot before the entrance to Castle Hordenhaal. It didn't seem to matter where you started from when you fast-traveled – the map almost always dropped you in the same location.

Chapter 35: Gathering the Troops

As Bernadette had feared, it was pitch dark when she arrived and nobody was stirring – the transit had evidently taken quite a few hours. This was one case where it would have been faster (though tiring) to travel under one's own power between Skarhalfn and Hordenhaal, provided one could fly. Sighing, feeling quite tired and hungry, she made her way up the stairs to the castle's main entrance.

Nobody was manning the guard stations on either side of the door, and the enormous double doors were locked. But when she rapped firmly on them, they were soon opened to her from inside. One of the castle servants smiled and nodded to her. "Glad to see you made it back all right, Fireblood," he said. "Come this way, they're waiting for you."

Bernadette was led down the stairs to the Great Hall, where their host and hostess and most of the group she'd brought with her were relaxing in front of the huge fireplace. She suspected the hour was very late, and she was touched that they would all wait up for her. Mothris was missing, but he was young and needed his sleep.

Andrion was on his feet in an instant, striding to meet her and throw his arms around her. Mmm! Then he stepped back and looked into her eyes, seeking news. She smiled at him. "I found where they landed," she said. "Let me drop a few things and, yes, I'm starving again. What's to eat?" He grinned at her, and gestured toward a small table that had been set up in front of the fire.

On it was a tray with an assortment of covered dishes, and a jug of water as well as a bottle of wine. "For me?" her face lit up, her younger self peeking through. Bernadette dropped her heavy pack and hurried around to plop herself down on a comfortable seat in front of the table, as the others clustered around her. As before, the first order of business was a long drink of water.

Next, she began lifting the lids. The food in the dishes was not hot, not this many hours after suppertime. But it was far from cold, either – and it smelled delicious! The rest of the group were forced to stifle their impatience (which they did with good grace, as they had all been relaxing while she did the hard stuff) until Bernadette had wolfed down enough of the food to quiet the painful rumbling of her stomach. Oof, she thought, as she took another long drink of water and then poured herself a glass of wine to sip.

Raising the glass to her lips and taking a swallow (a decent red, served at the proper room temperature of sixty degrees F.), Bernadette turned her head from side to side. "What?" she said, as if she had no idea what they were waiting for. "Did you want something?" Her impish grin left no doubt that, despite the hardships of the past hours, she was in good spirits.

Finally, she set the glass down and relented. "It seemed to take around three or four hours to fly over there. I can fly a little faster than Andi can, since I'm bigger. It appears he was nearly starving by the time he reached Skarhalfn. There was evidence of a noticeable reduction in the local walrus population, right at the spot on the shore you first reach if you fly straight there from here."

Faces around her nodded in understanding. "After he'd gotten his strength back, it appears he flew along the shore and found an old burned-out settlement. From the look of the place it may have been a walrus-hunting operation with maybe fishing thrown in, twenty or thirty years ago. It's been ruined for quite a while, though. There was evidence that all three kids had spent the night there, cooked and ate some walrus meat, then headed out on foot in the morning. The place is called Walrus Cove, and we can all go there by map now. But I need to get some rest first."

There was laughter and murmurs of "so do we!" all around the circle.

"Yes," Nerissa said rising. "Now that our dragon has returned to the fold, it's time we were all in bed." It certainly seemed like a good idea to Bernadette. Now that her belly was full, sleepiness was invading her limbs. Andrion threw an arm around her, giving her an affectionate squeeze, and they walked together to their quarters bidding the others good night.

In the morning, by special arrangement of Andrion, Bernadette awakened to find that a small (but considerably bigger than what he could produce magically) portable bathtub had been delivered to their room and was being filled with hot water by a parade of serving women. Her eyes lit as she looked in delight at the tub, then at her husband. "You did this? Oh, I love you so *much!*" Aw, he knew that.

Some time later, warm and clean and pink for the first time in days, Bernadette donned fresh clothing. Along with her wooly layers she put on armor, expecting that they would soon be needing it. From what she'd seen of Skarhalfn, it was bigger and much fuller of life than one might have expected from its far northern location.

After a delicious and hearty breakfast the company gathered to thank their hosts and say goodbye to everyone, Bernadette and Andrion extending invitations to Nerissa and Radigar to visit them in Waterdon with their family after this crisis was averted. Then Bernadette gathered everyone around her, and in a few seconds of subjective time they all found themselves standing exactly where Andi and his companions had stood some days earlier: on the desolate shore halfway between the abandoned jetty and the ruined buildings of Walrus Cove.

The trip had taken quite a few hours, and it now looked to be late afternoon. Bernadette led the party up the shore to the ruined village, and showed them where the kids' tracks led, up a trail to the north. "I wonder if this trail goes all the way to Mrzhgradfendz?" she asked no one in particular. Andrion answered her.

"It doesn't seem likely, unless the people here in the village had some reason to go there regularly. Or perhaps, the leukalfar we assume are living there now regularly come down to the coast?"

Bernadette frowned as she considered the question. "The Ankhrazana are nearly unique among leukalfar communities," she said. "They look just like leukalfar everywhere so their ancestors must have taken shelter with the dypalfar and been living underground like all the other leukalfar we've ever seen. But at some point they came out of their caves, and began living under the sun again. You know, the leukalfar call all the rest of us humans – men and alfar – 'Sky People' because we live under the sky. Which they don't. I doubt a tribe of leukalfar living beneath a dypalfar city would be running around outdoors unless they couldn't avoid it."

"The trail must lead somewhere, though," Andrion replied after giving it some more thought. "It's not that long before dark, and I for one am hungry again – as it's apparently been a good hour since we ate breakfast. Do we set off now, or camp here for the night and leave in the morning?"

A chorus of "Let's eat!" burst out around them, and Bernadette sighed. She had hoped to get started following the children's trail, but reason must prevail. It would hardly do them any good to set out tracking on an empty stomach and find themselves in the middle of nowhere a couple of hours later with the sun setting and it being too dark to see anything.

Anja and Lars selected a ruined house of their own for sleeping the night, though they gathered first with Bernadette, Andrion, Lifa and Mothris for a communal dinner from the stores they'd brought. They had packed well and taken on additional provisions at Castle Hordenhaal, and their first meal (gathered around the nearly-intact fireplace where Andi and his companions had smoked walrus meat a few days previously) was a convivial affair.

Despite the anxiety many of them felt for the missing kids, this was a bit like a fun (albeit chilly) adventure. For a while after eating, they all sat around the fire talking. Mothris was fascinated to be spending time with this party of older people, so different from those he had grown up among yet so similar in many ways to his own tribe. Finally the young couple bid them good night and retreated to their private quarters, while the rest of them bedded down near the fire where they'd cooked their supper. There was some quiet conversation before they all dropped off to sleep.

The morning came icy cold, and Bernadette (as had been the case through much of her adult life, it seemed) was the first to arise. She'd slept well bundled-up with Andrion in a warm double bedroll, covered chin to ankle in long wooly underwear and with thick woolen socks on her feet. Now she hugged her husband to her one more time and gave him a kiss between the eyebrows that was intended to both express her affection and encourage him to wake up, before slipping out of the bedroll.

By the gods, it was cold here! The heat of all these bodies sleeping close beside the fire should have done something to relieve the cold, and it probably would have – if the place had had a roof. She supposed it was a lucky chance that they weren't all covered in six inches of fresh-fallen snow, as she struggled into additional clothing and hurried to build the fire back up to a roaring blaze.

Bernadette filled a kettle with water, and in a few minutes there was tea to drink as the members of the rescue party began to wake up and crawl out of their bedrolls. By now the sun was up over the horizon, and it looked as though it would be a brilliantly clear (and deathly cold) day. Perfect weather for tracking their wayward kin.

Chapter 36: In Mrzhgradfendz

Andi, Meri, and Fjuri followed on Ghrztum's heels as he entered through the massive dypalfar metal doors of his home city. Leukalfar guards stood in the chamber inside, flanking the doorway a few paces off. They made to greet him, then reacted in astonishment when they saw who was accompanying him.

Each of them was armed with a chitinous leukalfar sword, which they drew. The one on the right, the senior of the two, barked "Halt, Ghrztum! Who are these strangers you have brought with you?" Ghrztum, towering over the guard by nearly two feet, smiled down at him with his unsettling snow troll grin.

"Relax, Berandis!" he said. "These are friends – emissaries from the Ankhrazana! I found them in the forest and brought them along to meet the tribe."

Berandis, who looked to be of middle years – though it was hard to tell, with leukalfar – let his sword fall at his side but did not relax. He acted as if he doubted what Ghrztum had told him. "The Ankhrazana? The tribe that lives in sunlight? That's just a myth! And anyway, these two big ones are clearly Sky People. I suppose they told you they were leukalfar?" Andi got the sense that Ghrztum's adoptive tribe might possibly regard him as big and stupid, though the Waterdon kids hadn't found him to be lacking in intelligence.

Andi spoke up at this juncture, hoping to smooth things over. "I am Andreas Drakespring of Waterdon, and this girl of the leukalfar is my adopted sister, Merelle Drakespring. We are friends with the Ankhrazana, who do indeed live under the sun in the Canyons of Stone, far to the east and south of here. The Ankhrazana's Chanter, Gryndor, told us of Mrzhgradfendz and its wonders, and we journeyed here with my friend Fjurbund Steadfast to see it for ourselves." It was more or less the truth.

He, too, towered over Berandis – and probably outweighed him by twice. The gate guard, presumably a member of the society of Sentries, hadn't failed to note that in addition to his size Andi appeared to be well armored and was carrying an enormous, powerful-looking bow as well as a long dagger at his belt.

Berandis pondered for a moment. He'd known Ghrztum since the troll had been brought here from outside by his Gleaner parents – an enormous, fur-covered baby. Many at the time had thought Indinala and Skarnoris were insane, taking in a snow troll. But the boy had proven to be more human than anyone expected, and he was now a valued member of the tribe. He decided to delegate the decision about admitting these strangers to someone else.

"All right, Ghrztum," Berandis said importantly. "These strangers are your responsibility, and they'd better behave themselves. Go and report to Keeper Arctoris, and we'll see what he has to say about it. Can't say I like the idea of Sky People in Mrzhgradfendz, even if they can speak like leukalfar."

"Thanks, Berandis," the troll responded casually. "I'll just stop off and get a party of Gleaners up here to bring in my load from the sledge first."

Before Berandis could respond to this unilateral revision of his "orders," Ghrztum turned and led his party of visitors away. They hurried down a flight of steps and turned left, then went down a corridor and through another set of doors before seeing any more people. Meanwhile, Andi had been looking around.

After their adoption of Meri, the Drakesprings had stopped questing into the lower levels of such places, anxious to avoid having to kill any leukalfar. They had visited the upper levels of some of the ruined cities though, long since emptied of hostile automatons, as Andrion searched for dypalfar artifacts for his research. Both Andi and Meri had been along on a couple of these "shopping expeditions" – including that trip to Undernight. There'd been no fighting involved, no danger to the children; but they'd had a chance to see what dypalfar ruins were like. Andi was amazed at how very nearly pristine Mrzhgradfendz was by comparison.

"Ghrztum," he said, coming up beside their enormous companion, "how is it this place is in such good condition? I've never seen a dypalfar city so free of fallen masonry, everything looking like the dypalfar just packed up and left yesterday."

Ghrztum smiled, proud of his home city and pleased by the compliment Andi had paid to it.

"This city harbored a large population of leukalfar who were not enslaved," he explained. "According to Liamdor, our Chanter, the Resistance Movement was strong and well-entrenched. Not a week went by that the hidden fighters did not rescue another of our people from enslavement. It's likely that, though the dypalfar everywhere all departed at the same time, the ones here were particularly anxious to leave before they should be overrun. After they were gone, the free leukalfar left behind took over – and we took care of the city we had inherited."

"Liamdor also says," the troll went on, "that in other places around Iscandia and Darkreach the earth often shakes – especially in the area of Og Vulanz. But here, not even the oldest among us can remember an earthquake. So, nothing to knock down our walls, I guess."

As Ghrztum was finishing his explanation they passed through another set of doors and began to see more people walking around, going about their business. Without exception they stopped what they were doing and stared, waving back in a distracted fashion when Ghrztum waved and called greetings to them. The troll seemed to be deriving a huge amount of enjoyment out of being the center of attention and causing a sensation as they walked further down into the labyrinthine city.

They turned at last into a large room with shelves lining the walls and a stone platform near the door behind which stood a particularly elderly-looking leukalfar male. Behind him, many others could be seen working in the room – adding items to shelves or taking them down, repackaging bulk supplies, and so forth. This appeared to be a central storage area for foodstuffs. Ghrztum led them up to the counter and said, "Greetings, Omondis."

The wizened fellow peered up at the troll from behind his counter, then around at the three visitors. He seemed a little less flappable than some others they'd encountered, as he then remarked calmly, "Greetings, Ghrztum. You are back from your foraging, then?" Ghrztum smiled and nodded.

"Yes, I had some help bringing back the sledge as you can see. It's waiting at the bottom of the front steps."

Omondis nodded, then stepped away to speak with half a dozen of the workers in the room behind him. They soon set off in a group, going back up to the city's main entrance to retrieve what Ghrztum had brought them. Any leukalfar could withstand being out under the sun if it was necessary – but few of them were comfortable doing so.

After the workers had departed Ghrztum set about making introductions. "Omondis, these people are Andreas Drakespring and Fjurbund Steadfast of the Sky People, and Andreas' adopted sister Merelle Drakespring. They heard about us from the Chanter of the Ankhrazana, and came here to see Mrzhgradfendz for themselves. I met them while I was foraging in the woods and brought them along. They have some amazing tales to tell." To Andi, Meri, and Fjuri he added, "Omondis is the head of the society of Gleaners to which I belong."

"Greetings, visitors," the old man replied formally. "It has been long since any Sky People have come to these shores, nor did I ever dream I would be speaking to some. Long before young Ghrztum here joined our tribe, some of us Gleaners would venture out hunting though no one wanted to. Once I saw some Sky People, carrying many sacks away from a cave far to the south of here. But I did not approach them. I think it likely they would not have wanted to talk."

Andi smiled at him. "I'm afraid you're right about that, Omondis. Many among my people do not even realize that the leukalfar are their fellow human beings, with language and family life much as they have. Likewise I think most of the leukalfar have been shut away too long, and don't know how much our races have in common." The expression on Omondis face suggested he could hardly believe what he was hearing. After a couple of heartbeats he responded, though.

"I am very glad to meet you, Andreas Drakespring. I have the feeling you are going to bring about some changes in the attitudes of both our peoples. Now if you will excuse me, I have much to do."

Though the writing of the leukalfar language had fallen into disuse after their enslavement, they still had some ways to keep track of things besides memorization. Omondis had several sheets of what looked like parchment (possibly made from goatskin), and on it there were columns of tally marks beside simplified pictures of food items. Evidently he was keeping track of what food supplies were stored here, what were taken away, and what new ones were brought in by his Gleaners.

Ghrztum led them away again. "You will meet my parents later," he told his companions. "They are busy in the mushroom caverns now, but we will go to our quarters and sup with them later. For now, I guess I had better take you to see Keeper Arctoris." After his intensive language lessons last night Fjuri was picking up more and more of what was being said, and he now asked haltingly, "Arctoris... boss man?"

The troll considered the question as they continued walking. "Boss? Not exactly. We don't have people who can make everyone do what they say, but some people are more respected and will be listened to. The Keepers are the most respected of the societies, and Arctoris is the eldest and most respected of the Keepers."

He continued to lead them down long corridors and staircases, through doors, and into what appeared to be a completely different wing of the sprawling complex. The Mirskhrazana, Andi realized, seemed to have occupied Mrzhgradfendz in a way far beyond anything he had heard about from his parents. They had explored countless dypalfar ruins, and always they had found leukalfar camping like cockroaches in the cities abandoned by their dypalfar masters – rather than living in them as the dypalfar had before them.

Eventually they came to a door that appeared to lead into an apartment, rather than a workspace. And instead of simply opening that door, Ghrztum knocked on it. It was shortly opened by a leukalfar woman who seemed to be of a similar age to Madira, back in the Canyons of Stone. She had an air of youth about her. "Greetings Amdara," the troll said respectfully.

The young woman smiled in a friendly fashion at Ghrztum, then spotted Andi, Fjuri, and Meri spread out in a circle behind him and looked startled. "Ghrztum!" she said. "What brings you here, and with such strange companions?"

The troll smiled shyly at her. "These are some people I met on my recent foraging expedition. I've been asked to bring them to see Keeper Arctoris."

All three of the young travelers felt a bit of anxiety. Even Fjuri, who was still only picking up about half of what was being said around him, sensed that they had reached some kind of a turning point. If this Arctoris guy looked them over and said they were all right, then they'd be in. And if he didn't, then what? He thought that Ghrztum was their friend, but he didn't for a minute think the troll would go against his entire tribe to defend three strangers he'd recently found wandering in the wilderness.

Best case, they'd be turned out on their ears and Andi could fast-travel them home. Being defeated seemed a lot better to Fjuri than being killed out of hand, and though he was big and strong and good with a blade he had no illusions about the three of them, even with Andi's battle magic, being able to fight (or even *find*) their way out of Mrzhgradfendz if the Mirskhrazana were turned against them.

Amdara stepped back from the door, and gestured the four of them to come inside. "Father is just finishing his midday meal," she said quietly, and led them deeper into the apartment. "Ghrztum," Andi murmured softly, "I think it might be a good idea not to mention the dypalfar portal right away. Maybe you could just say we're here as emissaries from the Ankhrazana?" The troll turned slightly, and to Andi's surprise winked at him. Trolls use winks? He couldn't imagine the eyeless leukalfar would use the gesture.

They were ushered into a spacious chamber where one of the plumper and more aged leukalfar the kids had ever seen, swathed in rich-looking robes, sat picking at the last scraps of a meal. His head rose as they came in, led by his daughter, and he did not look pleased. The annoyance changed to surprise and anxiety as he realized that some very strange people indeed had come into the room.

"Father," Amdara said quietly, "Ghrztum has come with some travelers that he found while foraging. He wishes to speak with you." Arctoris waved his daughter away dismissively. He might not be a "boss man," but he certainly had an air of authority.

"Ghrztum, why have you brought these people here?" he demanded in unfriendly tones.

Ghrztum dipped his head respectfully. "Honored Arctoris," he said, "These travelers have come to us from the Ankhrazana. Andreas Drakespring of the Sky People of Waterdon and his sister Merelle Drakespring, born of the leukalfar, have journeyed here with their friend Fjurbund Steadfast, who is still learning our language. They have been told of the wonders of Mrzhgradfendz, and have come here to see it for themselves. I ask permission for them to guest here while they explore our city."

Way to go, Ghrztum, Andi thought. There'd been no mention of the dypalfar portal. If anybody knew more about it, it was probably this guy. But he didn't think it would be a good idea to bring it up right off the bat – especially since, according to their friend, it was something of a state secret.

"Greetings, honored Arctoris," Andi said, stepping up and imitating Ghrztum's gesture of respect. Lay it on thick, he thought. He sensed the Keeper was used to being treated like a lord, and he'd certainly had plenty of interaction with Iscandia's elite before. Eorls and Reman dignitaries had paid tribute to his mom as the savior of all Terris, after all. "My sister and friend and I hope we will be made welcome in your city, so that we can return to the Ankhrazana and tell them of its grandeur. Never have I seen a more wonderful example of an intact dypalfar city!"

Why, these were nothing but a trio of kids, Arctoris realized. The girl, clearly one of his own race though the one called Andreas claimed her as his "sister," couldn't be more than twelve. And from what he'd seen of the Sky People in his long life, the two tall

217

"warriors" weren't old enough to be accounted adults. He relaxed, tension easing out of him as his fears receded. That these people were here, claiming to be sent by the fabled Ankhrazana, was surprising. But he didn't think they posed a threat.

"Thank you for coming to see me, Ghrztum," the old man said. "I greet you, Andreas and Merelle Drakespring and Fjurbund Steadfast," he went on – nodding to each of them. "You are welcome to stay here in Mrzhgradfendz, while you learn more about our city and the Mirskhrazana. I hope you will be able to bring back a favorable report to the Ankhrazana." Turning to Ghrztum, he added "You will find them quarters, of course?"

Ghrztum smiled. "I thought I would take them home to meet my parents. We have a large apartment, and we should be able to find room for them there."

Arctoris nodded. "Very well, then." To the three travelers he said, "Enjoy your stay in our city."

Andi wasn't quite done with him, thought. "I hope," he told the old leader, "that we will have a chance to speak more together while we are here. I am sure that as the foremost among the Mirskhrazana's Keepers you must have knowledge far deeper than that of the average person in the tribe. And perhaps we can talk as well with Liamdor, your Chanter?"

He was acutely aware that time was running out. Surely Mom and Lifa were on their trail by now, perhaps with others along – and if they didn't have something to show for it by the time their parents caught up with them, there was going to be hell to pay. Okay, Andi realized, there was probably going to be hell to pay no matter what. But he really, really, wanted to have proven this was a worthy quest before the bill came due.

Ghrztum considered Andi's words, and put in a tentative offer: "Perhaps after I have spoken with my mother we might be able to arrange to have you and Liamdor come and guest with us for the evening meal, Keeper. I will send a runner soon with an invitation if I can." The old man nodded. He was nearly as eager to pump these young people for information as they were to do the same to him (though he knew it not) – and Liamdor, he knew, would not want to miss the opportunity. "Very well," he told them. "I hope to be seeing you this evening."

Chapter 37: A Pleasant Evening

Once again the three travelers trailed behind their enormous, furry guide like chicks following a hen, as he led them through more corridors and turnings. Perhaps because Mrzhgradfendz was so much more intact than any other dypalfar city he'd visited, it seemed to Andi that the place was much easier to get lost in. He doubted he'd be able to lead them out if for any reason he, Meri, and Fjuri had to flee. Nor was he sure that Meri's presence or his ability with the leukalfar tongue would have been enough to keep them out of trouble without Ghrztum vouching for them.

The place was dimly lit by the ever-burning dypalfar lamps he'd known since earliest childhood. Papa Andrion had appropriated quite a few of these from dypalfar ruins he'd visited and installed them in Drakespring House for the convenience of the residents. Only the bedrooms didn't have them, so that people could have darkness to sleep in if they preferred. Andi and Fjuri were glad of these. The leukalfar could have done without them – though Ghrztum would have had as much trouble as Andi and Fjuri would, navigating in complete darkness.

The troll and his adoptive parents, it turned out, lived much higher up in the city (most of which was below ground level, a plus as it kept a uniform cool temperature year around) than where the quarters of Arctoris and his daughter had been located. This less-desirable location seemed to suit them well enough, however, and it meant that they'd been able to have a much larger suite of rooms for their small family (with one very large member) than they would otherwise have been able to obtain.

Nobody was home when they arrived. Ghrztum unlocked the gleaming metal door with a key that he kept in the pouch on his belt. Though the troll had no need of clothing to protect him or keep him warm, pockets were another issue – and he had several useful items slung about his person on the leather harness he wore.

"This is it," he said, gesturing around at the stone room. "Home sweet home." The kids looked around them with interest, having never seen a dypalfar dwelling that was occupied by people before their visit to Mrzhgradfendz. Andi and Meri, who had seen many bare rooms in dypalfar ruins, were surprised to see that fur pillows, presumably stuffed with dried grasses, served as cushions on the stone benches.

First thing, Ghrztum led the three kids off to another area of the apartment, which proved to be a bathroom of sorts. There was a large stone tub (though not as large as the one in Andi and Meri's home, actually), currently sitting empty, and a basin against one wall with a spigot protruding from it. The troll grinned at their expressions as they examined the room.

"We're lucky to have this bathroom," he told them. "Not all the apartments in the city have running water inside them, so some people have to draw water from the public fountains and bathe at the public baths. I guess the drawback is the noise, but you get used to it." Indeed, there was a fairly loud noise of whirring machinery that was much more noticeable here than it had been near the entrance to the apartment.

The basin had a broad rim, and on it rested a small dypalfar bowl containing what looked a little like sawdust. "Just turn on the spigot and wet your hands, then dip them in the bowl and work up a lather. That's soap plant roots. You can rinse the shavings down the drain after your hands are clean."

Huh, Andi thought, stepping up. This was pretty similar to the water system at home, not surprising since Papa Andrion had designed it based on dypalfar technology. After all four of them had washed their hands, Meri asked about a chamberpot and was led to a small enclosure in the room, wherein a funnel-shaped hole around six inches across was set into the floor. "When you're finished, just rinse it down with a bucket of water," Ghrztum told her. The others used the facilities as well, with still more hand-washing, before they returned to the living room.

Ghrztum seemed to be particularly delighted to be playing host to his new friends, and he urged them to take seats while he went to get them all something to eat. The kids still had some of their travel rations, even a few smoked walrus steaks, in their packs; but all the rest of the elk meat had been left on the sledge to be added to the tribe's communal stores. Andi supposed it was only fair. Were they not expecting to be fed from those same stores during their stay here?

While Ghrztum was absent from the room, the three talked quietly among themselves in the common tongue. "Ghrztum is so nice!" Meri said. "I really like him, and he's kind of cuddly too." Andi grinned at her. The idea of a snow troll being cuddly was kind of ridiculous, but she did have a point. Their new friend was sweet-natured, from what they'd seen of him so far, and that fur looked like it would be soft and warm.

"I don't know about old Arctoris, though," Andi said. "He was looking at us like we were either an army come to ransack his city or a trio of fat goats wandering into the sights of his bow."

"Is that why you didn't mention the portal, then?" Fjuri asked.

"Partly," his friend admitted. "But also, if the portal is the big secret the Keepers are keeping, I doubt he would appreciate it if I started blabbing about it within earshot of anybody besides another Keeper. I hope to talk to him privately about it this evening, if we get the chance."

Ghrztum returned with a large and handsome tray that appeared to have been fashioned from mandimant chitin. On it were heaped an assortment of foodstuffs. He'd noted that the two boys seemed to have appetites far in excess of what you might expect for creatures their size, and guessed that it had something to do with the fact that they were still growing. So he'd loaded up.

"We all missed the midday meal," he told them, "but there's plenty of food in our larder. Dig in!" With that he took his own advice, plucking a familiar-looking piece of leukalfar flatbread from a stack of them and rolling some chunks of a firm, white meat into it along with a sprinkling of chopped vegetable matter and a dollop of red-colored, thin sauce.

The boys didn't need to be asked twice, though as they reached for the sauce he warned them "The sauce is pretty spicy. Better taste a little before putting it on your food." Both boys had been exposed to the fiery cuisine of Zahar (where the climate frequently had meat turning only hours after butchering, and plenty of spices helped to cover up the "off" flavor) by eating at the

Bathing Maiden, where throughout their lives Lev Ciabalo had been wowing the Waterdon region with dishes the locals had never seen before. And they were very hungry, as well. They both decided the sauce was fine, and loaded up wraps themselves.

Meri, considerably more hesitant, first took some of the dried apples she recognized. Then she tried some of the flatbread. Unlike the coarse, grainy texture of the flatbread they'd enjoyed in the Canyons of Stone, this was pale, smooth, and slightly sweet. Quite good, actually! After devouring one plain she put a little of the white meat (which looked a bit like ocean fish) in another one with some of the vegetables. She decided to skip the sauce, though.

For some time there was little conversation, just the sounds of chewing and swallowing and occasional murmurs of "Mm, this is good!" Halfway through his third wrap and beginning to be full enough to resume showing some manners, Andi said "Thank you, Ghrztum! This is very unfamiliar but very delicious. You mentioned you don't have grain, so what are these flatbread rounds made from?"

Ghrztum smiled. "It's a type of tuber that grows in the deeper caverns," he said. "The plant aboveground flourishes in the light of a certain type of dypalfar lamp, and according to Liamdor these tubers were a major food source for the dypalfar. You can eat them baked or cook them and then grind them into a meal, which can then be made into flatbread. My people probably made their bread from grain, before we took refuge underground with our betrayers."

He spoke as if he were truly a leukalfar, and Andi supposed that in a way he was. Meri was certainly much more a child of Waterdon and the empire than she was of these tribal dwellers in the depths below dypalfar cities. "Sort of like potatoes, I guess," he replied. "And the meat? What is that?"

"Oh," the troll replied smiling, "that's mandimant."

There was an audible choking sound from Meri, and both Andi and Fjuri stopped chewing for a moment. After Andi had gotten a grip on his reactions, he said "So, they're not poisonous to eat?"

"Oh no," came the reply. "You have to be careful when you're cleaning them because various parts of the innards are loaded with poisons. The Priests who perform chemia use those in crafting potions and poisons. But if properly prepared the flesh is as you see it, mild and nourishing. They are our livestock, you might say – though we don't practice agriculture as it is said we did millennia ago."

Meri felt a little ill – but she observed that Andi and Fjuri, after a slight hesitation, had continued eating. They must have concluded that they'd already eaten quite a lot of the mandimant meat with no ill effects, and she supposed they were right. So she did the same. Just when she thought that she was coming to know her birth people, after time spent with Myrkra and Mothris and their kin in the Canyons of Stone, she met another leukalfar tribe who lived quite differently. And likely the leukalfar tribe from which her actual birth parents came had still different ways. Mom had said she had been found in a cave complex far, far below a dypalfar ruin in the mountains on the eastern edge of Iscandia.

After the food had all been demolished and everyone was comfortably full, Ghrztum produced a pot of warm tea and they sat drinking it as they talked casually, picking up some of their discussions from the night before. It doesn't seem to matter where you go, Andi thought – people everywhere drink tea.

They'd been enjoying themselves for quite some time, sharing stories with their new friend, when the door opened and a pair of leukalfar came in. The man was only slightly taller than the woman, and they looked neither young nor old. Andi supposed that once a member of the alfar races was fully mature it would be a long, long time before they began to look aged.

Ghrztum was on his feet in a moment, calling "Mother! Father! We have visitors!" The two stood looking at the three strangers in their living room, seeming a little uneasy but not exhibiting as much shock and surprise as had some of the other members of the Mirskhrazana they'd encountered since arriving here. Perhaps a couple open-minded enough to adopt a baby troll were less likely to be xenophobic?

224

Formal introductions were in order. "Mother, Father, I met these travelers on my last foraging trip and it turns out they were sent here by the Ankhrazana, looking for Mrzhgradfendz. This is Andreas Drakespring and his adoptive sister Merelle Drakespring, and their friend Fjurbund Steadfast." To the kids he said, "This is my father, Skarnoris, and my mother, Indinala."

The visitors all rose as well, nodding their heads and greeting Ghrztum's parents politely. Fjuri had mastered enough of the leukalfar tongue by now, having heard very little else spoken in the past couple of days, that he was able to chime in on the chorus of "Greetings" and "Pleased to meet you."

Indinala took the lead in the conversation that followed, and Andi got the sense that it was she who ran things in the household. Her husband seemed to regard her with love and respect, but was shy about addressing the strangers in their midst. "Greetings, Andreas, Merelle, and Fjurbund. Welcome to our home. Has our son shown you much of our city?"

As Indinala was the spokesperson for her household, so Andi tended to fill that role for their little group of would-be adventurers. Fjuri was the eldest, but he was naturally shy and reticent – and Andi was not! "Thank you, Indinala. Your son has taken us to visit with Keeper Arctoris, as well as to the Gleaners' storeroom. We're hoping we might get a chance to meet your Chanter, Liamdor, this evening. In a way we were sent here by Gryndor, Chanter of the Ankhrazana."

Ghrztum explained to his parents some of how the three wanderers had come to be here, and that he had suggested to Arctoris that he and Liamdor might be invited here tonight for the evening meal. Indinala, as a working mother (though her son was well and truly grown now and a member of the tribe's workforce as were she and her husband), was not thrilled to learn that in her absence she had suddenly picked up another five guests for dinner. But she rose to the occasion brilliantly. She was excited by the arrival of these exotic travelers and burning with curiosity about Merelle. Besides, having Arctoris and Liamdor as dinner guests was an honor in itself.

She smiled – an expression which, despite the fearsome-looking leukalfar teeth, made her look younger. "It's a good thing that we brought extra food home with us then," she told her hulking son. "Perhaps you had better go and get a runner to invite Liamdor, and tell Arctoris that the invitation is confirmed."

The troll bent to hug his mother and plant a kiss on her cheek, then told his guests "I'll be back in a couple of minutes." He left by the door they'd come in through, apparently going to find a "runner." Andi guessed that juvenile members of the tribe might be pressed into service running messages.

"Please excuse me while I get my dinner preparations organized," Indinala said to their guests.

"Just let me know if you want any help peeling or chopping," Andi replied disarmingly. He'd often helped in the kitchen, especially when Papa Erik was doing the cooking, and he was feeling a little guilty about just dropping in out of the blue and imposing on this nice family's hospitality.

Indinala looked surprised, but said "Thank you. I'll just make sure I have everything for my menu, and then you can help me in the kitchen." She was flustered. Sky People right here in their living room, speaking the language of the people, and with a leukalfar girl identified as an "adoptive sister"! Did that mean that the Sky People boy Andreas had been adopted by leukalfar? After all, she had been moved to adopt the orphaned baby troll after Skarnoris had killed its mother, defending the carcass of a deer he'd killed.

In all the leukalfar tribes, there surely must be other women who would have taken in a baby of the men (for clearly Andreas and his friend Fjurbund were not alfar) in similar circumstances. When she'd plucked up Ghrztum and taken him to her breast, no one had even believed that trolls were capable of learning human speech, human ways. How many had resented her for bringing him into their midst, and how many warned her that he would just have to be killed when he grew bigger and began to behave like the savage beast he was!

She smiled somewhat bitterly to herself. She'd endured a lot to raise that boy, and he had repaid her a thousand times over with his love, his endearing ways, and his abilities that benefitted the entire tribe. There might still be some in the tribe who whispered resentfully when Ghrztum or his parents were not in hearing – but no one could deny that her son was a useful and valuable member of the Mirskhrazana.

Skarnoris, who was laden with a heavy pack, followed his wife into the area of their spacious (if somewhat chilly, this close to the surface) apartment that was set aside for food preparation, and set the pack down so she could go through its contents. One benefit of being members of the society of Gleaners, the family always had plenty to eat and also got first crack at any surpluses that appeared.

He quickly returned to the living room where their guests were seated, talking quietly among themselves in an unfamiliar language he guessed to be the common tongue. The Mirskhrazana were doubly isolated from the rest of Iscandia society, here on their remote island; but thanks to the Chanters, they knew much of what life had been like in the days before the wars that led to the Betrayal.

He took a seat on one of the fur-padded stone benches and addressed the large youth who seemed to be the little group's leader. "So, Andreas, you have come from the Ankhrazana?" Andi launched into an edited version of their story – Meri's adoption by his family in Waterdon, their trip to the Great Temple and months spent studying the leukalfar language and culture, the visit to the Canyons of Stone in which the existence of this city was revealed. Again, he avoided mentioning the rumored dypalfar portal.

Ghrztum soon reappeared, reporting "The message is on the way. We should expect Liamdor and Arctoris, and Amdara as well, in about two hours' time." He rejoined the party in the living room, and in a while Indinala returned and sat with them too.

"Andreas was just telling me how he and his sister came to speak our language," Skarnoris told his wife as she took a seat beside him. "Merelle was found orphaned in a warren of caves inhabited by a tribe of the leukalfar far, far to the east of here, and Andreas's mother adopted her into the family. She was just an infant, and had never met any of her people until this past spring."

Well there goes *that* idea, Indinala thought. Still, it pleased her nearly as much to know that a mother of the Sky People was willing to take in a foundling leukalfar girl. From the way the boy acted around his sister, he truly regarded her as a beloved member of his family despite the obvious physical differences between them. After twenty years spent defending her "different" son from the cruel taunts of hostile tribe members, she could sympathize.

That got her thinking: should she have sought out trolls so that Ghrztum (the name meant "thunder," a dypalfar word that had wandered into the leukalfar tongue during their long captivity) could learn the language and ways of the people who had given him birth? But Indinala didn't know how that could possibly happen. From her observations of snow trolls, they had no social structure. They must surely have language, else her boy could not have so readily learned to speak. But they were so hostile, and so huge, there seemed no way they could even approach a snow troll without getting into a fight to the death. Perhaps this was something the boy could do on his own, now that he was fully grown.

After perhaps half an hour's further conversation, Indinala excused herself to get started on dinner preparations. Andi and Ghrztum (who was also feeling a little guilty about inviting a horde over to the house without okaying it with Mother first) joined her, to act as kitchen helpers. Meri would have liked to help too, but there wasn't that much room in what passed for their kitchen; and Fjuri begged her to stay, to help in translation. His facility with the leukalfar tongue had made great leaps forward, but it was still hard to discuss anything beyond the simplest of everyday situations.

There was a table in the food preparation area, and Indinala sat her hulking troll son and the tall Sky People boy at it with paring knives and bowls of tubers, vegetables, and herbs. After giving them instructions on what needed to be done she left them to it, and set to work with a large bowl, mixing up dough for flatbread.

Without the elasticity provided by the proteins in wheat and similar grains, the standard Iscandia breads raised with yeast were not possible. The Mirskhrazana did have some chemical leavening agents, however, and Indinala added some of these to the tuber flour to make a thick batter. She began turning out stacks of hot, slightly risen griddle cakes, softer than the unleavened flatbreads they'd eaten at the midday meal.

In a large pot she soon had a stew of goat meat simmering, accepting some of the herbs Andi had chopped to throw into it. The vegetables and tubers would go in after the meat had cooked to tenderness. Happy that things were well in hand, and excited at the prospect of hosting these three visitors as well as two of the tribe's most prominent citizens, Indinala began talking with her two helpers as she continued making griddle cakes.

"So, Andreas, did your mother have very much trouble with the people in your... town, is it?... when she adopted a leukalfar child?" Andi considered a moment, still peeling tubers, before he spoke.

"That was part of the reason Merelle and I went to the Great Temple," he replied. "Waterdon is small by comparison with this city, but it receives a lot of visitors from all over Agena and there are always a few idiots who would think Merelle was an enemy – or would just say cruel things to her. But my family is... special, especially in Waterdon. All the local residents who knew our family would never do anything to hurt Merelle. She's a part of our family, just like our other sister and our little brother." Once again, he stopped short of going into details about Mom (let alone him) being able to turn into a dragon, which meant he also couldn't mention Mondi or their other eighteen dragon siblings.

"Special?" Indinala asked, flipping another griddle load of the light, fluffy flatbread rounds.

"Mom's The Fireblood," Andi replied – hoping he could admit that much without having to explain all the rest of it. "She has an inborn power to learn and use dragon spells," he explained. "I don't know whether you knew that dragons had come back to Agena around seventeen years ago?"

Indinala nodded. "We have seen some of them here, though usually only one at a time. The Chanter had told us of their history, but everyone thought that they were extinct forever. There was no explanation of how they had suddenly returned. This was more than ten years after the last of the Sky People left the island. No one has seen any dragons near here in around the last five years, now."

Aha, Andi thought. So it probably was about thirty years ago the mine and coastal settlement were abandoned. He hadn't thought they looked all that ancient. "The dragons were brought back by the dragon lord Tarragin, firstborn of all the dragons," Andi told his audience. Both Ghrztum and his mother were gazing at him in rapt fascination.

He went on. "Tarragin had been trapped in another plane of existence by some ancient Norse heroes, who had poisoned him so that his ability to regenerate his magical abilities was almost completely destroyed. Thousands of years later, it seems, Tarragin regained enough power to return to our universe. He started using his powers to resurrect the dead dragons that were buried all over Iscandia."

Indinala jumped to pull the last batch of griddle cakes off the fire, as they were close to getting scorched. "By Apoldros!" she exclaimed, making a gesture with her right hand that was familiar to Andi from his days as an acolyte at the Great Temple. "You must tell all of this to Liamdor, every detail! This is stunning information!"

Andi smiled at her, finishing with his tubers and starting on some vegetables. "It all worked out okay, though," he assured her. "Mom turned out to be the one prophesied in the ancient texts to finally defeat Tarragin. He hadn't even been back for a year before she and my two papas tracked him down to Asengard and killed him for good. Of course, by then dozens of dragons were roaming the land again – so the problem has lingered on." He stopped short of adding, "Until recently." Damn, it was a good story and he loved telling it – but he didn't want to reveal too much to his hosts. Even though they'd been nothing but kind and courteous to him

and his companions, he wanted an ace in the hole in case
something... bad... happened.

After all the chopping had been done Indinala shooed them
out of the area, back to hang out with Meri, Fjuri, and Skarnoris so
she could get the table ready for eating at. Unlike in the Canyons
of Stone, where the Ankhrazana ate seated on mats around a
central fire pit, the Mirskhrazana had stone tables, benches, chairs,
and elegant dypalfar metal tableware – all courtesy of their
departed masters.

Shortly after Andi and Ghrztum had returned to the living
room the other guests arrived. Arctoris and Liamdor were both
members of the society of Keepers, and both highly ranked enough
to rate quarters in the favored lower reaches of the city. As they
were practically neighbors, they had chosen to come together –
accompanied by Arctoris' daughter Amdara.

Chapter 38: Revelations

The room was getting crowded, with a further three adults. Liamdor was introduced to the young visitors, seeming to regard them with fascination. Shortly thereafter they were all called into the dining area, which as at Drakespring House combined cooking facilities with the table on which the family ate their meals.

Some unfamiliar ritual words were pronounced over the meal by Indinala and Skarnoris in concert, as the heads of the household. Then they all dug into the meal. It was different from anything the Waterdon kids had tasted before, but proved to be good. As a small child, Andi seemed to recall, he'd been somewhat picky about what foods he ate. Food at home was good, and food at the Maiden (where the family ate often, whenever nobody felt like cooking) was even better. But there'd been times, visiting friends at mealtime, where he'd been leery of what was being served.

While he had that child's memories, lately Andi had a hard time believing he had once *been* that child. These days, he would cheerfully eat anything that would put a dent in his seemingly perpetual hunger – and have two servings if it tasted all right. Accompanying the meal was a slightly fizzy beverage that Andi thought was probably some kind of beer. It tasted odd, and he missed the milk he usually drank at home. He'd had none for most of the past several months, whereas at home (what with them having two milk cows) it was a staple of his diet. Ah, well.

Following the meat-and-veggie-rich stew, served over the griddle cakes, Indinala produced a sweet that was nothing like Andi had ever seen before. It was sort of gelatinous and pink, cut up into squares and sprinkled with what he thought was probably some kind of nuts from the forests on the island. It tasted pretty good and he had two squares, thinking as he washed them down with more of the beer or whatever it was that he hoped it wasn't made from mandimant.

After supper Ghrztum and Fjuri volunteered to do the washing-up, freeing Indinala and Skarnoris to play host to their distinguished guests. Now we get down to it, Andi thought. When they had gathered in the living room, and compliments had been conveyed to Indinala for the delicious meal, Liamdor collared Andi and demanded (in a jovial sort of way) to be Told All.

The old fellow was the plumpest leukalfar Andi had yet met, to the point where he would probably have been accounted pudgy even had he been a Norseman. That no doubt made him obese by leukalfar standards, but Andi supposed that a Chanter's life didn't offer many opportunities for exercise. He appeared to be less aged than Arctoris, but still well up there in years.

"It all started around seventeen years ago," Andi began, "when my mother first came to Iscandia from Auverne…" Around him the room fell silent, and even Meri (who of course had been hearing the story since she was old enough to understand words) was rapt as he told how Tarragin had reappeared in their universe and begun raising dragons and attacking small towns; how Mom, who had only come here seeking adventure after being bored out of her mind in Pied de Puce, had learned she was The Fireblood; and how she, with her two companions, had eventually gone to Asengard and defeated the Soul-Devourer.

Conversation resumed and swirled around as those in the room (of whom only Indinala and Meri had previously heard any of this) discussed the story Andi had told. To think, their entire world might have been destroyed and they would have known nothing about it until it had already happened.

Liamdor and Arctoris in particular were amazed by the tale, and discussed it quietly between themselves as the others were chattering. "What I want to know," Arctoris said, "is why this boy and his companions are here, now. And what does it portend for the future of the Mirskhrazana?"

"You know the Great Plan, Arctoris," the Chanter told his friend. "I realize it's been all but abandoned for the last few generations, but what if the Sky People could help? If we could bring a Sky People army to them, might the dypalfar not falter? They ran before…"

Arctoris' mouth twisted in a frown of denial. "You're a fool if you think that, Liamdor. The Sky People have been invading our homes and killing our Sentries for thousands of years. Do you think one boy with a leukalfar sister is going to turn them all into our allies? They'll pillage everything they can get their hands on, and if we let them through into the dypalfar paradise they'll pillage that, too. They can't be trusted."

Their discussion was pushed aside for the time being, as Arctoris turned to Indinala. "Might I trouble you, my lady, for some small drinking cups?" He produced a gleaming dypalfar metal flask from a pouch at his side. The leukalfar elder was richly dressed, by the standards of all of the leukalfar that Andi had so far met. So was his friend, the Chanter. Overall, the Mirskhrazana seemed to be civilized far beyond any others of their race that were known to the "Sky People." Arctoris smiled winningly, brandishing the flask. "I've brought along a little 'treat' for us."

Indinala smiled at him, and Skarnoris looked interested. She rose gracefully and went into the kitchen, where Ghrztum and Fjuri were having a jolly time washing dishes while the troll coached Fjuri on his leukalfar and poked fun at his stumbles in the recently-learned language. The two seemed to be enjoying themselves, and she doubted either of them really needed to participate in Arctoris' "treat." She smiled at them and told them to keep up the good work, then collected half a dozen small dypalfar metal cups from a shelf where they'd been stored upside-down to keep the dust out of them.

After Indinala returned to the group in the living room she set the cups out on the table, and Arctoris poured a glistening, slightly viscous purple liquid from his flask. Meri was curious, but she suspected this was one of those "grown-up" things – and when Indinala suggested she probably would not like this drink, she was happy enough to be left out.

Arctoris leaned toward Andi, proffering the cup. He seemed to have filled Andi's rather more than the others on the table, perhaps as an honor to a guest. "This is something unique to the Mirskhrazana," he said. "There may be other tribes with something similar, but this was developed right here in Mrzhgradfendz after the departure of the dypalfar. Our chemiasts discovered its making thousands of years ago, and it has become a drink for *very* special occasions among us. We call it *ghrztma*."

Andi eyed the cup with a certain amount of concealed (he hoped) suspicion. What was *in* this "very special drink"? Well, everybody else was drinking it and at bottom his physiology wasn't a lot different from that of the leukalfar or any of the other human races. He smiled, thanking the old Keeper, and took a sip. Wow, it was delicious! A little bit sweet, a little bit tart, a little bit… warm, somehow. It slipped down his throat and into his stomach, already beginning to feel less than full. It had been at least half an hour since he'd last eaten, after all.

"This is amazing, Arctoris!" Andi declared, forgetting to be overly formal. Even in the bosom of their families the leukalfar seemed positively stilted by comparison to his own folk, though it was clear they loved each other. He knew he should be handling Arctoris with kid gloves, but the old guy seemed friendly enough. Hadn't they all just had a nice dinner together?

Before he knew it his cup was empty, and when he set it down Arctoris filled it up again. Andi noticed he was still working on his *own* cup. Well, Andi was after all much larger than any leukalfar he'd ever met, and a lot younger than the old Keeper. "So, Andreas," Arctoris said, as Andi began drinking down more of the delicious ghrztma (funny, that almost sounded like their troll friend's name). "How is it that you have a leukalfar girl for a sister?"

Andi was feeling wonderful. Dinner had been delicious, Ghrztum had proven a good friend to them, his family had welcomed them into their home, and now two of the most prominent members of the Mirskhrazana were treating with him as friends. He felt he must pay them back by telling them everything about himself and his family. Then they would understand how important it was for leukalfar and the rest of humanity to put aside their differences. There was that other thing, the dypalfar portal, but he needed to discuss that privately with Arctoris later.

"It was when I was about five," Andi said. "The ancient dragon Sneyagflug, who had helped my mom and her companions get to Asengard to kill Tarragin, came and told Mom that dragons were going to go extinct because the last female dragon had been killed. He told her he needed her help, see, but he was really tricking her into... well, that all happened later. The thing was, she went off looking for a special chemia book with my papa Andrion, who's a mage, and they were down under some old dypalfar ruin when they ran into some leukalfar down there who were trying to kill them."

Andi blinked and looked around him. How had his cup gotten empty? He thought it had been full just a little while ago... Arctoris, following his glance, upended the flask and poured the last little bit of the ghrztma into Andi's cup. Andi grinned at him blearily, and said "Thanks, Arctoris. Man, this stuff is really good. Anyway, there was a fight and then Mom and Papa Andrion found out that one of the leukalfar she'd killed was a woman and she had a baby. She was really sorry, she'd just been defending herself, but now this baby was an orphan and it was her fault. So she and Papa Andrion took her back home with them after they found the book, and Meri's been part of our family ever since."

Andi smiled at his sister, and was surprised to see her facing him, rigid. Eyeless the leukalfar might be, but you could still tell when they were staring at you. Oops. It was possible that Mom had never actually mentioned to Meri that the reason she was an orphan was because Mom had killed her birth mother in a fight. What was the matter with him? He felt as if his tongue had just started flapping loose without his brain being connected to it.

He rose from his seat and stumbled over to where Meri sat, enfolding her in his arms. "She never told you?" he asked in Common. Meri choked back a sob.

"No! How could you all have lied to me like that?" Andi, through the haze that seemed to have engulfed his brain, sensed that Meri was more furious than devastated. After all, she had no memories of her birth mother – only ones of happy times growing up in the large, loving Drakespring clan.

Andi hugged his sister tightly and planted a kiss on her head. "Think about it, Squirt! Mom loved you so much, and she felt so guilty about killing your parents even if they *were* trying to kill her – and if she hadn't she and Papa Andrion would have been dead, and it would have been me and Riki who were orphans." Technically, of course, they would still have had Papa Erik; but he didn't mention that. "Mondi and Sigi would never even have been born! She just couldn't bring herself to tell you the complete truth, and I only knew about it because I was old enough to understand what people were saying when she and Papa Andrion brought you home. It wasn't for me to tell you that – I love you, and I didn't want to hurt you or the love between you and Mom."

She'd been stiff in his arms, but now Meri melted and embraced him back. "You're right, Andi," she said into his chest. After a long hug, she pulled back and looked up at his face. "Are you okay?" she asked dubiously. "You're acting a little strange." He looked down at her, joy and relief that his slip had not produced anything more than a momentary anger showing plainly on his face. Meri was going to be all right.

"I'm fine, I promise," he told her – giving her one last squeeze before returning to his seat and his conversation with Keeper Arctoris.

"It's all right now," he said apologetically. "I hadn't realized that Mom never gave Meri the full story." Arctoris nodded sagely.

"So, young Merelle grew up as a member of your Sky People family. And then what happened?" Andi went on to relate all the details of their trip to the Great Temple, which of course involved an excursion into the story of Mom, Papa Andrion, and Aunt Nerissa (at that time, an ancient vampire) going to the Eparchy after The Staff of Apoldros before he was born.

Liamdor was fascinated by all this, and kept prompting Andi for more details – which he was happy to give. "But this all happened before you were born?" he asked. Andi nodded. "Oh, I really must speak with your mother! And this 'Papa Andrion' you speak of?"

"He's one of my two fathers," Andi explained. "Mom couldn't choose between the two men she loved, so she got special dispensation from Aderos – or so the story goes – to marry both of them. Anyhow, they've been happily married since before I was born so I guess it's worked out OK." He got some funny looks at that, but it was hardly the first time.

"The thing is," Liamdor went on, "your stories are absolutely priceless and as they bear directly on the leukalfar they deserve to be part of the Lore. But your knowledge of the events is at best second hand. You were not even born when some of these things happened. For a Chanter to incorporate a story into the Lore, they must first be delivered to him or her by one who witnessed the events. And you say your parents are still alive and well? If only I could speak with them!"

Oh, you might get the chance to do that, Andi thought. He was beginning to feel a little more clearheaded, it now having been some time since the last of the ghrztma had been drunk. He supposed that if Mom and one or both of his papas showed up here looking for their missing kids, Liamdor might get more of an earful than he wanted.

"Perhaps, Liamdor," Andi said hesitantly, "you might travel with us to the Great Temple and visit with the leukalfar of the Ankhrazana. They could tell you much, not only as it bears on my family's story but about the history of their own people. I know you'd like Gryndor, their Chanter."

Liamdor smiled at him and sighed. "Look at me," he said. "I am old, and I am fat. I fear such great travels would be the death of me."

"Not with a magic map!" Andi said, pulling the map from his shirt. "My father Andrion made this for my mother, and if I'm standing where I can see the sky and am not under attack it will take me anywhere that I've been before, while in company with it. I could take you, and anyone else of your tribe that would like to come along with us, back to the Great Temple in what will seem like the blink of an eye. Much more time will actually have passed," he added, "but all it will take is a good meal and a night's sleep and you'll be fully restored after the journey – no days of dangerous travel."

Both leukalfar elders were staring at him fixedly now, looks of surprise and speculation on their faces. "May I see that more closely?" Arctoris asked, reaching out a hand, and Andi passed the map over to him. "The magic maps are closely linked to the person controlling them," he explained. "If you were to take it and try to use it by yourself, it probably would not take you anywhere."

A thought occurred to him. "Have you ever been down to the abandoned mine, a little over a day's walk from here? Or to the ruined village on the coast?" Andi asked. Arctoris nodded, still holding the map spread out in his hands. On the island, only the city in which they sat was marked on the map. Further afield, a handful of the major cities of Agena were marked.

"So," the old elf said, working it out, "If I'm not with you, I could use the map to take me to the mine or the village. But not to these other places."

"That's right," Andi said, "but only after you'd walked to the mine or the village with the map in your possession. The magic is peculiar, and even though my papa actually made this map he doesn't completely understand *why* they act the way they do. It's just how they are."

In the course of their conversation earlier it had come out that Liamdor too, while he held the special office of Chanter, was also a member of the society of Keepers. That made sense, as if there were any secrets the Chanter was privy to that the Keepers didn't want distributed to the general population, swearing him to secrecy on the subject was their only hope. Ghrztum and Fjuri had finished cleaning up after the meal and rejoined them, squeezing in along the padded benches and becoming part of the general conversation. Andi, Liamdor, and Arctoris were no longer the focus of the group's attention, as other conversations had sprung up among the people in the room.

Andi leaned across the table, facing Arctoris, and said softly, "Keeper, there is something I have not mentioned before – the main reason my companions and I have come here. I think it would be better if we discussed it in private. Might we go to the kitchen for a few moments?" Intrigued, Arctoris and Liamdor rose and

239

followed the Sky People boy into the next room, where they gathered at the now-clean table. The others noticed them getting up, but were distracted by their own conversations and paid them little mind.

Though they were alone in the room, Andi continued to speak softly as the three leaned together over the table. "Gryndor told us of the departure of the dypalfar," he said. "How they used the power of the Joining to coordinate so that every member of the race seemed to vanish at once. And how all of them used the machines created by Dzurman to open portals to another world, a plane perhaps of the Netherworld where the dypalfar could live in peace, free from the assaults of their enemies."

Arctoris in particular was looking uneasy, guessing where this might be going; but Liamdor nodded, saying "Yes, yes. Thus is the Lore that has been told by the Chanters from that day to this one. Only those of us who had managed to escape captivity were left behind." Andi fixed them both with a look, hoping to spot their reaction to what he said next.

"And Gryndor told us that here, far beneath Mrzhgradfendz, was one machine that was not destroyed after the dypalfar had fled through its portal. That here, a portal was still open and could be used to travel to the dypalfar's refuge."

Arctoris sat rigid, his worst fears realized. "Who else have you told of this?" he thundered. "Does anyone else know?" Andi started back, shocked at the old alfar's vehemence. Just how big a deal *was* this secret, anyhow? True, he and Meri and Fjuri had been riveted by the discovery – but Mom and the rest of his family at Drakespring Farm had shrugged it off as something not important enough to pursue.

"No one knows but me and Meri and Fjuri," he lied. He was *not* going to get Ghrztum in trouble, after all the troll had done for them. "Plus of course obviously Gryndor told us this story, and he's probably told others about it too. But the way he put it, it was just a story – not Lore, because it had not been passed down to a Chanter from an eyewitness."

Liamdor, considerably calmer than was Arctoris, nodded. "That's right," he said. "Just a story. I suppose that you've heard some wild stories about your own family, eh?" The boy's tale of the legendary deeds performed by his mother and her consorts seemed like a wild story itself, but he was inclined to believe it was true – or at least that the boy had been led to believe it was. He really needed to talk with the boy's mother, and the others who were there!

The old Chanter was making headway toward encouraging Andreas to believe that he'd been led on a wild goose chase by a fanciful tale, when Arctoris suddenly spoke up. He was sitting rigid, and looked pale even for a member of his darkness-dwelling race. He spoke tensely, as if through clenched teeth. "It is true," he said, so quietly that Andi had to lean closer to hear him.

"Arctoris!" Liamdor gasped, alarmed.

"No, no… it is best that he knows the truth," the elder Keeper replied. He fixed Andi with his eyeless stare. "Your Ankhrazana Keeper told you, did he not, that all of Dzurman's machines were destroyed save one?" Andi nodded, intent on what Arctoris was telling him. "Did he also tell you that the machine has an off switch?"

Mind racing, the boy blurted out "then you *haven't* been guarding it for the past three thousand years, preventing a dypalfar party from coming back through to destroy the machine? Why, then, all the secrecy? The society of Keepers? What is the point?"

Liamdor looked fearful, Arctoris insulted. "No," he said coldly and quietly, "we have not been standing guard on an open portal for the past three thousand years. Much of that time, the machine has been turned off and the portal closed. But it has been opened, many times. Over the generations this has been the closest-held secret of the Mirskhrazana, and it is from the ranks of the Keepers that volunteers have been taken – to enter the portal and try to make contact with our enslaved people."

Andi was agog. "And… ?"

"And, none of them has ever come back to report. We don't know what happened to any of them. The plan was to go in

241

silently, to sneak through the corridors of what we presume is a dypalfar city the mirror of this one, and to bring back a sympathetic member of our race with information we could use to plot the final overthrow of the dypalfar. We left the portal open for many days each time, guarding the heavily locked and barred door behind which it sits. There was to be a signal if our agent returned, so we could open the door. But it never came."

"The dypalfar must be aware of the situation then, must know that this machine was not destroyed and their paradise is not safe from invaders," Andi said, working it out.

"Exactly," Arctoris went on. "After many failed attempts, we decided to call a halt to our efforts. We hoped that as generations of dypalfar passed and no further attempts were made to breach their sanctuary, that we would be forgotten and would have better success years later. For most of my lifetime no tries were made, though the Keepers maintained the Lore. We became in truth something of a fraud, doing nothing more than continuing an apparently useless tradition. But we were biding our time."

The old Keeper reached across the table and seized Andi's hand. "I beg you, do not speak of this to any of the Mirskhrazana. If it were widely known what we are trying to do, our chances for success would be ruined forever. Some twenty-three years ago, we opened the portal again and found only a large, empty room. There were some stone furnishings but no carpets or other woven goods, as had been seen by observers when agents were sent through in the past. The door leading out was locked, and could not be opened. We even tried banging on it, prepared to run back through and close the portal if it suddenly burst open. But there was no response. Every few years since then we have tried, and always it has been the same though the dust grows thicker. It is as if no one is there anymore. Or perhaps the dypalfar decided to deal with our incursions by walling off the chamber on which the portal opens."

Liamdor gave his colleague an unreadable look, which was returned by the older alfar. "If you like, I will show you and your sister and friend the portal. Then perhaps you can be satisfied, and return to the Ankhrazana with the true tale." Andi's face brightened. It was disappointing to learn that the way was now closed off, possibly forever (though even stone could be shifted with the right tools). But that the tale of the portal's existence was true, that the portal could be opened at will, that was beyond amazing!

"I would love to see the portal!" he responded with enthusiasm. Arctoris favored him with the sort of the smile the old and wise give to the young and inexperienced.

"Shall we say, tomorrow morning? I will be at work in the Keepers' sanctum, but I can send a runner to lead you and your companions there."

"Terrific!" Andy exclaimed. He was so excited at the prospect, he could hardly imagine sleeping until then. Though he was beginning to get a bit of a headache.

Just then Indinala entered, carrying the cups from which they'd all drunk the ghrztma to the kitchen to be washed. "Oh there you are," she said. "I wondered where you three had gotten off to."

Andi was put on the spot, but Arctoris said smoothly, "I had more questions about the adoption of Andreas's sister, but I didn't wish to discuss it in her hearing. It seemed she was upset earlier by the revelation of how she came to be an orphan." Indinala looked a little woeful, but nodded understandingly. Ghrztum, too, had not been told that it was his adoptive father who had killed his birth mother.

They all left the kitchen together and returned to the living room. "Well, Arctoris said, "I am old and the hour is getting late. I thank you, Skarnoris and Indinala – and you too, Ghrztum – for your hospitality and the chance to converse with your guests. I've invited Andreas and his companions to come and visit at the Keepers' Sanctum tomorrow. There should be a runner here for them fairly early in the morning." Farewells were said, and the two elders went on their way.

"I thought that our visitors might sleep in my room," Ghrztum told his parents. Turning to Andreas he added, "There are three additional stone platform beds in the room where I sleep, though we don't have any more mattresses." "No problem," Andi replied, "we can use our fur bedrolls." While the other guests were taking their leave he had surreptitiously applied some healing magic to himself, and was now feeling a lot better. That drink, ghrztma, had made him feel very odd for a while.

Ghrztum's parents bid them goodnight, and they took turns using the bathroom before retiring to the bedroom where the troll slept when he was at home. His sleeping platform had a leather mattress (stuffed with goat's wool, he said) on it but the others were as bare as any Andi had seen in the several dypalfar cities he'd visited. "So is it true the dypalfar just slept right on the stone without any kind of padding?" he asked Ghrztum. His friend grinned at him.

"That's what Liamdor tells me," he responded. "When we leukalfar took over the city we preferred to use some padding on the stone. Leukalfar aren't as well-padded by nature as the other alfar races are. But supposedly the dypalfar thought that sleeping on a rock-hard bed was good for the back and posture."

As they prepared to lie down, Ghrztum went over to an oil lamp sitting on a small chest of drawers and blew it out. As at Andi's home, there were no ever-burning dypalfar lamps in the bedroom. "I'm going to have to go to work tomorrow morning," their friend rumbled as the four of them lay down and began trying to get comfortable for sleeping. "But maybe after your visit to the Keepers' Sanctum we can spend some more time exploring the city together. There are a lot of places I'd like to show you."

"Sounds great, Ghrztum," Andi said sleepily. "G'night."

Chapter 39: The Dypalfar Portal

In the morning all of them were up bright and early. At least, Andi assumed it was morning. There were no clocks, nor did they have a view of the sky. But from the low hum around them the activity level of Mrzhgradfendz had risen. The leukalfar might be just as comfortable in pitch darkness as they were in daylight (possibly more so), but they had been day-dwellers before the Change and a few thousand years was not much time for evolution to work. The Mirskhrazana maintained a night shift for some jobs that needed to be done around the clock; but most of the tribe's members still worked during the day and slept at night.

Indinala and Skarnoris were up before them, smiling on their visitors, and Skarnoris was in the kitchen preparing breakfast. As in Andi's family, it seemed, the couple shared cooking duties. "Would you like to bathe this morning?" Indinala asked somewhat shyly. A suggestion that someone needed a bath might well be taken the wrong way.

Andi considered. He was used to bathing pretty regularly, with the wonderful facilities at Drakespring House. Fjuri, for whom baths at home usually involved a wooden washtub and kettles of water heated over the fire, didn't mind going for a week or more between baths. Certainly they were all filthy, having been camping out for the better part of a week. It was Meri who piped up first, "Oh yes please, Indinala! I would very much like a bath."

Indinala led the girl, to whom she had taken quite a liking (a baby girl, stillborn some twenty years ago, was probably the main force that had brought her to adopt her son), into the bathroom and showed her how to use the tap. There was a glowing gem-like boss above a spigot. "How hot do you like it?" she asked, and Meri replied "Sort of medium. I've gotten used to hot baths at home." While Andi had been deep in conversation with the two Keepers last night, Meri had been entertaining their hosts with stories of everyday life with her family in Waterdon.

Indinala put her palm on the gem and twisted it to the right. The gem had been glowing a pale blue, but the color changed now to yellow, then orange. Meri watched in fascination, though to her leukalfar sight the color change registered as one of intensity – the light getting brighter as the dial turned. This device had been created by and for the dypalfar, who had color vision. Indinala pushed the boss inward, and water began flowing powerfully out of the tap and into the tub. Its bottom drain was blocked by an intricately decorated dypalfar metal plug.

Indinala put her hand under the running water and nodded, satisfied. "You try it," she told the girl. "See if it's all right." Meri put her hand hesitantly under the water that was flowing out.

"Ooh!" she said. "It's a teeny bit warm."

"Good," the woman replied. "The water will cool as the tub fills, so if it comes out a little too hot from the spout it will be just right when you get in." She handed over a stack of folded cloths. They weren't nearly as luxuriant as the bath linens Meri was used to at home, but they looked like they'd do the job.

Indinala opened the drawer in a small cabinet in the room, and took out a little earthenware bottle with a stopper. "Here is some liquid soap, much nicer than the stuff we use for washing hands. Just push the button to turn off the flow when you have enough water for bathing. Maybe after you're done you can get the boys to wash, too," she suggested slyly. Her own son was a special case, being covered in more-or-less self-cleaning fur; but she had noticed that for some reason males seemed less willing to bathe on a regular basis. She gave the girl a little hug, then left the room.

Some time later all three of the travelers had bathed, washed their hair, and put on clean clothes. The boys were surprised at how much better they felt, now that they'd undergone the ordeal of soaking in hot water and scrubbing themselves down with soap. They were served a nice hot breakfast by their hosts, a sort of porridge into which nuts and fruits had been stirred. The liquid floating atop it, which helped to cool it and thin the consistency, could not possibly be milk even if it looked a lot like it. Andi thought it was best not to ask what it was, a notion Meri and Fjuri were in agreement with.

Just as they had finished eating and were washing their own breakfast bowls, a young leukalfar boy arrived at the apartment.

Indinala and Skarnoris were making ready to leave for their work with the Gleaners, which again today would involve trekking far down into the city's mushroom gardens, and cheerfully greeted the youngster after opening the door to him. "So you're running today, Shindor!" Skarnoris said. "Have you eaten?" Parents of a child were of course responsible for seeing them fed, clothed, and raised up in the traditions of the tribe. But with their communal economy, any tribe member – especially a Gleaner – might look to the welfare of a hungry child.

The boy, who looked to be close to Meri's age (and showed some interest in her) delivered a grin full of sharp-pointed teeth. "I had breakfast a couple of hours ago, Gleaner. But I wouldn't mind a snack, if you're offering!" Runner duty fell to all young members of the Mirskhrazana, once they were old enough to know their way around the labyrinthine city yet still too young to have joined one of the societies. It was a taxing activity that could work up quite an appetite.

Skarnoris smiled back at the lad, and produced a sort of roll-up: one of those puffy griddle cakes, like the ones served at dinner last night, rolled with nuts and dried icefruit into a cylinder you could eat with one hand while you were walking (or running). "I have to go and consult with Omondis so I can plan my next foraging run," Ghrztum told Andi, "but I'll be free this afternoon. After you're finished visiting with the Keepers I hope you can return here so I can show you more of the city."

Andi smiled up at the troll. "That would be great, Ghrztum. We probably won't be able to stay here very long as there are other places we're supposed to be, but we can certainly spend the rest of today here and leave in the morning tomorrow." Ghrztum's furry face fell a little as he realized his intriguing new friends were planning to leave so soon.

"But we can come back again," Andi promised him. "Now that I have Mrzhgradfendz on my map, I can go from my house in Waterdon to the front door of the city in what seems like a few seconds, whenever I want."

"And have a lengthy discussion with Berandis, no doubt" the troll remarked with a half-smile.

"Maybe I'll just get him to send a runner," Andi suggested. "To Arctoris, or one of the other Mirskhrazana we've met on our visit. I think that in the future, leukalfar people will be getting to know more of the Sky People and realizing we're not all bad – and maybe some people of the Mirskhrazana could come home with me so my own people can learn the leukalfar are not just skulkers at the bottoms of dark caves."

Indinala and Skarnoris wondered at this speech, as did Ghrztum. The boy was right. This was not just a jolly visit with some chance-found, unexpected friends. This was very possibly the beginning of a new era, one that would change their lives forever. They all hoped that change would be a positive one. Their lives were not bad, and they were content with them. But there was certainly room for improvement!

They all parted at the door, Indinala and Skarnoris going off together toward the corridors that led down to the mushroom beds, while Ghrztum headed for the Gleaners' central storerooms and Shindor led the three visitors off in still another direction. He was a little goggle-eyed at the tall Sky People he was guiding, but Meri was familiar enough and it was mostly her he engaged in conversation as he led them down stairways and ramps, going ever downward.

Shindor was the first leukalfar boy nearly her own age that Meri had yet had a chance to talk with, during the short time since she had been reintroduced to the people of her birth and learned their language. He babbled nearly nonstop, proudly directing the visitors' attention to points of interest and discussing random details of life within the warren that was his home.

Leukalfar kids had relatively little chance to interact with their peers, as there were so few of them – but they sought each other out, creating their own little society within the one formed by their parents and ancestors stretching back for centuries. Among people with lives so long, childhood and adolescence was a brief, vivid phenomenon.

For some time now, they had seen few other people moving around the corridors. This wing of the sprawling edifice was only for the housing of the Dzurman Device and those who tended it, and no others but the society of Keepers had business here. At last they came to an imposing set of double doors in the usual elegantly-ornamented dypalfar style.

The doors were locked, and Shindor rapped upon them in a pattern of long and short sequences that suggested a code. Andi, intrigued by anything secret, automatically committed them to memory. Slowly, the doors opened before them and they were greeted by a pair of armed and armored leukalfar who looked more like members of the Sentries than of the Keepers. Keepers often started as Sentries, Andi recalled Ghrztum mentioning.

"I'll leave you now," Shindor told them. "When you are ready to return to the residence of Skarnoris and Indinala, just have them ring. If I'm not on some other mission I'll come and get you again." He grinned cheekily, a strange expression on the usually impassive leukalfar features. Andi smiled at the boy, and slipped him a gold guilder. Likely the coin of the empire was not in use here, where everyone shared all that was needed for life; but it was a pretty, shiny thing and he thought Shindor might treasure it.

"Thank you, Andreas!" the boy cried, seemingly very pleased indeed with his "tip." With that he took his leave, as energetic as he'd been when they started their journey.

"I like him," Meri informed her brother after the boy had dashed out of sight. "Maybe we could take him home for a visit?"

"We'd have to ask his parents of course," Andi pointed out. "But we'll see. There's going to be a lot of visiting back and forth in the future, I'm sure."

"You're expected," one of the guards told Andi. "Follow me, please." These fellows were the least expressive members of the Mirskhrazana they'd yet met, seeming neither curious about the visitors nor hostile toward them. Down a corridor and around a couple of bends they entered a spacious room with a collection of interesting equipment and machine parts stacked on shelves along one end of it. A middle-aged leukalfar was working at a stone bench, and on the far side of the room was a dypalfar metal desk at which Arctoris was seated.

As they approached, led by the guard, Andi almost tripped over a little dypalfar bug that came whizzing past them, its eight jointed metal legs ticking on the stone floor as it scuttled along. He was astounded. Since they'd arrived here, they had seen no sign of any dypalfar automatons. While the Drakespring kids had not encountered any of these in hostile situations, they had spent many happy hours at the old elf Miurlion's dypalfar museum, which shared a roof with the eorl's palace Dypendwelve in Alfenstein. There they had seen every type of dypalfar automaton yet discovered, all deactivated and safe to explore.

It stood to reason, Andi figured, that after three thousand years of constant occupation by the Mirskhrazana the city would have been completely freed of hostile automatons. There had to have been a finite number of them left behind, and one by one they would have been attacked and destroyed by the new residents. Yet here was one intact, in excellent condition – yet not trying to attack them.

Arctoris rose to greet them. He seemed to be in an excellent, almost a jovial mood this morning. "Welcome!" he called to them. Noticing the interest with which all three kids had focused on the scuttling mechanical bug, he smiled. "You're wondering about the automaton, I'll bet," he said. "Let me introduce you to my colleague, Gylabris."

Dismissing the guard back to his post, Arctoris led them across to the far end of the large room where the small leukalfar they'd spotted on their way in was bent over the stone workbench. "Gylabris," Arctoris said expansively, "I'd like you to meet our young visitors." He beckoned to each of them in turn. "This is Andreas Drakespring and his sister Merelle Drakespring. They and their friend Fjurbund Steadfast have all journeyed here from Waterdon to see Mrzhgradfendz, and to learn of the secrets we keep here." The elf, who somehow gave the impression of being myopic (a good trick without eyes!) peered at them in something approaching alarm.

"Er!" he said. "Um, glad to meet you, I'm sure. You must excuse me, I am very busy. Insko!" he commanded, and the dypalfar bug that had been scurrying around the room rushed over to stand before him. "Deactivate," he commanded the creature, and it froze in place. The glowing blue gem in the center of its "head" faded to gray.

"Wow!" Andi declared, dazzled by the trick. "How did you *do* that?" Gylabris preened under the boy's enthusiasm, and from being taciturn and fearful he became talkative, pleased to have an audience.

"It has taken many years," he said, "but I have finally figured out how to get them to take orders in Leukalfar. They were all designed to understand Dypalfar originally, of course, but though we probably knew the language three thousand years ago it seems everyone has forgotten. Not much call for it, eh?"

He picked up the device that he was working on at the moment, turning it from side to side so that Andi could admire its intricacies. "They were all destroyed, for the most part. Broken because they were attacking people, what else could we do? But the pieces remained. It has been my life's work to gather the parts of these automatons and teach myself how to put them back together, how to 're-program' them so that they would not attack us, and could be controlled. It's all in here..." he said, pointing at a recess within the gleaming carapace where a magical essence vial sat. "It's not just mechanism, it's magic!"

Andi and Fjuri were both fascinated, and could happily have spent the next several hours talking with Gylabris and learning the secrets of the automatons. But they were here on a mission even more compelling, and one that soon brought them back to the reason they had come here. "Thank you, Gylabris," Andi told the elf. "We would very much like to learn more about your work. But first, there's something else we need to do." How could they only stay here another day? But if they didn't get out of here soon, Mom and Lifa were going to catch them. He knew they would, inevitably – but he was eager to postpone the confrontation. He still thought he must have been half-insane to go on this expedition, but it certainly seemed to him as if it had been worthwhile.

"I look forward to it," Gylabris said. Now he was beaming, happy beyond words to have been treated with the respect he knew he deserved – even if it was only by some very strange young men of the Sky People. His own colleagues mostly dismissed him as a harmless nut, his little automatons curiosities with no practical uses. Just wait until he got the robon working!

Arctoris put his hands together and nodded at them, saying "Indeed. If you will come this way?" Though either of the boys was head and shoulders taller than him, the old elf had more than enough gravitas to dominate the situation and they fell meekly into line behind him. It wasn't until the three travelers had been well underway this morning, under the guidance of Shindor, that Andi had softly told Fjuri (and later, Meri) what Arctoris had promised him, the reason for this trip to the Keepers' Sanctum.

Though they had already blabbed to Ghrztum about the possible existence of the portal, Andi felt he must keep his promise to the two Keepers to tell no one else about it. Let Ghrztum think, for now at least, that the rumored portal had not existed after all and the secret the Keepers held was something else entirely.

They went down several corridors, wherein they found a few Keepers going about whatever business they engaged in – since they were not required to stand guard on an open portal, as Andi had first believed. Some seemed to be involved in weapons training, others in recitations of Lore. Likely Liamdor had an apprentice or two for the job of Chanter, and would be training them here. At last they came to another set of tall double doors, twins to the ones through which they'd entered the Sanctum. Arctoris produced a ring of keys from a pocket in his robe and inserted first one, then another into paired keyholes.

The doors swung open, and the group found themselves confronted by half a dozen guards. They had snapped to attention when the doors opened, but Andi could see disappointment on their faces. They must have the most boring duty in the tribe, he mused – standing guard day after day on a machine that was only turned on once every few years, from what Arctoris had said.

The guards all saluted Arctoris and greeted him respectfully, looking at his companions with a mixture of curiosity and unease. They must be all right, if the boss was escorting them here. But they'd never seen a stranger-looking bunch. What was this unfamiliar girl of their race doing with two hulking Sky People youths?

"These visitors are ambassadors from the Ankhrazana, and from the Sky People of Waterdon," the old Keeper said to the room in general. "They learned about the portal from the Chanter of the Ankhrazana, so I am showing it to them. This should just take a few minutes." They walked to the far side of the medium-size room, where a somewhat smaller single door stood barred.

One of the guards lifted the bar for Arctoris, and he then took out his keys again and opened the lock. He gestured for Andi, Fjuri, and Meri to walk in ahead of him, then turned before going through the door himself. "Bar it behind me. You know the code, and do not open the door unless it's given. Understand?"

They nodded at him, with a chorus of "Yes, sir!". The rare times when the portal was in use were the most excitement they got in their working lives, and they'd been well drilled about procedures.

The room was smaller than Andi had expected. This must have been a bit of a bottleneck three thousand years ago, if the dypalfar were to have tried to move their entire population and all their possessions, livestock, and slaves through the portal in a single night. Likelier, he thought, was that the portal had been in operation for years as scouts and construction crews had gone into the new world, preparing the way for the day when the last of their race would leave Terris forever. It must have been as closely-guarded a secret among the dypalfar as it now was for the Mirskhrazana.

There was only the one door into the stone-built room, and at the far end of it an enormous machine stood. Built all of gleaming dypalfar metal and looking far more complex than even the largest

of the automatons Andi had seen, the bulk of it sat on the left side
– up against the stone wall on the far side of the chamber. Pipes
and bars went across the top at a height of perhaps fifteen feet, and
more of the machine was joined on the far side leaving an opening
close to twenty feet across between the two sections.

Though the room was smaller, the machine itself was a lot
bigger than they'd expected. Rendering one of these inoperable
would clearly have been a major job, not like stomping a dypalfar
bug into scrap metal. The three kids were staring at the machine,
trying to take it all in, as Arctoris walked past them to what
appeared to be a control panel on the left side.

"Here it is," he told them with a hint of pride in his voice
(though certainly he personally had had nothing to do with the
machine's creation), "the last of the devices of Dzurman. You can
say many bad things about our former masters, but I think you
have to give them credit for the quality of their workmanship. This
has been working flawlessly, powered by an unknown energy
source, for over three thousand years."

So had many thousands of devices in dypalfar ruins all over
Iscandia, but the kids were still impressed. No other dypalfar
devices they had seen possessed the power to create a rift between
worlds. Arctoris reached into an inner pocket of his robe, and
produced an object that was familiar to all three of his companions:
a dypalfar attunement sphere. "Hey, my mom has one of those at
home," Andi remarked. Arctoris gave him an appraising look.

"Really. How very surprising," the old Keeper replied. "This
one, of course, is only the key to unlock the control panel. One
must still know the sequence to open the gate – and a different one
to close it."

He touched the sphere in four specific spots, and the
machine's control panel came to life with glowing lights and
buttons. "How did the Mirskhrazana find out how to turn the
machine on and off, then?" Andi asked, his curiosity piqued.

"According to the story as passed down by our Chanters,"
Arctoris replied, "there were two dypalfar volunteers who came
through to close the portal and destroy the machine. One of them

had the sphere on his body, which we found after the party of our ancestors who stormed the door and broke into the chamber had killed him."

"The other, it seems, lost his nerve and begged for his life. He provided us with the codes and in exchange, we let him go free – into exile, alone, on this island. Perhaps he built a boat and went to the mainland, or perhaps he was eaten by one of your friend Ghrztum's early ancestors. It's not reported what became of him, but one thing is certain – he was a traitor to his people. The dypalfar, it seems, were ever treacherous."

As he spoke, Arctoris had been pushing the glowing buttons on the control panel in a particular sequence. Though Andi was paying attention to the story, his eyes followed the pattern and he created a mnemonic, a mental image, to help him commit it to memory. He had no idea what use he might make of the information, but you never could tell. Mom and Papa Erik were always saying that learning something was never a waste of time.

When the sequence was completed, the control panel glowed with green lights all across the top of it. "It takes a moment to power up," Arctoris explained, as they heard a deep rumbling sound that started low before rising higher and higher in pitch. "One can only imagine what energies must be needed to create this rift and hold it in place, or where those energies are coming from. But once the connection is made…"

Even as he spoke, the stone wall showing in the area between the two sections of the device vanished as the space filled with coruscating light that swirled wildly in colors of purple, red, yellow and green before steadying into a slightly flickering sheet of energy. The view through it, though distorted, showed a room similar to this one but two or three times as large, with a pair of doors visible at the far end. There was no sign of any life.

"Go ahead," Arctoris urged them, "walk through. You can tell the Ankhrazana, and your people in Waterdon, that you actually stood in the dypalfar world. Take a look around the room and you will see it is as I have told you. The portal opens onto a part of the dypalfar's sanctuary that has been abandoned, and possibly walled off."

Walking into a dusty, long-abandoned room little different from many they'd seen in dypalfar ruins throughout Iscandia didn't sound very exciting. But still, it was in another world, the paradise the dypalfar had found for themselves. And perhaps someday, Andi thought, they could return here with a small army of stonemasons and warriors, and break through whatever obstructions the dypalfar had used to barricade this back door.

So, simultaneously eager and tentative, Andi, Meri, and Fjuri stepped into the portal and through it. There was only the slightest tingling as they walked through, as you might get if you were standing near a lightning strike. Even the stone floor, though of a different design, was the same height as the one they'd left behind so there was no stumbling. After walking a few feet into the room they turned back to look at Arctoris, dimly seen in the chamber they'd left behind. "Go ahead, look around!" he urged, waving them on.

Sure, why not? Andi wanted to study this room in detail, learn everything it could tell him. And who knows, perhaps they might find some object he could take home as a souvenir? He didn't think anybody would mind. They walked on down the room's central corridor. It was flanked by stone counters similar to those they'd seen throughout Mrzhgradfendz (and in other dypalfar cities, as well).

One of them had a number of small objects spread out on it, and Andi went over to it to examine them. Some of them were unfamiliar, others as prosaic as plates and cups. And were those crumbs of… food? Meanwhile, Meri had gone closer to the walls to admire a tapestry that was hanging there. She had not been there when Arctoris had told Andi no cloth had been seen in the room, so did not realize anything was amiss until she heard a gasp.

She turned her head to the sound and found herself looking at two largish, bearded elves. They were sitting cross-legged on the stone floor behind one of the counters, and had not been visible to the three intruders while they were walking down the central aisle.

They were wearing armor reminiscent of the dypalfar armor Mama and Papa Erik often made, and they had a meal spread out between them.

They were both staring at her in shock from pale blue eyes, and then one of them spoke to her in an unfamiliar tongue. Across the room, Andi and Fjuri began moving toward the sound of his voice. When he got no response, he switched to accented leukalfar: "Slave? What you doing here?" Slave?

As Andi and Fjuri converged on the spot where Meri was standing paralyzed by fear and confusion, the elves (guards, they must be) were surging to their feet and drawing short swords, preparing to advance on the little leukalfar girl and these two who looked like men were supposed to – though no living dypalfar had ever seen one in person.

The three of them were utterly unarmored and each carried no more than a dagger by way of weapons. Andi had been trained in some of the most lethal battle magic, but he had never killed a sentient being and wasn't anxious to start doing so – even if, in the tales he loved so much, all three of his parents and Fjuri's as well had killed dozens of bandits, renegade mages, and other human foes.

So, he did the thing he hoped would buy them enough time to get out of there: he cried "Kraf-Luft-Struung-Wund!" The dragon spell sent the two dypalfar (he assumed) guards tumbling end over end along the corridor between the wall and the stone counters – in the direction of the doors. Then he grabbed Meri by the hand. "Back to the portal! Let's go!" he shouted. The three of them dashed for the far end of the room, only to be brought up short in front of a blank stone wall. The portal was gone.

Chapter 40: On the Scent

"Over here," Anja called, from partway down the slope. They'd been following the kids' trail all morning. The confrontation with the bear had left its marks, though the animal itself appeared to have wandered away and they had not met it. Further on was evidence of a lunch break, which the rescue party thought seemed like a good idea. From the evidence the kids had been eating more of the walrus they'd apparently killed before leaving Walrus Cove to follow this trail, but the adults had come much better provisioned and were able to eat slightly stale, definitely cold sandwiches wrapped in waxed paper. No fire needed, and they were soon on the move again.

Now once again the tracks were confused as if something had disrupted the young adventurers' journey. Bernadette saw blood in the snow and her own blood ran cold, for a moment; until she spotted the stiffly frozen, blood-smeared corpse of an enormous snow cat lying where it had fallen some days before. Little scavengers had been at it, and it was looking much the worse for wear.

After Lifa and Bernadette had inspected the area in more detail and picked up the trail again, convinced that the cat had not laid a claw on any of their kids, the party continued on its way. This was why Bernadette wanted to stay on the trail. Who could say what might have befallen their loved ones, as they hiked along this perilous path toward the unknown dypalfar city?

They saw no more signs of conflict as the kids' footprints ran straight along the beaten path. Tracking in snow was certainly a lot easier than doing so on bare rock. The party stayed alert, as it was clear there were many dangers on this island. Lars reported he'd caught a glimpse of a lone wolf through the trees, paralleling their course; but it must have decided six full grown humans were beyond its ambitions.

"I think this is an example of what happens when there's a land bridge that later becomes submerged," Andrion said to Bernadette as they walked along. She was one of the few people in his life who always seemed to welcome his scholarly lectures, one of her qualities that had cemented his love for her early in their relationship. A powerful mage he might be, and a well-muscled man of action as well; but at heart he was a man who loved knowledge above all else except his wife, his brother Erik, and their children.

"Everything we have seen so far looks just like members of the same species on the northern part of the mainland," he pointed out as a surprised rabbit dodged across their path and fled up the hill from them for a few dozen yards before scrambling into some dense bushes. "That must mean that this island was part of the mainland, or at least reachable from it, until relatively recently. It hasn't been isolated long enough for the creatures that came here to evolve into different forms."

Bernadette smiled at him and stepped closer to give him a squeeze. Andrion was a still a very good-looking man, but it was his mind she truly loved him for. That and his surprising emotional vulnerability. "I do believe you're right dear," she replied as they continued along the trail – all the while staying alert for threats. "Do you think perhaps the land bridge was still there when the dypalfar occupied this Mrzhgradfendz?"

He continued walking, eyes on the trail as he considered. "It's possible, I suppose," he answered at last. "But three thousand years is just an eye-blink in geologic time. It might well be that the place was already an island when they chose it for the site of their city. Perhaps they hoped its isolation would protect them. But the Norsemen, and others among their enemies, are no strangers to seafaring. And that's not a bad harbor down there where we came in."

Conversation ceased for a while as the trail rose more steeply, forcing them to use their breath for climbing. Lifa, older than Bernadette by a few years and more sedentary in her daily life, found herself puffing and falling to the rear. Damn, she thought. It was so infuriating to have her legs run off by her daughter, not to mention Andrion – a few years older than she was.

But he'd been working at maintaining his physical condition for years, whereas she had just been doing the usual sorts of things a Waterdon housewife did: cooking, cleaning, laundry, sewing, running up and down the steps to Wyrmshalla on errands… She was not in *bad* shape, but there was no denying she was not the woman she'd been seventeen years ago. She hoped to hell she was up to the task, if push came to shove on this quest to bring back her only son.

The sun was well on its way toward the western horizon when the party came over one last rise to find the tracks they were following (along with the trail on which they were marked) veering off to the east and heading downward. They soon arrived at the abandoned mine site, and followed the kids' tracks toward the sagging door of the mine entrance.

The tracks went in and more came out, so that meant they were not going to find their offspring here. But Bernadette would be willing to bet they'd spent the night here – what, two nights ago? She had to assume that with Meri along, they would not have been able to make as good time hiking as had she and her party of adults. Meri's shorter legs would have slowed their pace, and her child's lack of stamina would have forced more frequent halts for rest. Her heart ached as she imagined her little stranger out here struggling to keep up with her big brother and his even bigger friend. Oh Andi, why did you do it?

After some consultation the members of the rescue party concluded that it made no sense to push on further today, as this was likely the only decent shelter to be had for hours in any direction. So they went inside. Bernadette furnished magical light until torches were found, and they saw plenty of evidence of recent occupation by the three missing members of their clans.

The party used the same campsite the kids had used, lighting a fire for warmth and comfort (and to boil water for tea) but once again making a meal out of the stores they had brought along. They talked long into the evening before sleeping: about the kids, about what they might find when they finally arrived at the dypalfar city, about life in the Canyons of Stone. This last diversion was brought to them courtesy of Mothris, who for almost the first time in his life had become the center of attention for a group of adults. He found the experience unsettling but, ultimately, enjoyable.

In the morning, washing down trail bread with a cup of tea, Bernadette briefly considered going dragon and flying up to Mrzhgradfendz with Mothris on her back. His abilities with the leukalfar tongue should keep them out of trouble long enough for her to change back to human (and into her clothes), then fast-travel back to this mine (which had appeared on her map as soon as they'd arrived here, she had discovered) and collect the rest of the party.

Then it occurred to her that while this ploy might assuage her anxiety to find her wayward children, it would not actually speed things up. In fact, it would presumably slow them down. The map would deliver her and Mothris back here, and return the group to the dypalfar city, in the amount of time it would take to walk here and back. She sighed. The map did not take into account a map holder's ability to fly, she'd learned. And she could scarcely airlift the entire party. So they might as well walk it, and be able to see by the trail exactly what the children had encountered on their trek.

The path they'd been following was gone, and the tracks began moving across country in the direction of the dypalfar city to their north. How fortunate, Andrion thought, as he shouldered his pack and set off, that no snow had fallen since the kids had come through here. He was also glad of a general lack of blizzard activity right now, come to think of it.

They had been walking for several hours, following the clear tracks of their quarry, when at the juncture of a small stream and an even smaller one they saw the kids' tracks veer sharply up the hill, along the banks of the rivulet that dashed down the hillside. About halfway up it they began to see blood, but there were other tracks here – deer or elk – and no one was worried. "I'll bet they didn't pack enough food," Bernadette puffed as she and her party forged up the hill, "so they've probably been foraging." She and Andrion exchanged a glance, both thankful that all of their children had been taught to hunt.

The tracks of children and cervid crested the hill and continued across a flat area where the snow sat deep. Meri's tracks disappeared for a while, probably as she was carried by one of the boys. The party climbed another slope, and suddenly they all stopped dead as they beheld the unmistakable, enormous tracks of a snow troll.

The blood drained from Bernadette's face as she beheld the evidence of the confrontation. Andrion too went pale beneath his tan. A much larger pool of blood had formed at the spot where the children had met the troll. But, wait... Truthfully, Bernadette and Andrion would be surprised if the combined might of their son and his powerfully-built friend Fjurbund had not been enough to defeat a snow troll. They were large, but they were just wild creatures with no weaponry beyond what nature had given them and a ferocity that was not matched by any great intelligence. Yet, what had happened here? There was no sign of a battle...

In short order, the party followed the trail and began to piece together events that made no sense. Andi, Fjuri, and Meri, in pursuit of a wounded deer, had met a troll. They had all stood for a while over the immobile and bleeding deer, and then they had all walked off together. Their trail led to a scene of slaughter, but Bernadette, Andrion, and Lifa had already concluded that it was none of their children who had bled here. It appeared the now-dead deer had been gutted and bled, probably skinned as well. Frozen gobbets of viscera were scattered around, along with the tracks of creatures like wolves and foxes.

The trail continued to a broad ledge, with a tunnel leading to a very nice cave. I wouldn't have minded using this for a dragon nest, Bernadette thought irrelevantly, except for the temperature... The inner cavern showed signs of frequent use, though nobody was in residence at the moment. "I'll bet the kids spent the night here," Andrion said. The rest of them agreed. It was only mid-afternoon, and a look at the map convinced Bernadette that they should be able to reach Mrzhgradfendz by nightfall, if they pushed on now.

"Look," she said, pointing to a double line grooved in the snow. In amid the tracks were the footprints of the troll, and over them the footprints of Andi and Fjuri.

"I don't know how it's possible," Bernadette said, "but I think that the troll was not an adversary. It seems to have teamed up with the kids and taken them, along with a heavily-laden sled of some kind, through the snow in the direction of the city." They had never heard of anyone being able to tame a troll, but somehow it must have happened. Maybe the leukalfar had that magic Andrion had read about, the spell that would bind wild creatures as friends and defenders.

"I'm for pushing on," Lifa said, ferocity shining on her still-beautiful features. The rest of them, even Mothris (who as the junior member of the group, had often felt as if he were just along for the ride), agreed – and they began following the plain trail that would, they all expected, take them to Mrzhgradfendz.

It was a longer trip than they'd hoped, and they were forced to stop for rest and food a couple of times along the way. Their constant motion kept them warm, but maintaining this pace required a lot of fuel. Even pulling trail bread from their pouches and munching on it as they moved, washing it down with water from the skins they kept close to their bodies lest they freeze, was not enough. Lifa was well into her forties, Andrion nearly fifty. They could not push on without some rest.

Thus sunset was not far off as the party approached the city of Mrzhgradfendz, shining above them on its hilltop and glinting in the rays of the westering sun. They all paused for a moment to take it in, hardly believing they were finally near their goal. Now an entirely new set of problems was theirs to enjoy.

"Let's keep moving," Bernadette said. The sight of the city had only renewed her determination to reach it before nightfall, and Lifa felt the same. To hell with what reception they would receive on their arrival – let's get this over with! The long northern dusk was still on the land as they approached the city entrance. The place looked deserted. The party gathered before the front doors, conferring briefly before trying to open them. Had there been any difficulty, Andrion could have had them open in a second or two; but they yielded and swung inward without any magical intervention.

In front of them, two astonished guards gaped at the party that had pushed in through the doors they guarded. Before a couple of days ago, there had been no one through those doors that was unknown to them during the time either of them had been alive. Now, it seemed, the Sky People were invading in force – and these ones were *not* accompanied by a familiar member of their tribe. They also appeared to be large, heavily armed, and armored.

Mothris was pushed to the front. This was his moment, time to do his bit before the alarm was sounded. "Greetings," he said, calling up the speech he had memorized. "These people and I have come to Mrzhgradfendz as emissaries of the Ankhrazana. We are seeking Andreas and Merelle Drakespring, and the Sky People boy Fjurbund Steadfast."

Nobody had drawn weapons, and Berandis (so *close* to the end of his shift, too!) suspected they would not, just yet. He turned to the junior guard at his side, and said "Call runners. I need Arctoris, and send somebody for Ghrztum as well." Inandis ran for the nearest doorway as if his life depended on it.

Chapter 41: Arctoris

Arctoris turned toward the barred door and stepped to it, calling to his mind the complicated series of knocks that would signal the guards on the far side to open it. Behind him the device of Dzurman was silent and dead: no lights showing, the stone wall between its pillars nothing but a stone wall.

After he'd completed the sequence he cried out, "Open up! Hurry!" in moments the guards on the far side of the door had removed the bar and unlocked the door. His was not the only set of keys to the doors in this, the innermost sanctum of the society of Keepers. As the startled guards opened the door before him (the keyhole on the inside had long been filled in) he stepped through, saying "Dypalfar! They came through the doors and captured the visitors!"

His audience was in shock. Most of them were not that old, and in all their lifetimes there had never been anything on the far side of the portal but an empty room. Arctoris had them half convinced the dypalfar had launched an offensive, and would soon be battering down their doors. They hastened to lock and bar it behind the elder Keeper as he came out into the anteroom.

Arctoris had not lingered long enough to learn that dypalfar guards had indeed returned to the room on which the ancient portal opened. In all his many years on Terris the place had remained lifeless, and he had no reason to expect that to have changed. As soon as the three visitors had moved a little distance from the portal, he had shut down the machine. All he knew was that he had eliminated a threat to his power, to the very way of life his tribe had enjoyed for nearly three thousand years.

He regretted that they had been so young, these strange intruders in his city. And perhaps he felt a pang as he considered their death agonies, trapped in that small room without food or water. But what were the lives of three strangers, who had come here uninvited, compared with the wellbeing of the Mirskhrazana and the comfortable lifestyle they had enjoyed these past millennia? They had a system that worked, and Andreas Drakespring and his companions would have brought destruction to everything they knew. Now, they were gone – and life would go on as before. It would be years, perhaps decades, before the portal was opened again – and those he had trapped on the other side would be nothing but dust.

Chapter 42: Questions

Bernadette, Andrion, Lifa, Anja and Lars paced around the entryway to Mrzhgradfendz, impatient for answers. "Ask him if they've seen the kids!" Bernadette commanded Mothris. Berandis had held his ground, though it was clear these people could have swept him aside with no effort had they a mind to do so. Inandis, scarcely more than a boy, returned in a couple of minutes, panting, to report that runners had been sent. At this hour, likely both Arctoris and Ghrztum were at supper, and it might take a while for them to arrive.

Berandis shuddered at the young leukalfar visitor's question, clearly a result of a command from that smallish but fierce-looking red-haired Sky People woman. He did not relish breaking the news to these people that the ones they sought were lost. He'd admitted them through this door only a couple of days before, but the word had gone out around midday yesterday: the three young visitors had sadly fallen victim to a freak accident while visiting the mysterious Keepers' Sanctum. Secrecy surrounded everything about the society of Keepers and their secluded area of the city, but rumor said the three youngsters had vanished without a trace in a brilliant flash of light – not even dust remaining.

Ghrztum had been devastated. It was he who had found the foreigners wandering in the woods south of the city, who had befriended them and brought them with him when he returned home after his most recent foraging expedition. The troll, whom many younger members of the Mirskhrazana were coming to think of as just a somewhat different fellow tribesman, lived with his parents not that far from the entry – and he was the first to arrive.

He'd outrun the young girl who'd been sent to bring him here, arriving out of breath and staring at the group of people who stood in the entryway. Emotion nearly swamped him as he beheld them. Beyond a doubt, the red-haired woman and the tall, brown-eyed man must be the parents of his friend Andreas. And the dark-haired (though now silver-streaked) woman with the deep blue eyes must be the mother of Fjurbund. Andreas had not mentioned to him that he and his companions had run away from home, that their parents might be out looking for them. But now that he saw them standing there, it became obvious. How could he not have realized it?

For their part, the six members of the rescue party who had come so far and so fast were riveted at the sight of a full-grown snow troll, slung about with leather harness, staring at them with tears welling up in his dark eyes. Then he spoke, and their amazement grew. He addressed Mothris, who he expected would be able to understand him. He had never met a member of the leukalfar race who did not speak the leukalfar tongue.

"I'm sorry, so... sorry. I didn't realize that your children were here without approval." Ghrztum hung his head, tears running down into the fur on his cheeks. Mothris, aghast, translated. Bernadette shoved aside the issue of a civilized troll who spoke the leukalfar tongue, focusing instead on *what* he had said. "So sorry?" Tears? What had happened to her children?!

While Ghrztum, Mothris, Berandis and the five Sky People visitors were laboriously piecing together the events of the past couple of days, Arctoris arrived on the heels of Shindor. The young runner had been tagged for the duty of fetching the old Keeper, and had run like the wind down the many corridors to the elder's comfortable residence. Arctoris, riveted and horrified by the news, had come here as swiftly as his old bones could carry him. He was now having trouble catching his breath.

Apoldros forfend! These could be none other than the parents of young Andreas, and the older woman looked like she might be the mother of Fjurbund though he saw no likely candidates for the boy's father among the group. Disaster seemed to be piling on disaster since those accursed youngsters had arrived, and now his carefully-constructed explanation for their disappearance was teetering on the edge of destruction.

Grief and despair were battering at Bernadette's mind, trying to find their way in and destroy her. Could her children have really come all this way safely, only to die in a "freak accident"? A wall of disbelief was her defense. Though terror that the story might be true threatened to engulf her, she presented a face of white-faced anger to the old leukalfar who was wearing what looked like some kind of ceremonial robes. Mothris was still talking, translating what the troll was saying. This fellow who had just come up was Arctoris the Keeper, whatever that was, and he was the source of the story about the kids having been "vaporized."

Andrion put an arm around her as she turned to face the newcomer, who from the respect he was being accorded must be some kind of authority here. Looking up at her husband, she saw his face was pale, his expression bleak. Gritting her teeth, Bernadette told him in an undertone, "Don't believe it for a moment! Somebody is lying here, and I think it's *him*." She gestured slightly toward Arctoris. The expression that had passed over his face for a moment as he came in and saw them had been one of panic.

"Mothris," Bernadette demanded, her inability to communicate directly with these people infuriating her still more, "ask this Arctoris exactly what happened, and when." There was an exchange in leukalfar that went on between the leukalfar youth and the elder for a couple of minutes. Mothris face was contorted in grief, as he heard what the old Keeper had to tell.

But when he turned to face Bernadette, Andrion, and the rest of the rescue party, his face had hardened. "He says that Andreas, Merelle, and Lifa's son Fjurbund (whom Mothris had never met, though Andreas had talked about him) were welcomed here as guests. The troll there, his name is Ghrztum, met them out in the woods by where the deer was killed, and took them home with him. He's a member of the tribe, it seems, though I assume he's adopted. Then after Andreas talked with him night before last, Arctoris invited the kids to come visit in the special part of the city where only the Keepers are allowed to go. That was yesterday."

Bernadette seized on that. "Keepers?" she asked. More back and forth between Mothris and Arctoris, then the boy reported "He says they are one of the societies within the tribe. They are the ones that train the Chanters, and they are also the keepers of something down there at the bottom of the city that's a big secret. He can't tell me what it is, on account of his vows." After another glance at Arctoris, the young leukalfar added "I think he's lying about something."

This made no sense. If the Keepers' work was so secret they could tell no one, why would the old man have invited the kids down there for a tour? They were children! What was to stop them from blabbing about everything they'd seen to the next person who struck up a friendly conversation? Unless... maybe there was only *one* big secret locked up behind doors, and it had been all right to show the visitors the rest of the operation... One big secret, like maybe a portal to the dypalfar paradise?

Andrion's mind was running in the same channels Bernadette's was, and he bent to say quietly to Mothris, "Ask him if the secret they are guarding is the last remaining portal to the dypalfar world." That story again! Mothris hadn't been nearly as convinced as Andreas had that Gryndor's story had been anything more than a tale. But then he didn't have Andreas' long association with magic maps and their properties.

Mothris relayed the request to Arctoris, and the result was startling. The pale old leukalfar's face flushed, then grew even paler and contorted in fury. "Silence!" he roared. "You must not speak of this, here in the entryway to the city." He looked around at the intruders, fairly quivering with rage (though fear was certainly an element of it). "Come with me, all of you. We must talk in private."

The numbers of free leukalfar living in hiding within Mrzhgradfendz had been large compared with those in other cities, but they had still been far fewer than the dypalfar who had been its official inhabitants. Millennia later their population had grown but was still not enough to use all the space available to them. Arctoris stalked off down a corridor to an empty room nearby that he sometimes used if he needed to be working closer to the city's entrance.

His quarters far below were much more convenient to the Keepers' sanctum, but he didn't want to have to travel all the way back there if his work kept him in the upper levels for a period of days. It had a bed, a washstand, and some other amenities including a fireplace. It was cold and noisy up here, compared with the comforts further down.

He unlocked the door and ushered them inside, then bade them to sit. His mind was racing. His fellow Keepers had all been told that the dypalfar were guarding the portal again, and that the young visitors had been taken and presumably killed. Furthermore, it would now not be safe for them to re-open it for several more years, lest the portal be overrun and they be subjected to an invasion by dypalfar. Over many years without much outside contact, the Mirskhrazana had strayed far from the warlike lifestyle practiced by most leukalfar tribes. In all the tribe there were only a couple of dozen Sentries, usually on guard duty at the main doors or in the Sanctum; and a few weapons-trained members of the Keepers.

The story Arctoris had given to Ghrztum and his family, which was in general circulation throughout the city, was that while visiting in the Sanctum they had been the victims of a freak accident involving one of the mysterious dypalfar devices Gylabris was always tinkering with, which had blasted them into nonexistence with a single discharge.

People outside the Keepers were an ignorant lot, and were willing to believe almost anything of their long-departed masters. The dypalfar had built this city, and so many marvels within it. Why not a disintegration ray? Right now, he wished there *was* such a thing – one that he could turn on this lot of angry-looking Sky People and their leukalfar stripling translator, and make the problem go away once and for all.

What could he tell them? The leukalfar kid looked like a good breeze would blow him over, clearly not a warrior. But the two tall and muscular men and three well-armed (and angry-looking) women were not just going to roll over without a fight. If they thought he was lying to them, they might very well extract the truth at the point of a sword. And he wasn't entirely convinced the entire Guard Corps of Mrzhgradfendz would be adequate to defend him. Had he realized that one of those women could turn into a large dragon at will and that the older man, her consort, was a powerful battle mage, he would have abandoned that hope entirely.

Finally, Arctoris hit on a story he hoped they might believe, one that might make these bereaved parents go away and leave them alone. Speaking slowly and with many pauses so that the youngster (Mothris, he'd learned, a member of the fabled Ankhrazana) could translate, he told them "You are correct. As I believe your son Andreas was told by the Chanter of the Ankhrazana, Mrzhgradfendz houses the last working example of the devices of Dzurman, the machines that created the portals through which the entire dypalfar people fled to what we believe may be a plane of the Netherworld."

There was some conversation among the Sky People as Mothris relayed this information. Then Arctoris continued: "Throughout the time since the dypalfar departed, when we remaining free leukalfar wrested control of the device from those sent to destroy it, the Keepers have stood as an organization dedicated to guarding the secret of the portal. Our mission is to one day go through the portal, overrun the dypalfar – at least the ones in the city on the far side of it, if not all the dypalfar in that world – and free our enslaved people."

His audience was now looking at him with more respect, appreciating the plausibility of his tale. After all, it was nothing but the truth. Indeed, he had not lied to Andreas at all about the portal or the Keepers' role in using it while protecting the secret of its existence. Not until the very end. "Many times over the years," he went on, "we sent volunteers hoping to infiltrate the dypalfar city on the other side of the portal. They were to bring back one of the enslaved leukalfar so that we could gather intelligence to plan our invasion. But though it seemed the portal was not guarded on that side, once our volunteers had passed the doors at the far end of the room they were never seen or heard from again – at least, not by us."

"We concluded that the dypalfar were alert to the danger posed by the portal and were guarding the area too closely for anyone to get past," he continued. "So we left it turned off for many years, in hopes that we could lull them into believing there would be no more attempts. The alfar have long lives, and we were prepared to wait them out. Yet when finally we turned it on again, after I had become head of the Keepers, we found nothing."

They were all staring at him as he picked up the tale. "We found nothing but the empty room on the far side of the portal, the doors at the far end of it locked tight. We couldn't pick the locks or break through them, and there was no response to our knocking. Not that it would have been a good response, I'm sure, but we were desperate! After several such visits over a period of decades we concluded that until we can mount an invasion in force, with equipment to excavate stone, there will be no entry into that city beyond the portal. We have no such resources."

"And how do our kids fit into this?" Bernadette asked, after Arctoris' last sentences had been translated.

"Andreas asked me about the portal, and I begged him to tell no one," the elderly Keeper replied after her question was relayed. "I think he, Merelle, and Fjurbund had become good friends with young Ghrztum, and I was afraid that the secret we've been keeping all these centuries would be let out. The disruption this would cause could destroy the Mirskhrazana and our way of life. I explained to him what had happened with the portal in recent years, and offered to let him and his companions see for themselves that the portal was now just a dead end. I hoped that he would return to the Ankhrazana and tell their Chanter what he'd seen with his own eyes, so that the conclusion to that tale could be incorporated into the Lore."

"The next morning, your children came to the Sanctum of the Keepers and were admitted. After touring the place and seeing some of the work that we carry on – it's not all just guarding the portal, of course – I took them into the guarded chamber where the device is hidden. It requires a special attunement sphere to activate it, then a series of buttons to be pressed for the portal to be formed. To turn the portal off again, a different series of buttons is pressed and the device shuts down. One only needs the sphere to awaken it," Arctoris explained.

The old Keeper had now regained his self-control, and the mantle of power and command – which he had worn since long before any of these upstart visitors were born – came flooding back to him as his panic subsided. It made him still more convincing as he went on with his tale. "I opened the portal and we saw through it just what had appeared at the last several openings: an empty room, bare of furnishings beyond double rows of stone counters. In the past we had filled the heavily barred room with armed guards, prepared should the dypalfar have been maintaining a vigil. But so many times we had found nothing, I didn't think it was necessary. As it happens" – at this his face fell and he gave them a look of deep regret – "I was wrong."

"All was as before, and I led our young visitors into the room so they could see for themselves," Arctoris continued. "Young and eager, they hurried ahead of me to explore the room. There are some differences in evidence, between the architecture you will find here and in other ancient dypalfar cities, and what is to be found on the far side of the portal. Then suddenly we were set upon! Armed guards sprang out from both sides of the room, hidden behind the counters and seemingly lying in wait for us – though how they could have expected our arrival I cannot imagine. I was knocked to the floor, but your young men – Andreas and Fjurbund – were larger and stronger than our attackers. And though unarmed, they began to struggle with them. Trying to save Merelle, I think."

The attention of all in the room was rapt, caught up by the story and waiting for its conclusion. "I was disregarded, just a feeble old leukalfar lying senseless on the floor as far as the dypalfar guards were concerned. As they rushed to join their comrades in subduing Andreas and Fjurbund, I rose to my feet and dashed to the portal. As I reached the device, I could see that your children had all been subdued and the dypalfar were now making for the portal. Had they reached it, they might have beaten down the door and launched an invasion, killing or enslaving all within Mrzhgradfendz. I had no choice – I quickly pressed the sequence to shut down the machine, killing the portal." He hung his head as if in shame, forced to doom the young visitors in order to save his entire city.

The translation of this brought much discussion among his audience. Arctoris waited a few moments, for the reaction he knew must come. The boy Mothris, after talking with his companions, said "This is a very great disaster, but we have come here to rescue Andreas, Merelle, and Fjurbund. You must open the portal for us so we can go and get them back."

The old Keeper let his face fall further. Crocodile tears were unknown to the leukalfar, after thousands of years without eyes; but he managed to look completely woeful as he said "If only I could! I would have gathered guards and gone to the rescue immediately. But after closing the portal and regaining my breath I felt around my robes and realized that I no longer had the attunement sphere. It must have fallen unnoticed to the floor of the chamber on the far side. Without it, the portal is closed to us… forever."

Faces fell around the room as this final detail was made known to them. Bernadette gave the old Keeper a cold, appraising look before huddling with her team for a discussion. In another minute, as Arctoris continued to sit on the stone bench looking sad, Mothris addressed him once more. "This is very distressing news, sir Keeper. Very distressing indeed. We have all traveled long today, and we must eat and rest. Then tomorrow I think we may go searching for another attunement sphere. If, as it is said, each of these devices of Dzurman was activated with one, it may be that another can be found deep in the ruins of one of the many dypalfar cities in Iscandia."

Perfect, Arctoris thought. They'll go away, filled not with rage and grief but with determination to find a sphere that will let them reclaim their children. And likely they'll be years at it if they can ever find one at all. I've never heard a whisper that any part of a Dzurman's device survived, other than the one we have here. And if they do show up with a sphere that works, I can just "fail" to make it work with the power-up sequence "because this isn't the right sphere." Congratulating himself on a brilliant ploy, he rose to his feet.

"I am so very sorry," he said, counting on Mothris to provide translation. "We truly had no way to know that the dypalfar had once again begun guarding the portal. I will see if I can find you some accommodation for the night. Then I suppose, in the morning, you will want to be off on your search for another attunement sphere."

As they stepped through the doors they found the enormous snow troll, Ghrztum, standing in the corridor outside. He knew where the Keeper had taken the visitors, and had been waiting for them. He nodded to them, to the Keeper, and then said to Mothris, "I am deeply sorry for what happened to Andreas, Merelle, and Fjurbund. I would like to take you to meet my mother and father, and I think we will be able to feed you dinner and give you a place to sleep tonight. Will you follow me?"

Chapter 43: Answers

After the translation and a general assent they parted ways with Arctoris, thanking him for telling them the true story, and fell into line behind Ghrztum as he led them along the corridor toward his family's apartment, not that far away. Bernadette was fascinated, and could hardly wait to meet the troll's "mother." Though the leukalfar were feared and hated throughout Iscandia nobody had ever denied they were human – they made clothing and tools and weapons and houses, they practiced animal husbandry with the mandimants. So adopting Meri had been a safe bet. But what must it have taken for a leukalfar woman to adopt a baby troll? And who would have guessed he could grow up to be as human as anyone she had ever met?

It was late, but Indinala had not yet started preparing supper. The runner's arrival had thrown their household – already in mourning over the loss of their young friends - into an uproar. She and Skarnoris had been sitting in the living room, sipping tea and anxiously waiting for their son to return and report what he'd learned.

They were stunned when Ghrztum returned with a retinue of five Sky People and one young leukalfar trailing behind him. Indinala rushed to embrace her son, on whom she now came up only a little above the waist. Fortunate that the dypalfar, who were if anything a little shorter than most of the other alfar races, had favored high ceilings! "Mother," he rumbled, "I have brought the parents of Andreas, Merelle, and Fjurbund here. We need to feed them and find somewhere for them to sleep."

Indinala's gaze immediately flew to the leukalfar youth among the group. Having heard Andreas's story she guessed that the Sky People would not have the leukalfar tongue, and this boy must have been brought as a translator. She approached him, palms up in the traditional gesture of welcome. "Greetings," she said with a slight smile. "I am Ghrztum's mother Indinala and this is my husband Skarnoris. Might I know your name?"

For the first time in many days, Mothris felt almost as if he were home. This tribe, the Mirskhrazana, lived far differently than did his own – but life here seemed to be in many ways similar to the way leukalfar acolytes lived in the Great Temple of Apoldros. He had seen signs here, signs that told him the worship of their god had not been forgotten among these people as it had been among many other tribes of the leukalfar.

"Greetings Indinala," Mothris replied formally. He was, as his mother might put it, "a nice boy." "I am Mothris son of Urgnis and Myrkra of the Ankhrazana. I thank you for your hospitality." Formal introductions out of the way, Indinala scurried to the duties of a hostess – leaving Skarnoris, whose culinary skills were not as great, to take care of interacting with their guests in the meantime.

Mothris had enjoyed his moment of being the person actually being spoken with, but now it was back to being the translator as Indinala said, "I am sure you must be starving! Please sit down, and I'll bring some refreshments."

Ghrztum was tempted to go help his mother in the kitchen, in order to avoid painful interaction with the bereaved parents of his late friends. But why did they appear to be acting so normally? They seemed if anything somewhat determined, not wracked with grief to learn that their children had been killed just the day before they had arrived to rescue them.

This was soon cleared up, as they all sat down. More teacups were found and everyone got a little before a new pot was started. Holding Mothris' hand, silently thanking him for the service he was performing (and wishing for the hundredth time today that she knew the leukalfar language) Bernadette looked Ghrztum in the eyes. The troll looked down at her sadly, his own dark eyes red-rimmed. "Ghrztum," she said, "you believe that Andreas, Merelle, and Fjurbund died in a tragic accident. Yes?" He nodded sadly after hearing the translation.

She smiled at him. The resemblance between Andreas and his mother was strong, and the man with her could only be Andrion, Andreas' blood-father. Father and son had been stamped from the same die, though Andreas's hair was dark auburn not brown. "It's not true!" she said. "I must ask that anything I say here will not leave this room." Bernadette peered around at Skarnoris and then back at Ghrztum as Mothris translated what she'd said.

Indinala came in at this juncture with more tea and a large platter of cold foods, appetizers as it were. These included several fruits, mushrooms, some hard-baked bits of flatbread with dipping sauce, and what looked like little chunks of a firm, white flesh like some kind of ocean fish – also intended to be dipped, it seemed. The party, who had not eaten in hours, fell on the food with a general lack of concern for what it might actually be. Nobody here but us humans, after all, and what one can eat should be safe for another.

As everyone else began eating Bernadette looked up at Indinala, whose name she caught during the exchange earlier. She'd listened to enough of the leukalfar tongue, with running translations in Common, that she was beginning to make some connections though her facility with languages (other than dragon tongue, which had been handed to her on a plate along with the draconic body she sometimes inhabited) was not as great as Fjuri's. "Thank you Indinala," she told their hostess. "I think that you should hear this too, but you must not tell anyone else."

Ghrztum and his parents, after understanding the request, all agreed. The three were fairly burning with curiosity to know why Andreas's mother, whom they assumed should be devastated at the news of her son's death, was smiling and looking determined instead. "Arctoris told us," she revealed after getting their vows of silence, "that our children are still alive. The secret the Keepers hide deep below Mrzhgradfendz is the last remaining portal to the world where the dypalfar fled three thousand years ago. And Andreas, Merelle, and Fjurbund are trapped on the other side of it."

This revelation both elated and astounded Ghrztum and his parents. Like everyone else who'd been fed Arctoris' threadbare story of a "freak accident," they had accepted it. With sorrow in their case, since they had known the three young visitors and liked them. The troll exploded in joy. "I knew it!" he declared. "I just knew they could not be dead!" In his enthusiasm he reached across the table with his enormous furry paw and took Bernadette's hand. She smiled up at him and squeezed it back.

Some hours later the appetizers had all been devoured, as had more substantial fare in the form of a game stew with flatbread wraps. Andrion, whose many years of studying ancient tomes had given him more of an insight into other tongues – particularly those of the archaic alfar races, was beginning to make attempts to converse directly with their hosts. Bernadette still didn't feel like she could reliably formulate a sentence, but she was beginning to pick up a lot of what was being said.

They had eaten the evening meal in the kitchen, then returned to the living room after supper for little glasses of a fruit wine and some sweets that seemed also to be made from whatever fruits were available on the island. Icefruit, Bernadette suspected. She had spent much of her adult life studying chemia and the ingredients used in it, as well as the herbal properties of Iscandia's plant life.

Now it was time to get down to it. The wine had relaxed her a little, taking some of the edge off her driving urge to go plunging after Andi and Meri. Time for some strategy. She addressed everyone in the room, counting on Mothris to translate for Ghrztum and his parents. "Earlier this evening," she said, "the learned Keeper Arctoris told us the sad story of how he was forced to close the portal in order to prevent a dypalfar invasion of Mrzhgradfendz. And how he then discovered that the attunement sphere needed to reopen the portal had fallen to the floor when he was knocked down by the dypalfar guards in the room on the far side of the portal."

Andrion squeezed her hand. He knew what was coming, and he suspected Lifa at least must guess as well. After her words had been translated, Bernadette looked around the table before speaking again: "He was lying through his pointy little teeth! He never saw my son fight dypalfar guards!" Her look of ferocity was matched by a gleam of menace from Andrion's usually warm and friendly brown eyes.

Bernadette's words had been a shock to their hosts, less so to the other members of the rescue party. They all knew Andreas – and as they reviewed in their minds Arctoris' story of the brief battle in the room beyond the portal, it was plain that he had made the whole thing up. In the best way he knew how – which meant Arctoris did not know Andi was a battle mage, did not know he was fireblood.

Ghrztum had been following Bernadette's train of thought. "That's right!" he said. "Arctoris told you that Andreas and Fjurbund were unarmed and struggled with the guards, then were overpowered?"

"So he did," she said briefly after the question had been relayed.

"When we were staying in my cave after we met," the troll explained, "he used a fire spell to thaw out some frozen rabbits. And he said he was good at battle and healing magic. I don't think a mage with battle spells would just be 'struggling' with people who were attacking him."

Bernadette grinned at him, once more astounded at the intelligence of this person – a member of a race she had always thought were nothing but large, ferocious animals. Indinala had truly done the world (and perhaps the snow troll race) a service, when she took in this bouncing baby boy. "You got it in one!" she crowed. "I don't know exactly what Keeper Arctoris is up to, but if he lied about that you can bet he lied about the rest of it. I think we need to go pay him a visit."

Chapter 44: Beyond the Gate

As Andi, Fjuri and Meri skidded to a halt before the blank stone wall that stood where moments before the portal had been, the two dypalfar guards were collecting themselves from where they lay sprawled on the floor. The Gale dragon spell was unlikely to kill anyone who wasn't already close to death, but it did have a way of putting a temporary halt to an attack. Realizing they'd been betrayed (or had Arctoris spotted the guards and panicked, closing the portal to prevent the dypalfar coming through?), Andi now turned to their foes. There were just two of them, and they were not yet back into fighting form.

Raising both hands, he fired dual bolts of lightning – broad bands that shocked the hapless guards into temporary paralysis without doing any permanent harm to them. The idea that he might very well find himself forced to choose between killing another human being or getting killed himself was beginning to work its way into his mind – but he was determined to postpone that for as long as possible. When you were reading about it in stories, it was all glamor and glorious deeds and excitement. The reality of leaving someone, a person with his own life and loves and dreams, lying dead on the floor – was something else.

"Quick!" he called to his companions, "Get their weapons!" The three of them fell on the stunned guards and each of the boys took one of the short swords. Before they could regain the power of movement the two hapless dypalfar (Real dypalfar! Andi thought in amazement, as he bound one of the guards hand and foot with leather strips cut from his cloak) found themselves immobilized. They were armored in dypalfar metal, but had been armed only with the short swords and some daggers.

Andi had heard one of the guards address Meri in accented Leukalfar, and he thought it likely that some at least of the dypalfar must know the language – in order to communicate with their leukalfar slaves. It would be in their interests if most of the slaves didn't understand the language of their masters, permitting the masters to converse in front of slaves without their secrets being revealed. The whole concept repelled him. Other than the dypalfar betrayal and enslavement of the leukalfar, there had been no slavery in Agena for many thousands of years.

It seemed they were going to have to explore the dypalfar city (something Andi had dreamed of doing since he first heard Gryndor's tale – but not under these circumstances!) whether they'd intended to or not. He looked down at the elder of the two trussed guards, who was glaring up at him with hatred. The two looked similar enough to be brothers, somewhat stocky-looking alfar with long pointed ears, black hair hanging loose to their shoulders and tied back around the ears with small braids, long beards the same color as the hair on their heads, blue eyes lighter than Riki's, and skin as pale as any leukalfar's. "You," he said in leukalfar, trying to seem tough. He was bigger than the guard, at least. "What's on the other side of that door?"

The guard sneered up at him. "An army of armed guards waiting to take you into custody, *threkzal*," he replied in leukalfar, his tone one of defiance and scorn. Andi didn't recognize that last word and assumed it was an insult in the dypalfar tongue. He suspected they were not going to get a lot of cooperation from these two, but without them he doubted they'd be able to get through the door unless maybe they could cut their way through. Now that he thought of it, that might be an option – or maybe a way to elicit a more helpful attitude.

The two recalcitrant captives were lying in the room's central aisle, leaning up against one of the stone counters that ran down either side between the aisle and the walls. Back against the wall where the remains of their meal sat, scattered in the confusion, two dypalfar metal shields stood propped against the wall. "Fjuri," Andi said in Common, "could you please bring me one of those shields?"

Fjuri's expression said he wasn't following Andi's plan, but he went along with the request. Andi took the shield with a word of thanks and then, speaking once again in leukalfar, mused as if to himself "Hmm, nice work. My mother makes some pieces like this." Looking down at the guard who had spoken before, he asked casually, "What would you say? Is this shield somewhat thicker than your armor?" It was, by nearly double; but the guard only glared in response.

The bound guards were sitting near one end of the stone block. Andi walked over and propped the shield up against the far end of the same block. It was roughly rectangular, so it stood up all right. Then he readied a combination of spells that, so far as he knew, were practiced only by him and his father: the "metal cutting" interlinked weaves of fire and lightning that Andrion had first used to cut dypalfar metal pipe before Andreas was born.

In moments the shield glowed white-hot where the interwoven spells had struck, and in another couple of moments glowing liquid metal flowed out the bottom as the weave (which Andi had adjusted to about the size of an arrow shaft, for increased intensity) cut an ever-growing hole in the edge of the shield on the side nearest the two guards. Their blue eyes, up-tilted like those of all alfar, grew wide with fear.

"My, my," Andi said thoughtfully. "Imagine what that would do to a human body. Why, it would just go right *through* armor, wouldn't it." He felt a little bad about doing this to their captives, but he figured it beat actually killing them. The helpless guards were now white as sheets and quivering in terror. It was one thing to die gloriously in the heat of battle, and another to be threatened with a hideous, painful death while trussed up like a chicken for the spit.

"Th-the key," the more talkative guard stammered, "it's in my pocket! And you need to know the knock to get through... but I can't get it tied up like this."

Andi considered the problem. "Fjuri," he said, "see if you can get his armor off him without untying him." The tall, well-muscled lad bent to the guard and dragged him over onto his side, then unbuckled the breastplate. After a couple of minutes he had managed to strip the breastplate and greaves from the guard without untying the bonds – leaving him in his heavy dypalfar boots and a tunic and short trews he'd been wearing under the armor.

"Might as well do the other one, too," Andi suggested. With a frown of concentration Fjuri stooped to his task and soon both guards, still immobilized, were lying there in their underwear. "Which pocket?" Andi demanded.

Feeling even more vulnerable without the armor – though Andi's demonstration had clearly shown how much good that would have been against his battle magic – the guard immediately replied "right side shirt pocket."

Andi bent over him and retrieved the key, an elaborate-looking thing. "And the knock?" he asked. The guard's face looked blank for a moment, as if his mind were far away. Then he focused on Andi again. His terror seemed to have receded now that it appeared they were not going to be tortured or killed. These were just kids, he realized – not hardened killers.

"Knock three times fast, pause, knock once, pause, knock once again" he said, "and the bar will be opened." Was there a glimmer of satisfaction in those tip-tilted, pale blue eyes?

The boys had been furnished with the best armor they were capable of wearing since they were four years old, all of it lovingly crafted for them by Andi's mom. They felt naked going out into what they had to assume was hostile territory unarmored. If only they had put on their armor before setting out for the Keepers' Sanctum! All of their armor, along with their weapons and packs, was back at the apartment of Ghrztum's family.

They had the guards' swords and shields. Could they wear their armor as well? For some minutes they tried. The larger of the two guards was only a little smaller than Andi, and he might have worn it but it would have been uncomfortable and not provided the coverage it should have. And that would still have left Fjuri and Meri without any protection. In the end, they decided to leave it behind.

After Andi had knocked and the door had been opened, the plan was for him to mow down the guards on the other side of the doors with Gale (which shouldn't be all that difficult, considering how these two had fallen), then run like hell and see if they could pick up armor for all of them and perhaps a bow for Meri, as they lost themselves in what would probably be a typical dypalfar city with its crisscrossing corridors and hidden recesses.

The three of them were sure that help would be coming, if they could just stay out of the clutches of the dypalfar here long enough for that help to arrive. Andi and Meri knew their mom wouldn't be fooled by whatever story Arctoris was putting around, and soon the portal would be opened again. But likely not before these guards were due to be relieved!

Fjuri took one of the shields, sword in hand. Andi took the other shield, the one with the hole in its edge (it had now cooled again) and slung it over his shoulder as he kept a sword in one hand and the key in the other. He approached the door, ready to use the key and begin what he hoped would be their escape. Meri stayed behind them both. As he did so, the door was flung open and a swarm of armed dypalfar soldiers came running into the room, surrounding them before he could make a move! He, Fjuri, and Meri were the targets of a dozen drawn bows. There was no magic Andi could think of using that would get them out of *this* scrape.

They let the swords and shields drop to the floor, and in moments the bound guards had been cut free and were getting to their feet. His face triumphant, his voice once more filled with scorn, the guard Andi had so recently terrorized said in leukalfar, "So, *threkzal,* it seems you have never heard of the Joining?"

Chapter 45: Persuasion

It had been too many hours since they had slept, and everyone in the rescue party needed a rest. So after their plotting session they all went to lie down in their bedrolls – some on the stone platform beds, others on the floor. Bernadette and Andrion shared a double bedroll on the floor, groaning at its hardness. Not that the beds were much better! He enfolded her tight in his arms and murmured into her ear, "Don't you worry about a thing, Berni. We're going to get them back." She smiled drowsily in the darkness and kissed him, then rolled over and fell into a heavy sleep almost at once.

When she woke again all was darkness, the silence broken only by the low, constant thrumming of the dypalfar machinery at this level of the city. Soon all in the room were on their feet, lights had been lit, and they were quietly getting ready for the assault on the home of the lying Keeper Arctoris. As ever, Andrion was the last one up.

Indinala and Skarnoris, alerted by the activity though they were planning to go to their jobs as usual this morning, helped them gather supplies and equipment for the trek. If all went well, they would be going from here into the portal to rescue their missing children; so they needed to bring along all the food, water, and other items they would need for the operation.

Ghrztum outfitted himself as though for a hunting expedition. For not only was he to be their guide through the labyrinth of Mrzhgradfendz to the home of Arctoris, he planned to accompany them through the portal to rescue his friends. The idea that the old Keeper's lie might have covered something as simple as the ambush and murder of the young visitors was not something any of them were willing to dwell on. And after all, it's not as if it were that easy to ambush and murder someone who could fling you across the room with a dragon spell, burn you to a crisp with battle magic, or simply turn into a dragon and bite your head off.

The troll was one of very few Gleaners with any experience at killing. He usually relied on the weapons he'd been given by nature, but having been raised as a human being he had others at his disposal as well: a razor sharp dypalfar dagger, a stone-tipped wooden club, and a leather sling with which, with his long arms, he could hurl a small round rock with deadly force and accuracy. He put on the leather harness on which these were hung; and strapped on a stiff boiled-leather breastplate, one he'd made himself, to add some protection across his chest.

Indinala and Skarnoris were fearful as they beheld their usually gentle young son looking warlike and determined. He had been the joy of their lives, and now he was going off to kill or be killed. Would they ever see him again? Despite their anxiety they were as angry at Arctoris' perfidy as he was, even as the children's parents were. The kids had meant no one any harm, and had guested under their roof. And then the old Keeper had done… something… to them by treachery. It was if they themselves had betrayed the laws of hospitality.

The corridors were mostly empty as Ghrztum led the party down through the many levels to the one where Arctoris, and others of his exalted rank, had his apartment. As they walked, the troll's mind was seething with suppressed fury. He had been crushed, utterly devastated, by the news that his new friends had died. Horrified, shocked, and racked with guilt when their parents arrived, and he realized that he had been aiding a trio of under-aged adventurers on a completely unauthorized expedition. Aiding them to their deaths, as he saw it.

Then, to learn that it was all a lie, that one of the most respected members of his tribe had done away with the young visitors in order to further his own narrow ends – without a care for the effect it had had on Ghrztum and his family – made him consider murder for the first time in his short life. Yet still, when at last they arrived at the door, Ghrztum murmured quietly to his companions "Arctoris shares these rooms with his daughter Amdara. I am sure she has known nothing of this, so please don't hurt her."

"Don't worry, Ghrztum," Bernadette said after Mothris had translated the warning. She was beginning to understand more and more of what was said in the leukalfar tongue, but still lacked the understanding of grammar and syntax that would let her make herself understood in that language. "We don't intend to hurt anyone, not even Arctoris." Her expression as she said this seemed to belie her words, as her eyes had a murderous glint.

The door, unsurprisingly, was locked. "I'll handle this," Andrion said quietly and stepped to the door. As he laid a hand on it there was a faint glow and a slight click, then the door swung quietly open. After more than sixteen years as Magister of the Academy at Eisenstag, he had a broad arsenal of tricks at his disposal, including some learned from the University of the Magical Arts in Remus. But this was a spell he'd first acquired even before Andi had been born.

The seven of them, Ghrztum in the lead, crept as quietly as possible into the apartment's front room, and as quietly closed the door behind them to avoid drawing attention. "It's this way," the troll murmured, heading off toward the right. Amdara slept in a much smaller room on the opposite side, seemingly in thrall to her father's needs for care and companionship and unable to marry or start a life of her own while the old man lived.

Once again Andrion took the lead as they entered the spacious sleeping quarters. The area was dimly lit by ever-glowing dypalfar lamps. It occurred to him that the leukalfar when they slept must have some way of turning off their psychic vision – something he had never thought to discuss with his adopted daughter.

This room, like many in dypalfar residences, may once have contained several stone platforms. But the Mirskhrazana valued comfort more than had their departed masters. Only a single large stone bed, cushioned with a wool-stuffed leather pad, occupied one wall of the room while elsewhere there were dypalfar metal stands and chests, and a sort of settee.

Andrion stood over the sleeping old elf, lying on his back with his mouth open and his long ears drooping in repose. With a slight wave of the hand he cast a brief paralysis spell over him. Then in an eye-blink Bernadette was there beside him, sharp dagger held at Arctoris' throat as with her other hand she slapped his wizened cheek and he awakened.

289

Mothris was standing on her other side, and had been coached with what he was to say. "Ssshh!" he warned. "Don't make any noise, or we may be forced to harm your daughter."

"Amdara?" the old Keeper gasped weakly, the paralysis already wearing off. "No! Don't hurt her. I will be quiet."

As Bernadette kept the dagger at his throat, Mothris hissed "Your story was a lie. We know you did not see Andreas fight dypalfar guards. So what really happened?"

The situation of being trapped in his bed by this party of fierce and determined-looking warriors was enough to strike terror into anyone. But the old Keeper had not gotten where he was today, after centuries of growing power, only to be cowed by a group of mere men. Well, and one angry-looking snow troll, too.

"I'm sorry," he said softly, as anxious as they were that Amdara should not wake and come to see what was the matter. "I lied about seeing them fight. After the guards left me I just turned tail and ran for the portal, then without waiting to see what was happening beyond it I closed it as fast as I could. I was terrified, panicked! Can you forgive me for being a fearful old man? Everything else is just as I told you, I swear it!"

After hearing the translation Bernadette rose from her crouch, flummoxed. Was he telling the truth now? She had counted on the effect of their surprise visit to terrorize the old Keeper into spilling the truth. But had he been less frightened than they'd hoped, and just altered his lie after she had tipped him off about what part of the previous lie they didn't believe? The dagger was still held above Arctoris' throat, ready in case he should attempt to rise and call out.

They all stood there in a silent tableau for a moment. Then Andrion had an idea. "Let me," her murmured to his wife, gently putting a hand on the arm that held the dagger. She looked up at him questioningly, her sea-gray eyes huge and dark in the dimness of the bedroom.

Another of the spells Andrion had learned at the University of the Magical Arts was Befriend, and in a few seconds he had cast an enchantment on Arctoris. For nearly five full minutes, the Keeper would be inclined to regard Andrion as his dearest friend, someone he was eager to please. The tricky part, of course, was that this had to be done through an interpreter since the two "bosom buddies" had no language in common.

"Mothris," Andrion said quietly, "I need to work quickly with you. Our friend Arctoris and I have to have a talk, and it needs to proceed with as little delay as possible. But please be sure to convey to him my friendliness and warm regard, all right?" The lad wasn't sure what the Sky People mage was up to, but he was willing to step up. He'd gotten an awful lot of practice in translating the past day or so.

Smiling broadly at the Keeper, who was still lying flat on his bed but looking up at Andrion with a sort of bemused fondness, Andrion said "My dear Arctoris, please sit up. We are all friends here." As Mothris translated, Andrion gave his "friend" an arm and helped him to rise. "Can I get you anything?" Andrion next asked.

The old elf had been sleeping in underwear, and he gestured toward a hook on the far side of the room. Smiling, he said "Thank you. Could you hand me my robe, please?"

After Arctoris was more comfortably attired, Andrion said "Arctoris, there is something I very much hope you can help me with. It would mean so much to me if you could just tell me what really became of my son and his companions. I promise, I won't tell anyone else." The rest of the party had drawn back a little in the dimness, and though they were all in easy hearing of anything that was said the effect of the spell on the old Keeper had him narrowly focused on his dear friend Andrion. The leukalfar boy helping them to communicate was somehow included in the spell, so he had no fear in telling him anything.

"Ah, yes," Arctoris said, gesturing Andrion and Mothris to step still closer though they were already almost on top of him. "I would greatly appreciate it if you could keep the secret, for it would bring much harm to my people if it were known. I'm so sorry, I felt very bad that it had to be done, but as soon as they went through the portal I closed it behind them. I couldn't have them going out and telling the world about Mrzhgradfendz and its portal to the dypalfar world, of course. It would have brought destruction on us all."

Andrion and his companions were riveted at this news, once it had been translated. "So," Andrion asked his "friend," "there were no dypalfar guards attacking?"

"Oh no, of course not," Arctoris replied with a happy smile. "The place was just as deserted as ever. They're probably getting a little hungry and thirsty now, but they're perfectly fine. I was going to just leave the portal closed for a few years, then everything could go back to the way it was. Nothing personal, I hope you understand."

"And the attunement sphere?" Andrion asked next. "Not lost, then?"

"Dear me, no. It's over there in the chest where I keep it when not in use. Very good lock." As soon as this piece of information had been translated, Bernadette was over at the chest like a shot – lockpicks in hand. She lacked the spell that let Andrion open any lock with a gesture, but over her years of tomb raiding she'd gotten quite good at opening locks without magical intervention – and she didn't want to wait. Her heart was singing with joy. Her children were alive, were fine! Temporarily trapped in a parallel dimension, true, but not held captive by a horde of xenophobic dypalfar.

Andrion spotted Bernadette about her task and smiled to himself. He, too, was feeling exultant. What a relief, after everything they had been through, to learn that the kids had endured nothing worse than a day and a night spent locked up in an empty room. "Arctoris," he said quietly, letting his smile spread across his face. "I have just the solution to your problem. We are all men of honor, and we promise not to reveal your secret. It's only of interest to archaeologists and dypalfar scholars, in any case, since as you say the room beyond the portal has been barricaded and abandoned. We'll just go now and open the portal, get the kids out, and be gone. You can believe me when I tell you, when we get through with those young scamps they will never *dream* of telling a soul about what they know."

Confusion was beginning to pass over Arctoris' face during the translation of Andrion's long speech – and realizing that the spell was about to wear off, Andrion renewed it with a wave of his hand. Another few moments passed as the old Keeper's brain, recently realigned in its train of thought, processed the request. He sprang to his feet. "Yes!" he declared, "that is an excellent idea." He glanced in the direction of the chest, just in time to see Bernadette (who had been working with her picks the whole time they were talking) raise its lid and produce the sphere with a triumphant smile.

"Ah good, my friend," Arctoris rasped. "I see that your wife has already gotten the sphere. Let us be on our way to the Keepers' Sanctum then." The party, now eight strong, trooped out of the apartment making as little noise as possible, and the old Keeper led them down the hall to their right. Only he knew the way, and Andrion and Mothris stayed close beside him. Andrion was careful to renew the Befriend spell every few minutes, as the journey on foot to the Sanctum in the deepest depths of Mrzhgradfendz took quite a while. It wouldn't do to have Arctoris suddenly come to his senses and wonder what he was doing out here with all these people!

As they set off Bernadette pulled out her notebook and began marking their path again. Years ago her ljosalfar friend Senalie, one of the proprietors of The Golden Thread in Sylvanian, had put her onto a supplier for the graphite drawing sticks she used in her trade. They were much more convenient than pen and ink, allowing you to take notes anywhere. She had hastily sketched their path in a sort of shorthand on the way here, and now continued to make note of the turnings – just in case they needed to find their way out again without a guide.

Eventually they came to the main entry to the Keepers' Sanctum. While most of the Mirskhrazana were not up at this hour, or were just arising and getting ready for the day ahead, the Sanctum was guarded twenty-four hours a day. Arctoris, overflowing with goodwill after repeated doses of Befriend, smilingly ushered them through the checkpoint and along the corridors to the guarded room that led into the room with Dzurman's device in it.

The guards were all quite astounded to see their boss here at this hour, and accompanied by a motley group of Sky People, the troll, and one skinny leukalfar youth. But he'd shepherded a group of Sky People here only a couple of days before, so perhaps the two occasions were connected. Besides, he was clearly not under any kind of duress. If anything, he seemed to be in a better mood than any of them could remember seeing him in before.

At last, they were standing in the chamber with the device, the door locked and barred behind them. This was unbreakable procedure set down over the millennia, so that if a hostile invasion were to be launched through the portal it would quickly find itself stopped cold. The relatively narrow doorway was highly defensible, and a large contingent of additional guards could be brought should there be any attempts to break down the door.

Andrion wondered idly about the effects of being put under repeated Befriend spells over the course of time. Arctoris was beginning to look a little punch-drunk, as if his level of euphoria were increasing to the point where he was no longer just best friends with Andrion, but eager to extend the milk of human kindness to everyone in his sight. As he stood there weaving slightly before the device, a happy grin on his face, the rescuers gathered for a brief, quiet conference.

"So," Andrion said, "we just open up the portal and the kids come staggering out. Then we ground them all until they're thirty, after hauling them home – right?"

"Sounds good," Bernadette replied. "But I want to do a few things first just in case there are any surprises. Could you get Arctoris to slowly show you how it works while I take notes?"

Andrion stepped over and took the old Keeper by the arm, standing head and shoulders above him. "Arctoris old friend," he said warmly, "I am very impressed by this marvelous device you have and I'm eager to see how it operates. Could you please show me, very slowly, how it is done?"

Warming under what he saw as praise from his dear friend, the elderly elf smiled and said "Certainly. Could Bernadette hand me the sphere please?" She had been unwilling to part with it on the journey here and had tucked it into her pack.

She handed it over, then stood watching as Arctoris explained the procedure. "See you press this button and this one on the left side, then press and hold down this one and this one on the right." Before them the lights on the control panel came up and they heard the humming as the device came alive. Bernadette quickly sketched the sphere, indicating which buttons. They were of different colors; which made it easier for her, with her color vision, to remember than it was for the leukalfar.

Again, she sketched the control panel and noted which buttons were pressed and in what sequence as the old Keeper operated the controls. When the portal sprang to life and the view of the room beyond came into focus, they all stared at it raptly. But the room appeared empty. "Does sound pass through the portal?" Andrion asked Arctoris through Mothris.

"Oh yes, though there is a distortion of light across the boundary sound, people, weapons, anything can pass as if there was nothing between this room and that one." He smiled again glancing up at his friend like a dog seeking a pat on the head. Remind me not to overdo the Befriend spell, Andrion thought to himself.

"Andi! Meri! Can you hear me?" Andrion boomed in his deep baritone. There was no reply.

"Fjurbund!" Lifa shouted angrily. So near to reclaiming her beloved son, her fury at him for running off and putting them through all this was beginning to come to the fore. She and Bjorn had never beaten their children, a practice popular among some families in Iscandia. Fjuri was getting a bit big to whup, in any case. But she'd think of some punishment that was far, far worse.

"Wait here," Bernadette said to Andrion, "and make sure your buddy there stays friendly. Come on Lifa, let's take a look." They approached the glimmering portal gingerly, then stepped boldly through to the other side. Just as Arctoris had claimed, the room was apparently empty. Down either side of a central corridor ran a series of the large stone blocks the dypalfar liked to use for tables or workbenches, and at the far end stood a pair of closed doors that looked very similar to the one on the doorway leading to the device's chamber.

The two women, both seasoned warriors if a bit out of practice in recent years, stalked carefully down the aisle peering to either side and occasionally calling out for the children. Only faint echoes came back to them from the walls and ceiling of the stone room. Bernadette noticed some objects on one of the stone counters and stepped closer to examine them. Were these bowls and dishes that had recently held food?

Just then, two heavily armed dypalfar guards, who had been crouched in hiding behind the stone, burst forth to attack her and she dodged back out of their reach. "Eiz-Nehm-Bild-Stalz!" she cried, and the two forms halted in an instant – turned, for a moment, into solid blocks of ice.

Seeing the confrontation, Anja, Lars, and Ghrztum dashed through the portal to join them and in the few seconds before their adversaries regained their senses they had the two dypalfar (surely, what else could they be?) disarmed, stripped and bound. Andrion burned to join them, the habit of coming to his wife's aid in battle ingrained in him after all these years. But he needed to stay with Arctoris, lest they all find themselves in the kids' situation.

He was now coming to realize that the old Keeper had told them the truth as he knew it – but it not been all the truth. Seemingly, the dypalfar *were* once again guarding the portal. He wondered why they'd kept only two guards here, but then reasoned that two were enough to sound the alarm. If it was true they could talk mind to mind, these recent guardsicles might have alerted a much larger force on the other side of that door to the intruders, as soon as they heard him shouting through the portal.

Bernadette, Lifa, Lars, Ghrztum, and Anja wrestled the cursing guards to their feet and half hauled, half marched them back through the portal. While her companions kept an eye on the captive dypalfar Bernadette got out her notebook again. "Have him close the portal, please," she asked her husband. Andrion had just hit Arctoris with another dose of Befriend, and the old elf was so eager to please he even helped to carefully mark the correct button sequence for shutting down the machine. In moments the portal had vanished, the machine had gone silent, and the pale blue eyes of the two captive guards were bugging half out of their heads as they realized they had just become trapped in the world their ancestors had fled – millennia ago.

Chapter 46: Plan B

They all gathered in the chamber, which was no more than twenty-five feet from one end to the other and only marginally wider. "What the hell are we going to do?" Bernadette asked. She wanted more than anything to simply go back through the portal, break down that door, and rampage through the dypalfar city on the far side of it until their children were found. If she had to raze every foot of it from sub-basement to the ground, that's what she would do. But that wasn't going to work. They needed to plan. Once again Mothris was pressed into translating as Andrion acted as the group's spokesman.

"First thing, I think," Andrion replied, "is to set up some local support. Arctoris my friend, would you kindly use your key and secret knock on the door there so we can go back out into the Sanctum?"

"Gladly! A wonderful idea," the old elf said; and in moments the door was open and the ones guarding it were standing mouths agape to discover that the party they had admitted earlier had now been joined by two half-naked, trussed-up elves who from their appearance must surely be dypalfar. No other race of the alfar combined that black hair, pale skin and eyes, and the ability to grow a long, thick black beard. Most alfar, the leukalfar among them, didn't even need to shave to maintain a smooth-faced appearance.

Bernadette had taken note of the secret knock, as well. It was beginning to look more and more as if these notes would be needed, and in the near future. "The room on the other side of the portal has been put under watch by the dypalfar again," Andrion told those standing around nearby.

"Yes," one guard spoke up, "we know. Arctoris told us how your children were taken captive. Why would you open it again, knowing this?"

Aha, Andrion thought. Um, let's see… "Could someone get these two captives locked up?" he asked, and a couple more guards who'd arrived were tasked with marching the bound dypalfar off to separate cells. They both had some fluency in leukalfar, and after giving their ranks declined to supply any more information. Andrion doubted their resistance would last long after they'd had a dose of the medicine Arctoris had been guzzling for the past hour.

Now, he turned back to Arctoris. Despite the serious turn of events the old Keeper was still smiling slightly, seeming not to be completely aware of his surroundings. "We need to go and speak with some of the other Keepers about this, and now. Will you lead the way, please?" Smiling, Arctoris beckoned them to follow and led them down the corridor to the area where he kept his office – across the room from where Gylabris worked on his automatons.

Soon all of the senior Keepers who were at work this early were gathered around, and Andrion gave Arctoris another shot of Befriend . He was starting to feel a little guilty about robbing the old elf of his volition, but desperate situations called for desperate measures. With Mothris translating, Andrion addressed everyone in the room. "As my friend Arctoris told you before, the dypalfar have once again begun guarding the room on the far side of the portal. Our children were taken, and Arctoris wisely closed the portal before the dypalfar could swarm through and invade Mrzhgradfendz. We are determined to try to rescue them, however, so Arctoris kindly agreed to open the portal for us again. After all there are seven of us, and we are well armed."

There were little gasps around the circle. All had thought Arctoris quite reasonable in announcing that the kids were sadly lost, and that the portal must now stay closed. Yet two days later he agreed to open it again? These Sky People must be persuasive indeed. Not to mention insane with concern for their children, if they were willing to go up against an entire city of dypalfar to try to save them.

"We have captured two of the dypalfar guards, and I believe that they speak and understand the leukalfar tongue."

"They do," Mothris said in an aside as he was translating this speech. "I heard them cursing us and demanding to be released as they were being hauled through the portal."

"I intend to interrogate them," Andrion went on, "and we will learn as much as possible about the city on the other side of the portal and what might have become of our children. Then we will launch an expedition to retrieve them. After we have gone through, the portal must stay open and the door to its chamber heavily barricaded lest any dypalfar try to storm it while we're searching for the kids. Can we rely on you to do this?"

He was addressing all of the Keepers in the room, really, but Arctoris was the senior among them and still heavily under the influence of Andrion's spell. "Of course, friend Andrion," he said. "It is the least we can do for you after allowing your children to be captured." His emotions seemed to be in a happy fog, but somewhere down deep his mind was squirming in remorse that he had intentionally stranded the young visitors with the intent that they should die of thirst and starvation. How could he have done something so horrible to the children of his dearest friend?

To his companions, in Common, Andrion said "I'm afraid this is going to delay us, but we must have more information before we go back in there or our efforts are going to be futile. Those guards are going to tell us what we want to know, but in the meantime I think we might want to have something to eat and maybe a little more rest." Getting Mothris to translate once more, he asked the room in general "Is there anything to eat here? We got up early and skipped breakfast this morning."

A voice near the back of the room spoke up, and a small, middle-aged leukalfar in a Keeper's robe came forward. "We have a dining area for staff," he told them through Mothris, "and I'm sure we can find you something to eat there. I'm Gylabris, by the way. I was very sorry to hear about what happened to your son, I assume that he is Andreas? Very nice young fellow, and very interested in my work."

"Your work?" Andrion asked politely, though his stomach was growling and the mention of food had seized his attention. Ordinarily, everything about this incredibly well-preserved city and its civilized leukalfar inhabitants would have fascinated him. Who knew how much knowledge they might be able to impart about the dypalfar and their technology? But at the moment he only wanted to hold his son and daughter in his arms again – oh yeah, and eat some breakfast.

Gylabris began leading them around a corner and up another corridor to the dining hall, and the smiling, stupefied Arctoris followed in their wake. "I have made it my life's mission to unravel the secrets of the dypalfar automatons," the little leukalfar explained through Mothris' translation. "I have been gathering the pieces of the ones broken over the centuries, studying them, and trying to get them working again – but re-programmed so that they will obey our commands, and not attack us."

Andrion looked at him in amazement, distracted from his hunger. "This is fascinating, Gylabris! You must tell us all about it while we are eating. At the moment, I'm afraid I'm about ready to faint." Seemingly no Befriend spell was needed on *this* Keeper. He was so delighted to meet people with a genuine interest in his work, that he was already beginning to think of Andrion as a dear friend. They reached the dining hall and went to a counter, behind which a member of the society of Gleaners was handing out food. Not everyone within the Sanctum were Keepers, though you must be one (or the guest of one) if you were to go through into its innermost chambers.

Andrion renewed the Befriend spell on Arctoris one more time, then requested "Could you have whichever of the two prisoners appears to be the most senior given a robe to put on, and brought to a small room where we can interrogate him? It should have some light, a small table and a couple of chairs, and a solid door with no windows. Maybe a storeroom of some kind? And offer him some food and water." The old Keeper smiled happily at him, and soon told off one of the guards that had accompanied them to do as his friend had asked.

As they all gathered at long stone tables eating the food that had been provided, Mothris sat between Andrion and Gylabris, translating as the little Keeper explained the projects he had been working on. "Insko, my first successful project, is just a bug. I have programmed him to respond to simple commands, and he's been trained to attack if he identifies specific threats that I have defined for him. At the moment I have him prowling the corridors looking for rats and shria. We get quite a few of them down here in the deeper corridors, especially in the wintertime. I'm planning to loan him out to Omondis, the head of the society of Gleaners, once the snows start in earnest this fall."

Andrion, his mouth full of what tasted like venison stew wrapped in a smooth, slightly sweet piece of flatbread, raised his eyebrows on hearing the translation. As soon as he could speak again he said enthusiastically, "This is wonderful! I have spent most of the past sixteen years studying dypalfar devices and I would love to spend some time working with you – maybe when this is all over with, eh?" Gylabris smiled back. Despite the serious threat posed to his city, he was willing to brush aside any anxiety at the prospect of having someone, even if it was a member of the Sky People, so interested in what he was doing. His colleagues in the Keepers had given him bare tolerance and no encouragement.

Andrion finished devouring another bite of the hand meal. In a way, it was almost like a sandwich. Thinner bread, true, and the filling was warmer and more liquid than you could ever achieve between two slices of bread. But it was good. Maybe they should mention it to Remy or Lev, after they got home. Lev's mania for marketing was now such that he was talking about opening a second Bathing Maiden in Roma, and perhaps one in Auverne as well.

A thought occurred to him. "I suppose if we're going to work together, Gylabris, I had better learn to speak the leukalfar language. If my son could pick it up in a few months I should be able to master it as well. I've studied many languages, but most of them were dead ones and there was nobody to discuss pronunciation or idioms with." After that had been translated Gylabris smiled secretively on both Mothris (of whom, as Andrion's proxy, he was becoming fond as well) and Andrion.

"If my latest project works as I hope it will," he said smugly, "you might not have to."

Andrion took a large drink of what seemed to be sweetened cold tea, washing down the last of his meal. He hadn't yet been offered any alcohol here, and wondered whether the leukalfar used it. He had never heard of a human society that didn't. On the other hand, this was supposed to be breakfast. He leaned toward Gylabris, peering at him, and asked "Your latest project?"

"Kziintke!" the little Keeper replied with pride. "My master work! I found him many years ago, already disabled, standing at attention in a tightly locked storeroom. Unlike nearly all of the other automatons here, he was never violently destroyed and his most delicate mechanisms were unharmed. I had only recently begun my work, and for many years I was afraid to work on him. He is, after all, a robon about the size of our young friend Ghrztum down there." Several places down the table, the young troll was impressing the visitors with the size of his appetite. It appeared he might be able to give Andi and Fjuri a run for their money.

"A robon!" Andrion cried in astonishment. Those pinnacles of the dypalfar automaton hierarchy, made to resemble enormous muscular humans in heavy armor, were the biggest peril to be faced by adventurers hunting treasure amid the ruins of dypalfar cities. They could be anywhere from around Andrion's height of six-foot-two to a staggering twenty feet tall, and like all their kin they were inimical foes – programmed to destroy all intruders or die trying.

Gylabris had never been happier. A geek in a world of priests, smiths, and grocers, he had never before found someone who shared his passion, felt the excitement and potential of his life's work. Instead of "yes, yes, excuse me I have business to attend to" Andrion was practically hanging on his every word. Had the little Keeper ever had the opportunity to meet more people outside his tribe, he would have found that Andrion's attitude was much less rare among the races of men. Those short-lived, fast-breeding, dynamic people were always interested in anything that might give them an edge.

In that moment, he decided he would do anything he could to aid Andrion and his companions in the recovery of their missing children. They *must* have the opportunity to spend more time together, to learn together – and that would not happen if their visitors were lost forever in the world beyond the portal.

He lurched to his feet. "I am very close to completing my work on Kziintke, and I must hurry if he is to aid you in your quest!" he announced breathlessly. "I will return as soon as possible. You will be interrogating the dypalfar guards?"

Mystified, Andrion replied "Yes, we must get to that now that we've eaten. Your 'Kziintke' is going to aid our quest?"

"No time to lose!" Gylabris cried, halfway out the door. "I will see you in the room leading to the chamber of the device!" With that he vanished at a run down the corridor.

Andrion and Mothris exchanged a glance. "He's a very friendly fellow," Mothris volunteered.

"And a bit eccentric," Andrion replied. "He reminds me a little of some of the older mages at the Academy. They get so wrapped up in their work, they lose track of the fact that the rest of the world has no idea what they're talking about." He rose to his feet, observing that the rest of the party had also finished eating and were following his lead. "Let's go make friends with the dypalfar, shall we?"

Chapter 47: Intelligence

During the meal and the conversation with Gylabris the five-minute time limit had elapsed on Andrion's latest Befriend spell on Arctoris. Yet the old Keeper had sat at table with them, mechanically munching on some food, without seeming to come to his senses. He was staring into space as if half asleep, and had not spoken to anyone in some time. Andrion surveyed him worriedly. The old rascal might have plotted to kill his son, but he didn't wish him permanent harm. Likely he was a valued resource for his people, if a bit obsessed with keeping the status quo.

He applied the Befriend spell one more time, and Arctoris turned to look at him. "My friend," Andrion said, "I must apologize for having roused you from your sleep so early. I see now that you are tired, very tired. And I think that you need a nice, long nap. Is there any place within the Sanctum where you might rest?" After this had been translated one of the guards who had accompanied with them spoke up.

"Keeper Arctoris has a room here in the Sanctum where he sleeps sometimes if there is not time for him to return to his home. Shall I escort him there?"

Andrion smiled beneficently. Years of command as Magister had given him a sureness, an expectation that he would be listened to and obeyed. This did not precisely apply when he was home, of course… "Thank you, uh…" "What is your name, please?" Mothris asked, and the guard responded "Simdis, sir." Andrion had picked up on that and went on, "Simdis. Please take care with Keeper Arctoris, as I fear that the recent events may have been traumatic for him. If he should become disordered in his mind, please keep him calm. I trust that the rest of the Keeper guards will continue to follow his orders that, once we have gone through the portal, the portal will remain open and the door leading from its chamber kept shut and barred."

"Yes sir," Simdis responded after hearing the translation, and led the half-dazed old Keeper off in the direction of his room. The attunement sphere had been transferred from the pocket of his robe to Bernadette's pack. Andrion had his fingers crossed that when the effects of the repeated Befriend spell had dissipated (assuming they ever did!) Arctoris would be too disoriented to effect any reversal of those orders. If he did, they were all in a lot of trouble. For a moment he toyed with the idea of spot-welding a dypalfar shield (a couple of which they currently had) over the control panel on the device. But suppose they came through in a hurry, and had to cut through that without damaging the machine?

Another guard led them to the room that had been selected as an interrogation chamber, and the seven of them were ushered inside. One of their dypalfar captives, looking alert but hostile, sat bound to a dypalfar metal chair, his hands free. He was drinking a glass of what Andrion assumed was water, and on a plate in front of him were the remains of a meal of some kind. He set the cup of water on the table and glared up at them menacingly as they came inside.

Andrion thanked the guard and asked him to wait right outside the door. Then he walked to the table and sat down in the chair opposite the prisoner, Mothris at his side as the others spread out around the room. The prisoner craned his head and stared at the troll for a moment, then brought his pale gaze back to the man who was obviously in control of this interrogation. He was firmly determined to reveal nothing.

Andrion smiled at the man across the table and gently cast the Befriend spell. A feeling of reluctance, as if he had dipped his hand into filth, passed over him as he did so. He had learned this spell as he had learned so much in his life, because he had an insatiable thirst for knowledge and because, as his brother Erik said, no learning is ever wasted. But to use it repeatedly to turn a thinking, self-willed human being into a mass of fawning jelly, was repellent to him. He had only to remind himself *why* he was doing this, and pressed on.

"Hello," Andrion told the prisoner, as Mothris translated. "I hope that you found the food satisfactory?" The captive nodded, an expression of confusion making his pale blue eyes look innocent as a baby's. "I apologize for the inconvenience, but my son and

306

daughter are missing and we must find them. My name is Andrion Drakespring. May I have yours, honored dypalfar brother?"

His resistance swept aside by the Befriend spell and Andrion's courteous approach, the guard replied "My name is Kagrenzkar, of the clan Brazkram," he replied, looking considerably more friendly than he had a couple of minutes ago. "I am very pleased to meet you, Kagrenzkar Brazkram," Andrion replied. He was coming to find that certain things enhanced the effectiveness of the Befriend spell, including smiling, respectful and friendly forms of address, and frequent use of the subject's name. His skin crawled.

"I am sorry to tell you," Andrion went on, "that a couple of days ago my very foolish son and his two companions went through the portal and into your world without any guidance. I was wondering if you had any word of what became of them."

"One of them was of the slave race, right?" Kagrenzkar asked, "And the other two young men of perhaps Norse or Galise ancestry?"

Stifling a grimace, Andrion replied "That would be them."

"Oh," Kagrenzkar replied smiling, anxious to please, "they were taken by the large guard force that was notified through Joining by the portal guard, and imprisoned within Mrzhandtham."

Some three hours later Kagrenzkar, now looking as dazed as old Arctoris, was led back to his cell with a happy smile on his face. All these people were his friends, and life was wonderful! He could hardly wait to get back home to his comfortable cell, though he would probably want to remove that unnecessary pad from the stone bed before lying down for a nap. Though it had not been that many hours since he got up this morning, for some reason he felt really sleepy.

Andrion, Bernadette, Lifa, and the rest of their team were escorted back to the room that led to the chamber with the portal device. Bernadette's notebook, of which only a few pages had been filled before they started this journey, was now almost full up with diagrams, maps, and notations. Kagrenzkar, their new Best Friend Forever, had even drawn some of them himself. They were thankful that his command of the leukalfar language was so excellent.

By now, all of them were beginning to understand the leukalfar tongue. Listening to it spoken immediately followed by translations in Common had led all of them to make connections. Poor Mothris had needed to be supplied with drinks on several occasions and once a session of healing magic from Bernadette, so raw had his throat become from almost nonstop talking. He was probably the most tired of all of them. But their labors for today were far from over.

They found Gylabris waiting for them, beaming and nearly vibrating with excitement. "It worked!" he crowed as soon as he spotted them. "Kziintke is a success! This is the greatest achievement of my life, and I am giving him to you to help you in your quest!" Andrion and Bernadette were both taken aback. He hadn't had much time to fill her in on his earlier conversation with the little leukalfar mechanist, beyond a mention that he was trying to activate a dypalfar robon to aid their cause.

In the corner Kziintke stood, one of the smaller robons they had ever seen. Its design seemed different, somehow, its head bigger in proportion to its body. It stood around seven feet tall, roughly the same height as Ghrztum. "Kziintke?" Andrion asked.

"It's an old dypalfar word," Gylabris explained. "A few words in their language survive in ours, mostly words that imitate sounds – like the name of our young troll friend there." He pointed at Ghrztum. "His name means 'thunder' or perhaps, the sound of thunder. Kziintke's name means the sound of 'clink.' It seemed appropriate…"

Momentarily embarrassed, hoping that his new friend Andrion's companions would not think him too silly, Gylabris called to his creation. Not really *his* creation, of course. Some long-dead dypalfar had designed the automaton and made him what he was. But Gylabris had brought Kziintke back from the dead, had reprogrammed him to obey new masters. It was no small accomplishment.

"Kziintke!" the little Keeper called, "come here!" The robon, which had been as immobile as any deactivated automaton to be found at the bottom of Undernight, awoke and stood to attention. Its eyes alight, it walked over to the group and then stood, awaiting further commands. Then it spoke and everyone in the room except Gylabris nearly fell over in shock.

"Your command, Master?" it asked in flawless but mechanical-sounding leukalfar.

Bernadette, Andrion, Anja and Lars had all had extensive experience questing in dypalfar ruins. They had encountered dozens of dypalfar automatons, from the little knee-high bugs to towering robons, and they had never heard any of them utter so much as a mechanical squawk. By all the gods, what magic was this?

"First language Common, translate to leukalfar," Gylabris said crisply, high as a kite on the stir Kziintke had caused.

"Yes, Master," the robon replied in Common, followed almost immediately by the translation of that phrase in leukalfar. The rescue party, and everyone else in the room, were so astonished that pandemonium broke out for a few minutes. Gylabris very nearly achieved Nirvana, had such a concept been postulated on the world of Terris.

Andrion, the eldest and most educated (if not always, necessarily, the wisest) among the rescue party, was the first to get a grip on his astonishment and begin delving into the mystery. "Can I address Kziintke myself?" he asked Gylabris, then listened as the robon, not Mothris, translated the question. Gylabris replied in leukalfar, and Andrion had already picked up the affirmative response when Kziintke said, in the common speech (curiously clipped and lacking in inflection, but perfectly understandable)

"You may speak to me and I will relay what you say to my master. But only my master may give me commands."

"This is very useful," Andrion said after another few moments. The idea of a machine that could speak and communicate with humans, and translate between languages, was so huge that he could hardly wrap his mind around it. But he was eager to do so. In his visions, the entire world would become a better place as a result of the technology of the insular, cruel dypalfar – applied in a humanistic fashion with an eye to ending war and famine, and bettering the lot of every person on Terris.

"Oh, there's more" Gylabris assured them. "Kziintke is trilingual. He was supplied by his builders with the common tongue, the leukalfar tongue, and the dypalfar tongue. I think he must have been built at a time when the dypalfar and the leukalfar acted as allies, but commerce among them and the encroaching Norsemen had not yet been halted by war." Andrion pondered this statement for a moment, as translated by the automaton.

"Then you mean to send him through the portal with us?" he asked. "To translate with those who do not speak leukalfar?"

"Ah yes," Gylabris replied. "And not just his language skills will aid you. Look at him! He was designed to be a warrior as well as a linguist!" Andrion eyed Kziintke up and down. Indeed, other than the overly-large head the automaton was a fairly typical robon. But he and his brother Erik, and their wife Bernadette as well, had turned more than one dypalfar robon into scrap during their time as adventurers. They were not invulnerable.

Andrion hesitated. Now that they had the information they needed to penetrate the dypalfar stronghold they were eager to get on with their mission, to find the missing kids before they were taken even further afield – or killed out of hand. They needed to get moving! "Gylabris," he said, his voice freighted with emotion the little Keeper heard – though it was not reproduced in Kziintke's translation. "Kziintke is unique. He is no more invulnerable to harm than any other of the dypalfar automatons, and we have Mothris to translate for us between Common and leukalfar. It appears many within that dypalfar city of Mrzhandtham are conversant in your language. Would it not be better to spare your creation from harm?"

To Andrion's shock, the robon replied without translating his speech or waiting for a response from the "Master." "I do not mind the risk," it said, the contrast between the mechanical sound of its speech and the meaning conveyed by it so profound that all who heard it were struck dumb, "For many ages I have awaited a purpose, and my new master has given me one. I wish to go with you and help you find your children."

Chapter 48: Captivity

As they were hustled through the door and into the next room by the guards surrounding them, Andi thought huh, that guy wasn't lying. There *was* an army of guards waiting to take them into custody. That'd teach him not to ignore what people told him when he asked... The room beyond was large, and filled with more people. The dypalfar all looked like first cousins somehow, every one of them with slightly waving black hair, pale blue eyes, and the men all had long black beards. They seemed shorter and more heavily set than other alfar races he knew, not fat by any means but less willowy. Their ears were as long and pointy, their eyes as tilted as any ljosalfar or sylvalfar he'd met; and he supposed that people much like these lurked within his own Galise ancestry.

They were hustled out double doors at the far end of the room to mill around in a broad corridor beyond, as someone Andi identified as an authority figure came forward. The martial-looking woman was flanked by a raft of associates, including – he saw to his surprise – several leukalfar dressed in what looked like livery of some sort. After surveying the three captives she barked a command to one of the leukalfar, in the leukalfar tongue: "Take the girl to the slave quarters. The others will come with me."

Two of the leukalfar nodded and seized Meri by the arms as she was thrust forward, screaming and kicking. No, he couldn't let them take her! They needed to stay together or they would never get out of here. Though the odds looked bad, Andi readied a spell he hoped might disrupt the guards surrounding them and give them a chance to break free.

The Terror spell might give them a few moments, he hoped – grabbing Fjuri by one wrist to exclude him from the spell as he prepared to cast it with his other hand. Without physical contact Meri would be affected too, but he figured he and Fjuri could scoop her up with them and be three corridors over before the spell's effects dispersed. It created a fear so deep your enemies could think of nothing but fleeing from you, until the spell's short life ran out.

Andi released the spell at last… and nothing happened. The female officer who had ordered Meri taken to the slave quarters looked right into his eyes and smiled. "Never met a magic block spell, have you?" she asked. Oh crap, magic block! This was a spell that was common in Remus, one Papa Andrion had learned at the University of the Magical Arts there. But it wasn't much in use in Iscandia. Andi didn't know how to cast it, and he had never witnessed its effects before. It was as if he simply had no magical energy, though he could feel it strong within him.

Like all born mages, Andi had an instinctive knowledge of his own reservoir of magical energies – one that told him precisely how much he had at any time. At this moment, he could not have lit a candle with fire. None of his magical energy was available to him. He could still have cast a dragon spell, he thought; but there was no dragon spell in his arsenal that would enable him to immobilize two dozen armed guards and a similarly-armed mage. His shoulders slumped in defeat, and he hung his head in despair.

Some minutes after Meri had been dragged off by the leukalfar slave guards, spitting and clawing like an infuriated smilodon, the troop escorting Andi and Fjuri arrived at a set of doors and the two captive boys, accompanied by the female officer and four of the two dozen, were hustled inside and into a cell. There was some discussion in a language Andi supposed was dypalfar, presumably purposely intended not to be understood by them. Then the doors clanged shut and they were left alone.

They sat there on the stone floor, panting a little. Good: they were alive and more or less uninjured. Bad: pretty much everything else. "Well, that could have gone better," Andi remarked to his oldest and closest friend. Fjuri's mouth creased in a smile even as his brows knit in frustration, and he stifled a laugh.

"Do you think?" he replied.

After a few minutes the two got to their feet and began exploring their options. Andi tested and found that the magic block spell had expired, leaving him free to use his magic. The cell contained two of the standard dypalfar stone beds and two buckets: one full of clean water and the other empty, presumably intended to hold their wastes. Well at least, Andi thought, they don't intend us to die of thirst.

Their environment was clean, almost sterile. The only opening in the stone walls was the door, a standard single dypalfar metal door with a lock Andi could presumably have cut through in a minute or two. But once they were through the door, then what? In the confusion and his upset over Meri's being taken away he had not paid close attention to the route that they'd taken to get here. And even if he and Fjuri could have found their way back to the portal, they couldn't leave until they'd found Meri!

"What happened back there, man?" Fjuri asked. He knew Andi had all kinds of magical skills, and he couldn't believe he'd just stood there and let them drag Meri off. To the slave quarters, had they said? The word hadn't come up much during his time of absorbing the leukalfar language, but he thought that was it.

"Aw shit," Andi replied, hanging his head. "Because Meri's leukalfar they think she's supposed to be a slave, and they took her off to the 'slave quarters' – wherever those are. I was going to blast them with terror, which would have made everyone in the room want to run away and hide for about a minute, but that bitch up front cast a spell on me that took away my magic."

Fjuri goggled at him. "They can *do* that?" he asked. Like both his parents and Andi's own papa Erik, he hadn't a magical bone in his body and no knowledge of the way magic worked, either. Andi shook his head.

"I'm afraid so," he replied mournfully. "It might not be a spell everybody can do. I got the idea that woman was something like a general or a commander. So I should be able to use magic to break us out of here – but I don't think we'd get much further than the door of our cell."

"Yeah," Fjuri mused. "Those guards we captured know that you can burn through metal with that spell, and by now probably everybody in this place knows about it too. I'm surprised they left us in here." There was a window in the door, but it was covered by a latched metal plate on the outside so they had no way of knowing how many guards might be out there.

They sat on the stone benches, they paced the narrow confines of the cell. They drank from the one bucket and made deposits in the other. Footsteps were heard, and a narrow slit Andi had not noticed before opened in the bottom of the door to admit a tray on which were two bowls of a gray porridge-like substance with mysterious objects floating in it.

As they were both fairly well starving by now, they ate every scrap of it and looked around for more. It wasn't all that bad, actually. Just as the two boys were about to lie down on the hard stone and try to sleep, having run out of topics of conversation, there was the sound of many booted feet outside the door and it was opened. As they heard the lock click, Andi once again felt that sensation as if his magic was on the other side of an invisible, impenetrable barrier. There was that tough-looking woman again, and this time she held in her hands a glistening dypalfar-metal object that resembled a decorative torc.

It was jointed so that it could be opened and slipped around his neck, then clicked together. As it did so, a jewel on the locked end lit up. Andi could just catch the red glow if he peered down his nose, and supposed it must make him look demonic. He wondered if they might get a chance to see a mirror. "There," she said, with the air of a mother who had just dealt with a toddler's mud-streaked hands, "there'll be no further battle magic from you."

Damn, Andi thought, I should have used a dragon spell on her before she got this thing onto my neck! Though probably that would just have resulted in him and Fjuri getting shot full of arrows. They were all facing in the direction of the jail entrance now; and the woman took her position at the head of the group, Andi and Fjuri in the middle of it with armed soldiers (they really seemed a lot more heavily armed and armored than you would expect for ordinary guards) on every side. "Let's go," she ordered, and led the way.

Chapter 49: The Interrogation

They had not bound the boys' arms, and if there had been anyplace for them to run to Andi supposed he could have gone dragon and gotten them away. But the corridors were only just big enough for his dragon form, with no room to get airborne – and on the ground as a dragon he could not move all that quickly. And what if the collar was magically unbreakable, and it strangled him? It simply wouldn't work. Well, these people hadn't killed them so far. Perhaps they didn't intend to. He hoped!

This time they were both paying close attention to their surroundings, trying to memorize the layout. Andi had an idea that the corridors leading down to the portal room were those off to the left, remembering this intersection from when they'd been hustled through here hours before. Eventually the party fetched up before two large and magnificent dypalfar metal doors, and in the anteroom beyond them they halted as there was a shuffling and some discussion in the dypalfar language. All but two of the soldiers guarding them peeled off – either to wait outside the doors or report for some other duty.

As this was going on the boys looked around the room with curiosity. This was really the first time they had had an opportunity to examine a room in a dypalfar city occupied by living dypalfar, and there were many differences in décor between this city and Mrzhgradfendz. The leukalfar there seemed to prefer comfort in their surroundings, but had few strictly decorative items in their homes. Here, there were several vases (though empty of flowers) and other items with no apparent practical use.

Andi stopped and stared as his eyes fell across the other occupant of the room, who had been sitting bent over a metal desk writing on a stack of papers as they came in – and was now sitting stock still, staring back at them. By the gods, she was beautiful! She looked to be around Andi and Fjuri's age, which for an alfar girl probably meant she was a little older.

Like all the dypalfar they had seen so far she had pale skin and raven hair, flowing down in glistening waves past her shoulders. Her blue eyes were darker than most, almost violet in color. They were enormous and almond-shaped, up-tilted, with thick black lashes. Her mouth, surely the most lovely mouth Andi had ever seen, was wide and curving, medium-full lips like an elven bow in a deep rose shade, currently half-open in surprise as she looked back at them. At him, actually.

Rezira Bagrum had been working on the paperwork she'd been assigned for hours, and the tedium was such she'd been ready to fall asleep at her desk. Now she sat staring in amazement, every nerve alive, as she beheld the two captives who had entered the room with her mother and a unit of soldiers. *These* were the invaders Mother had told her about? She'd said they were boys, and Rezira had been expecting striplings like her younger brother Karzeno. They had supposedly been accompanied by a leukalfar girl of around Karzeno's age, so that would have made sense – though why an "invading force" should consist of three unarmed children made no sense at all. Were the leukalfar across the portal in Mrzhgradfendz now letting kids play with the portal device?

But these were no children! They were taller than all but a few full-grown men she had met, and the darker one considerably more muscular as well. He was very tall and manly, to be sure, but with his black hair and blue eyes somewhat darker than her own he might almost have been one of her own people. Give him some time to sprout a black beard and grow that hair out a little more to hide the lack of pointy ears, lose that tan, and he could have passed for an outsized citizen of Mrzhandtham with no trouble at all. Boooring!

But the other one! A little more slender than his friend, but that hair! And those eyes! In her whole life (all almost-seventeen years of it) she had never seen anyone with deep auburn hair and warm brown eyes. Since fleeing to their own plane of existence all those millennia ago, the dypalfar had become as homogeneous as a flock of goats. You almost needed name tags to tell one from another.

Those warm brown eyes were gazing at her now with wonder and a sort of longing, and Rezira gasped and mentally shook herself. She saw with a frisson of surprise that he was wearing a magic-block collar. There were probably no more than three of those in existence, and that this one had been brought from the vault in which it was stored must indicate the "boy" was a powerful mage. She saw only the slightest down of a beard on his face, and she was sure that males of the races of men all grew beards on their faces when they reached adulthood. She'd read all the books. How could someone not yet grown have such powers?

The shuffling of the guard contingent was completed, and the commander realized that her daughter was staring raptly at the two captives when she still had an inch-thick stack of reports to get through. "Rezira!" she said sharply, and the girl started and picked up her pen.

"Yes, Mother?"

Raising an eyebrow, the Commander told her daughter, "You'll have plenty of time to study the invaders later on. They'll be our guests here for quite some time to come. I believe you have work to do?" "Yes Mother," the girl said and bent to her task again, eyes downcast. It sucked being the daughter of the youngest commander the Great Army of Mrzhandtham had ever known.

Despite their situation, Andi had a faint smile playing about his lips as they were ushered into the office behind the bossy commander lady, their two remaining guards keeping them in tight control. He hadn't understood any of their exchange, since it had been in the dypalfar tongue; but he got the sense that the girl was the commander's daughter. They looked a lot alike, for one thing. More so than any dypalfar looked like any other, that is. But where the daughter was young and beautiful, the mother seemed ageless and more handsome than pretty. Probably it was mostly her attitude. She made his own mom, the world-famous badass and literal "dragon lady," who had slain Tarragin and saved the world, seem like a pussycat.

Szursta Bagrum took a seat behind her desk and smiled somewhat tightly up at the two captives in what she hoped was a disarming manner. She was much more comfortable with simply issuing orders and having them obeyed. "Please be seated so we can talk," she told the boys in Leukalfar. The initial report from the captured portal guards had indicated that one of them, at least, was fluent in the slaves' tongue. And since they had a girl of the slave race with them, she supposed it made sense.

The guards reinforced her request by pushing Andi and Fjuri down onto the two chairs that sat on this side of the desk. Was she about to interview them for jobs as clerks in a counting house? The whole setup here, including the desk outside and the paperwork that stunningly beautiful girl (sigh) was doing, reminded Andi of that.

After they were seated the woman leaned forward a little, once again with an attempt at a smile that looked about as friendly as a smilodon's. "My name is Szursta Bagrum," she told them, "and I am Commander in Chief of the Great Army of Mrzhandtham – that is the name of our city here, on this side of the portal," she added at their blank looks. The other races of humanity always seemed to have trouble with Dypalfar, one of the reasons why most who had dealings with the slaves learned Leukalfar instead of the other way around. Not that the leukalfar were exactly human anymore…

"I would like to know who you are and why you came here," she went on. "Well?" Fjuri was picking up some of this, but being a captive and confronting a strange woman didn't help his shyness any. He remained speechless, and Andi jumped into the gap.

"I'm Andreas Drakespring and this is my friend Fjurbund Steadfast, of Waterdon" he told her formally. "Fjurbund doesn't understand this language, only Common." It was mostly the truth.

"Waterdon?" she asked, surprised. The dypalfar were deeper in lore than any of the other races, and they had taken most of their knowledge with them when they fled. She knew of the place, in the way that a resident of 21st century Earth might know of the Colossus of Rhodes. It was ancient history. But she did know it was a long, long way from the portal in Mrzhgradfendz. "What are two boys from Waterdon doing here, if I might ask?"

Andi gave her his most fetching grin. It was similar to one his father occasionally used on his mother, and it certainly worked on her when *he* did it. In Andi's experience, when he tried it, it was not always enough to forestall Mom's wrath. It wasn't all that successful on Szursta either, though she did give a half-smile in response as he said "We were adventuring. I was supposed to be going back to my studies in the Eparchy, but we had heard about the portal and we wanted to see if it really existed."

Szursta's brows knit. "So, you were *playing hooky*?"

"Essentially," he admitted. "It was a stupid stunt, and I am going to catch hell from my mom, but it seemed like a good idea at the time." He hoped that he was right about Szursta being a mom. Maybe she would have some sympathy, if not for him and Fjuri then at least for their mothers.

"And what about the girl of the slave race?" the Commander asked next. "Why was she with you? She is not one of ours. Do you Norsemen and Galise now also keep the leukalfar as slaves?" Andi's face flushed dark at the words, as he struggled to bite back his anger. The thought of Meri thrown into the slave quarters, and the idea that he or his people would *own* other human beings as if they were cattle, was so offensive that he was almost glad of the collar. Without it, he might have fried the woman on the spot.

Through gritted teeth, Andi replied "That girl is my sister. She was found as an orphan and adopted into my family when she was a little baby, and until a few months ago she had never met any other leukalfar. Nor did she know their language." Szursta's eyebrows went up, and she sat back in her chair. Clearly, she had struck a nerve. And that one of the slave race should have been taken in and raised as one of the family by a woman who, judging from this boy's appearance, was probably Galise... very odd.

Well, she was trying to make nice here. Unlike Andi's father she had never had the opportunity to acquire the Befriend spell, nor did the more ordinary sort of charm come easily to her. Andi, on the other hand... "My friend and I only wanted to see your wonderful city. The leukalfar on the other side of the portal have quite a civilization actually, and one of them kindly offered to let us go through the portal for a look at the room on the other side. We thought nobody would be there, he said nobody had been for years, but then your guards surprised us and I guess he panicked and closed the portal with us inside. We didn't mean any harm."

"I only reinstituted the practice of guarding the portal room after I became commander," Szursta told them. "So likely your leukalfar friend had reason to believe it would be unguarded if no one had tried recently. For years, the little buggers were always trying to sneak spies into our city. We believed they were looking for a way to free our slaves. But then the attempts just stopped, and everyone thought that the device must have broken. I knew they were wrong."

She seemed to take some pride in having the foresight to guard against leukalfar incursions through the portal. Andi supposed that without that, the Mirskhrazana might very well have succeeded in their attempts at some point. "Well," he went on, "that's my story. We were just three kids exploring what we thought was a deserted room in an exotic world, and ran afoul of your guards. We weren't trying to invade your city, or hurt anybody."

Szursta was thoughtful. The boy was so... endearing, so plausible. She had to remind herself of the terrified Joining broadcast by the guards after this innocent-looking youngster had knocked them across the room and then immobilized them with some kind of battle magic, before threatening to burn holes through them with a mysterious type of spell none of them had ever seen before. How could this sweet-seeming, handsome boy be that kind of a powerful mage? Was he really an adult wizard using a glamor spell?

Well, whatever sort of magic he had at his command he was helpless without the key to the magic block collar. And he couldn't be using a glamor spell with the collar on, unless he had one with a permanent effect that did not have to be maintained. It seemed that there was nothing to do for the time being but pass this information along to Leader Degranac, and find out what he wanted to do with them.

As Szursta was about to rise and request that the soldiers return the boys to their cell, Andi spoke up again. "If you don't mind my asking," he said with a look of disarming earnestness, "you mentioned you are the Commander in Chief of the army. I thought the dypalfar came to this world to escape war once and for all. So why do you need an army?"

A bitter smile quirked her lips as the commander replied, "It is precisely so we can continue to escape war. For as you will know young Andreas, when you are older and wiser, it is ever the way of humankind to seek advantage over their fellows – by force, if necessary. This world is truly a paradise, overflowing with plants both useful and beautiful, strange animals that proved easily domesticated, and no sentient beings before we came here with our slaves. But it is much smaller than the continent of Agena. In order that our paradise should not be destroyed, and so that we can grow enough food to feed our people and slaves, we have built our cities deep in the earth."

"Just like before…" Andi said, thinking about what she'd told him.

"That's right," she nodded. "Before our underground fortresses protected us from a sea of enemies, some of them religious fanatics who hated us because we did not worship their gods. Now, they provide living space for our people while the land above remains unspoiled. Except for our grain fields and plantations, our herds of meat animals, you might wander above and never guess that people lived here. Well, and except for the leukalfar farm laborers and their dypalfar overseers," she admitted.

Andi was stunned. It didn't seem like such a bad way to live, really, keeping most of the land intact instead of paved over with roads and the dwellings of men. "But the threat that makes you arm yourselves?" he asked, getting back to the original topic.

"Ah, yes," Szursta replied. "The threat is from within, I fear. Within our race, at any rate. Slaves do all of our labor, with only the jobs requiring a lot of education being performed by dypalfar. Many young men and women are eager for action, so they happily accept weapons training and become members of the army. Indeed, we require that all young people perform service to the city between their twentieth and twenty-fifth years."

Waiting patiently, happy that he had gotten the commander to open up, Andi looked at her with friendly interest and she went on.

"The cities of the dypalfar in Agena were spread far and wide, across two provinces. Because of our power of communication, the Joining, we were in some ways united as a people. But there were differences. When we all came to this world, after years of preparation, the residents of each city moved into a new city on the other side of whichever portal they had come through. Because of the relatively small land area of our little plane of the Netherworld, these cities are clustered much more closely together than they were in Agena. But still, we do not mingle. We have become like relatives who never see each other, and only communicate by letter."

"You mean you can't just read each other's minds all the time?" Andi blurted out.

"Maker, no!" Szursta laughed, "What a thought! Packed together as we are in our cities, our minds would be deluged with every passing thought from everyone in the vicinity – what they were having for breakfast, the disagreement with their wife, their need to empty their bladders – we'd be driven insane inside a day. The Joining only works as a reaching-out. Those of us most skilled in it can send thoughts to a single selected mind many leagues away, or broadcast to everyone within range. It was thus that the signal was given for our final move through the portals to freedom."

Yeah, Andi thought bitterly. Freedom for the dypalfar, not for the leukalfar. These people had so many accomplishments, so much to offer the world. How could they be so wrong-headed? Putting a couple of things together, he went on "So, you and your distant relations don't get along so well?"

Szursta frowned, surprised at his perception. Then she went on, "Indeed, young Andreas. Though face-to-face meetings between citizens of different cities here are rare, each of the cities sees the others as a potential threat. By maintaining a strong army, and making sure the other cities all know about it, we prevent any one of them from getting ideas about coming over and taking what is ours."

Now Andi was stunned. *What?!* The dypalfar seemed to have been locked up with nobody to talk to but themselves for too long. The neighbors are going to come over here and take your stuff, which is exactly like their stuff? When you're all members of the same cultural group and should be working together, maybe getting a little diversity going? He suspected that the dypalfar had committed the biggest mistake of their lives by coming here, cutting themselves off from the rest of humanity. The world of Waterdon was vibrant, alive with a mix of different people and ideas passing through it all the time. Here, everyone and everything was just the same, over and over again, for thousands of years.

"I suppose a strong army helps keep the slaves down, too?" he asked casually. Szursta's smile vanished and her lips (really a lot like the lips of that girl in the outer office, Andi realized) went hard, compressed into a straight line. Clearly, she hadn't appreciated the comment. "Sorry," he said with an apologetic smile. "There is one other question I'd like to ask you, if you wouldn't mind."

Szursta got a grip on her irritation. Why should it bother her that this stranger boy pointed out the obvious? They had found the ideal way in which to live, with their slaves and their automatons in this perfect little world, and there was no reason it should ever change. Anyone who said otherwise was just a troublemaker, someone who had not yet been taught to understand the way in which things should be done. She yanked her mouth back into a sort-of smile and said, "Yes?"

"That girl in the outer office who was working when we came in," Andi said. He hoped if he laid it on thick enough he'd get a straight answer. "She's so beautiful, and she looks so much like you. Is she your daughter?" Szursta's smile became genuine for a moment. She was very proud of her children. How many other dypalfar women had produced not one but two beautiful, healthy babies – and then gone on to achieve the pinnacle of power in their chosen profession? Most alfar women of whatever race rarely managed more than a single child, but she felt she might have had three if she hadn't been busy achieving her military ambitions. She was a very competitive woman.

"Ah yes, Rezira," the Commander answered. "She is my pride and joy, and already working with me in administrative matters. But I have another child as well, a boy. My duties as commander, of course, prevent me from spending as much time with my children as I would like." Wow, Andi thought. It looks like I pushed *her* button. He knew that the alfar didn't pop out nearly as many kids as did the races of men, so that short-term at least the men were gradually outstripping the elves in population back in Agena. She must be proud as punch to have two kids *and* high office. He'd need to think about how to use that.

Andi was not normally so manipulative, though he had the skills for it. He felt bad about getting over on people and didn't usually try to do so in his daily life – but here he was a captive, surrounded by enemies, and he was going to use any tools he had at his disposal to get himself, Fjuri, and Meri free and safe and back where they belonged. These dypalfar were welcome to their "paradise" – much good it was doing them.

"Thank you for your kindness, Commander Bagrum," he told Szursta, smiling into her eyes. Szursta felt a slight flutter at the pit of her stomach. What *was* it with this boy? Her studies of the races of men told her he was likely no older than sixteen, from the lack of facial hair. Had she not been busy building her career and had gotten around to motherhood sooner, she might have grandchildren his age.

Feeling uneasy, she said somewhat curtly "Guards, take them back to their cell. Oh, and make sure they have something to eat."

The guards saluted and exited the office with Andi and Fjuri tightly controlled between them. The boys were taller than either of them, and were it not for the fact they were utterly unarmed and unarmored they might have tried to make a break for it. Andi, at least, was pretty sure he knew how to get from here to those corridors that led to the portal room.

As they came back out and the doors closed behind them, Rezira arose from her desk. She'd made almost no progress on those reports, straining to hear what was being said behind the doors of her mother's office. She hadn't been able to make out more than one word in three, but it did seem as though Mother had done a lot of the talking. She'd thought the boys were here to be interrogated? It made her wonder.

She hurried to the center of the room before the group could reach the outer doors, saying imperiously "Wait! I would have a word with the prisoners!" The guards, two of Szursta's handpicked troopers, knew that Rezira was damn near second in command around here. She was a brat, really, but her mother doted on her and if she wanted to speak with the prisoners it was best to let her do so before she threw a fit that would bring Mother out to see what the fuss was about.

She looked up into Andi's face as if she was trying to penetrate into his soul. For a race with mind-to-mind communication, he supposed, men or other alfar might be a disappointment in the intimacy department. Their minds were ever a locked door. She was petite, shorter than his mom even, and at this distance so meltingly lovely that he could scarcely speak. Mister Smooth became Mister Um-uh as soon as an unfamiliar, attractive, young female came into range. He fervently hoped that was something he was going to grow out of.

She bored into his warm brown eyes with her deep violet ones, and said in perfect leukalfar "I am Rezira Bagrum. You are?"

Unable to stop gazing into those bottomless eyes, Andi replied "Andi... uh, Andreas Drakespring." The leukalfar formality allowed for no nicknames, no diminutives. Rezira savored the name in her mind as if it were flowing off her tongue. It had a certain rhythm, could have used a few more hard consonants... but she liked it!

"Andreas..." she murmured, and seemed almost to melt. Andi, in shock, half expected her to fall into his arms. What the? In another moment the young woman had become all business again. She leaned a little closer and murmured so softly he barely caught it himself – and he was sure the guards, keeping a little distance, would not have heard a thing – "I will see you later. Keep an ear out for my coming."

Chapter 50: Invasion

"It's the magical essence, I'm sure of it," Gylabris was saying, as Andrion and the rescue party sat gaping at the words Kziintke had just uttered. "All of the automatons use magical essence vials of course," he explained. "The bugs and rollers mostly rely on lesser magical essences to fuel their self-directed behavior, and they act much as animals do. Most of the robons use more powerful magical essences, and they frequently seem to exhibit more intelligence than do their smaller kin. But Kziintke has a vial containing the magical essence, the soul, of a sentient being – a human or perhaps one of the other humanoid species such as gatti or saurions. In a way he *is* that person in a new body, one of metal. So of course he has sentience and his own ideas about things. Am I right, Kziintke?"

"Not exactly," the seven-foot, gleaming automaton replied in its mechanical voice, speaking in leukalfar as Gylabris had. "I do not remember inhabiting another body. I remember when you awoke me, but nothing before then. I am as my dypalfar creators made me, and as you remade me. But I live, and I think, and I am." The automaton then repeated this all in Common for the benefit of those who had not understood the previous speech.

"Amazing," Andrion said almost under his breath. Not only were trolls people, but machines could be people as well? As angry as he was at the kids for their escapade, he was coming to feel that this trip had been worth it. Provided they got their children back safe, of course. "Well," he said aloud, "Our interview with our new buddy Kagrenzkar revealed that it's the same time on the other side of the portal as it is here. I think it would be a good idea if we didn't go over to Mrzhandtham until the middle of the night, when there will be fewer soldiers on duty and fewer non-combatants wandering the corridors. So we might as well all get some rest."

Sleeping quarters were found for all of them except Kziintke, who needed no rest, and they napped for several hours before arising and eating another meal. Feeling much more up to the task at hand, the group gathered in the room before the door to the portal chamber. Arctoris, they'd learned, was still sleeping. Feeling a twinge of guilt, Andrion hope the old elf would eventually wake up – and that he'd still have a mind when he did so. He didn't know of any previous case where a subject had received so many hours of nonstop Befriend.

Kziintke and his master Gylabris were awaiting them when they arrived. The automaton's metal face was of course incapable of expression, but the little Keeper was beaming at them. "I certainly wish you a safe trip," he told them. "I personally will join those keeping watch here, making sure that the door is secured and listening for the knock that will signal your return. Kziintke, while you accompany our friends you will take orders from Andrion. Is that understood?"

"I will do so," the mech replied.

"Thank you Gylabris," Andrion said, then looking around him at the rescue squad added "Time to go, people. Everybody ready?" There was a chorus of assent, and the door guards pulled back the bars and opened it to admit them. "Barricade it tight," Andrion admonished them as he went through, his words quickly translated by Mothris. "While we're out in the city searching for the kids the portal will be wide open, and almost anything might come through."

The guards saluted, and after the last of the party was inside the portal chamber the door was closed behind them. They could hear the sound of the bars being thrown shut, then scraping as if heavy objects were being piled up. As this door would be the only thing standing between Mrzhgradfendz and a full-scale dypalfar invasion, Andrion hoped it would be enough.

Bernadette produced the attunement sphere from her pack and got out her notebook, to make sure that she got the power-up sequence correct. She thought she had it nearly memorized, but she wasn't sure what the result of entering it incorrectly would be. Other dypalfar devices she'd encountered and had to open using trial and error had been fault-tolerant, but suppose this one had a security feature?

The portal sprang to life before them and they stood looking into the long room beyond. As on the previous occasion, it appeared at first glance to be empty. "There's no way they haven't re-manned it after we kidnapped their guards," Bernadette murmured to her companions. "Anja, you and I will go in first and get up onto the counters on either side nearest the portal. Try not to make a sound, and maybe we can take out some of the guards with our bows before they realize we're here."

They were both expert marksmen, Anja having been trained by Bernadette in archery since the girl was no more than six. They crept through the portal, crouching low. Both of them had honed their sneaking skills in many an aptrgangr-infested dungeon, and there was scarcely a sound as they boosted themselves up onto stone counters on either side of the room. From this vantage they could see that heavily armed and armored soldiers were hiding behind counters on both sides, down toward the far end of the room. There were three on either side, and it appeared they were dozing.

They were awake. But standing guard on an empty room for hour after hour, long into the night, had taken its toll on the guards' alertness and they had failed to notice that the portal was now open. Before they could get on their feet, one on either side of the room was down for good and the others were sprouting arrows from armor or shields. The daimonic bows and arrows Bernadette crafted at her famous Fireblood forge packed a serious wallop.

As soon as the guards were roused the rest of the party surged through the portal to join the fight. Undoubtedly, guards on the other side of that door at the end of the room would have been notified of their arrival by their fellows using the gift of Joining. Andrion only hoped that the rest of the troop would not burst through the doors and join the fight before they'd had a chance to disable these.

Mothris, whose only weapon was the bow, also jumped up onto a counter where he was out of the melee and could choose his shots. Ghrztum, a terrifying sight to the dypalfar soldiers, ran into the room swinging that huge club. Stone against dypalfar metal armor was not a good choice, but with his long arms and the length of the weapon his opponents couldn't get near him with their swords.

Ghrztum sent one soldier's helmet flying, then knocked the man out on the next swing. As he did so another of the dypalfar guards slashed frantically at him from behind; and though the troll's hide was tough it sliced through and left a cut that stained the white fur with red. "That hurt!" Ghrztum roared, spinning to face his back-stabbing adversary. He brought his club down hard on the man's arm, breaking it through the armored bracer, and the sword dropped to the stone floor with a clang. But the stone head of the club broke, as well, leaving the troll with only a big stick (and his dagger and sling) for weaponry.

Andrion shot a burst of electrical energy from both palms that took two of the soldiers off their feet, hurling them against one of the stone counters and leaving them stunned. Then he whipped the daimonic warhammer he was carrying off its baldric and tossed it to the troll. "Ghrztum, catch! I think you can make better use of this than I can!" Wincing a little at the pain from the wound in his buttocks, Ghrztum grinned ferociously and plucked the weapon out of the air. He hadn't understood Andrion's words, but the meaning was clear.

With Lifa and Lars using swords and Kziintke laying about him with his dypalfar metal arms, it was only moments before all of their foes had been dispatched. Bernadette was quick to apply healing magic to Ghrztum, closing up the painful and bleeding wound and leaving him feeling much better than he had even before the fight had begun. Healing magic could have that effect. Then she went around checking on the rest of the party for anything that needed healing, before seeing to the fallen dypalfar.

In her younger years Bernadette had been a cheerful killer, slaughtering bandits with glee and sending vampires and undead aptrgangr back to their eternal rest with scarcely a qualm. After she'd become a mother her pacifist streak had gotten stronger, though – and while she was willing to kill as many enemies as necessary to protect her children, she didn't want anyone to die if it wasn't necessary.

Three were beyond help, but the other three lived. They'd been knocked out, but had no life-threatening injuries; and before long they also had no weapons or armor, and were securely bound. Gathering the team behind him, Andrion stepped to the door and opened the lock with a moment's concentration. Then he sent a beam of actinic energy, flames and lightning intertwined, down the center line between the doors from top to bottom —severing the bar that had held them closed.

Andrion had a few words with Kziintke, and the automaton stepped forward and gave the doors a shove. The hinged side remained attached to the door frame on each, but the other side flew into the next room where a ring of awestruck dypalfar soldiers stood staring in disbelief. Their shock increased when he spoke to them in dypalfar, as Andrion had instructed him: "We are here to rescue the children. Lay down your weapons and we will not harm you."

There were only eight of the invaders, and though the troll and the talking robon sent icy fingers of dread through their hearts, there were two dozen of Mrzhandtham's finest troops in the room – nearly the entire night contingent, called here by a sending from their fellows who'd been standing duty in the portal chamber. "Yeah," their commanding officer called back scornfully, also in dypalfar. "I don't think that's going to happen. You come any closer and we'll kill you all." Kziintke relayed the reply to Andrion in Common, and he sighed. It had been worth a try.

"Berni," he said quietly, "think you could get us a little running room?" he gestured to the ranks of soldiers packed closely in the doorway just beyond the open doors. She gave him a tight grin and stepped up to the front of the group, saying quietly to her companions behind her "Get ready for action." Then she faced their opponents, took in a deep breath, and cried "Kraf-Luft-Struung-Wund!"

It was rare that The Fireblood had such a good target for the Gale dragon spell. Nearly every soldier in the room beyond them was shoved back and sent tumbling. Those in the rear were crushed between the stone wall and their colleagues in front of them, knocked senseless. Even those whose landing was cushioned were somewhat stunned, and before they could regain their feet their foes had rushed fully into the room and were upon them.

Ghrztum wielded the daimonic warhammer Andrion had provided him with glee, breaking bones and knocking out opponents right and left. "I *like* this weapon!" he roared. In these close quarters Bernadette slung her bow on her back and drew her sword, a daimonic short sword she'd enchanted to burn, shock, and siphon stamina from anyone struck with it.

Anja, too, had switched to a blade, fighting beside her lover as Lars used the superior reach of his height and his daimonic longsword to knock back their enemies. Her mother Lifa stood on her other side, giving as good as she got. Only Mothris among them had nothing to do, and Bernadette yelled at him, "Mothris! Run for the doors and wait for us in the corridor!"

The dypalfar soldiers were too involved fighting off their foes to worry about one skinny adolescent leukalfar non-combatant sneaking around them to the doorway that led out to the corridor beyond. We should have left him back in Mrzhgradfendz, Bernadette was thinking. With Kziintke to translate, there was no reason to put the boy at risk. She sincerely hoped she would be able to return him to Myrkra unharmed.

Whenever Andrion had a good group of their opponents in his sights he hit them with a dual-wielded blast of lightning. Dypalfar metal was a reasonably good conductor of electricity, and frequently this would knock them senseless for a while. Before they could get back up, Kziintke would come by and club them over the head – putting them out of the fight.

In a couple of minutes all twenty-four of Mrzhandtham's Finest were lying scattered around the stone floor, senseless or injured so badly they were no longer able to put up a fight. Some of them were probably dead, but Andrion couldn't bring himself to worry about it. They'd been offered a chance to surrender, after all.

All of the rescue party were still on their feet and there didn't seem to be any serious injuries. Bernadette wanted to inspect them all and apply healing as needed, but she was getting very anxious about reinforcements arriving. "Come on people!" she cried, "Let's get the hell out of here before more of them show up!" She had her notebook out and was studying the map, searching for the route that would take them to the prison block where Kagrenzkar had said he believed the prisoners had been taken. He had not been on duty when the kids had arrived. They found Mothris waiting anxiously for them in the corridor, his bow ready to take down any more guards that might come from that direction. Soon they were all moving off at speed, making as little noise as possible.

Behind them in the portal room's antechamber one figure arose from amid the heaped bodies. Corporal Zrstan Ingmandzam was in shock. He could not believe that his entire unit had been wiped out by a handful of invaders. Some of his comrades were still alive, he thought – he could hear them groaning. But his orders were clear. The invasion must be stopped before Mrzhandtham was overrun, and the doors guarding the portal room had been disabled.

After sending a mental message to headquarters to report his actions, he staggered across the room clutching his broken arm, stumbling over the bodies of his fellow soldiers as he made for the switch on the wall. Below it a series of buttons was set, and he tapped in the code before pulling the switch. Machinery rumbled, and then grinding and rumbling filled Zrstan's ears as the room's entire ceiling fell in – burying him and the remains of his troop of soldiers, along with the entrance to the portal chamber, in a mixture of enormous stone blocks and rubble. The portal might remain open, but no more invaders from Agena would be coming through to their city.

Chapter 51: The Leukalfar Resistance

As they'd hoped, coming here in the middle of the night meant that they encountered few people wandering the corridors as the rescue party hastened along the turnings – climbing staircases and ramps as they made their way from the portal chamber in the depths of the city to the prison block, several levels up, where they hoped they would find the kids. Maybe they would be able to free their children and come right back down here without getting into any more fights, Bernadette hoped. She was conscious that they were invaders here, with no real right to come into the city, and the dypalfar had every right to fight them. It wasn't like going after bandits, and she regretted every life they had just taken.

The ever-burning dypalfar lamps were everywhere, providing dim illumination. Ahead of them in an otherwise-unoccupied corridor they spied a small figure, a leukalfar woman from the looks of her. She was down on her hands and knees scrubbing the stone floor, a bucket beside her. "Mothris," Bernadette said quietly to the leukalfar boy, "go down and talk to her about why we're here. We don't want her getting into a panic and running to tell some dypalfar she's seen invaders, or we may have an army down on our heads."

He nodded shyly and headed toward the woman at a slow lope, his big feet making little sound on the flagstones. The leukalfar woman's long, pointed ears picked up his movement though, and she ceased her scrubbing as she got to her feet to look at him. "Quiet, boy," she hissed at him. Then as he got closer she realized she did not know him. "I don't recognize you, boy. Who are you?" she demanded. Up close, she reminded Mothris a bit of his mother.

He put his hands out and said softly "Greetings, Mother (a term of respect for any woman above puberty if you didn't know her name), I am Mothris of the Ankhrazana." The woman drew a blank, then realized he was referring to one of the ancient tribes of the leukalfar. Many of their customs had fallen into disuse during the millennia in which they had been enslaved here in their dypalfar masters' "paradise."

Putting a few things she'd heard lately together, she spoke quietly. "You are one of the invaders? From beyond the portal?"

"We're not really invaders," he told her. "We're just looking for some lost kids. Two big Sky People boys and a leukalfar girl. Have you seen them?"

"Ahhh," the woman said with a sort of sigh. "I have heard that the boys are in the prison block two floors up." She gestured. "But the girl was taken to the women's slave quarters, and I have spoken with her. Merelle, of the 'Drakespring' tribe?"

"That's her!" Mothris said excitedly, smiling at the woman. She smiled back.

"I can take you to her, but you will have to get past the guards and unlock the doors. Do you have help?" She peered around him, and immediately spotted the rest of the rescue party hanging back – far down the corridor.

"We didn't want to scare you," Mothris explained.

"All right then, I'm not scared," she remarked drily. "Ask them to come forward."

Rather than shout in the corridor, possibly rousing more guards, Mothris hurried to his companions and said quietly, "It's all right, she's not going to raise the alarm. She says Merelle is in the slave quarters." Bernadette and Andrion both flinched at that. Their little girl, locked up and enslaved. Different though she might be, they loved her as one of their own. The party hurried back down the corridor to join the woman, who had now tossed her scrub brush back into the bucket and stood awaiting them.

Palms out she said "Greetings. I am Umina of no tribe. Or perhaps you might say, of the free leukalfar. I am one of the leaders of those of us who fight here to free our people from bondage." So, a slave rebellion had continued here among those the dypalfar had taken with them when they crossed the portal to their new land. It must not have been easy for them to make headway, if the leukalfar were still enslaved three thousand years later.

With Mothris translating, Bernadette addressed the leukalfar woman. "Greetings, Umina. I am Bernadette Drakespring, mother

336

of Andreas and Merelle Drakespring. I understand you know of Merelle's whereabouts?" Umina peered up at her curiously. Bernadette was not a tall woman, but Umina stood no more than five feet in height.

"Her mother. She said she had been adopted by the Sky People, and I see that it is true."

Bernadette had more questions. "Free leukalfar? Are you and your 'tribe' truly free, Umina?" The woman smiled somewhat grimly at her. "I come and go much as I will," she told them. "But my masters believe me to be still enslaved. I work to raise a revolt that will bring them down and free us all forever. But it is very hard. What one of the dypalfar knows, all may learn in moments. You cannot hold them captive, but if you kill anyone there are reprisals. My fellows and I have been doing this all our adult lives, and still the leukalfar are enslaved. But we are free in our hearts, if not in our bodies."

As Mothris translated this all remained silent for a moment. It was hard to say whether Kziintke, built to serve a master, could have any understanding of the human longing for self-determination; but the rest of them felt deeply for her and wanted to help her even as they hoped she would help them.

"Come," Umina said abruptly, "and quietly. I will take you to the women's slave quarters where your Merelle is being held. There are guards and the door is locked, but I think that you shouldn't have much trouble with them. I believe the time may have come for us to rise up at last." With that she turned and led them back down the corridor where she'd been scrubbing the floor (or perhaps, pretending to as a cover for something else?), and along a series of mostly narrow, dim corridors and back stairways.

As they followed her, Bernadette's mind was in turmoil. How could they not help Umina in her cause to free her people? But what was a full-scale slave revolt going to do to their chances of effecting a safe rescue of the children? She supposed they were just going to have to play it by ear and hope for the best. This motto had stood her in good stead when she was younger, but age and experience had left her reluctant to leave things up to chance if planning and forethought could produce a better result.

Miraculously, or perhaps by Umina's design in the route she chose, they encountered no dypalfar guards during their journey to the quarters of the female slaves. The dypalfar wanted complete control over their slaves' breeding, and while babies and children were allowed to remain with their mothers, fathers were left completely out of the picture until sons were old enough to be moved to the men's quarters. Their daughters, they never knew.

Umina motioned to them to halt before going around the next corner, and murmured "The door and the guards are around the next turn and perhaps fifty paces down the corridor." She peered at Bernadette and Anja, both of whom had their bows at the ready. "Are you any good with those?" she asked, not failing to note the quality and gleaming lethality of their appearance though she didn't recognize that they were daimonic weapons. Bernadette understood the question and nodded, replying in leukalfar "Good enough."

Umina nodded as curtly and said "I'll distract them. If you both shoot at the same time, maybe they will both be dead before they have time to use the Joining to raise an alarm." This time, Mothris quietly translated her words so that all would know the plan. They waited for a minute as Umina, bent and seeming somehow much older than she had been a moment before, hefted her pail of water and began hobbling down the corridor around the bend. They waited until they heard her speaking with the guards, then Bernadette and Anja slipped silently out into the corridor.

Bernadette was standing to Anja's left and she motioned to her to take the guard on the right. Down at the far end of the fairly short corridor, on either side of a set of barred double doors, the two guards were bent over Umina. They seemed to be giving the woman a hard time for coming to be let in at this hour, and she was complaining loudly "It's not *my* fault! They want the floors all clean and dry for the Masters when they get up and go about their business. When else am I to clean, without leaving wet stones for them to tread on? Take it up with my overseer, it was *her* orders!"

The guards didn't much like being lipped by this wizened little slave, and they both stood with hands on hips glaring down at her. Neither of them was wearing his helmet, figuring that they could better see what was coming at them bareheaded. They'd have plenty of time to pick up the helmets and put them on if they saw armed invaders rushing down the hall.

They never saw Bernadette and Anja, though, and in one instant each guard's brain was penetrated with an arrow that came in at the temple and went all the way through their heads before being stopped by the metal doors. They collapsed soundlessly to the floor, and now it was Umina looking down on *them* with satisfaction. It seemed that Apoldros had finally decided to answer her prayers!

Bernadette motioned to the rest of the party, still crouching in the side corridor, to come out. They all hurried down to meet with Umina at the doors. "Do you have a key?" Bernadette asked her quietly.

"No," the woman replied shortly. "I have... *other* ways of coming and going from these chambers."

"No problem," Andrion said. He had understood from the context what was going on, and approached the doors. In moments the twin locks were sprung, and the doors to the women's slave quarters fell open.

Chapter 52: In Bondage

The doors opened on a broad antechamber with narrow corridors running off of it in three directions. No one was there. "Are there any dypalfar here?" Bernadette asked. That Joining ability was a real danger, as even a glimpse of them by a single dypalfar could bring the whole city down on them.

"No," Umina replied smugly. "There are those among us who are trusted by the Masters and are given better treatment, more food in exchange for acting as overseers to us within the quarters where we sleep and eat. I think that, having made us as we are, the Masters now see us as repellent, subhuman, and they dislike having any more contact with us than necessary. We may have to do a little more fighting, but I don't think anyone here can raise an alarm."

The leukalfar woman set her bucket and brush on the floor beside the doorway and, walking upright now, strode to the rightmost of the three corridors. "Come," she said quietly. "Let us find your Merelle." The corridor ran for a long way, with many doors off of it. One at the end opened onto a large dormitory room, with stone beds several times the width of what they were used to seeing in dypalfar dwellings spotted along each wall. On each of these, as many as a dozen leukalfar, women and children, were curled in sleep.

Down at the end of the room furthest from the door a much smaller bed sat, and on it Meri was curled in dejected misery, sobbing quietly to herself. She was shackled to the bed by one ankle, and on a chair at the bedside a relatively tall and burly-looking leukalfar matron sat watching over her. "Stop that sniveling," she hissed at her charge. "If you wake anyone I'll have you beaten again." Meri gasped and stifled her next sob, sunk in despair. Would Andi and Fjuri ever come? Would she ever see Mama again?

Umina was leading them down the corridor between the rows of enormous beds, but when Bernadette saw through the dim light that it was her daughter there, she broke from the group and ran down to where the matron was now standing over the helpless girl, threatening her with violence. This leukalfar woman was taller than she was if not as broad, and she was armed with a rod of dypalfar metal with a knob on the end. It looked as if it might be capable of breaking bones.

With her left arm, made strong by years of archery and working at the forge, Bernadette seized the woman by her sinewy elbow and dragged her away from the bed where Meri lay. As the astonished matron tried to make sense of this apparition, she hauled off with a right cross and hit her *hard*, right in the middle of her face. The woman dropped as if she had been poleaxed, knocked cold. Then Bernadette kicked her with a booted foot for good measure.

Meri had uncurled and was sitting up now. "Mama?" she said in a small voice, not sure she could trust her vision. Then, "Mama!" a squeal of joy. Spurning the unconscious matron, Bernadette leaped onto the stone bed to enfold her daughter in her arms. Tears of joy were running down her face.

"Baby, oh baby, did they hurt you?"

"I'm all right, Mama," Meri said in a muffled voice, pressed against her chest.

Andrion was at their side and in another moment he had the shackle open before taking his turn to hug and kiss their daughter. "We've got you back," he said gruffly. "Everything is going to be all right." Meri struggled out of his embrace for a moment to look up at her parents.

"Andi and Fjuri? Are they all right too? Where are they?"

"We're getting them next," her mother assured her, "but we met Umina and she told us where we could find you so we wanted to come get you first. Look what we brought!" She hefted an object that Meri seized on with glee.

"My pack! And my bow's here too! Oh, thank you!" The clothing she'd been wearing when they were captured had been taken away and replaced with the shapeless gray shift that was standard garb for all of the slaves in Mrzhandtham. But Meri had soon dug some underclothes from her pack and then put on her custom-fitted leather armor over the top. The clothing change made her feel 100% better.

Meanwhile, the rest of the group had stripped the nicer, green shift from the back of the matron – along with her rod, her badge of office – and torn it into strips with which they bound and gagged the woman. They hoisted her up onto the bed and fastened the shackle tightly around her ankle. Meri went around the group exchanging hugs with Lifa, Anja, Lars, and Mothris. Ghrztum picked her up bodily in his long arms, squeezing her against his furry chest – armor and all. Then he let her back down, a big grin on his face. He was so glad to see his little friend alive!

Meri was a bit taken aback to see a dypalfar robon among the party. Obviously it was not hostile, but what was it doing here? She was astounded when it bent at the knees to bring its face closer to hers, eyes glowing, and said in mechanical but flawless leukalfar, "Greetings, Merelle Drakespring. I am Kziintke. I am glad that you are well."

Meri responded automatically with "Greetings, Kziintke. Thank you." Then she turned to look up at Andrion.

Her papa smiled down at her and put an arm around her shoulders. "Kziintke was awakened by a friend of ours among the Mirskhrazana. I think you and the boys met him – Gylabris?"

"Oh yes!" she said, her outlook brightened by the memory. "He had the cutest little dypalfar bug running all over the place."

"That's him," Andrion replied. "He has been working on bringing Kziintke back to life for a very long time, I think. Probably longer than I have been alive. Kziintke is not exactly an automaton. He's more of a metal person."

As the family reunion had been going on, Umina was on the move. She saw the arrival of this curious rescue party as the opportunity she had been waiting for her entire life, and she intended to seize it. She ran from bed to bed, rousing the occupants. "Arise, arise!" she called, "The day is at hand! The guards are dead, so take up your weapons and gather in the hall. We must free the other women, and then the men!"

A large percentage of the women and children in the room seemed to be in on the plot, and many of them were soon brandishing objects that might be used as weapons: broomsticks, kitchen knives, rocks. Anything they could lay their hands on had been hidden away, waiting for the day when it might be used to gain their freedom.

As the dormitory's occupants headed for the corridor, intent on going door to door and rousing each of the other dormitories' residents in turn, Umina turned back to the rescue party. "You came through the portal at the bottom, right?"

"You know of it?" Bernadette asked. "It's sort of a well-established rumor," the older woman replied. "None of us have ever beheld it, as it has been heavily guarded. Besides, I gather that it can only be opened from the other side?"

"True," Bernadette replied. "I assume you intend to lead your people through the portal to Mrzhgradfendz, the city on the other side?"

Umina hesitated for a moment. It was all coming true, and it was little hard for her wrap her mind around it. Then she spoke again. "Yes, it is our only hope for freedom. Even if we here were able to slaughter all of the Masters within Mrzhandtham, they would certainly broadcast their troubles to the other dypalfar in this world. Likely the differences they have with them would be forgotten, and multiple armies would arrive at our doorstep. We cannot simply barricade ourselves inside this city, as all of our food comes from above. We must go with you back to the other world, there to seek a new home."

Bernadette was excited and horrified at the same time. A city-wide slave revolt could certainly work to distract the army from their small party and their mission to reclaim the boys; but there was no way they could just slip back through the portal and then close it leaving these people to die or be returned to slavery. And getting them through to the other side, then dealing with finding them homes, was going to be a nightmare. Time to focus on the problem immediately at hand, then. She drew Mothris close to translate as she and Umina engaged in a discussion.

"Umina," Bernadette said, as she and her party prepared to leave and go looking for that cell block once again, "you seem to have your people well-organized, and soon you will have gotten everyone out of the women's quarters. You plan to go then and free the men?"

"Yes," the woman replied. "We should easily be able to swarm under the guards and they will undoubtedly have the keys on them. But they will probably call for help using the Joining. Then we'll see how well the Great Army of Mrzhandtham does against an army of angry slaves."

Bernadette was horrified. "Your people may outnumber them, but they are armed and armored and have been trained in fighting. Many of you will be killed!" The leukalfar woman shrugged.

"We have been treated like animals, to be discarded at need, since the time when your remote ancestors were first mastering the working of iron. We will kill as many of them as we can, and some of us will die. And when their soldiers are no more, we will flee to the portal and freedom."

"You know the way, then?"

"I have been down there, as far as the guarded room which they say lies before the room in which the portal opens. It is heavily guarded, but perhaps not now?" No flies on this one, Bernadette thought. Their very presence reflected a distinct reduction in the guard population down there near the portal.

"We left some dead, some tied up, and some unconscious or severely injured," she admitted. "Those will have called for help, of course. I think they believe we are the forerunners of an invading force, though. They are guarding against more people coming in through the portal from the other side, not from those seeking to escape. At least not yet."

Umina looked thoughtful. "And *will* any more be coming through from the other side?" she asked. Bernadette was surprised at the question.

"No! The door beyond the room that houses the portal device is locked and barricaded. We came through only to rescue our children, not to turn this city on its ear."

"Huh," came the disappointed reply. "Well, I guess we'll just have to rely on ourselves, then – and some help from you, perhaps?"

"Get your people to the portal as soon as possible," Bernadette told her. "If you are able to pass through into the room beyond it, not many will be able to fit inside it. And I or my husband Andrion must be there to give the signal for the door to be opened. We must go now to free my son and my friend's son from their imprisonment. Then we will meet you there."

Chapter 53: The Jailer's Pretty Daughter

The really bad thing about being locked up in this cell, Andi thought, was that it was just so gods-cursed *boring*! He and Fjuri had been thrown back in here after their interesting (and informative) interview with Commander Bagrum. To their surprise and delight, more food had been brought – better, more substantial food which they'd devoured with enthusiasm.

After that they had talked for a while about what they'd learned. Fjuri had actually picked up quite a bit of what had been said, but discussing it helped them exchange insights, as well as giving them something to do to pass the time. "Three thousand years ago," Fjuri said, "my Norse ancestors were living in sod huts, dressing in fur, and just starting to figure out what to do with iron. And at that time these dypalfar were doing pretty much exactly what they're doing now. It's like they decided they'd gotten it right and there was no need to ever change anything again."

"Exactly!" Andi cried. "They've gone stagnant, and it's killing them. Give them another three thousand years and they'll probably dry up and blow away, if their slaves or their fellow dypalfar don't end up killing them all first. They need to start interacting with the rest of humanity, before it's too late."

They thought it was probably mid-evening by now, and having nothing better to do they lay down on the hideously uncomfortable stone beds and went to sleep. It *had* been a long day. Hunger woke them, and they sat on their beds stretching and feeling the aches that had sprung up as they slept. There was no way to tell what time it was, as they were far underground and the ever-burning dypalfar lamps looked exactly the same always.

Or perhaps there *was* a way to tell – through the metal cell door they soon heard the sounds of activity, footsteps approaching. A tray was thrust through the slot at the bottom of the door, accompanied by a gruff voice saying in leukalfar, "Breakfast! Eat it up." Eat it up they did, and it was surprisingly good. The climate on the surface above them must be much more equable than the one outside Mrzhgradfendz, as there were scrambled eggs, actual leavened wheat loaves, some kind of fresh fruit that was tart but delicious, and sizzling patties of what they thought might be pork sausage. It was a feast!

"Commander Bagrum must have taken pity on us," Andi remarked to Fjuri around a mouthful of succulent sausage.

"I think she liked you, you dog," his friend replied smilingly, "and so did her daughter!" Andi flushed pink. He seemed to have picked up that trait from his mother. They sent the tray back through the slot, and later on a couple of heavily-armed guards came in and exchanged their buckets for another full of clean water and one that was empty.

Alas, that was the highlight of the day. They spent hours discussing their situation, the lovely and mysterious Rezira Bagrum, old times in Waterdon. They got down on the floor and did calisthenics, tried to conduct wrestling matches in the narrow space between the beds. "What I wouldn't give now for a musty old tome of forgotten knowledge," Andi groaned, as they lay on their stone beds staring up at the ceiling after a relatively light lunch of bread rolls, cheese, and fruit.

Andi's papa Andrion, who had taught both the boys to read and cipher, had always been big on those musty tomes. He must have gotten his enthusiasm from his own papa, old Francois Lamonte. While Andi had a thirst for knowledge, he preferred to get it in more interesting ways than spending hours with his nose in a book. Lessons learned at first hand, like smithing with papa Erik or chemia with Mom, always seemed to stick better.

By what they presumed was late afternoon, judging from the renewed growling of their stomachs and the apparent time elapsed since lunch, Andi was almost ready to try going dragon and pushing their way out of the cell. The magic block collar, as it had been called, seemed to place a thick barrier between him and a part of himself that had always been there, almost from his earliest memories. It was driving him mad.

Dinner came again, this time more bread rolls and enormous bowls of a savory stew. It was delicious, and again they devoured every drop. What else was there to do? After eating they talked some more about their situation. Andi was wondering what Rezira had meant, when she said that she would see him later. An entire boring day had gone by, and nothing. He was considering talking loudly with Fjuri about some imagined plot, with the hope that the guard might report the activity and they would be called in for another interrogation by the commander. But suppose she wasn't so nice next time?

Eventually they slept again. Andi awoke from a deep dream of home and family to find the cell door swinging open – and Rezira standing there, robed and hooded and looking unbelievably mysterious and beautiful. "Shhh!" she warned. "Don't make a sound. I have come to free you." Still half asleep, Andi was having a hard time getting his thoughts in order.

"Rezira, what have you done?" he finally managed to ask. She smiled at him beguilingly, a look that nearly short-circuited his brain on its way to parts lower down.

"Just drugged the guards," she murmured back. "Mother made sure that my education was complete, including magic and chemia."

She stepped closer to him, sending him into a state of near paralysis. As she reached up toward his throat, she said softly "Hold still. Just a minute now…" With a click, the magic-block collar parted from around Andi's neck and for the first time since it had been put on he could feel his magic flowing within him. Just out of pure joy he reached up and a globe of magical light blossomed above their heads.

"Oh, that's so bright!" Rezira gasped. "Are you trying to draw more guards?"

"Sorry," he stammered, looking down at her and falling into those violet eyes as into an abyss. She was as lost, gazing into his warm brown ones until Fjuri spoke up.

"Uh, maybe we should be going?" Andi snapped out of it. They had no baggage to gather, nothing but the clothes on their backs, and were soon moving out of the open cell door and through the jail area.

A pair of guards within the block itself were seated at a table, dozing. Another pair, similarly asleep, were at a table outside the jail's outer door. "Sorry it took so long to get back to you," Rezira said with a smile. "You would not *believe* how hard it was to get Mother's key for the magic-block collar. And as soon as she wakes up, she's going to notice it's gone. So we need to get moving!"

The girl led the two friends along a corridor, seeming to know exactly where she was taking them. None of this looked familiar, and Andi didn't think they had been here before. The corridors were deserted, and clearly it must be the middle of the night. After a while Andi said "Um, Rezira... I'm really grateful to you for taking off that collar and getting us out of prison. But *why* are you doing this?"

She halted for a moment and turned to look at him, her lovely eyes sparkling in the blue glow of the ever-burning dypalfar lamps that lined the corridor. "Because I believe in the cause of leukalfar freedom – of course, silly! My people wronged the white elves just so they could enslave them, and for thousands of years they have been suffering in bondage. It's not *right* to own other human beings, and even after all we did to them the leukalfar are still human. It has to stop!"

Laudable sentiments, and it thrilled Andi to the core that this beautiful girl was on the side of Right. But he was still having some trouble seeing the connection between breaking them out of prison and freeing the leukalfar. "Uh..." he said, but got no further as she went on, "That's why you and your friend came here through the portal, right? You're here to free the slaves? Mother has been telling for years about how the leukalfar on the other side of the portal were always trying to come here and do that, so it stands to reason that's why you're here. You're not leukalfar, but you came with a leukalfar girl, so..."

She peered at him, and Andi felt utterly unable to speak. Damn, her beauty was so distracting, and he so much wanted to appear a hero in her eyes. But he just had to tell the truth. How could he lie to this goddess, this angel? He put his hands on her shoulders and looked deep into those eyes. "Rezira," he said softly, struggling not to lose his train of thought, "the leukalfar girl is my sister. Fjurbund and I came to Mrzhgradfendz, the leukalfar city on the other side of the portal, because we'd heard about the portal and wanted to see for ourselves if it existed."

She stared at him, so heart-stoppingly beautiful he could barely breathe. "Your sister?" she asked uncomprehendingly.

"My mom adopted her as a baby," Andi explained. "She had never met any other leukalfar until this past spring, when she and I went to spend time at the Great Temple of Apoldros, in the Eparchy. We learned to speak the leukalfar tongue there, and talked to an old leukalfar Chanter who told us about the portal."

Rezira cast her eyes down, freeing him from imprisonment. She said softly, "Oh." Looking down at her bent head, the glossy black locks flowing down, Andi was seized with the desire to plant a kiss on that head, to banish all her troubles and make everything be all right. As he stood rapt, her mind had been working – and abruptly she looked up again, her eyes sparkling with joy and those divine lips wreathed in a smile.

"It's all right, then!" she declared. "Of course, when you got here and realized that the local leukalfar were trying to free your sister's people, you had to step in!" To his astonishment, she stood on tiptoe and reached up to plant a sweet kiss on his cheek. "And you're going to succeed," she went on smilingly, "with my help!"

Don't wake me up, Andi thought dazedly. This girl was like a hurricane, and he didn't want the storm to end. Nonetheless he had to ask, "Where are you taking us?"

"To the armory, of course," she said as she turned on her heel and began once more leading them along the corridor they'd been following. She stopped again, and turned. "One thing," she said, with the air of someone mentioning a teensy problem that should be no trouble at all, "there are guards on the armory, and I think that they might not just let us go inside and get arms and armor. Can you use your battle magic on them?"

About this point Fjuri spoke up. "Um, Andi? What's your girlfriend up to, here?"

"She's not my girlfriend!" Andi insisted, at the same time he was thinking oh, if only she was... "She's taking us to get some arms and armor, and I think she expects us to help free the leukalfar slaves. But that's where they were taking Meri, so we should be able to rescue her and free the slaves at the same time. Okay?"

Both of them were eager to get back into arms and armor. They'd spent most of their childhood years wearing the latter and learning how to use the former, and they felt naked without them. Even though Andi had powers beyond belief even while standing there in his birthday suit, he felt more comfortable somehow with metal plate between him and the bad guys. And a bow or a sword in his hand wouldn't be a bad idea, either.

As they approached yet another dimly-lit corridor, Rezira halted them and whispered, "The armory is around the next corner. There should be two guards on the doors. Can you take them down?"

"No problem," Andi whispered back, considering. He *really* didn't want to kill anybody, but if he did anything besides kill the guards instantly they would call for help, and bring down soldiers on their heads. But maybe they just needed to buy some time...

"Wait here," he said softly to Fjuri in Common, and again to Rezira in leukalfar. Then he rounded the corner silently and approached the guards. They had not heard his footsteps, and were standing looking straight ahead, bored with their duty. So much military readiness, so little reason for it – the dypalfar's attempt to distract their young people with imaginary threats had failed, as had so much of their culture since they had fled from Agena.

"Eiz-Nehm-Bild-Stalz!" Andi cried, and the two guards became statues of ice. He had only moments in which to knock them out before they would return to consciousness and sound the alarm. "Fjuri, help me!" he cried, and both his friend and their young dypalfar ally came rushing around the corner. "What did you do to them?" Rezira asked, aghast at the sight of the motionless guards.

"I just turned them into icicles for a moment!" Andi cried anxiously. "Fjuri, get his sword out of the scabbard and hit him over the head with the hilt! We have to knock them out before they come back to consciousness and call for help!" Understanding what Andi needed, Fjuri grabbed for the hilt of the guard's short sword. Heavy dypalfar armor, dypalfar short swords, and dypalfar shields seemed to be standard issue for the soldiers of the Great Army of Mrzhandtham. They appeared to prefer conformity in all things.

Augh, the hilt of the sword was so cold it burned his palm as he attempted to pull it from the scabbard! Andi and Fjuri had been left in the comfortable, casual clothes they'd worn for their "fun field trip" to the portal a couple of days ago, and Fjuri grabbed a handful of his tunic, using it to protect his hand as he once again seized the hilt of the sword. It was frozen in place, but the muscles he had developed after spending months doing construction work overpowered the bond in a moment. He wrenched it to the side a little, twisting as he pulled at the hilt – and with a "tink" the ice-cold sword slid from the scabbard.

Fjuri's tunic wasn't long enough to let him lift the now-freed sword, wrapped in the hem, up high enough to bring the hilt down as a club on the frozen guard's head. He squatted quickly, setting the sword on the floor, then peeled the tunic up in one smooth motion and whipped it off over his head. Then, wrapping the tunic around his hand and arm, he bent and picked up the sword again. He brought it down with force on the guard's head, several inches below the level of his own. And the guard... broke.

Rezira's eyes had been drawn by the sight of Fjuri removing his tunic, and they had widened at the sight of those muscles. Maker, this "boy" of the Norsemen needed nothing but a bit of facial hair to be accounted a man! Impressed though she was, Fjuri still failed to overthrow the attraction she felt toward Andi. She was an elf, and elf men are not musclebound. Then he brought that sword down on the guard's head, and her mind shattered in shock as the man shattered at her feet.

Andi's eyes went wide with horror at the sight of frozen pieces of guard flying across the stone floor. As Rezira turned to retch, the sword he'd been unsuccessfully trying to remove from its scabbard finally yielded as it and the man bearing it softened, the effects of the Freeze dragon spell wearing off. He hadn't removed his shirt, instead using a tiny flicker of fire spell to bring the hilt to a temperature where it would not freeze his flesh. Now, as the guard stood swaying, he brought it down and the man fell to the floor – knocked out by his blow.

The bits of the guard Fjuri had inadvertently broken into pieces had thawed at the same time as his living companion had, and Fjuri too was standing to one side vomiting up whatever was left in his stomach, these several hours after his supper. The sight of those glistening gobbets of human flesh sent a jolt of nausea through Andi too, but he stifled it.

They needed to get what they came for and get out of here, go find Meri and get the hell out the portal before they were captured again! He put his hand on his friend's arm. "Fjuri, it's all right," he said urgently. "It was an accident. I'm sorry, I didn't know that was going to happen." Fjuri stood up, gathering himself. His eyes were red, tears running down his cheeks. He had never killed anyone before.

Next Andi put a hand on Rezira's shoulder as she bent, still retching. "Rezira! I didn't mean that to happen, but it did and now we need to get moving before the other guard wakes up. Come on, let's go!"

He'd half expected her, this frail and beautiful elfin flower, to have dissolved into useless hysteria – but after taking a couple of shuddering breaths, tears staining those beautiful cheeks, she said "You're right. Let's hope it's the *other* guard with the key in his pocket."

It was. In another few moments they were inside the armory, a good-sized but far from cavernous room lined with sets of armor, boots in piles, racks of those short swords, piles of shields. After pawing through the stacks for a few minutes Andi and Fjuri had found breastplates, greaves, bracers, and boots to fit them. Each of them took one of the short swords and a shield, more for the appearance than because they liked the armaments.

The remaining guard, whom they had dragged inside the room, began to stir and Andi knocked him out again with another blow to the head from the hilt of the sword he now bore. He wished he owned something like a long-lasting sleep spell. The biggest prize of their foraging was a pair of dypalfar helmets, of the antique design still popular in this antique city. Each bore the molded likeness of a stylized dypalfar warrior, completely obscuring their features. Other than being a bit on the tall side, and with Andi's reddish hair tucked up under the helmet, the two boys were now indistinguishable from any soldier in the Great Army of Mrzhandtham.

Before leaving the guard (along with the gathered bits of his unfortunate companion) locked inside with the weaponry, Andi gave him one more tap to the skull. He hoped the man would recover. Outside, he turned to Rezira. "If we're going to free the leukalfar – including my sister – we need to get to the slave quarters now. Which way do we go?" She smiled at him, seemingly fully recovered from her earlier shock.

"Follow me," she said.

Chapter 54: To the Portal

The rescue party, Bernadette with her notebook leading the way while Andrion watched her back (as he had done so many times during their years together), made their way cautiously through the corridors leading to the cell block where they hoped they would find the missing boys. Meri was walking in the very middle of the group, protected on all sides by heavily armed adults who would gladly lay down their lives before they would let harm come to her. She felt triumphant, safe, on top of the world. And more than a little hungry, too. Part of her punishment for having a Bad Attitude after being dumped in the slave quarters had been going to bed without her supper.

Ghrztum, shortening his strides to walk beside her, looked down and said "What's the matter, Little One?" She looked up at him.

"Have you got anything to eat?" she asked. He rummaged in a pouch hanging from the left side of his harness and came up with a flatbread wrap. It was tiny in his hand, but a good-sized hand meal for Meri and she seized it eagerly – sinking her teeth into it without even asking what it was.

"Mrmph!" she exclaimed, chewing as they continued walking along, "This's good!"

"Roasted nut paste and icefruit jam," he said, smiling down at her. "Need a little water?" Swallowing the sweet but somewhat sticky concoction, she took the skin from him and washed it down with a sigh.

"Thank you, Ghrztum. I love you."

The troll felt heat rising in his face beneath the fur. The Mirskhrazana, like most humans, loved their mates, their parents, their children, their friends. But as in most tribes of the leukalfar, these sentiments were very seldom expressed aloud. He felt both delight and embarrassment as they continued on their way.

They began to hear shouting and the sound of pounding feet as they made their way through the city, but their small party managed to avoid any confrontations. Bernadette wished she had enough invisibility potions that she could just make them all disappear until they got where they were going. The difficulties involved with helping the entire leukalfar population of Mrzhandtham escape beyond the portal were still to come; but for now all she cared about was finding the boys.

At last they came to the area marked on her somewhat sketchy map, the cell block where Kagrenzkar said that Andi and Fjuri would have been taken. Bernadette halted them behind the corner and Andrion stepped close to consult. They were expecting at least a guard or two out front, and probably more inside. And as always, there was the problem of disabling them all at once so that none could call for help. That damned annoying power!

Silent and sneaky, Bernadette stuck her head around the corner and beheld the entrance to the jail. There was a table set outside, with a couple of chairs. On those chairs sat two guards – their heads down on the table, snoring loudly. Bernadette leaned back around the corner and met her husband's gaze. "The guards are asleep!" she exclaimed in an undertone. What the?

After thinking about it for a few moments Bernadette said softly, "Wait here for a moment. If you hear anything that sounds like a dragon spell, come running." Andrion squeezed her shoulder and nodded. Moving with the stealth that had once enabled her to stand within touching distance of enemies undetected, Bernadette crept closer to the guards and inspected them. They were out like a light, drooling onto the tabletop – and from the looks of the liquid in their cups, they had been drugged.

Bernadette put a hand to the door they were supposed to be guarding, and it swung open. Unlocked! What had gone on here? Inside the jail, a medium sized room had half a dozen doors leading (one might presume) to cells. In the middle of the room was another table like the one outside, also supplied with two chairs and two dead-to-the-world guards. One of the cell doors stood slightly ajar, but she found nothing inside to tell her what occupants it might recently have held.

The other five cell doors were shut and locked, but peeking through the covered slots in them revealed them to be empty. She supposed the dypalfar were a law-abiding folk, and they didn't often find themselves locked up in jail. Who knows, perhaps this cell block had been completely deserted for decades before her son and his companions had arrived to disrupt things.

Strolling back out, no longer making any attempt at stealth, Bernadette called to her companions. "The coast is clear," she said. "It looks like somebody already sprung the boys. Either that or they've been taken away for interrogation in the middle of the night. But there are four out-cold guards here who would suggest otherwise."

The rest of them came out of hiding and explored the area. Just to make sure, Andrion opened the locked cells. They were dry, dusty, with no sign of any occupation. The one with the open door had some waste left behind in a bucket, and some crumbs on the floor that suggested a meal had been consumed here a few hours before.

"This has to have been where the boys were kept," Bernadette said firmly. "From the looks of the other cells this jail doesn't often have any occupants. And I can't imagine the dypalfar authorities would send for the prisoners to interrogate them in the middle of the night and then leave all the guards like this." She nudged the guard collapsed at the side of the table nearest her, and he fell from his seat to the floor – still snoring. She picked up the cup and sniffed it, her chemial interests aroused. She knew of no potion that would produce this effect, so perhaps it contained some ingredient that grew here in this plane of the Netherworld and not in Agena.

"If somebody's helping the boys, maybe they'll take them to the portal," Andrion said. "And even if they don't, I think we had better go there and check to see what's happening. Aren't your leukalfar slaves all supposed to be heading that way? And I don't like wandering around these corridors with Meri. I'd like to see her safely through the portal as well."

"You're right, Andrion," Bernadette replied. "Let's go see if we can get Meri through and start the guards opening up the door. Then we'll be ready to begin moving the slaves across."

It sounded as if the slave revolt was getting up to speed as they began navigating the corridors, stairways and ramps that would take them down to the portal. Once they halted, clustered in the dark space between two of the ever-burning lamps, as the sound of many booted feet running came to them from up ahead.

A huge troop of the Army's soldiers, fully armed and with weapons drawn, hurried along the corridor ahead of them – running right past the one in which the rescue party waited, willing themselves to invisibility. Not a single soldier glanced in their direction, intent on reaching their goal. When all was silence ahead of them they continued on their way, even more alert for trouble. "Looks like somebody must have given the alarm," Bernadette remarked quietly. "I hope Umina is getting her people down to the portal room, and they're not just up there getting slaughtered."

With murmurs of agreement the party continued on their way, following as she, map in hand, led the way down to their goal. When they at least reached the bottom level, they could hear a commotion as of many excited voices, and picked up their pace. Bernadette closed her eyes briefly and said a sub-vocal prayer: "Gods, *please* let us not be running into a pitched battle!"

There was no battle. Ahead of them, packed into the corridor so tightly that the rescue party could barely approach the room where they'd fought the two dozen guards earlier, was a small horde of leukalfar. They all seemed to be women, some of them with babies in their arms or accompanied by a small child. Once again Andrion got Kziintke to be his PA system, and shortly the automaton's mechanical voice boomed out in leukalfar: "Please clear the path! We are here to let you through to other side of the portal and freedom!"

Women moved aside to form a narrow pathway down which the party approached the double doors of the room in which they'd left those disabled guards. An older woman, whom Bernadette recognized as one of Umina's lieutenants, turned at their approach. Her face was a mask of near-panic, verging toward despair. "What is wrong?" Bernadette demanded, voicing the phrase in leukalfar.

"We cannot go to the portal," the woman replied. She gestured toward the jumble of stone blocks barring the way ahead of her. "We are lost!"

Chapter 55: The Commandoes

Now that Andi and Fjuri were clad as members of the Great
Army, and accompanied by the daughter of the commander of that
army, Andi figured they would just be able to stroll over to the
slave quarters and collect Meri, then go back to the portal room.
By now surely someone must have realized Arctoris' perfidy and
opened it again. And Rezira had brought along a pack loaded with
supplies – if need be they could barricade themselves in the portal
room until it opened again.

He was wrong. As they approached the corridors leading to
the slave quarters, they were overtaken by a large troop of Great
Army soldiers running in the same direction they were headed. Its
commanding officer barked at them in dypalfar, "What the hell are
you men doing just wandering around? Fall in line now! The
slaves are trying to escape!" Andi of course didn't have a clue
what had just been said, but Rezira stepped in.

"These men are escorting me!" she replied haughtily. "They
are my personal bodyguard. I will send them to help you after they
have returned me safely to my quarters."

The harried officer, in a panic to get his men to the scene of
what the Joining had described as a riot, didn't stop to wonder why
Rezira should need escorting back to her quarters at four in the
morning. Or to consider that her quarters, in the apartment of
Commander Szursta and her consort, were nowhere near this
corridor and in the opposite direction. He saluted her with a smile
(unseen behind his helmet) and said "Yes, Ma'am!" Then he and
his soldiers hurried off.

"The slaves are escaping?" Rezira asked after the soldiers had
departed and they were hurrying down the corridor once again.
"How did you two manage that while locked up in jail, might I
ask?" Andi had to assume it was just a coincidence, at first. Surely
leukalfar slaves must have been plotting to obtain their freedom
ever since the Great Betrayal. Maybe the ones here in
Mrzhandtham were just better organized?

Then another thought occurred to him, and as soon he
considered it he knew he had hit on the truth. Mom and Lifa, and

probably some other people, had come to rescue them. And somehow they'd learned that Meri was in the slave quarters. Might they still be there, in a battle with the Great Army? "Hurry!" he shouted to his companions as he burst into a run, "We need to get down there now!"

They rounded a corner to behold a scene of chaos. Many leukalfar were racing past them, running off into other corridors as they tried to escape the dypalfar soldiers who'd been sent to round them up. Others were trying to buy time for those fleeing by fighting, with anything that might be used as a weapon – or, in a few cases, with the soldiers' own swords confiscated from them after they had been knocked to the floor.

There were quite a few soldiers down, but armored as they were few had serious injuries and most would be back in the fight before long. Many leukalfar lay on the stones as well – and it did not look like they would ever be getting up again. "That's the women's quarters, where they were taking your sister," Rezira said, pointing. "And all the fighting is going on down by the men's quarters.

A few more leukalfar ran past them, headed in the direction from which they had come. "Wait!" Andi called to them, but they flinched away from what they took to be a pair of soldiers and ran off down the corridor as fast as they could move. "We're not going to get any answers with these helmets on," Andi said, and took his off. Oh, that was better – now he could actually see where he was going.

Fjuri also took his helmet off as they approached the now deserted-looking women's quarters. Two dead guards flanked the wide-open doors, the fletchings of a Daimonic arrow standing out from the temple of each of them. "Mom's been here," he said to Fjuri, then translated it into leukalfar for Rezira's benefit.

"Your mother did that? She sounds a bit like *my* mother."

Weapons sheathed, they made their way into the women's quarters and met an elderly leukalfar woman coming out. She stared at them, trying to make sense of these clearly non-dypalfar men dressed as soldiers of the Great Army. Andi quickly spoke to her, "Don't fear, Mother. We are not soldiers. We're looking for some more Sky People like us, who would have been here rescuing a leukalfar girl that was taken captive. Do you know anything about them?"

"Yes, I saw them," she told him. "They were here... I don't know, perhaps half an hour ago? There was a woman leading them, it seemed, but I have never seen a stranger group. Sky People, some huge white beast that walked like a man, a leukalfar boy, even a dypalfar robon. The boy said they were going to rescue her son and his friend from the jail downstairs, and then meet us at the portal so we can escape to your world and freedom."

"I'm the son!" Andi told her, riveted at the news and wondering at her description of the party with Mom. The "huge white beast" must be Ghrztum, and it made him smile to think that their troll friend would have insisted on joining the rescue party. "And this is my friend. What about the fighting, down the hall?"

The old woman began to look anxious. "After we had freed the women and children, those of us bold enough stormed the doors of the men's quarters and killed the guards, then opened the doors and began rousing the men. But of course the guards had called for help before they died. We had been trying to get as many of our people as possible away to the portal, but then soldiers started arriving. If something is not done soon, I fear many of our men will be trapped or killed. Now if you will excuse me, it is time for me to flee. I may be old, but I would still like to taste freedom before I die." With that, she walked out past them and left Rezira, Andi, and Fjuri staring after her.

"Andi, you've got to do something!" Rezira exclaimed. "Those unarmed leukalfar don't stand a chance, and I don't think the soldiers care whether they kill valuable property. Their blood is up, and this is their first real chance to use their military skills." Ugh, Andi thought. Using "military skills" on underfed, unarmed slaves dressed in ragged shifts.

"Let's go, then," he told her. Fjuri understood well enough. "Rezira, you're unarmed and wearing a dress. I don't think you should be out there. Once the soldiers realize we're the enemy, they're likely to start attacking you, too." Rezira bridled at the suggestion that she was a useless female.

"I have other resources, you know," she said haughtily. "My mother didn't get to be Commander of the Great Army by being good at knitting, you know. And she's tried to teach me everything she knows."

"Like using weapons you don't have?" Andi asked, frustrated that she would not just do what he asked and stay out of harm's way.

"Like I'm a *mage*, idiot!" she snapped. He was so dreamy, but what a stubborn dolt he could be, sometimes.

"Oh," he said, kicking himself for not realizing it. Szursta was the one who had cast magic block on him, and all the alfar races were supposed to have an aptitude for magic. "Sorry," he replied, then added "You don't happen to have a really good paralysis spell, do you?"

Less than fifteen minutes later the three of them, gasping for breath, closed the door on the men's quarters and broke the keys off inside the locks. All of the leukalfar slaves had now departed, those not affected by the paralysis spell helping to carry off the ones who had fallen, caught in the melee with the soldiers, when Andi had cast it wholesale across the entire rear half of the corridor.

Rezira was in awe. It had taken him only a minute to learn the spell, and then he had done something with it she hadn't thought was possible. He had fine-tuned the effect, somehow, and with an outpouring of power she could scarcely believe, had dropped everyone in that end of the room in a motionless heap.

The spell lasted for five minutes, long enough for them to begin moving among the heaped bodies gathering up swords. As more of the male slaves emerged from the slave quarters, they joined the effort. Before they were finished disarming all the soldiers a swarm of escaping leukalfar had dragged all of their fellows away, giving Andi an easy shot to cast the spell again.

While all of the leukalfar who had been struck down found themselves able to move again, and as many as possible of the slaves began heading for the bottom of the city and their portal to freedom, the three youngsters worked as fast as possible stripping weapons, shields, and helmets from the motionless (but conscious, and furious) soldiers. All these were thrown into the slave quarters before the doors were closed. Andi didn't doubt that when these soldiers could move again they would soon figure out how to get them open and retrieve their weapons; but he figured it would buy them some more time.

He had just cast the paralysis spell on the motionless soldiers one more time when they heard the sound of many booted feet hurrying their way. Uh, oh. It would take him a couple of minutes to recoup the magical energy he had just used, so he wouldn't be able to paralyze this next batch. Much better to be gone when they arrived.

"Come on!" he shouted to Fjuri and Rezira, and they ran off down a corridor away from the sound of the oncoming soldiers.

"Where should we go?" Fjuri asked. "Back to the jail?"

"I don't think so," Andi replied as they moved down the corridor at a trot, heading for the nearest flight of stairs. "They will already have been there and realized we're gone, and I think the sleeping guards will be enough to tell them we weren't taken by the authorities. Let's head for the portal."

Chapter 56: At the Gates

The three hurrying youngsters soon began to catch up with
some of the leukalfar slaves. The men had had less time to flee
before soldiers arrived, and had had to fight to get free. Of those
not killed outright, many were injured and being helped along by
their friends and companions. The trio stopped several times so
that Andi and Rezira could apply healing magic, enabling the
refugees to move more quickly and avoid getting caught by the
soldiers who were sure to be on their trail before long.

Then they dashed on, and as they got closer to the room where
all the soldiers had come from when the Waterdon kids had first
been captured, they found their way blocked by a sea of leukalfar
slaves – all close to panic as they struggled to escape but could not
move forward. What was holding things up? True, the door into
the Keepers' Sanctum from the chamber with the portal device in it
was not all that wide – but things should not be at a standstill!

"What's the matter?" Rezira asked. "Why are we stopping?"

"There's something up ahead preventing the crowd from
moving forward I think," Andi said as he peered over the crowd.
He and Fjuri were the tallest people in the area, and he could see
almost all the way to the entrance of the portal chamber's
anteroom. But what was going on? People seemed to be frantically
milling around, carrying rocks and rubble out of the room and
passing it to others to move it further from the doors.

"We need to get down there and see what's going on!" Andi
said anxiously. Rezira's lips curved in that heart-stopping smile,
and she cast a spell ahead of them. Then she spoke up loudly "You
must move aside and let us pass." Like the sea parting before the
prow of a boat, the leukalfar ahead of them squeezed in toward
either side and a path opened up. As the three of them hurried into
the gap and toward the doors, Andi asked "What was that?"

"Command spell," the girl said smugly.

Huh, Andi thought, useful for people who keep slaves I
suppose. The whole idea of the culture Rezira came from repelled
him, though he was fascinated by their technology and lore. But
she wasn't like them, she was working to help free the slaves. As

they approached the doors Andi spotted a couple of dust-coated figures struggling under huge broken stones, passing them in a relay out through the doors where the massed leukalfar slaves took them and passed them on out to the edges of the crowd.

After handing off her stone one of the dusty women looked up and spotted him. "Andi! Oh thank the gods, you made it."

At almost the same moment the other figure, which turned out to be Lifa, said "Fjuri!" and scrambled past their helpers to seize her son around the waist. "Oh son," she said, tears cutting streaks in the dust on her face, "I am so glad to see you safe and sound!" Fjuri, tears running down his own cheeks, hugged his mother tight. Then she looked up into his face and added, "And I am *so* going to kill you when we get home!'

"Don't just stand there, come on!" Bernadette said after thoroughly hugging and kissing her boy. As thoroughly as that heavy dypalfar armor allowed, at least. "The ceiling came down in here – I suspect it was some kind of security measure. We've been trying to clear it out for the past half hour and we've taken out most of the small stuff and the bodies, but the biggest blocks are right in front of the door to the portal chamber. We need your muscle!"

As the boys went into the room, which now had a large cleared path from the doors to a mountain of stone blocks in front of the doors leading to the portal room, Bernadette realized that they were accompanied by a small, very pretty dark-haired girl. "Andi, what is this dypalfar girl doing here? Is she a hostage?"

"Oh no, that's Rezira. She's actually the daughter of the commander of this city's army, and her mom's probably going to be breathing down our necks in another few minutes. I'll explain later, but right now we need to get through this." To Rezira, he said "Unless you've got a 'disintegrate stone' spell or a telekinesis spell that will lift blocks this size, you'd better stand back out of the way."

Rezira looked stricken. Here they were, so close to achieving the goal she'd held for at least a year. It had been a grand adventure, but now it looked like the slaves would be recaptured,

Andi and Fjuri and probably his mother and all their friends would be imprisoned and executed, and she would be in *big* trouble with Mother. Father was no problem. He was probably the handsomest dypalfar male ever born to the residents of Mrzhandtham, but he was also an amiable dunce with no ambition whatsoever. The perfect consort for Szursta Bagrum, and he had given her two beautiful children as well.

She backed out of the way and watched anxiously as the boys joined the group's strongest members – Ghrztum, Kziintke, Andrion, and Lars – at the pile of huge blocks barring entrance to the portal room. The doors were buckled where stone had piled against them. A gap around a foot wide between them showed that the portal at the far end of the room was still open.

The men, troll, and powerful machine all did what they could, but they were down to the last and largest few blocks and it was impossible to get a good enough grip on them to do team lifting. If they'd had a few hours to work on the project, they could have rigged ropes and pulleys – or perhaps melted the stone into slag with battle magic and then waited for it to cool. But the soldiers were coming!

Andi had an idea, and he was pretty sure it was the only thing that would work. Mom had told him how the power of dragon spells was magnified when multiple users of the spells combined their efforts. And dragons (those that knew the spells) could cast the same one repeatedly with only the briefest interval between to recharge – the power of the spells growing with the dragon throughout its lifetime. He stepped back out to the entrance of the room, calling "Mom!"

Everyone was pushed out of the room to stand over by the doors, urging the crowd back. Rezira was able to help with that, using her command spell on those nearest the door and urging them to tell those beyond. Even as the room was being cleared, Bernadette was starting to peel out of her armor and helping Andi with his. Rezira, near the entrance, was peering in at them, frank curiosity on her face. "Turn your back!" he demanded, and she blinked at him but obeyed. What were that boy and his mother doing in there?

As Bernadette and Andi removed the last of their clothes, Rezira peeked back again. Hmm, she thought, not bad. Gee, his mom looked pretty good for a Galise her age, too. Andi had been facing away but turned to the door one more time, flushed an interesting shade of red, and yelled "Back off, everybody!"

Andrion, Lifa, and the rest of the rescue party from Waterdon knew what the two were doing, and they knew things were going to get very crowded in that room in the next minute. Better give Bernadette as much space as possible. As one, the two firebloods cried "Mon-Drache-Ein-Korp!" Rezira squealed and jumped out of the way as an enormous red-scaled tail tipped with spikes came snaking out the door at her feet, bringing with it a reek of sulfur and musk.

She gaped in disbelief. Inside the room, where her crush and his mother had been standing naked just seconds before, a large red dragon and a smaller bronze one now stood facing the pile of blocks that prevented anyone from going through to the portal. Her ears were split the next second as the two scaled creatures cried in unison again, "Kraf-Luft-Struung-Wund!"

The sound itself seemed as if it might be strong enough to knock over stone blocks. But this was sound with magic behind it, the ancient magic of the *drachen*. The twin doors buckled further and ripped off their hinges, flying into the room beyond. The blocks at the top of the stack rocked and tumbled down, opening a space maybe three feet high at the top of the doorway.

"Again," the larger dragon said to her son, and again "Kraf-Luft-Struung-Wund!" split the air. More of the blocks tumbled away now, some of them flying far into the portal chamber. A third time they cried in unison, and the blocks that had made the doorway impassable were now scattered in a single layer over the floor of the room beyond, no longer a barrier though they would certainly impede progress.

"You might as well change back, Andi" the larger dragon said. "Oh by the way, we brought your pack with your regular armor and weapons – it's over there in the corner." She nodded her huge head to indicate where the pack lay on a pile of small rubble.

"Great, thanks Mom!" he said enthusiastically, and cried "Drache-Mon-Zur-Heim!" Once again, a tall and slim/muscular young man stood there. He glanced at the door and met Rezira's eyes, as she stared at him in disbelief. "Like what you see?" he asked cheekily, and now it was she who flushed pink and turned away.

He dashed for the pack and in another minute or two was in his favorite set of elven armor. He'd been wearing this stuff, one set after another, since he was a little kid – and he had felt like a beast of burden lugging that dypalfar armor around. Those dypalfar soldiers must be strong if they wore it all the time he thought, as he strung his bow and hung a quiver of daimonic arrows over his shoulder.

Meanwhile, Bernadette had used the immense power of her armored head and serpentine neck, pushing with her huge taloned feet, to bulldoze the remaining stones out of the way of the doorway. It was far too small to pass her body, but the room beyond was big enough to contain her so she quickly transformed into human, walked through the doorway, transformed back to dragon, and finished pushing stones away toward the walls until there was a good-sized clear path through the center of the room to the portal. She stuck her draconic head through the door and called to Andi, who had just finished dressing, "Start sending them through!" He hurried to do her bidding, anxious that those in the rear of the crowd would be taking damage from arriving troops at any moment.

Back in human form, Bernadette ran through the cleared doorway and scooped up her clothing and weapons. She went back into the corner of the room to get dressed, and when her garb was completely back together she slung her pack over her shoulder. She'd be needing the book when it was time to close the portal, but that was not likely to be for more than an hour yet –judging by the size of the crowd of leukalfar slaves waiting to get through. Already dozens of the slaves at the head of the line, mostly females either old and infirm or accompanied by children, had crossed the portal and were crowding the chamber on the other side of it.

"Mothris!" Bernadette called desperately as she realized her error. "I need you to translate for me." The boy, too willowy to be of any use with the massive blocks, had been directing traffic a few paces from the entry doors while Meri had worked with him.

Now he told her, "Stay here" and worked his way through the antechamber to meet Bernadette at the portal. "I need to go in there and get to the barred door, so I can signal the guards in the Keepers' Sanctum to open it and let us through. Come with me!"

He nodded, anxiety written plainly on his eyeless features, and they pushed into the portal. The room was already packed almost solid! Mothris called to everyone, "Please move aside and let Bernadette through. She must get them to open the doors so we can all go inside." The women in the chamber, looking even more anxious, pulled aside as much as they could. Bernadette unslung her pack and tossed it to the boy.

"Mothris, can you see if you can tuck that over there by the device's control panel, so I can get it and close the portal later? And then please go out and tell everybody no one else through the portal until the door is opened." He nodded and gave her a tight smile, and now unencumbered by the bulky pack she wriggled through the crowd and reached the door.

The code knock needed to tell the guards to open the door was graven in her memory, and she delivered it then waited. Nothing. Beads of sweat breaking out on her forehead and putting still more streaks in the dust on her face, Bernadette was about to repeat the knock sequence when she heard noises on the other side of the door and a muffled voice called in leukalfar, "Who is there? Is it you?"

Kind of a stupid question, she thought, but said in that same language "Me, Bernadette! Bernadette! Open the door!"

Chapter 57 : Traffic Jam

With the way to the portal open at last and Bernadette on her way to get the door through to Mrzhgradfendz opened, Andrion and the rest of the rescue party (save Mothris, who had gone to help Bernadette communicate with the leukalfar slaves), stepped aside and began letting people move through the doorway. They were joined by the three people they'd come to rescue, Fjuri busily trying to change back into his regular armor as they talked. He was plenty strong enough to wear heavy armor, but felt much more comfortable in his own. As they all stood there, they held a quick conference.

"Kziintke, please translate everything we say," Andrion commanded the automaton. Then he spoke to the group at large. Most of them spoke only Common, some only leukalfar, and a few multiple languages. "I'm sure the Great Army of Mrzhandtham must be right on our heels by now, and the slaves at the back of the line are going to be defenseless. We need to get back there so we can try to delay the pursuit and keep the slaves from getting killed. Any ideas?"

"I know what can help," Andi said as the robon's translation went on seamlessly. He looked at it in awe, burning with curiosity. But that was one tale that was going to have to wait. "Rezira, this is my father Andrion Drakespring. He taught me nearly everything I know about magic. Papa Andrion, this is Rezira Bagrum. She is the daughter of the Great Army's commander, Szursta Bagrum, but she is opposed to slavery and she's been helping us. She was the one that busted Fjuri and me out of prison."

Andrion eyed the girl appraisingly. Maybe all the dypalfar weren't bad, after all. And he could see at a glance how his son might have fallen head over heels in love at first sight. What a beauty! She almost looked like a petite female version of Lifa and Bjorn's son Fjuri, with her deep blue-violet eyes and raven locks. To Rezira, Andi went on "Can you teach me that command spell? I think it'd be a good idea if you stay here and help direct traffic so the leukalfar don't start trampling one another in their panic to

371

escape. Plus, I'd like you to watch my sister." He beckoned to the leukalfar girl at his elbow.

Once again Rezira glared at him in resentment, but he murmured to her (thus avoiding the translation being broadcast by Kziintke), "We're going to be fighting back there, and some people are probably going to die. Do you want to be using battle magic against your own mother?" She winced. This was the part of the adventure she hadn't really thought through. It had all seemed so romantic, freeing the boys from prison and leading the slave revolt (or so she imagined it, little realizing the work the slaves themselves had been putting into the project for generations). But now she was up against it. Was she going to throw in her lot with Andreas and his friends, and become an exile in his world, a traitor to her own people? Or sneak back with her tail between her legs and face the music? At the moment, the first option seemed more desirable.

Andi picked up the command spell as quickly as he had the paralysis one, though with less enthusiasm. Soon a wave of people were squeezing themselves against the walls of the corridor in their eagerness to make way, as they'd been Commanded. Andi led the way and Andrion, Lifa, Ghrztum, Anja, Lars, and Kziintke followed, leaving Rezira in charge of traffic control as they waited for the exodus into Mrzhgradfendz to begin. It was a pretty important job, she realized, but she still wished she could stay by Andreas' side. What if something happened to him?

The crowd was still waiting for the door on the other side of the portal to open, so they could all start making their getaway. People were nervous, but for the moment nobody was trying to push into the room Rezira guarded and she looked down at the leukalfar girl by her side. She seemed a lot better fed than most leukalfar the dypalfar girl had ever seen (no point in overfeeding slaves, was the general consensus among her people), and carried herself differently too. More like one of the dypalfar – back straight, head high, hands on her hips. She seemed to be annoyed about something.

"So you're Andreas's sister Merelle, huh?" Rezira asked, making conversation to ease tension as they waited and also hoping she might learn more about that fascinating, infuriating young man. Meri peered up at her with an expression of caution on her face. So far, she hadn't met any dypalfar she liked. She'd been around elves her whole life, was one herself – but these people were just... *wrong*, somehow. Still, Andi had said the girl had gotten them out of jail and was helping them to free the leukalfar slaves. She must be all right.

"That's me," she said. "And that army commander who had me dragged off to be chained and beaten in the slave quarters is your mother?" Ouch.

"I'm sorry," Rezira said, smarting but wanting to establish a rapport. "Mother is pretty much a force of nature and there's nothing I can do about her. But I'm here helping, aren't I?" She smiled down at the girl who, after looking up at her for a moment, gave her a wry smile in return.

"So, what's the story with the dragon thing?" Rezira asked casually. The question elicited a smirk. As often as Meri herself had been the object of fear and disbelief, that was nothing compared with the reactions of people the first time they saw her mama or older brother turn into dragons. "They're fireblood," she said. "Do you know what that means?"

The dypalfar's lore held no prophecies concerning dragons, though they knew the beasts of old. Reading about them in her studies, Rezira had wondered if such creatures had truly existed. There was nothing that large and fierce here, let alone all of those things and sentient as well. "I've never heard of it," she admitted to the child beside her.

"Your people have been gone a long time, I guess," Meri admitted. "A few things have happened in Agena since you left and one of them was the birth of a line of humans with a special link to dragons. When my mama was young, before she married my papas, dragons had been gone for thousands of years but they were just starting to come back. They were flying around all over the place and killing people. Then it turned out mama was this person they called 'The Fireblood.' She met my papas and they helped her fight the main dragon, who was prophesied to destroy the world. I guess it wouldn't have affected *you*, I think it was just our world."

Rezira stared at the girl in amazement. Clearly, there was going to be a lot of catching up to do. And if she stayed here, in the stagnant "paradise" of her people, she would never learn about any of it. The history of the dypalfar since their arrival here was barely worth mentioning, let alone writing books about. Essentially nothing of note had happened for the last two thousand, five hundred years.

"But, turning into dragons?" Rezira asked. "Is that part of being fireblood?"

"Not exactly," Meri explained. "Being 'fireblood' is hereditary, but apparently it's only passed on to one of each fireblood person's children – or maybe their firstborn, we don't know. Andreas is the first child my mom had. She's had two more, my sister Erika and my brother Sigmund, who's a little younger than me, and neither one of them is fireblood."

Rezira was beginning to feel a little impatient. When was her question actually going to be answered? Still, she was picking up more information about Andreas's family. The idea of living in a family with four children in it seemed absurd to her. Even growing up with a younger brother had made her unusual among her peers.

"Anyhow," Meri went on, "not too long after Mama found me and brought me home she got involved in a quest to save dragonkind from extinction. There were no females left and people kept killing the dragons that were attacking their farms, plus old Tarragin was gone so there were no more dragons being brought back from the dead." She looked up at her rapt audience of one, though others within hearing were also listening with interest. What a tale!

"Sorry it's taking so long, but it's complicated! And it all happened when I was just a baby, so I don't actually remember any of this stuff. This big old dragon Sneyagflug that had helped Mama and my papas defeat Tarragin came and asked her to help him. But what he didn't tell her was that he was setting her up. With a potion and a certain spell, what they call a dragon spell – you heard some a little while ago – anybody who was fireblood could turn into a dragon. So he tricked Mama into becoming a dragon, and then she agreed to have dragon babies with him so there would be more females and dragons wouldn't become extinct. After which he got her a different dragon spell so she could turn back."

Meri looked up at the petite dypalfar girl as if to say "there you have it." Rezira could hardly grasp the story, and wouldn't have believed it for a minute if she had not just actually witnessed Andreas and his mother changing back and forth between dragon and human – not to mention knocking enormous stone blocks out of the way with those "dragon spells."

Just then a voice could be heard calling from the portal chamber. "It's open! Let's start getting 'em through!" Mothris shouted, as he'd seen through the murky surface of the portal the door to the room beyond swing open, and the crowd of leukalfar women inside the chamber with the device in it surge forward. As he called out, he stepped aside and let the milling crowd in the room with him begin to move through the portal.

What he could not see, as he continued directing traffic through the portal, was Bernadette. She had been standing nearly flattened against the door by the press of bodies behind her – and when the door finally opened she had fallen forward, sprawling on the stone floor beyond the door. The panicked leukalfar women, scarcely believing they had reached freedom and desperate to run to where they could be safe from the pursuing dypalfar, trampled over her and she was tripped over, kicked in the head several times, and eventually left unconscious on the floor.

Gylabris was among the Keepers who had come running when word was passed that the door had been unlocked and the signal given. He spotted the fallen woman and collared a couple of the guards, who were standing back in astonished pleasure to behold the stream of leukalfar women that had been unleashed when they finally got the door open. Some of them were quite young and comely!

"That's Bernadette!" he told them sharply, "My friend Andrion's wife! Quickly, get her out of there and take her to safety!" He was horrified that anything should happen to one of his new friends, now that they had seemingly performed the miracle of completing the mission which had been the central purpose of the society of Keepers for the past three thousand years. These could be none other than their long-lost brethren, the enslaved leukalfar stolen by the dypalfar when they fled to their new world.

The guards shouldered their way into the press of fleeing women and dragged Bernadette to safety. She was armored, but had not been wearing a helmet and it seemed she had sustained a concussion. "Take her to one of the chambers where she can rest!" Gylabris ordered the guards. They had no healers here and no healing potions, but some would be sent for as soon as they had time. For now, the rest of the Keeper guards gathered in readiness for what *else* might come through the portal.

Chapter 58 : Battle at the Gate

The hordes of escaping leukalfar slaves were packed tight in the corridors on the bottom level of Mrzhandtham, up the staircase to the next level, and spilling out into another corridor – filling it from side to side and rounding a corner before beginning to thin out. At the juncture, a wall of heavily-armored dypalfar soldiers filled the corridor, and they were hacking at the unarmed and helpless leukalfar before them.

They didn't particularly want to *kill* these people – slaves were valuable property, and killing them all would have netted the same result as letting them all escape. They just wanted to fight their way through these mobs and try to reach the portal, try to stop them all from fleeing to the world on the other side.

Suddenly the soldiers in the first rank, battling hard against leukalfar slaves who refused to just lie down and die – instead fighting them with sticks, rocks, agricultural implements and anything they could get their hands on – spotted an armed party running down a narrow path that seemed to open like magic through the crowd ahead.

As they approached the dividing line between the army of fleeing slaves and the Great Army of Mrzhandtham, which stretched wall-to-wall down the corridor as far as they could see and presumably went around the corner and up the stairs beyond it, the defenders spread out into a line. It was a thin line – the corridor here was some 30 feet across and there were but 8 of them.

Andi and his father stood side by side in the center of the line, no more than ten feet back from where the dypalfar were, for the most part, just mowing down the defenseless slaves. "Rezira taught me a really good paralysis spell," Andi told Andrion. "Do you know one you didn't mention to me?"

"What is it?" Andrion replied, and Andi responded by casting it in as broad an arc as he could manage, knocking down everyone from wall to wall and to a depth of around twenty feet.

Andrion smiled at his son, picking up the nuances of the spell just from watching it cast. There was likely no one on Agena more knowledgeable or more adept at magic than he was. "Good one,

Andi!" he said, "like this?" and he hurled the same spell from wall to wall for a further thirty feet, almost back to the corner. That ought to slow them down a little.

Andi turned to look behind him at the slaves who, he noticed, were continuing to edge along the corridor. Did that mean the door beyond the portal had been opened? Were they starting to move? He sincerely hoped so. He called to the leukalfar closest to him, "Come help! Save your comrades before the soldiers come back to life!" These last of the slaves, the ones at the very end of the line, were mostly the oldest and slowest. But some of them were those who had helped him, Fjuri, and Rezira collect the paralysis-stunned leukalfar outside the doors of the men's slave quarters. In a minute or two, all of the still-living but immobile slaves had been gathered up, slung over shoulders, and were being carried down the corridor behind them.

A gap opened up between the line of defenders and the Great Army, as the slaves hustled with their burdens down the corridor behind them. They could do this! All the slaves could escape through the portal, while they held the enemy with a series of paralysis spells. No one would be hurt, no one would be killed – and then they could scamper through the portal themselves. They would leave their enemies lying unable to move, close the portal behind them, and everything would be fine!

The mass of leukalfar behind them had moved perhaps 20 feet away down the corner when the soldiers before them began to move again. Paralysis left you fully aware, but unable to use your muscles – no movement beyond the autonomic (heartbeat and respiration), no speech. Andi wondered whether it affected that Joining ability the dypalfar had. He wished he had thought to ask Rezira about that, but guessed it probably did not.

The paralyzed leukalfar carried by their fellow slaves were now able to move again, and were set down to resume walking on their own feet. Facing the defenders, the soldiers were once again stirring. During the five minutes they had been out, more soldiers had come around the corner to find their path completely blocked.

The only way for them to proceed was to walk on the bodies of their fellows.

Some of them had begun trying to do so, as the pressure of more troops built up behind them. With a sinking feeling Andi wondered, how big *is* the Great Army of Mrzhandtham anyhow? He suspected he wasn't going to like the answer. The two mages in the party unleashed their paralysis spells again, Andi taking the near ranks while Andrion took everything up almost to the corner. As the soldiers before them fell again, they all turned to look behind them. The army of slaves had vanished around the corner!

"Let's move back to the corner, people," Andrion ordered, and Kziintke relayed the order in leukalfar. Only Ghrztum was in need of the translation. As they made their way down and took up a new line facing up the corridor to the next bend, they saw that the leukalfar were now nearly halfway down to the bend after it, and the staircase leading to the next level down.

This is really working, Andi thought, his heart soaring in elation at the way things were going. As much as tales of adventure had captured his imagination as a child, he had to admit that he was more of a lover than a fighter. He momentarily envisioned stepping up to the ranks of temporarily frozen dypalfar soldiers and asking them, "Can't we all just get along?"

The soldiers were stirring again, and the combined range of Andrion and his son was not quite enough to reach to the next corner from the one at which they stood. Behind the line of defense, the crowd of escaping slaves seemed to be moving at a good clip – they must be pouring through the portal like a torrent! Andi hoped Meri and Rezira were safe.

As they stood holding the line, a new group of soldiers could be seen shuffling to the front near the far corner, just beyond where the soldiers affected by the spell were lying immobile. Oh crap, they had bows! Up until now Andi had not seen any sign of variation in the armaments of the Great Army. Like so much of dypalfar society, that too had been uniform – every single soldier, whether male or female, issued with the same sort of armor and bearing the same shield and short sword. Where had they gotten these archers from?

Andi whipped out his bow and fired back, and one of the enemy archers standing some fifty feet away fell with a yelp. Anja, too, began shooting. But they were two archers against ten, standing in a line across the width of the corridor. All of the defenders fell to the ground, presenting no targets, as arrows flew past overhead. In this underground passageway, with a ceiling no more than fifteen feet in height, archers could not shoot into the air to drop their arrows on your head. It was a small blessing.

"Papa," Andi said. "I was hoping we could just keep paralyzing them until all the slaves had gotten through. Is there anything that would reach farther?" Andrion considered. In his years as Magister he'd developed at least a passing acquaintance with every form of magic known in Agena.

"I can't just wipe them out," he replied. But I can delay them." He turned his head and saw that the mass of leukalfar slaves had already turned the corner and disappeared down the relatively narrow staircase behind them. "Let's get around the corner and out of those archers' sights first, shall we?" Kziintke translated, and was the first to stand. His gleaming metal form drew some of the archers' fire as the meatier members of the party crouched and dodged around the corner to the relatively short corridor that led to the staircase.

"I don't think these spells will work for you much," Andrion told his son as they stood on their feet again. "You've never really done anything with conjuring. But I should be able to bring some allies to our cause for a few minutes. Enough to create some excitement in the ranks, at least."

With a wave of his hand a shimmering female form made all of fire appeared in the air before them. Then it flew in the air around the corner, and began shooting fireballs at the line of mobile foes down at the far end. "Wow," Andi murmured, "a fire demon." They were so beautiful, these lithe denizens of the Netherworld. Interesting that they could be called from the plane of the Netherworld to which they belonged to a completely different one, as he assumed this to be. Szursta had said that it was.

Andrion called forth three more of the fiery creatures, then a couple of hulking frost demons and a trio of menacing daimonic knights – in full daimonic armor. His fund of magical energy was beyond belief, as was the speed at which it regenerated. He had been actively practicing magic for well over half his life, in addition to which he wore magic-enhancing enchanted items from head to toe. Being married to a woman who was not only one of the foremost smiths in Iscandia but also one of its most skillful enchanters, was not a bad thing.

Meanwhile the rest of them retreated down the short corridor to the stairway. Here they were at a disadvantage, with their enemies above them; but the distances were short enough that Andi and Andrion between them should be able to blanket the stairway and the corridor beyond it with the paralysis spell. Behind them, the mass of fleeing slaves was reaching the bottom of the stairs.

There was another hundred feet or so of corridor, with another bend in it, between the bottom of the stairs and the entrance to the anteroom. They were almost there, they could do it! The conjured daimons and demons, though soon enough defeated or fled back to the planes of the Netherworld from which they'd been summoned, threw confusion into the ranks of the army and even after the paralyzed soldiers had regained their ability to move it was another few minutes before the Great Army of Mrzhandtham was ready to advance again. As with the Befriend spell, it appeared that repeated doses had a cumulative effect. Those soldiers who had been downed three times were finding that their muscles ached and felt weak, making it hard for them to push on.

But reinforcements were on the way. As the throng of slaves pushed ever closer to the portal, their panic growing, and the thin line of defenders backed slowly down the stairs to the next likely strongpoint, an elite troop came up behind the rear ranks of the Great Army and pushed their way through. Commander-in-Chief Szursta Bagrum had been roused from her sleep by a generalized and frantic Joining call from the guards outside the men's slave quarters some two hours before. She was not in a good mood.

Her consort slept on, oblivious to such things. He was a pretty boy-toy, but discussing military strategy with him would have made as much sense as bringing up the subject with the leukalfar slave woman who swept their floors and scrubbed their toilets. She rose hastily and got into her armor, something she did not do every day. They were a great army, a mighty force, highly trained and provided with the finest of weapons – and in three thousand years they had never done anything more exciting than participate in the yearly Games, a competition among the various dypalfar cities of their little world. It gave the troops something to do, and helped to maintain the political status quo as observers from each city witnessed the strength their rivals could bring to bear.

There had been chaos when she emerged from their apartment, frantic to find that Rezira was missing. The girl was not responding to her Joining call. Was she dead, unconscious, shielded? Unknown to any but high-ranked mages among the dypalfar, there were ways in which to prevent an individual dypalfar from using the mind talk without killing them or knocking them out.

Barking orders right and left, Szursta had hurried to headquarters only to receive an overpowering Joining call from Leader Degranac that had occupied nearly a quarter of an hour of her time as she tried to explain to him what was being done. The frantic guards' Joining call had flooded the minds of almost every citizen of Mrzhandtham, but most were unequipped to deal with it. The entire city was awake now, and a goodly percentage of them were in a state of near panic.

Szursta was finally released from the mind-to-mind contact with their millennia-old Leader, son of the dypalfar lord who had ruled them at the time of the Great Exodus. Moments later her mind was flooded again as he broadcast a message to the entire populace of the city, assuring everyone that all was in hand. They should remain in their homes, the slaves would soon be rounded up, and all was well.

Right. The intervening time had been one disaster after another, as Szursta desperately sought word of her daughter while ordering troops to the scene of the slave uprising. Finally she spoke with a platoon commander who told her he had seen Rezira, in company with two soldiers of the Great Army, moving through the corridors near the slave quarters more than an hour before. She had since learned that the two captive boys were no longer in their cell, and the picture Szursta was beginning to put together did not look good. "Were these soldiers unusually tall?" she asked the lieutenant, who replied "Why yes, now that you mention it."

And now Szursta found herself catching up with her army as they pursued the last of the male slaves down the corridors heading toward the portal room. Her mind was in a white-hot fury, burning off the veils of a black despair that threatened to engulf her. All the slaves, nearly every one of those housed within the city (many who worked the surface fields were quartered above and were not involved in the revolt), were between her army and the portal. And from the way they were moving, she could only assume that somehow the safeguard, the rain of stone blocks intended to kill any invaders and block the portal forever, had failed. Oh, *why* had they not just walled off that entire wing thousands of years ago?

The defenders stood in a line at the bottom of the stairs, a glance behind them showing that the last of the slaves were rounding the corner and heading into the last stretch before the anteroom. They had only around a hundred and fifty feet to go, then they would be through the portal into Mrzhgradfendz, and on their way to freedom!

Andi and his father waited, still at the center of the line, for the corridor and stairway before them to fill with troops. Then they would cast their paralysis spell over everyone in front of them, and the fallen bodies would block passage for the army behind them. Maybe this time, five minutes would be long enough for the rest of the escaping slaves – and their thin line of defenders – to make it to the portal.

Troops came down the steps, swords drawn, and halted near the bottom confronting the mages and the rest of the combatants before them. Their experiences since the defenders first came up had made them wary. Andi was glad to see that the archers had not come with them. But as they anxiously waited for the corridor beyond the stairs to fill, there was a stir in the ranks and a surprisingly short figure, clad in a different and more elaborate style of gleaming dypalfar armor, came through the ranked soldiers to stand at the top of the stairs looking down at them.

She lifted the visor of her helmet, different from those of the troops, and glared down at them. "Hit 'em *now*, Papa!" Andi gasped, realizing their peril. It was too late – his magic had been blocked.

"That the Commander?" Andrion asked his son quietly.

"I'm afraid so," Andi replied as softly. "She's quite a mage, and she's got my magic blocked."

"Me too," Andrion replied shortly. "Stall for time."

Likely the magic-block spell would have a time limit – a minute, three, five? Then it could be re-cast of course, just as they had repeatedly paralyzed Szursta's troops. But she wasn't going to be putting any collars on Andi, not this time at least. Just maybe taking his head off so that collars were unnecessary, he realized. But if he could get her talking, they might be able to have a split second in which to cast their spells. Then they could stroll off through the portal, and close it behind them before the dypalfar army could move again.

"So, Commander Bagrum, we meet again," Andi said, hoping he didn't sound too ridiculous. The woman at the top of the stairs favored him with a look of anger and disdain.

"You little *threkzal*," she said, "You lied to me!"

"The dypalfar word means 'slave lover,'" Kziintke chimed in from the side. Ah, good to know.

"Lied to you, madam?" Andi replied, giving her his best Young Innocent look.

"You told me that you were three innocent children accidently stranded in our world. I was almost ready to let you go! And now *this*…" She gestured down the stairs, and the defenders realized that the last of the slaves had vanished beyond the final corner and must now be making their way to the portal.

"This?" Andi asked innocently. "This is none of *my* doing, or my friends' either. You have kept an entire race captive for thousands of years. Did you think they would just lie down and take it forever?" The slaves were escaping, but Szursta was so infuriated she could not forego the chance to have it out with this young man she had mistaken for someone's innocent son.

"The slaves may have gotten out of their quarters by themselves," Szursta admitted, "but you are providing them with an escape hatch back to Agena. You are stealing our property, and for that you will die!" Oh, not just yet please, Andi begged her in his mind. "But there is something else I need to know from you," the commander went on. "What have you done with my daughter? Is she dead?"

Andi laughed out loud, sending a knife of pain through Szursta's heart. What sort of young monster *was* this boy? As they spoke, Andrion was battering against the barrier that the magic-block spell had created. Being unable to use his magic was like being struck blind, or deaf, and it was driving him crazy. As soon as the spell expired, he was ready to blast everyone in front of him with paralysis.

Seeing the expression of desolation that crossed Szursta's face, Andi realized that she may have misunderstood the reason for his laughter. "I'm sorry, Commander, I didn't mean to frighten you," he said. How much longer until he could use his magic again, dammit? "Rezira is safe and well. She believes, as we do, that it is wrong to treat other human beings as possessions. She has been working with us to free the slaves, though that was never our intent in coming here."

Szursta gaped at him for a moment, momentarily at a loss. That her beloved daughter was alive was a huge relief, more than she'd hoped for. But Rezira, a traitor? She didn't want to believe it. As she stood there digesting Andi's words Andrion felt the veil begin to lift, and he reached within himself. Some flicker of his intent must have passed across his face though, for in another instant Szursta raised her hand and the barrier slammed down again. Neither he nor Andi could raise a trace of magic, and while all there were formidable warriors, they were outnumbered by about a hundred to one.

The Commander in Chief of the Great Army of Mrzhandtham had had enough of speaking to this wretched boy, and they needed to get moving before all of the slaves were beyond their reach. Addressing her troops, she ordered "If you find my daughter, take her into custody but *do not harm her!* We have one mission, and that is to bring back those slaves, no matter what. Go!"

Andrion and Andi exchanged a look, then shouted "Run!" and turned on their heels to dash down the corridor and around the bend ahead of the wall of heavily armed soldiers pursuing them. "Papa!" Andi gasped as they pounded along, "Should I go dragon and try to hold them off at the door? They'll never expect it!"

"No, son! Absolutely not! You are *not* sacrificing yourself."

Andi realized as they continued running that he truly had no desire to die in the battle to win the freedom of the leukalfar slaves of Mrzhandtham. It was not his fight. He hoped they would make it, and he would do what he could to help them, but going out in a blaze of glory in order to delay the army long enough for the portal to be closed didn't seem like a grand gesture he was willing to make at this point in his life. Maybe later… "Keep running!"

The last of the horde of slaves, pushing and shoving in a panic to reach the portal, had now all cleared the anteroom and were moving through the portal room. Ghrztum and Kziintke, the slowest of the party, fell behind and blocked the doorway of the anteroom to allow their companions a chance to run ahead. In the portal room, the last of the slaves were going through the portal and Rezira stood anxiously – clearly terrified, but holding her ground.

"Andreas!" she called as he came running into the room.

He hurried to her and embraced her hurriedly, then asked "Where is Merelle?"

"She's fine," the dypalfar girl replied. "I sent her through with a group of slaves around ten minutes ago. Your friend Mothris went with her to keep an eye on her."

He hugged her again. "Good! Thank you! Have you seen Mom?" Rezira looked blank. The term didn't fully translate into formal leukalfar.

"Your mother?" she asked, confirming what he'd said.

"Yes! Have you seen her?" She shook her head.

"I'm sorry," she said. "She went through the portal and got them to open the door a long time ago, from what Mothris said. But then she disappeared. Why?"

"She's the one who has the notes on how to close the portal!" he exclaimed. Then he grabbed her by the arm as Lifa, Fjuri, Lars, and Anja ran past through the portal. "Come on, we've got to go!" This was the moment of her decision. Andi fixed her with that warm brown gaze and pleaded, "Come with me, Rezira! The world of the dypalfar is dead. Come to where people are *living*!" She took his hand and ran.

Behind them, Ghrztum and Kziintke stood side by side holding the broad doorway of the anteroom against the Great Army of Mrzhandtham as Commander Szursta Bagrum hurled battle magic at them from several ranks back. The soldiers were packed so tightly in the corridor, it was hard for anyone to move. Andrion watched anxiously as the last of his people disappeared through the portal. "Fall back!" he urged his two remaining companions. "Hold the doorway to the portal room instead!"

The anteroom floor was still littered with fallen stone, and though the slaves and their rescuers had cleared a broad path through it there weren't many places for the troops to stand. Ghrztum swung the daimonic warhammer in broad strokes, daring any to come within range, while Kziintke used his arms that were as powerful and lethal as any warhammer. He wasn't armored, he *was* armor.

Andrion was still waiting for his magical abilities to be restored, but that damned woman must be just outside the anteroom and she had somehow managed to block him again. This was no good! And where was Berni? She was supposed to be staying close by, ready with her notes to press the sequence of buttons that would shut down the portal once all of their people were inside.

Ghrztum howled as a bolt of lightning caught his warhammer, singing his fur and causing the weapon to be thrown from his hand in an involuntarily spasm. He stepped back a pace from the relatively narrow doorway he'd been defending, gasping in pain. Kziintke shifted over a step so that he blocked the door alone, as the half-dozen Great Army soldiers in front of him (all that could approach him at one time, in this tight space) tried to get past his flashing, club-like metal arms.

"Go for the portal," he told Andrion and Ghrztum, "I will hold them while I can."

"Thank you, Kziintke!" Andrion called, as he helped the injured troll to the portal and through it. Entirely of his own volition, the robon launched into a loud stream of dypalfar, making his antagonists pause as his words reached them. "Give up," he broadcast to those attacking him and their fellows in the ranks behind, "it is no use. The slaves are gone, and you do not need them. Stand on your own feet, become a new and better race of dypalfar! We could have led the world, and instead we fled from it!"

Kziintke had been re-programmed by the leukalfar, but now he was speaking to the dypalfar soldiers, shouting at them, as one of their own. And it was not only the content of his speech, but the fact that one of their own automatons was speaking to them without being ordered to, that made the soldiers confronting him at the door let their sword points falter, falling back half a pace to gape. What manner of thing was this?

In a fury Szursta finally pushed her way through the crowd and stepped into the anteroom. "Why are you holding back?" she nearly screamed, close to snapping. Rezira had not been found. Had she fallen, or gone beyond the portal? As the soldiers surged forward again to the attack, Szursta raised both hands and dual-wielded lightning. The streams crashed together in the center of the robon's head, and he fell backward through the doorway to lie motionless on the stones. As the dypalfar ran past him and over him, his glowing eyes winked out.

No healer came for Bernadette. She awoke to find herself lying on a stone bed in a small chamber. Her head ached abominably, and when she tried to sit up the room spun around her. She got her feet on the floor but then bent over and retched, spilling what little remained in her stomach. She could not recall when they had last eaten.

Mustering her resources, Bernadette applied healing to herself. In moments her blurred vision went clear, the headache vanished, and she no longer felt like throwing up. Now, she was ravenously hungry. Her memory of recent events was hazy, and she looked around the room for her pack. How had she gotten here, anyway? There was a clamor outside the door as of many people rushing past. Were the slaves still coming through?

I've got to get out there, she thought. Must close the portal! She hoped that her pack, with her notebook inside it, was still where she now remembered seeing it last: tucked by Mothris beneath the control panel of the portal device. Cautiously, she opened the room's single door to look out into the corridor. Then she recoiled in horror and slammed it shut again, wishing she had a key so she could lock it and never, ever come out again. It was too late. She had failed! The Great Army of Mrzhandtham had come to Mrzhgradfendz.

Chapter 59: An Ending

Bernadette huddled on the stone bed, shivering in misery, until the sound of the passing soldiers had faded away. She had no idea how long she had been unconscious, or what had transpired while she'd lain here. Were her husband, son and daughter, all their friends, dead – fallen to the dypalfar army? And soon, that dypalfar army might be rounding up all of the Mirskhrazana along with their escaped slaves, herding them all back through the portal into bondage.

The leukalfar here in their city of stone greatly outnumbered the army, she suspected – but they were grocers, smiths, shopkeepers, scholars – not warriors. For thousands of years they had lived happily here, keeping their Great Secret and living in peace. Now everything was going to be swept away for them, and it was all the fault of her and her family.

Biting back a sob, Bernadette heard muffled cries coming to her through the solid metal door. "Berni! Can you hear me? Where are you?" Wiping tears away with the back of her hand, she was at the door and flinging it open in an instant.

"Andrion! Oh, Andrion!" She rushed to him, burying her face in his chest. "I'm so sorry!"

He kissed the top of her head. "It's all right Berni, the portal is closed now. Turns out Gylabris knew the sequence, though he wasn't able to get in there until the dypalfar stopped coming through. And we found your pack, with the sphere and the notebook in it..." He stepped back and handed it to her.

"Andi? Meri? Are the kids all right?"

"They should be," he said, "but we've got to get up there! When Mothris brought Meri through and you were nowhere to be found, they ran up and mobilized the society of Sentries. They're running all over the city, warning people of the chance that the dypalfar are coming, and arming anybody who's willing to defend themselves. Ghrztum and I were the last ones through, and since we couldn't close the portal behind us we rallied the Keeper guards to lock and bar the door to the portal room again. That held them for a while, and we were able to escort the escaping slaves on their way. We're trying to get everybody out of the city, to scatter and hide in the countryside beyond."

"And then you came back for me?" she asked. He nodded, squeezing her tight again.

"There wasn't anything I could do to stop the army by myself. That bitch Szursta dropped a magic-block spell on me every time I got close to them. So I waited for them to pass, then ran down here. The door was flattened and the guards were all killed, but Gylabris was inside the portal room. He explained how he'd had a couple of the guards take you to safety after you'd been trampled by the crowd. But those guards were dead now, so we didn't know where to find you. Thank the gods you were awake and could hear me call!"

"I just regained consciousness a few minutes ago," she told him. "We'd better get up there and see what's happening." She had to dig out the notebook and flip to the page with her map of the route between the Keepers' sanctum and the upper levels. As they hurried along, constantly climbing, they frequently encountered the bodies of leukalfar. Some were slaves, others of the Mirskhrazana. Any that still lived, Bernadette stopped to heal before they moved on.

The mass of escaping slaves, joined by residents of Mrzhgradfendz who'd chosen to flee rather than hide in their locked apartments or fight, surged through the corridors moving ever closer to the front doors of the city. At the head of the mob, runners had been pressed into service to guide them. They had been running forever, it seemed, running in a nightmare from an implacable foe that would not be left behind.

They were not far wrong. Szursta was in a near-panic herself. She and her troops had successfully gotten here before the accursed leukalfar of this city had managed to close the portal; but nearly every slave belonging to the dypalfar of Mrzhandtham was now running ahead of them. If they were not caught and brought back it would mean the end of their way of life. "After them!" she commanded, "Faster!"

The soldiers, who had been running all-out in full heavy armor for hours now, were nearing the end of their strength. The leukalfar slaves were underfed, but they were also unencumbered – and opening a bit of a gap in their frantic efforts to escape. The Great Army surged into the city's great entry hall to find the gates open and the guards fled, as the last of the horde of slaves ran down the steps outside. A cry of triumph rose up from the throats of the dypalfar soldiers as they beheld their quarry stumbling, beginning to falter as their reserves of strength were exhausted.

Bringing up the rear now, Szursta stood at the top of the stairs panting as she tried to get back her breath. Running in full armor was not a skill she had practiced much, the past few years. She heard a noise behind her and spotted that mage, the one she thought was the father of Andreas Drakespring. Together they had slowed her army in the corridors of Mrzhandtham, preventing them from rounding up the slaves before they crossed the portal. Damn the man! She hit him with a magic block before he could cast a spell, then with a jolt of paralysis. That would keep *him* down for five minutes, though she wondered where his son was.

The woman with him, who from her appearance must be the mother of Andreas, dropped beside her consort and checked to make sure he was alive. Then she stood glaring as Szursta waited for her magical energy to recharge. The paralysis spell she used took a lot of magical energy, and she could not understand how the two mages, father and son, had been able to drop dozens, hundreds of her troops all at once. She only knew how to cast a spell like that on one target at a time.

This woman was no taller than Szursta, and seemed no older though it was hard to tell with the races of men. She was wearing light elven armor – not nearly as strong as her own dypalfar plate. And she was armed with a bow, a short sword hanging at her side – none of which caused Szursta to fear. To her personal retinue, who had stayed with her as the rest of the army ran down the steps after the fleeing slaves, she said "Take her!"

Bernadette hadn't understood the dypalfar words, but she had a good idea of their meaning, and a flicker of a smile crossed her lips. Stepping closer quickly before the oncoming soldiers could open up too much distance from their commander, she cried "Kraf-Luft-Struung-Wund!" and watched in delight as Szursta and her soldiers flew through the air to tumble to the bottom of the steps – landing in a motionless heap.

She didn't allow herself long to gloat though, but immediately dropped her weapons and began stripping off her armor. This was getting to be a habit! Before Szursta had recovered from her fall, before Andrion had begun to stir again, she cried "Mon-Drache-Ein-Korp!" and took to the air.

Andi and Rezira came running down the corridor. The last of the Mirskhrazana had been warned, and it seemed that while they had been running around both the slaves and the pursuing dypalfar had passed them by. "Papa Andrion!" he cried on spying his father crumped in a heap on the stone floor. He bent to find a pulse, tried a little healing magic, but there was no response. "He's been paralyzed, I think," Andi said, rising to his feet. "I wonder if he found Mom?"

The two hurried through the door and immediately spotted the big red dragon in the air above the open space fronting the entrance to the city. She was swooping and diving over the field of battle as the slaves and fleeing citizens of Mrzhgradfendz struggled with the dypalfar soldiers attacking them. Only those soldiers' desire not to kill their quarry outright prevented the leukalfar from being slaughtered wholesale, but there wasn't a lot the dragon could actually do to prevent them from being knocked out and hauled off. She couldn't capture an army all by herself.

"Rezira!" a ragged voice called, and the two of them looked down to the bottom of the steps to see the commander and a small troop of dypalfar soldiers getting to their feet. Before Szursta could block his magic Andi shot a wide blast of paralysis on them, dropping the group once more to the snow-sprinkled packed dirt of the broad space before the steps that led up into the city.

"Mother!" Rezira called, and ran down the steps to kneel at Szursta's side. "Oh, Mother," she said sadly, tears running down her cheeks. "I'm so sorry, but this has to stop." Rummaging in her pack, she produced the magic block collar that she'd taken from Andi's neck all those hours ago, and snapped it around her mother's neck. It locked with an audible click, the red gem glowing to life. Then she stood again. Andi had quickly followed her. He gave the girl a little hug, saying "Thank you Rezira. I think you've just saved a lot of lives. Give me a hand with this armor? I've got to go help Mom."

Andi could have stood there and cast paralysis on groups of the fighting soldiers and their helpless (or nearly so; some *were* trying to fight back) leukalfar victims, but the battlefield was too broad for him to hit it all at once. And before he could recover his magical energy enough to cast it again, his first subjects would be only minutes away from regaining their power of motion. Furthermore, this time they had no helpers to drag away the leukalfar – every shot of magic would strike friend and foe alike.

Instead, he hoped that another dragon out there might be enough to cow and distract the dypalfar. Rezira blushed crimson again as he once more stood naked before her, turning her head to the side and backing away hastily as he went dragon and launched himself skyward.

"Mom!" he bellowed as he flew above the battlefield, "How can I help?" They were flying some hundred feet above the heaving mass of combatants, and hovered in midair for a conference. "We're not enough!" she called back to him. "We need reinforcements, and I think I know where to get them. SNE-YAG-FLUG!"

They flew on, diving on the soldiers and scattering them, breaking up the attack for a moment first here, then there. But though the dragon attacks were frightening, the dypalfar were determined in their mission and fought on. The two dragons were just another hazard, and they'd already figured out that they were not breathing flame on anyone.

Then there was a rush of wings, and the second biggest dragon anyone had ever seen since the demise of Tarragin came flying in from the south. "Schunmurte!" he boomed in his enormous voice,

"You called?" Bernadette circled around, greeting her one-time dragon consort.

"Hey, Red," she said. "Thanks for showing up! The people down there are a mixed bunch of leukalfar and dypalfar, and we're trying to save the former from the latter."

"Dypalfar! They are not extinct?"

"Huh," she replied, "people thought dragons were extinct. But I don't want anybody hurt. I'm hoping we can just terrorize them to the point where they'll stop fighting."

"Then we need more help," Sneyagflug said with a smile in his voice. In the years since he and Bernadette had begun the new era of dragon-human cooperation, there'd been little opportunity for some good clean fun of this sort. Iscandia didn't even have wars anymore.

"ZUUN-EN-WALT!" Sneyagflug cried, then "LAN-GE-KIIND!" Bernadette and Andi got the idea, and began Calling too, the names of the children of Sneyagflug and Schunmurte. "SCHICK-E-MAAD! DRACH-MON-DIEN! SNE-HIM-SEEL!" As each name was Called the dragon who bore it heard; and by the magic of the dragon spell, they were there: winging in to join their parents above the Battle of Mrzhgradfendz. All nineteen of them.

Now the sky was full of leathery wings, and the combatants on the field below were becoming alarmed. After greetings had been made, for it was seldom that they were ever all together these days, the dragons conferred. Then they spread out, blanketing the field, and cried in unison, "ANG-LOS-SCHER-FLIEG!" The Great Army of Mrzhandtham threw down their weapons in dismay, falling to the ground and begging for mercy.

Epilogue: A Beginning

Szursta Bagrum stood in the chamber of the portal device, watching in sadness as the last of the Great Army of Mrzhandtham marched through the portal to return to their home. The remaining slaves of that once-great city had come through here going the other way the day before, every last household slave and farm worker that had not fled when the slave quarters had been opened four days before. Now the Mirskhrazana were keeping their end of the bargain, the soldiers being brought back to defend the city before their dypalfar neighbors learned of the disaster.

The negotiations had taken two days of argument and debate in Mrzhandtham, after Szursta had stood near the portal, wearing the magic-block collar and restrained by leukalfar guards, and broadcast a Joining to Leader Degranac and all within the city of her birth. Rezira had stood nearby to verify that the leukalfar demands were being relayed correctly, that there would be no treachery.

After the slaves had all come through, and Umina had moved among them making sure that none had been held back, the soldiers of the Great Army had had their armor returned to them for the trip home. Weapons they would have to obtain from the armory, or more would have to be forged. The dypalfar had not forgotten any of their skills of making.

Now only Szursta remained on this side of the portal, no longer restrained. She and a delegation that included Arctoris, Gylabris, and the members of the rescue party (as well as those they'd originally come to rescue) stood in the portal chamber as Arctoris handed over the device's attunement sphere to the defeated dypalfar commander.

"We are at an end," he began formally. "The Keepers' work is accomplished, and there is no more need for the portal. You dypalfar are welcome to your world, a world where nothing ever happens. But I suppose something will be happening in your little part of it, eh? And it appears that we, too, will be seeing some changes made."

Szursta took the sphere and held it in her hand, smiling bitterly at the old leukalfar. In the telepathic discussions that had arrived at this agreement, it had been promised that she would suffer no reprisals for her utter failure. But she suspected that her brilliant military career was over. She gazed into her daughter's eyes, hurt and pleading in her own. She had been paralyzed but conscious and aware when her beloved daughter had committed that final act of betrayal, fastening this accursed collar around her neck.

"Rezira, please, will you not come home? I don't want to lose you!" Tears welled in Rezira's lovely violet eyes and ran down her cheeks, but she stood firm.

"I'm sorry, Mother, this is where I belong now. There's a whole world out there, full of new ideas and people who aren't exactly like us. Why don't you stay? You and I could set up shop as Agena's foremost dypalfar experts!"

Szursta cast her eyes down with a stab of pain. It was almost tempting, but *her* world was beyond the portal – full of the people and things she knew, the only world she had ever known. And she had a young son there, no more than a boy, who needed his mother. "This is goodbye, then," she said and awkwardly embraced her daughter while juggling the hand-sized sphere. "I will always love you."

With that she turned and, back straight, walked through the portal without another glance. Rezira watched her go, lower lip quivering, and Andi came to stand with an arm around her. "It's all right, everything will be all right," he murmured softly as Arctoris, in his last official act as head of the Keepers, stepped forward and pressed the button sequence to shut down the dypalfar portal. Forever.

As the portal vanished they all walked out of the room, idly closing the door behind them. It was a gateway to nowhere, now. Arctoris addressed the group of Keepers that filled the room, jovially declaring, "It's over. Time for the work to begin!" There was a spontaneous cheer, almost shocking from the formal, reserved leukalfar.

The Waterdon contingent made their way through the crowd, greeting people they knew and thanking everyone for their help. The Mirskhrazana, having been handed the wish they had held for millennia, had stepped up nicely. Before leaving the area on their way up to the apartment of Ghrztum and his family, Andrion asked "Gylabris, were you able to get Kziintke working again?" The little Keeper beamed, and gestured off to the right.

"I'll let him answer that," he said.

"Greetings, friend Andrion," the robon said in Common. "I trust you are well?"

"All the better for seeing you up on your feet!" Andrion declared, patting the automaton on one gleaming arm. Gylabris had not only replaced Kziintke's fried power cell, but polished out the dents he'd sustained at the fight before the portal. A pity it wasn't as easy to bring one's human companions back from the dead. Many had fallen, especially among the Keeper guards and Sentries.

The automaton joined them as they all made their way to Ghrztum's place. His parents smilingly greeted them, but the group was too large to fit into the living room and they spilled out into the corridor through the open doors. The troll had hugs for his young friends, and they all said their goodbyes. "We'll be seeing you before too long," Andi promised. With this place on three of their magic maps, they could come for a visit whenever they felt like it (with permission, of course).

The party walked out through the main entrance of the city into late afternoon sunshine, a cold breeze blowing as they stood atop the steps admiring the view. The dragons, large and small, had all long since gone back to their hunting grounds. Andrion stepped close to Andi and gave him a hug, saying "Mind your mother, son." Then he scooped Meri up and kissed her firmly. "We'll be back soon," he told her. "Give my regards to Edla, and tell her all about your adventure."

"I love you Papa," she said, kissing him back. "See you soon!"

Finally it was Bernadette's turn, and she fell into his embrace. They were not wearing armor for a change, and serious hugs were possible. Then she stepped back and fixed him with a gimlet eye.

"Don't you and Gylabris get 'distracted' up there at the Academy," she told him. "Erik and I and the rest of the family will expect you in *one week*. Right?"

For answer Andrion locked his mouth on hers and gave her a thorough kiss. Then he said "Yes, dear" mildly and stepped away from the rest of them.

He drew Gylabris and Kziintke close, just to make sure the map would bring them along. "You're going to like Eisenstag," Andrion promised the little leukalfar tinkerer. "The climate's a lot like here." With that the trio shimmered into nonexistence.

"Okay, gather 'round," Bernadette told the rest of them briskly. "Here we go."

Rezira pressed tight against Andi as the world darkened for a few seconds. She had begun her lessons in Common; and learning that everyone who knew and loved him called him by his nickname, now did the same. The group found themselves standing on a dirt road, partway down a long slope that led to a sparkling river backed with snow-capped mountains. The sun had recently risen above those mountains, and was casting a warm glow on the long, bulky farmhouse that sat on a rise above them. "There it is," he told her, pride and joy in his voice. "We're home."

The End (for now)

www.ingramcontent.com/pod-product-compliance
Lightning Source LLC
Chambersburg PA
CBHW071155250626
47159CB00001B/91